To Marianne

Enjoy the ride!
Kents S. Ching

Lucifer's Pride

Keats P. Currie

Order this book online at www.trafford.com
or email orders@trafford.com

Most Trafford titles are also available at major online book retailers.

© Copyright 2013, 2014 Keats S. Currie.

All rights reserved. No part of this publication may be reproduced, stored in a retrieval system, or transmitted, in any form or by any means, electronic, mechanical, photocopying, recording, or otherwise, without the written prior permission of the author.

This is a work of fiction. Names, characters, places, incidents and dialogue are the product of the author's imagination or are used fictitiously. Any resemblance to actual persons, living or dead, business establishments, events, or locales is entirely coincidental.

Printed in the United States of America.

ISBN: 978-1-4669-8604-6 (sc)
ISBN: 978-1-4669-8603-9 (e)

Library of Congress Control Number: 2013904752

Trafford rev. 06/25/2014

 www.trafford.com

North America & international
toll-free: 1 888 232 4444 (USA & Canada)
fax: 812 355 4082

For my brother, David
My angel
Love Never Forgets

> We pass your face,
> To a dark forgotten place . . .
>
> — Soul's Gate

Acknowledgments

I am grateful to Soul's Gate whose music inspired the writing of this book and whose lyrics were used in the telling of my story.

Chapter 1

Boom! A thunderbolt lit up the sky when it struck the decrepit elm at the corner of the street sending patrons of the gas station scampering for cover. "Ha, ha, you missed me . . ." Shane smirked with an insolent glance to the sky as he walked calmly through the puddles and entered the convenience store. A pale girl with greasy brown hair stood behind the counter looking half bored to death. Seeing Shane, she inhaled deeply in order to thrust her bosom out as far as possible and leaned in, "What can I get ya?"

Shane stared straight into the girl's eyes. *How, after two weeks of freedom, was it possible that he could still find a dog like her even mildly appealing?* Five years without a woman would change a man. He allowed his eyes to peruse her ample breasts. *Yep, a conjugal visit with her would have been a fantasy comes true. God knows I overlooked a whole lot more than a homely female face to get some action in the can,* he thought. He gave her his full dimple smile. The girl's face flushed a deep red and little beads of perspiration broke out along her hairline. *Well, maybe my standards have been permanently lowered* he decided, *but that just means more fillies on the field for the stud.*

"Zigzags," Shane said slowly and suggestively. Unnerved by the attention, the girl faced the handsome stranger with abject fear in her eyes and a frozen smile. Shane handed her a bill and gave her a suggestive wink, "What time do you get off tonight, honey?"

The girl's jaw dropped slightly as she sputtered, "Uh, eight."

"Great," Shane smirked lasciviously. "I'll give you a call later."

Making his way to the exit he left his eyes on the bedazzled girl, only relinquishing his gaze as he slipped through the door.

She will be fantasizing about being in bed with me all day long, he speculated as he strolled to his motorcycle. Women had always found Shane profoundly sexy but now, at age thirty-three, he knew he was at the top of his game. Standing six-foot four he projected a formidable presence due to a massive upper torso and well-developed arms—polished to perfection in the prison yard. His bright red hair created a halo of curls around his flat baby face. Large blue eyes and full red lips bestowed a facade of child-like innocence he never failed to exploit. A battery of psychological testing in prison had proven that his I.Q. was in the genius range but that did not impress him as important. Growing up in the streets had taught him that bullshit baffled brains. For him, having intelligence simply meant he could come up with a little better bullshit. He had a knack for charming women; in fact, he had a knack for talking anyone into just about anything. The con was his specialty and he kept it honed with dedicated practice—just as a butcher sharpens his cleaver. He had no intention of calling any woman today. He had bigger fish to fry. As a smug smile crossed his face, he jumped onto his bright red Low Rider and raced down the highway to meet James.

Shane pulled his bike up to the pool hall where he found James sitting at a small table on the sidewalk, smoking a cigarette and drinking an espresso. Tattoo ink covered the taut muscles of his upper arms and his shiny black hair was tied back in a pony tail that fell almost to his waist. He flicked his cigarette into the street and motioned Shane toward his black Impala at the curb.

"Hey man, this is it! I'm here to earn my patch. Let's get rollin'." James took the car wheel and floored the gas creating a dust up in front of the cafe.

"Did Snake ask you to do the job himself?" Shane asked, "Ya, he came up to me after church while we were all sitting around having a beer. Jonesy told him I was solid and my work was top notch. I've been workin' my butt off for the past seven months trying to earn some respect. This is my break," James stated with confidence.

"Thanks for bringing me in man," Shane said slapping James on the shoulder.

James paused thoughtfully, "Well, you cleaned up some messes for us when we were inside, and we all thought you'd make a righteous brother. The club can always use solid guys and once you make Patch you're set."

"I figure I'm ten years behind where I should be," Shane speculated. "Now I'm gonna be making up for lost time. Besides, if I ever have to go back in, I'm going as Pride—you guys were the only ones getting conjugal visits!" Shane laughed. James slumped into the seat, leaned his head back and looked up to heaven. "Wow, man, talk about getting laid—did we party last night after church!"

"Did you stay at the clubhouse?" Shane asked.

"Ya, there were about ten of us left, just having a brew when Nick came by with a new dancer from the club. This bitch was fuckin' gorgeous. Long blonde hair and that body! I gotta tell ya man, my tongue was just hangin'. Nick started laying out lines on the bar for her and after doin' a few, this chick is up dancing for the guys. Well by the time she had taken off her G-string, Sammy behind the bar had a hat full of numbers and we were drawing lots. Fuck man, she was unbelievable. The guys couldn't wait so she was doing two at a time." James closed his eyes and his breath became heavy.

"Did you fuck her?" Shane looked intensely at James as provocative images danced in his head.

"Oooh ya, we all did. What a wildcat. She really liked her coke and we kept the champagne flowing. But then, fuck man! I couldn't believe it! About three A.M. who comes in but Boots himself. He tried to make the meeting but his plane got in late, so he thought he'd drop in and say hi to some of the guys. Well, he takes a look at this chick in action and he's makin' moves on her. Shit man, she's off limits as long as Boots has laid his claim," James frowned.

"I helped body bag the last guy that pissed Boots off and he weren't too purty. I'm not about to get into the Vice President's bad books over some pussy!"

"Chin up James," Shane laughed. "He's legendary for going through broads like used Kleenex."

"True bro, but sometimes he hangs onto favourites for a while, even when he's clippin' every chick he meets. Look at Fancy—his Ole Lady. He's had her for almost thirty years. I can't get this chick—I think her name was Brandi—out of my mind. I would have looked her up at the club tonight. Fuck."

It was a clear moonlit night and they were edgy with anticipation. James pressed the gas pedal to the floor and a spark of enthusiasm rose in his beautiful blue eyes. THUD. A rabbit lay dead on the road.

The light receded from his eyes and once again those blue eyes were windows to nothing. He lit a cigarette. Both men were lost in their thoughts as they drove down the empty country roads.

James finally broke the long silence, "It's just a couple of miles up here. Fuck, I can't wait! This is my Patch. I fuckin' guarantee it." Shane looked at James and snickered. He remembered when he had that same youthful enthusiasm. It was a big job. If everything went as planned it could change their lives forever.

Shane loved this kind of action. Sitting behind a desk and kissing somebody's ass for promotions was not his style. He was a breed apart—a realization he had by the age of five—just as some people know they are meant to be on a Broadway stage. He sighed with frustration, "Fuck, I just wanna be able to have a beer at the clubhouse. You know? This gig better work. I have to tell you man, this lowly hanger-on shit does not sit well on these shoulders. I've been pumpin' iron like it's my day job for the past five years and I can't wait to get in there and earn my way."

James upper lip curled back onto his teeth and a tiny spark of enthusiasm reappeared in his eyes. "I hear you bro, but this one is mine. I made Prospect in five months because I kick ass and I'm good at it."

"Well, you know what they say on Oprah, 'Do what you love . . .'" Shane flashed his white teeth and a set of perfect dimples.

"You watch Oprah?" James asked as he shot Shane a look of disgust.

"Well, you know, the Old Lady has it on. She has to tune in to get her daily instructions," Shane chuckled.

"That's it!" James said as he turned off the lights and pulled into a driveway. The house was a big garage that had been converted into living quarters. Only the flicker of a television light hinted that there was anyone inhabiting the small shabby building. Shane walked up to the side door and found it to be open. They could see a man with long curly hair and a paunch bathed in TV light sleeping on an old blue couch. Beside it a few small children camped out on the floor with pillows and blankets. James moved swiftly to his target, grabbed the man by the neck, and lifted him up from the couch. A look of horror passed over the man's face when he realized what was happening and he lost his balance as he struggled to extricate himself from James' grip. The thud woke the little boy who was sleeping in front of the TV.

"Dad!" the little boy screamed as he witnessed his father being dragged through the house and out of the side door. Frozen to the spot, his face flooded with tears, the boy watched as another large man moved toward him. Shane pointed his finger into his face and snarled, "Shut up and stay put." Shane kept his eye on the boy as he walked to the door where he had a vantage point from which to monitor the action outside.

James had the man pinned against the house. "You think you can fuck Snake for fifty G's? You must be one stupid motherfucker . . . ." James fists pummelled the guy's stomach until he doubled over and fell onto the gravel driveway.

"I'm getting the money tomorrow! Tomorrow!" he pleaded as his breath was being kicked out of him.

"You fuckin' liar. Shut your fuckin' hole!" James hissed as he used his cowboy boots to kick the guy in the mouth. Pure glee danced in his icy blue eyes as he heard a tooth crack. Aiming for his mouth once again, he missed and kicked the man's nose. Blood spurted everywhere covering the man's T-shirt and James' cherished cowboy boots.

"Do you think I'm an idiot? I'm going to listen to you, you fuckin' piece of shit?" James pulled his leg back to give him another good kick in his lying mouth but the man was writhing around on the ground and, once again, James' foot missed its mark. The man's eye popped out and hung by some tissue to the side of his cheek. He tried to speak but only a groan escaped from the bloody hole in his face. The noise had alerted the rest of the family and a woman with long stringy blonde hair was now approaching the entrance door with three small children clinging to her in fear.

"What's going on?" she screamed as the children cried and whimpered.

"Stay back lady and keep the kids quiet!" Shane yelled back. The intense look etched on Shane's face struck the woman and her children dumb.

"Come on man, we gotta follow orders. Snake didn't say 'dead'," Shane whispered as he pulled James' arm to break his focus. James leaned over and screamed into the man's ear, "There won't be a tomorrow, asshole. You're gonna pay tonight."

James and Shane jumped into the car and disappeared into the darkness. The woman screamed at the children to stay inside as she ran out to where their father lay groaning in pain. The man tried to say something but because he was barely conscious with a mouthful of broken teeth, he only managed to gurgle. She leaned in close and whispered, "Tell me, Honey." The man inhaled deeply and tried to move his jaw which no longer appeared to be attached to his face, "No police!"

She understood.

Shane drove a mile down the road before turning on the car lights.

"Fuckin' Eh!" James screamed at the top of his lungs as he punched his fist into the dashboard.

"Beautiful job, man!" Shane looked at James and winked, "Straight up."

"Hey, wanna do a hit?" James asked eagerly.

"No way man, we gotta take care of business right now. We'll party later," Shane answered gravely.

"Did you see his fuckin' eye man? It was lying on his fuckin' cheek. That will teach that fucker some respect. Tryin' to take Snake for fifty G's. Night's not over either." His smile widened and a spark of fire danced in his eyes once again.

Shane turned the car lights off as they approached the small housing development in an isolated rural area. He parked on the grass beside the creek a short distance from the houses. The car was shrouded in darkness but as the pair walked up the road two hundred feet to turn onto the street that was lined with houses, they could see that getting to their target would mean they would have to walk under a street light. They looked at each other knowing that two men walking in the neighbourhood at two A.M. would arouse suspicion if they were spotted.

"Fuck it. Let's do it—I'm not turning around now," James whispered. He walked quickly to the second house on the right side of the street and turned sharply to head towards the back yard. They could see a light on in the living room at the back of the house. The picture window was open to allow the smell of cedar and pine trees in the backyard to waft into the living room.

As they crept closer they realized that they would not have to force an entry. Their target, a beautiful blonde woman with her hair in a ponytail, was sitting on a couch near the window with a phone to her ear. Her laughter echoed off the small forest outside the window, "Ya, Davey, I'm going to bed—I just have a hard time sleeping when you're working nights. Do you have enough to eat? OK, then, stay away from the coffee and donuts. Love you too. Bye, see you in the morning."

James pulled a Berretta out of his jacket and pointed it at the woman's head—now only four feet in front of him behind the window screen. POP. The woman was thrust to the floor with a thud. In a rare moment of uncertainty, James pushed the nozzle of the gun through the screen and had Shane boost him up to make sure that he had accomplished his mission. He watched as the woman's blood pooled quickly beside her head and seeped into her long blonde hair. Satisfied that the job was complete, the pair ran full out to the car, jumped in, and left the scene.

After driving about five miles, Shane pulled into a deserted lane, stopped the car, closed his eyes and let out a large exhale in silence. He turned to James and they hollered at the top of their lungs until they ran out of breath.

"Fuck man. I need a hit," James said as he took out a small packet of white powder and offered it to Shane. "You first bro."

"Na, I don't touch that shit," Shane said as he reached for his stash and his package of Zigzags. James lit a glass balloon of white powder, inhaled the white smoke deeply, and relaxed back into the car seat. After a minute or two they looked at each other and started shaking their heads in disbelief at how well the whole operation had unfolded. They gave each other a high five and gripped hands knowing that they would always share this moment of glory. It would change their status in the club forever.

"I have a feeling he will find that fifty G's for Snake when he reads his sister's obituary in the paper tomorrow morning. Oh, I forgot, his eyeball is on his nose," James laughed hard, releasing some of the pent up tension of the night.

"Hell, brother, it's all glory now. You make Prospect and I make Patch. What other job gives you instant power, respect, and all the pussy you can handle?" James asked with a grin. Shane flashed his dimples, "Just the United States Presidency my friend."

Chapter 2

It was a hot, humid June day in the town of Dover, New Jersey, just a couple of miles south of Highway 80 and thirty miles west of downtown New York City. Sherry had an hour left in her shift at Mick's Restaurant and Pizzeria, a small one cook operation that made some of the best pizza outside of Italy. She had been busy serving delicious dishes all afternoon and her hunger pangs were screaming too loud to ignore. When she noticed an untouched slice of pizza on a dish she was clearing, she decided she would squirrel it away and eat it on her way home. She blushed to think how embarrassing it would be to get caught eating leftover pizza since Mick, the owner and cook, was constantly offering her food while she worked. She suspected he knew how limited her resources were at times and all his teasing about a skinny waitress being bad advertising was just his way of circumventing her pride. As much as she appreciated his kindness however, she could not allow herself to lean on his generosity. Taking something she had not earned was unthinkable. It was not her way.

She thought about the incident earlier when two smart ass guys began pressing her to meet them after she finished her shift. Mick had politely, but firmly, told them to leave and not come back. Typically, Sherry could handle the flirtations and propositions from customers with a bit of dismissive humour. Today was the first time that Nick had been drawn into the problem she had been desperately trying to keep under wraps and panic struck her as she wondered if her job was now in jeopardy. She wasn't under any illusions—this job was the only thing keeping her life from falling apart.

In fact, Mick was aware that there had been a few incidences of harassment, but he also noticed that for every such incident, there were a hundred orders that came in just because Sherry was the new waitress. The men of Dover came into Mick's Pizzeria just to lay eyes on the most beautiful woman they had ever seen.

As Sherry waited for the last few tables to leave, she prayed her customers would be generous with their tips. It was a rare occasion that she went over budget but she had made an exception for her mother's birthday and spent her last fifty dollars on a pair of real gold earrings. She hated to admit to herself that her extravagance had an ulterior motive but deep down she knew the gift was a peace offering, or maybe even a pitiful gesture of submission. She just wanted to be accepted as any daughter would be, or should be, but as hard as she tried to stay in her mother's good graces there was more than the usual tension between them lately. The power struggle that defined their relationship was escalating and Sherry felt powerless to stop it. Her life had been dedicated to making herself small enough, hollow enough, and insignificant enough that she did not to pose a threat to her mother, but nothing seemed to work anymore.

She pictured her family standing around the kitchen table, the new gold earrings twinkling in the candlelight of the birthday cake as her mother made a wish for the family's future prosperity and happiness. In the next instant reality pushed away her happy little vision and her smile waned. *If only it were like that,* she said to herself wistfully. Her mother's birthday tradition was to give a birthday card that said, 'Present to follow.' Unfortunately, the tradition was that the present never followed. She had to admit that the ritual engendered a bit of anticipation even after it became evident that her mother never made the effort to buy a gift for anyone.

Sherry tried to maintain the traditions that the rest of the world cherished but her efforts always seemed to fall flat. Life had given her mother a hard shell and Sherry prayed that there would come a day when her softer side would show itself. Maybe today would be that day. Once again Sherry had made all the preparations in case those precious moments were to unfold. She would hope for the best despite the knot in her stomach that reminded her how sentimental occasions seemed to evoke feelings of resentment and scorn in her mother. She shook her head to make those thoughts go away; they seemed ridiculous.

She breathed a little deeper as she picked up the ten dollar bill and discreetly stuffed it into her apron. If only she could stop thinking! Thinking! Thinking! If she spent her days thinking about her situation and her inability to change things, she would go crazy. She knew she would only be truly happy when she got away, far away. But that wasn't possible. Not now. She had to cope with her situation until she finished this last year of college. Then she could make a plan. For now she had to make the best of things and find happiness in the moment. That, she reminded herself, must be her focus.

Sherry pulled the pizza out of her bag and ate it as she walked down Clinton Street toward her friend Natasha's house. At least she had one friend that could empathize with her life. They had more in common than they really cared to discuss. Natasha's parents like to drink and they were usually incapacitated by three in the afternoon. Sherry knocked on the door and Natasha greeted her with a big smile.

"Hey Sherry, how was your shift?" she asked.

"Fantastic! I made sixty-four dollars in tips. Looks like we may have groceries this week after all!" she laughed.

"Everything cool?" Sherry inquired hesitantly, knowing that Natasha's parents could very well be in one of their many crisis modes that would make a friendly visit impossible.

"So far so good," Natasha shrugged with a roll of her eyes. "Forget them. I've got something I want to show you!"

Natasha and Sherry had met at college and formed a strong bond of friendship as they came to appreciate the many obstacles each other faced in the pursuit of their dreams. Natasha had her acting, Sherry had her art, and they both had hope as well as trepidation that they could someday live life on their own terms.

Natasha pointed to the far wall in her brother's bedroom.

"Lenny put that poster up on his wall last week and I kept looking at it and thinking that the image reminded me of someone. Last night just before I fell asleep I put two and two together. Pull your hair back. I'm going to do your makeup and we're going to put on this wig." In half an hour Natasha had applied theatrical makeup to Sherry and pushed all of her long dark hair into a short, platinum blonde wig. Sherry squeezed into a knock-off of the famous white halter dress and looked into the mirror.

"My God!" Sherry gasped. "I see what you mean!" Sherry was looking at the reflection of the poster behind her head. She was a dead ringer for Marilyn Monroe.

"That's just hilarious!" Sherry laughed, "Can I borrow the wig for tonight? I made a cake for my mum's birthday and it would be fun to sing Happy Birthday to her as Marilyn Monroe."

"Oh, sure, keep it," Natasha answered softly as she stared at her friend with stunned disbelief.

"Sherry, you're so beautiful . . . honestly, you look like a movie star. You should be studying dramatic arts, not me."

"Thanks for the compliment Natasha, you're a wonderful friend," Sherry said as she gave Natasha a hug. She hesitated and then looked at Natasha with sadness in her eyes, "I can honestly say a career in drama has never interested me. I feel that I have had to act my whole life just to get by, and what I really want . . . is to be me, the real me, not someone whose identity is dictated by circumstance."

As Sherry walked up the steep hill along the familiar row of identical white houses on Prospect Street, she passed a crew working on the road. All work came to a halt as hoots and whistles echoed down the empty street. Sherry laughed and gave them a wave. She had to admit that she had brought this on herself, however, there were other days when she found the attention of men on the street less than charming and she would go home and vent her frustration on canvas. Recently her paintings were gruesome images of people with exaggerated sexual organs attached to their bodies or distorted images of sexual mutilation. These were her private collection; she did not reveal such evidence of her subconscious mind to her art instructors at school. She was aware that this was another glaring example of not living an authentic life but she did not feel ready to face the scrutiny that her true artistic expression would bring. Right now, the catharsis of expression was enough. Nothing made her feel more alive.

As she approached the house where her mother rented the downstairs flat, she saw an old red car in the driveway. Anguish gripped her stomach and she paused to gain her bearings. Peels of laughter emanated from the small front window. Regina Raleigh was in her element—she had an audience. Giving her their undivided attention were her new boyfriend of one month, Luke Howard, and her very old friend Karen Benson, along with Karen's common-in-law husband of fifteen years, Freddy Gibbons. At forty-two, Regina still looked remarkably young despite her many indulgences and her many years of indulging them. Her shoulder length light blonde hair, slim well proportioned figure, and impassive light blue eyes, bestowed a beauty that fuelled the narcissism that defined her life.

Karen had been a drug abuser and alcoholic since the age of fifteen and it was all recorded in detail on her face. Regina's friendship with Karen had started about twenty-two years before when Regina returned to the East Coast after her boyfriend, Billy Anderson was murdered. Billy had been a loud-mouthed, domineering, boor who thought he was just a little smarter than the rest of the world and the only man that Regina had ever truly respected. They had gone west so that Billy, a career criminal, could team up with a few guys he knew from a stint in Attica. Little did he know that his buddies were under police surveillance and that their first attempted bank robbery would be their ticket back to the pen. Billy was finding his place as an alpha male in the alpha male world of Chino State Prison society when someone objected strongly to his ambitions and stabbed him four times in the heart.

Regina returned to the east and rented a cheap room in a rough section of Brooklyn where she met Karen who also rented a room in the old house and turned tricks on the local corner for booze, speed, and smokes. With huge blue eyes that tilted up at the corners, very long legs, a prominent overbite, and dark brown freckles that covered her entire face, Karen was at a distinct disadvantage in her chosen field because every cop on the beat recognized her and remembered her every misdeed. Regina had her own corner and, being young and beautiful, did very well plying her trade despite the fact that she was pregnant with Brandi, Sherry's older sister. As her due date approached Regina had less energy to go out on what they euphemistically referred to as "dates" so Karen had generously helped Regina out when she could. After Brandi was born, Regina had a bout of maternal instinct and stayed home to nurse the baby for about two months. However, her restless nature soon kicked in and it was not long before she was looking for someone to stay with the baby while she partied or turned a few tricks. Regina finally left the house in the spring with seven month old Brandi when she hooked up with a new a boyfriend and moved to a better part of town. Freddy, Karen's husband, was a small man with dirty blond hair and bad teeth. His lack of intelligence and self-possession bestowed an aura of innocence that belied a more sinister nature. It had been a number of years since Regina had seen her old friends and she was wallowing in the attention.

Regina was re-enacting an encounter she had many years before with a particularly memorable john. Standing in the middle of the room, she had her skirt hiked up her thighs with her feet spread wide apart and her knees bent. Her audience of three was laughing hysterically as she entertained. Dirty plates of food and empty bottles of beer cluttered the old table. A cheap bottle of wine had just been divided among the company of four. Cigarette smoke hung in clouds of blue haze.

"Karen, you remember—he had that yellow Ferrari and he wanted us both to go back to his place so you sat on the gear shift—you remember!"

"No, Reggie, I don't remember the 90's." Karen responded with a look of complete sincerity.

Regina laughed and continued her story, "He takes us back to some ritzy condo and pulls out a wad of bills that would choke a horse and says, 'Three hundred dollars each for a shower'. Karen is sitting there like the Queen of Sheba with her glass of Dom, shaking her head no way, and I'm saying, 'Are you fucking kidding?' For three hundred bucks the shoes are coming off, the panties are coming off, and I'm climbing up on the glass table while he waits underneath and . . . ."

Sherry took in the scene at the kitchen table and suddenly felt like that vulnerable little girl she once was, arriving home from school to find her mother entertaining a bunch of drunks that made her skin crawl. And just like old times, her eyes automatically scanned her mother's eyes in order to assess the degree of intoxication that would set the tone for the remainder of the evening. Regina perused her Marilyn get up and gave her, **The Look.** This was a signal she was well acquainted with from childhood which used to mean she should disappear because uncle Freddy or some other lascivious loser was a little too interested in little girls. **The Look**, became a great source of pride for Regina who liked to point to it as an example of her superior mothering skills. Sherry never understood how her mother could not appreciate that a good mother would never allow creeps such as these into their home in the first place. The last thing she needed, then or now, was instruction to get as far away from her mother's friends as possible.

Regina, however, had never recognized any of her own shortcomings or, if she had, she certainly had never acknowledged them. She could turn on the charm whenever she was determined to impress someone but that talent was never extended to family members. Rarely did Sherry see anything except her critical cantankerous side. Maybe, she concluded, when you see yourself as perfect in every way you lose patience for the foibles of mere mortals.

"Hi aunt Karen, uncle Freddy. Nice to see you."

"Hi," Karen answered automatically from her drunken stupor. Freddy and Luke looked over at Sherry but were too dumbstruck to respond. Regina maintained an unblinking stare at Sherry's face—her nostrils flared and her jaw clenched.

"Happy birthday, mum! I hope you liked the earrings. Natasha was experimenting with makeup. I didn't know you had company," she said apologetically.

"Yep, OK Sherry, I was just in the middle of a story . . . ."

"Sherry!" Freddy said aghast, "Fuck I can't believe it's you! You grew up!"

"A bit of an understatement," Luke chipped in with a chuckle. Sherry could feel her mother's eyes throwing daggers at her but she dared not look over.

"Well, I better check on Lila," she said in an effort to extricate herself from her mother's wrath. As she left the room Freddy looked over at Luke and their eyes locked as if to say, "Do you believe what you just saw?"

Regina picked up on the tacit message of the exchange and the anger erupted into her veins as it moved up her neck and into her face. The uncomfortable silence was broken when Brandi, Sherry's older sister by one year, sauntered into the room wearing a pink negligee top that barely reached tiny matching panties. Sparkling in her ears were the earrings her mother had received as a birthday gift from Sherry.

"Well, good morning sexy!" Regina beamed.

"Hi aunt Karen, uncle Freddy! Christ, I haven't seen you in years. How have you been?"

"Great, just great!" Freddy's eyes lit up and his broad smile revealed a checkerboard of teeth in different shades of brown.

"Wow, you're all grown up too! We just saw Sherry. She came home done up as Marilyn Monroe." The vision of her sister dressed as Marilyn Monroe made Brandi uneasy. A look of fear brushed her green eyes.

"God I couldn't believe it! She even has a body like Marilyn Monroe only younger—you know, sexier," Freddy added enthusiastically. Brandi put her arms up into the air and began to gyrate her hips in a slow circular motion revealing her mid-section and a pink rhinestone belly ring.

"She might have a body but, believe me, she doesn't know how to use it," she retorted with defiance.

Relieved to be off the topic of Sherry, Regina chimed in, "This one is knocking them dead at the new Dancing House in the city. And— get this—the manager, Nick Pricello, is a top member of the Lucifer's Pride motorcycle club. When they saw her they hired her on the spot even without experience. She started two nights ago and the guys went nuts! She made a couple of hundred bucks in tips both nights. But, what can I say? She's got her mother's good looks . . . and that body! My tits were never that big even before I had kids. Hey, if you've got it, why not use it? And why give it away if they'll pay for it, right Karen?" Karen nodded and then wondered what it was she had agreed with.

"Can you imagine getting in with those guys? The Pride runs this fuckin' country now. Everybody knows the Black Cat—Lion Terkel—he's a household name. And they're loaded! I mean big money. Yachts, private jets, mansions. I'm so proud of this girl. If I was her age, I would be exactly where she is—girls have so many opportunities these days," Regina stated with complete self-assurance. Karen nodded in agreement.

"Wait mum—you won't believe what happened last night! After my set Nick took me to the Pride clubhouse to party. We were all feeling pretty good, and at about three in the morning this gorgeous fuckin' guy comes in called Boots. Nick said he was one of the leaders of Lucifer's Pride! He took one look at me and . . ."

As Sherry walked into the room and headed for the fridge, all heads turned in her direction. Brandi leered at her with an expression of unmitigated hate.

"What do you want Sherry?" Regina asked curtly.

"Just getting Lila some dinner . . . anything left?"

"I think it's all gone—just make her a jam sandwich," Regina said making a dismissive gesture with her hand. Silence fell on the room as Sherry grabbed a carton of milk and left.

"We don't discuss anything in front of her," Regina closed her eyes and shook her head with disdain. "She can't handle it." Freddy's eyes opened wide with disbelief.

"Fuck man, she's gorgeous. She's gotta be the most beautiful woman I have ever seen!" The room became even more silent.

Sherry closed the bedroom door on the noise of the party and a familiar fear settled into her stomach. Pain registered on her delicate features as she gazed down upon Lila colouring on her bed as Bugsy, Sherry's English Bull dog, watched attentively. Although Lila was her sister's five year old daughter, Sherry knew that in every way that mattered, she was Lila's mother. And everyday Sherry lived with the guilt that she was losing the battle to protect her as a mother should. The demands of work and school meant Lila was exposed to Brandi and Regina's criticism, contempt, and neglect. She knew what relentless rejection did to a child's spirit and she could see Lila becoming more and more withdrawn just as she had been at her age. Seeing Karen and Freddy had dredged up that old feeling of desperation that had permeated every moment of her youth and now history was threatening to repeat itself. *They won't win!* Her internal voice screamed. *Lila will not have my childhood!* As she hugged Lila tears welled up in her eyes and her heart ached for this child she loved so dearly. She made a silent promise to herself that she would use every ounce of strength she could muster to give Lila a better life.

Humble that it was, Sherry's bedroom was their sanctuary. Created by some inept carpenter, it was a six by ten foot space that featured a giant water heater in the corner and a door in the middle of a wall that led to a crawl space. Copies of Impressionist masterpieces decorated every inch of wall space. The Night Café at Arles by Van Gogh, which she had just finished the night before, glowed in the afternoon light. *She might be the poorest girl in town,* she thought, *but she had an art collection that would be the envy of most billionaires.*

Sherry constantly drew on her natural creative talents to make her life a little more pleasant. She taught herself to refit clothes from Goodwill for herself and Lila and she became skilled at creating meals that fed everyone on her very limited budget. But despite the fact that her talents and discipline made life better for the entire family, no acknowledgment was ever given. Regina did not appreciate being eclipsed by anyone. As she became older Sherry began to question the unwritten rule that none of her talents were ever to be acknowledged. Deciding to attend Art School was seen as an act of defiance by Regina—perhaps even a personal affront—and their relationship had taken a dramatic turn for the worse.

Sherry used pure willpower to draw her focus away from the circus on the other side of the door. *What was she accomplishing by dwelling on their parties, their irresponsibility, and their hateful ways? She could not make them care. She had to let go,* she told herself. *She had to stop allowing their problems to become her problems.* The reality was that, right now, this tiny space was all she had to give Lila. But, in this little space, they had some measure of peace, comfort, and beauty.

"How was your day at school, princess?"

"Fine."

"I'm glad. Listen, I'll just wash this funny makeup off my face and change so we can walk down to the store and get you something to eat."

"O.K. Meme," Lila responded using her nickname for Sherry. Just then Regina opened the bedroom door abruptly, "Ya, Sherry, give me a couple of bucks will ya?"

"Mum, we just don't have money for booze. I've got one more shift this week and I need the money for food . . ."

Regina interrupted, "Jesus Christ, why does everything have to be such a big deal with you?" She spoke slowly emphasizing every word as she rolled her head in circles.

"Brandi gets her pogey check next week and she will give you the money back if you are so concerned about it."

"But we need Brandi's check for the rent," Sherry said softly, her voice edged with desperation.

"Just give me the God damn money! Brandi is working tomorrow night and she makes big bucks in tips, not eight bucks an hour. God you're a pain in the ass . . . ."

Without another word, Sherry picked up her purse and gave her mother thirty dollars to cover the cost of a case of beer. She knew her mother would win; she always would as long as Sherry was living under her roof.

Sherry looked down at the pile of mail and bills that her mother had dumped on her dresser. She sighed and closed her eyes. *Not much longer.*

Chapter 3

The party was still going strong when Sherry and Lila returned from the grocery store. Brandi was basking in the glory of her new status as stripper and biker chick. Karen was so tanked she was nodding off while Freddy and Luke were revelling in the off color stories Regina was spinning to keep the party lively.

Funny, Sherry thought, *how despite all their pleas of poverty they always seemed to come up with enough money for a party.* She had noticed that Brandi had been hitting it hard lately and there was a new brightness to her eyes that did not come from booze. And an unfamiliar edge was creeping into her personality that made her even more obnoxious than before. At the same time, there had been a profound change in her lifestyle. It was so unlike Brandi to leave her bed and her TV unless it was to party. *She must need more money for drugs,* Sherry thought. *That would explain this sudden spurt of motivation to work that was so completely out of character.* Of course, she was working as a stripper and, knowing Brandi as she did, she wouldn't be surprised if she did it for free. Brandi was just like Regina in that respect—their desperate bids for attention had been a source of embarrassment for Sherry all of her life.

The party hit a note of silence as Lila and Sherry made their way through the kitchen to Sherry's bedroom. Lila found a book to read on the bed and Sherry glanced through the pile of mail on the dresser. Finally, the letter from St. James Hospital had arrived. She had discreetly asked her mother where she had been born without sharing the reason for her interest. She was not about to invite derision by confessing that she needed her birth time in order to study her astrological birth chart.

The letter read, "Dear Ms. Raleigh . . . We are assuming that you are now using your mother's name because there was only one live birth in our hospital on November 28, 1991. The birth time was 12:05 p.m." Sherry looked at the birth certificate for which she had paid twenty-five dollars. Beside the child's name it read: Sheherezade. *Darn*, she thought. *I've been sent someone else's birth time and I've wasted twenty-five dollars.* As she laid the copy of the birth certificate down on the dresser her eyes scanned the words Regina Raleigh. She picked up the paper and tried to sort out what she had read. Under Mother was listed: Regina Raleigh. Under Father was listed: Terrance Ivey. Under child's name was listed: Sheherezade Ianthe Ivey. Sheherezade . . . Sherry. *My name is Sheherezade* she thought. *My last name is Ivey.* She knew immediately that her mother was hiding something. Regina had always told Sherry that she did not know the identity of her father. Her mind floated back to the giant oak in the backyard of the old house where they once lived. After making sure the coast was clear she would climb to the very top and lose herself in girlish dreams—many of which were about the father that would come for her some day. *If only*, she thought. The idea of having a father to love her and maybe even a branch of family members that would accept her as she was filled her with yearning.

Sherry had always suspected that part of her mother's contempt for her was the fact that her father had been a john. She had never broached the subject with her mother, however, because she had never wanted to give her the satisfaction of retelling the story of her ignoble conception. Regina took such smug pleasure in reiterating the tale of how she had tried to abort Sherry, with the help of her own mother, that Sherry did not relish being the star of another family legend. Now she was so curious she could spit, but she knew it would be useless to ask Regina for the truth. Obviously, it was information Regina had hoped Sherry would never discover.

Sherry was still lying awake at two a.m. trying to imagine why she would have a name that her mother refused to acknowledge, when she heard groaning and laughing coming from another part of the house. She opened her bedroom door just a crack to make sure the sounds of distress were not coming from Lila who had a cot in Brandi's room. She soon realized, however, that the sounds were coming from the living room at the other end of the flat. She heard Brandi giggling and then she heard uncle Freddy's groan turn into a slur of words, "I'm telling you Brandi—I mean it baby, you are more woman than your sister ever thought of being." *No, it can't be,* she concluded.

Sherry could not believe what she was hearing. She searched her mind for an answer to why Brandi would be having sex with uncle Freddy. Brandi had boyfriends—more than her share. Sherry knew she had always been promiscuous, but uncle Freddy? He was not exactly a relative but he and aunt Karen were around all the time when they were kids. It just seemed so unnatural, not to mention disrespectful to aunt Karen. *God, she could be so disgusting,* she thought. Sherry's only real concern, however, was shielding Lila from such sordid behaviour. Sherry waited by the door so that if Lila woke and walked toward the living room, she could run interference. After some more laughter, Brandi went stumbling stark naked to the bedroom clutching what looked like a twenty dollar bill.

Sherry thought she had seen it all living with Regina but apparently she could still be surprised. She had heard the word slut whispered indelicately to describe her sister for years. *Maybe she was a nymphomaniac, if there was such a thing—but uncle Freddy?*

Perhaps all her loose behaviour was a search for a father's love, but if she were seeking love, why had she never reached out to her for companionship or affection to fill that lonely place? As much as Sherry tried to be a loving sister, Brandi had chosen to see their relationship solely in terms of an ongoing rivalry. Sherry was a teenager before she realized that every honour role grade, every accolade for artistic achievement, and every compliment she received for her beauty, struck Brandi like a knife in the heart. Regina's response was exactly the same and just as predictable. In her heart she knew she had never really had a mother or a sister—there was only hate on their part where there should have been love.

At 7 a.m. the next day, Sherry was serving breakfast to business people in the area. By three o'clock her feet were sore and she started to make the short walk home. She was tempted to say something to Brandi about her indiscretion with uncle Freddy the night before. *Oh God,* she thought, *where do I start?* She knew that anything that could be interpreted as criticism or reprimand from her would be taken as the ultimate insult and would send Brandi into a rage. Her purpose was not to preach morality to Brandi. She had long since given up trying to change anyone; that was a hopeless pursuit. Her only goal was to shield Lila from the sordid lifestyle that Brandi led.

Lila needed protection and love—two things Regina and Brandi could not, or would not, provide. Sherry's plan had always been to leave the madness and the hate behind as soon as she turned sixteen. But then Lila came along and now she was not leaving without her. Regina and Brandi exploited her devotion to Lila for all it was worth but Sherry knew that it would not guarantee her security. She had to be careful of what she said at all times. Even though she did the cooking, cleaning, and paid most of the bills, she knew that they would toss that all away for a dramatic show of their power over her. Power over people was the one thing they valued. It validated their belief in their own superiority.

I'm going to keep my mouth shut, she thought. *Nothing I say will change Brandi but I will be kicked out of the house if I get in Brandi's face and point out her shortcomings. They don't care if they hurt me and they don't care if they hurt Lila. I've got to avoid confrontation and focus on the one thing that matters: being with Lila.*

Sherry could see the red car still parked in the driveway and wondered if the party had started yet. There were no voices coming from the front room so she opened the door quietly thinking that everyone was probably still sleeping. It was like a tribal custom in their house that no one should ever be disturbed before they awoke of their own accord or a great deal of screaming would ensue. The bedroom doors were open, so she crept down the hall quietly and looked into Regina's room. She saw Freddy sitting on the end of the bed with Lila on his knee. A cold shudder gripped Sherry when she noticed his hand resting on Lila's thigh in an unnatural position. Freddy looked up and their eyes met. He knew that she knew he had evil intentions. Sherry composed herself, bent down, and put her arms out.

"Lila," she said enthusiastically. "I'm home." Lila jumped down from Freddy's knee and ran into her arms. Sherry grabbed Lila's hand and without a word turned and led her into their tiny bedroom. She planned to keep Lila there until these bottom feeders her mother called friends crawled back to wherever it was they came from.

About an hour later, Brandi, decked out in full regalia for her date with Boots, barged into Sherry's room.

"Come on Lila, we're going."

"Where are you going?" Sherry asked.

"Don't worry about it; it has nothing to do with you," Brandi answered in her best voice of condescension as she pushed Lila's head in the direction of the door.

"I said move Lila! Go and pack up some clothes."

"Pack up? Is mum taking her somewhere?" Sherry asked with apprehension.

"God, if you must know, mum had a little problem today and she's in jail."

"Jail! Again? For what?" A look of concern passed over Sherry's face.

"See, that's why we don't tell you anything. It's no big fuckin' deal. She went shopping with Karen and she got charged for boosting . . . but she'll get off. It might take a week to get the bail money that's all."

"So where are you going with Lila?"

"She's going to stay with aunt Karen and uncle Freddy until mum gets out."

"Oh no, Brandi, I'm here at night. You are not sending her with them!"

"I've got news for you sis," Brandi said with a smirk. "You're outa here too."

"What are you talking about Brandi?"

"Mum and I have just had enough of you." She started to emphasize every word and speak slowly as was Regina's style when she was attempting to be as rude as possible.

"No one can have any fun around you. You're just a pain in the ass . . . ."

Sherry reflected on the Marilyn Monroe costume and surmised she had crossed an imaginary line by garnering too much male attention.

"Look Brandi, if you and mum want me to leave, I will, but please, don't send Lila with Karen and Freddy! I walked in on Freddy this afternoon in the bedroom. He had Lila on his knee and his hand was under her skirt. I don't think anything happened but I'm convinced it would have if . . . ."

"Why? Because he's a friend of mum's and he likes to have a drink once in a while? Karen and Freddy have had very hard lives and they are good people. No one is trying to feel up Lila. Besides, she's my daughter, not yours—get a life of your own," Brandi sneered.

"I caught him looking at Lila as if she were a glass of water on a hot day. You have to believe me! I would never lie about something like that! Please, don't even think about sending her!" Desperation and panic were beginning to set in as Sherry was seeing her worst nightmare become reality before her eyes.

"She's going and you're going and that's final!" Brandi screamed as her smug look changed to one of pure hatred.

"Brandi you went through the same thing with mum's boyfriends and you know what it's like to live with that shame and humiliation. We have to protect Lila! We can't allow history to repeat itself," Sherry pleaded.

"What the fuck are you talking about? No one touched me! Now shut the fuck up and get out!" Brandi hissed through clenched teeth.

Sherry felt the grip she had on life slipping through her fingers but she thought she would try one more heartfelt supplication.

"You don't have to hide it from me, Brandi. You don't have to be ashamed of what someone else did to you. It's not our fault we were faced with fighting off all those losers that mum brought back to the house when she was drunk or stoned . . ."

"Mum likes to have fun! O.K.? She's a happy person. Not everyone wants to mope around looking for things to nag people about. You're such a fuckin' downer Sherry. I don't want Lila to be around you anymore because I sure as hell don't want her turning out like you. No one can stand you. You think you're hot shit and you're just a big God damned bore!" Brandi yelled at Sherry with a look of pure loathing in her eyes.

"You walk around here like little miss self-righteous, looking down your nose at everyone. You and your fuckin' paintings and your custom made clothes and your books. No one is impressed. We don't need your bullshit or your stupid waitress job."

"Well," Sherry screamed back, "You needed it last week and you needed all the money my other stupid jobs brought in over the years to feed you because you were too damned lazy to get off the couch! And what kind of fun are we talking about Brandi? Having sex with uncle Freddy thirty feet from where aunt Karen and your own daughter are sleeping? And that's not the best is it Brandi? The best is that you took money for it! A two bit whore just like mum, and aren't you proud of yourself!" Brandi was taken aback by Sherry's sudden aggressiveness but quickly recovered her imperious demeanour.

"Listen to Miss High and Mighty! If your father hadn't been paying for a quick fuck you wouldn't even be here. You're just street dirt!" Brandi screamed as her face turned purple.

"It's true I don't have the pure criminal pedigree you have Brandi. And with your drinking, drugs, stripping, and hooking, I'm sure your daddy would be truly proud. It certainly seems to impress mum. To tell you the truth, I'm thankful for any genetic material my father contributed to make me because God knows it's an improvement over you two losers!" Sherry was letting it fly for the first time in her life and it felt good.

Brandi's face twisted into an ugly mask.

"You fuckin' bitch! You parade yourself around here in a low cut dress and then you pretend you're little miss innocent after you get the guys all worked up!"

Sherry cringed with guilt as she thought back to her Marilyn Monroe get up. She was so used to being used as a scapegoat by her mother who did not take blame for anything, that she found herself searching for the logic in what Brandi was saying before she realized how ridiculous it was. *I will not buy into that anymore,* she thought. *Never again.*

"I am attractive Brandi and I'm sorry if that makes your world a darker place but that doesn't mean I am going to take responsibility for every hard-on within a ten mile radius. That was always your specialty. Remember how you used to take a run at any boy that found me attractive in school just so you could cope with the jealousy? Ya, I wasn't as stupid as you and mum liked to believe—I just let you try your best knowing that it would never be good enough."

"That's how much you know," Brandi fumed. "Mum and I used to laugh about how Jason, the guy you dated in grade twelve, used to meet me behind the bleachers all the time he was dating you."

Sherry's face drained of blood and her eyes looked out into space for a short moment. "That's it isn't it—it wasn't about the money—you just used that as justification. It was because he said I was beautiful. You had to have sex with uncle Freddy to prove to yourself that you were my equal. You are one sick bitch."

The truth hit home and Brandi started to shake with rage. For the first time in her life she was lost for words.

"Maybe you thought I was going to put up with your crap for a lifetime but I've got a news flash for you and mum—that was never my intention. Lila deserves a whole lot more than the life she would have living here with you hateful, self-absorbed losers. You know what I'm saying about Freddy is true and the pathetic part is you don't give a shit as long as you don't miss a date with some biker and your partying isn't interrupted. If you send her with that didler I will pick up the phone and call children's services and I won't forget the part about your glossy eyeballs. Now get your skanky ass out of my room!"

Sherry's plans had changed. She had made a decision. The universe would forgive her.

Chapter 4

Fancy McFarlane told her driver to wait in front of the building since there was a chance that she would be right back. Stepping out of the elevator onto the thirty-ninth floor occupied by Thunder Corporation headquarters, she removed her white mink cape and dragged it to the reception desk outside of the tall, curly maple doors that led to the office of Luigi Falcone.

"Tell him I am here," she said without looking at the girl sitting behind the desk. She hated to have to wait but she knew he always kept the doors locked.

"At once, Ms. McFarlane." The secretary grabbed the phone and tried to concentrate as fear undermined her focus.

The lock popped and the double doors swung open automatically. A twenty foot wall of glass faced the double doors, blinding anyone who was entering the office. His eyes spontaneously perused her long muscular legs that were prominently displayed by a red mini dress. After thirty years of trying, he had to admit he had never seen anything like them until he met the enchanting Miss Brandi the night before at the Pride clubhouse.

"Fancy! How are you doing?"

"I'm fuckin' furious Boots, just furious!" she whined.

Fancy liked to ignite reactions in people and she had a knack for pushing exactly the right buttons to do just that. Best of all, she liked to get a rise out of Boots. He was still beautiful but she always thought of him as he was so long ago with gorgeous blue black hair that touched his shoulders and flawless olive skin that contrasted her white skin when they were in bed together. Only one other man had turned her head more than Boots but that thought was too disturbing to recall and she shook her head to try to make it go away. It was bad enough that Jimmy's perfectly sculpted face still haunted her dreams.

Almost thirty years before Fancy had been a dancer in a bar in Philadelphia where Boots and his biker buddies hung out. She was young and beautiful with deep blue eyes and a long mane of curly blonde hair—but it was her fabulous body that would turn heads when she walked down a street. Small hips with firm round buttocks sat perched atop the most curvaceous legs Boots had ever seen.

They started a relationship which was innocent and passionate. She soon realized that it was not in his character to be faithful but instead of confronting him with his infidelity, she kept the knowledge to herself and held onto it like a get out of jail free card in case the day came when he found out that she had the same proclivities. The romance faded but a relationship of mutual benefit endured and she remained his official Old Lady. For Fancy it meant an identity that came with money, respect, and prestige. For Boots it meant never having to make a commitment to the women he seduced, bedded, and left for the next pretty face.

"I thought we were finished with this shit Boots! I can't believe how I was treated today by that bitch. I'm not taking it! Just because I'm your Ole Lady, I don't think I should have to put up with disrespect like that!" Fancy knew that if she could frame the insult in a way that made Boots think the disrespect was directed at him he would become angry enough to retaliate on her behalf.

Boots had come to the United States at the age of two with his parents who had emigrated from Italy. His father had always had a language barrier that prevented him from bringing the family out of poverty, and as a boy growing up in a small town, Boots' perception was that his family was looked down upon by the hoity-toity denizens. By the age of twelve his mission was clear and he would tell anyone who asked him what he wanted to be when he grew up: he wanted to be rich. He fought his way out of the small town making sure he laid a beating on anyone who even looked at him sideways. For that he earned the moniker, "Boots." As a boy of fifteen Boots met another boy adrift in the streets of Philadelphia named Lion Terkel. They became fast friends and soon found that they shared a love of motorcycles and a mutual ambition to rise above their humble beginnings. Greed fuelled their efforts to expand their power by organizing their band of friends into a criminal organization which they named the Lucifer's Pride Motorcycle Club. They had found the focus of their aspirations.

By the age of twenty-five he was rich. By the age of thirty he was filthy rich. Boots had successfully channelled his hatred for middle-class society into a driving ambition that took him to heights in his professional life even he had not imagined possible. He had done his best to bury the humiliation he experienced growing up and for the most part he had been successful. However, his vulnerability would resurface when he felt he had been disrespected. And then God help the person who was responsible for making his blood boil. Boots was merciless.

Fancy could tell by the way his lip was curling back over his teeth that she was hitting the nerve for which she had been aiming. She loved to be at the center of a brewing storm and she could not wait to see what punishment Boots would mete out to that condescending bitch. She was relieved to find she still had this power over Boots because she knew that it meant she still had a position in his life—one that he felt he had to protect.

"Jackie was with me when I went to see a dermatologist over in Newark yesterday. I made the appointment about a month ago under my real name. After we sat there waiting for half an hour, we noticed the girl behind the counter staring at us."

"Now she wouldn't be staring at you because you were wearing a couture suit worth thirty G's and five carat diamonds in your ears, would she Fancy?" Boots smirked.

"Oh, shut up Boots, I'm trying to be serious here," she cajoled.

"The receptionist, who is this little gen-ex cunt all made up like a five dollar whore, calls me over and says, 'Do you go by another name? Aren't you Fancy McFarlane?' I said, 'Yes, why?' She says, 'No reason, but I have bad news for you—the doctor is not taking new patients and she did not realize that you had not been here before.' I said, 'Well you better tell her to get out here because I'm not leaving.' She goes into the other room and the doctor comes out and says, 'What can I do for you Ms. McFarlane?' I said, 'You can keep your appointment with me. I believe you are cancelling because you just realized who I am. You must know that I am not the person you want to piss off.' Well, she apparently didn't like being told what to do so this prissy little doctor says to me, 'Sorry Fancy but I don't do tattoo removal.' And the other gen-ex bitch puts her head down to hide a smirk."

Fancy saw Boots' eyes darken.

"I leaned over the counter, got right in her face and I said, 'Oh, really? Well, I'll pass that little gem onto my Old Man'."

"What did they do then?" Boots' eyelids dropped and his gaze was tense.

"Let's just say it wiped the smirks off their faces," Fancy replied.

Boots took a breath and composed himself, "Fancy, why don't you just go see the doc? Shit, I've made him a rich man so that we don't have to use citizens."

"I knew you would say that Boots, but I needed a specialist for some Botox, and besides, I just don't like the way he looks at me."

Boots laughed, "Fancy you look good but you know you're a little out of his age range. He told me that his new girlfriend is sixteen but that's OK because she has the body of a twelve year old."

"God, I've heard that joke for twenty years—it would be funnier if there wasn't so much truth behind it," Fancy said with exasperation.

Boots became serious again,

"Well Fancy, if you're going to lay yourself open like that then you can't let these nothings get to you . . . it's just petty jealousy. Let me buy you the new SLS Mercedes Roadster. You'll love it. Before you know it the wind is blowing through your hair and you forget all about this stupid bitch. What color would you like? A friend of mine has a dealership in Jersey. I'll have them deliver it . . . by the way, what's the doctor's name?"

Fancy felt a tickle of anticipation but it was not for the car. "You know red is my color Boots. The doctor's name was uh . . . Lynn Bailey. Thanks for the car and thanks for trying to make me feel better."

"Well, it's my pleasure but I better get going. I've got a business meeting downtown," Boots interjected. Fancy surmised a business meeting was a euphemism for pussy and she envisioned the young thing with the twenty inch waist he would be with tonight. A twinge of jealousy swept through her but passed quickly as she lit a long white cigarette.

"Thanks honey," she cooed as she smiled seductively and swept out of his office.

Boots was going to the Harley Davidson dealership to put his order in for the newest model coming out in the spring. Nothing tickled him more than the prospect of a new bike except, perhaps, a new woman, and he was on a perpetual shopping spree for the best of both. He loved nothing more than to feel the air blowing through his hair on a ride but these days he used a car and driver most of the time because running his empire meant that he was always on the phone. Having hands free was now his greatest luxury and he was nostalgic for the carefree days of his youth.

"Mitsy, how are you sweetie?" Misty had been one of Boots' working girls in the early years who now managed a spa in Manhattan that was part of his chain called Thunder Spas.

"Ya, I know, we'll have to have lunch soon. Listen, I'm sending a girl over there today . . . a Miss Brandi . . . and I want her to have the best of what you've got. And, Mitsy, invent the Thunder Spa internal flush for the occasion will you? When I'm mowing her grass I don't want to be blowin' every guy in Jersey." Boots laughed his soft distinctive laugh that endeared him to every woman he met.

"Boots you're bad and you haven't changed one bit in thirty years."

"So they tell me, Mitsy. Gotta run. Take care."

"Hi Ziggy, do me a favour? Have Gail book an appointment for me with a Dr. Bailey. I've got a rash. She's in Newark . . . ."

Chapter 5

The limousine pulled up to the canopied entrance of the elegant coop on Fifth Avenue. The doorman told Brandi that Mr. Falcone was waiting for her upstairs and escorted her to the private elevator that led to the suite. An immaculately groomed woman in a business suit greeted Brandi warmly and escorted her through the marble entrance to a stunning living room decorated in shades of warm browns, terra cotta, and gold. One side of the room was a beautiful view of central park draped in exquisite silk.

"Can I make you a drink, Miss Brandi?" the woman smiled.

Brandi did her best to present an aura of sophistication, "Yes, a dry martini, please."

The woman left and Boots came rushing into the room his hand extended in greeting. Brandi was temporarily stunned. Too much champagne and cocaine the night she entertained the boys at the Pride clubhouse had left her unprepared for the vision before her. A moustache fell over full sensuous lips; his eyes were big, brown pools framed under thick arched black brows. He was the sexiest, most masculine presence she had ever encountered.

"Hi Brandi, how are you? I'm delighted you could join me." Lou Falcone was a master of self-deprecation—it was a major facet of his well-honed charm.

"Did you enjoy yourself at the spa? You look terrific!"

"I loved it! They treated me like I was Queen for a day."

"I just opened that location about a month ago. It's a far cry from the old massage parlours I used to run in Philly. I'm glad they took care of you."

The woman returned with a dry martini with a twist of lemon for Brandi, a martini with an olive for Boots and a delicate glass tray of tiny hors d'oeuvres which she placed on the table in front of the couch where they sat.

"Brandi, let me introduce my housekeeper Vivienne. She makes my life possible. I don't know what I would ever do without her," he smiled. "We'll eat in about half an hour Vivienne—if that's OK with you Brandi." He lifted his brows to invite her final approval.

"Perfect," Brandi replied giving him a sexy unbroken gaze.

Boots was surprised to see how beautiful Brandi was in the daylight. He had perused her profile against the streaming light of his living room when she first came in and was awestruck by her curvaceous legs showcased by a very short dress that revealed almost all of them. Now as he looked into her luscious green eyes and glimpsed her round breasts protruding from her strapless gold dress, he felt his knees get a little weak. Revealing clothes made the pursuit more exciting and Boots loved the pursuit. Once he reached the finish line and could declare a conquest, he started to get a little bored. A woman he could not possess completely was the only woman that could ever keep him amused. He had not met her yet.

A stout woman in uniform served a sumptuous dinner of roasted duck, grilled vegetables and salad, followed by plates of cheese, fresh fruit, and tiny pastries. They took their time over each course and sampled some rare wines that Boots decanted with great care and expertise.

"Try a pastry Brandi. They came over from Paris on my jet today just for you."

"You have a plane?"

"Just a little one . . ." Boots answered as he erupted into his inimitable laugh.

"How rich are you Boots?"

Boots enjoyed women with no social graces; it made the seduction less taxing and he was able to savour the experience. Only two things struck fear in the heart of Luigi Falcone and that was an educated, sophisticated woman and the thought of losing his hair.

"Oh, now Brandi, I don't even tell my accountant that." He pulled her close and kissed her on the lips for the first time. She had fallen in love by the first course, but that kiss sealed her fate. She wanted to own him. She ached to feel him inside her.

As they talked, kissed, and sipped cognac, Brandi felt her defences crumbling.

"How old were you when you had your first sexual experience?" Boots asked as he kissed her hand.

"I don't remember to tell you the truth. Mum had a lot of boyfriends and from an early age I was often an unwilling pitch hitter when mum was passed out drunk or stoned. I think I've blocked a lot of it out of my mind."

"Did your mother know?" Boots asked as his lip curled back slightly under his moustache.

"Once, when I was about twelve, she turned around suddenly while she was talking on the phone and I know she saw her boyfriend's hand up my skirt. If she had investigated further, she would have saved me a lot of pain, but she chose to ignore it and pretend it never happened. He hung around for another year and it wasn't because of her. I didn't tell anyone—I had no one to tell. It used to give me nightmares but I'm beyond that now. Before—when she pissed me off—I would throw it in her face but she would never admit that she ever knew anything was going on."

"Nice mother," Boots said sarcastically.

"No, she's good people. There's no point dwelling on the past and nagging her about what she should have done or known. It's old history. I've decided to put it behind me and just get on with my life."

Boots liked this girl. She had guts and she came from his world. He picked her up without saying a word and took her into his bedroom where he dropped her onto the bed. He unzipped his pants and his penis fell out unencumbered by underwear. Brandi's eyes widened when the sheer magnitude of his member gave her a start.

"What can you do with this?" he asked coyly.

Brandi looked up into his eyes as she grabbed his penis and touched it to her red lips. He allowed her to use her considerable expertise to make him even harder and then he took her into his arms and kissed her sensuous lips.

"Nick told me you had some special talent but honey you're unbelievable . . ."

Brandi thought back to the day she went to interview for the job at the Dancing House and ended up blowing three guys in the office who were doing the hiring. She wondered if that bit of fun with Nick and the boys was threatening to destroy her chances with Boots.

"I needed the job, Boots. I have a little girl to feed," Brandi implored.

Boots laughed, "Brandi, you are forgetting who I am. I make my own rules. I love sensuous women who know how to enjoy their own body. Obviously, you live life on your own terms as well and I respect that. You got the job and had a bit of fun. So what? No, the only problem I have with that scenario is that I wasn't there to watch."

His mouth moved down to her firm perfect breasts as his hand reached down between her legs. Brandi moaned as his tongue slowly found its way down the center of her stomach in a direct line to his hand which was gently massaging her vagina. Boots spread her long muscular legs and flicked his tongue in a rapid motion making Brandi shiver with excitement. When his heart was pounding so hard he could hear it, he pulled Brandi up on her knees and entered her from behind. The sex was almost savage—as if they could not get enough of each other's body. Brandi's vocalizations reached a loud pitch as Boots held her breasts and pummelled her rhythmically with fierce intensity. When her body quaked with orgasm, the room darkened and she felt as if she were on the verge of passing out. He held her tightly for some time, kissing her gently and whispering compliments into her ear until she slipped into oblivion.

The smell of coffee. The softest bed and silkiest linen she had ever felt. A cozy warmth by her feet. Brandi's mind found its way to consciousness and she became aware that she was in the sumptuous bedroom of Lou Falcone. She was surprised to find that she had not heard him leave but she was also relieved that he was not there to witness the present condition of her hair and makeup.

Feelings of euphoria and happiness washed over her body as she looked around the magnificent room. At the far end, a painting of a deformed female shape that could only be a Picasso, hung above a big stone fireplace. There was enough light streaming in that she could see an intercom on the wall beside the bed. She pushed the button that read STAFF. A soft voice came through, "Good morning Miss Brandi. May we serve you breakfast?"

Brandi stared at the intercom for a moment and then replied, "Yes, that would be nice, thank you. Oh . . . is Mr. Falcone here?"

"No, Miss Brandi. He always leaves about 7am."

"Oh, OK," Brandi replied.

Fuck this is living! she thought. She pressed the button that said DRAPES and suddenly the sky filled one complete wall. She jumped up to take in the breathtaking view of Central Park and then paused for a moment to ask herself if this was really happening. *This is the most magical day of my life and I don't want it to end. I want to stay in this reality forever.* A soft knock on the door surprised her and she jumped back into bed before a uniformed maid entered pushing a food cart.

"Good morning, Miss Brandi. Cook says that he would be delighted to prepare something else for you if this is not to your satisfaction. Just let him know over the KITCHEN intercom if there is something else you would prefer. Can I run your bath for you?"

"Yes," Brandi replied with an air of importance. The maid arranged the cart so it hung over the bed like a hospital server, removed the food covers, and poured the coffee.

"If I can be of any service, please let me know," she smiled as she excused herself to run the bath water.

"I will. Thank you."

Brandi examined the silver tray laden with food and decorated with an antique vase filled with a dozen small pink roses. There were crepes oozing with orange custard, bacon, freshly squeezed wheat grass, and an assortment of pastries. She spread a warm croissant with Devonshire cream and raspberry jam and bit into the delicate layers of pastry. A heavenly taste flooded her senses and she could only guess that she was enjoying a pastry that had been prepared in a foreign country and flown in by plane. *Even his food has had experiences I haven't had,* she giggled. Brandi's heart started to pound when she picked up a napkin and saw a gift wrapped box. She ripped open the paper to find a bottle of JOLIE MADAME perfume by Balmain and a note. Her hands were shaking as she read:

Brandi,

> *This is my favourite perfume and I want it to remind me of you. I hope you enjoy your Champagne. I'll call you as soon as I can. Counting the moments until I can touch you again.*
>
> **Boots**

Brandi opened the bottle and sprayed a little into the air. She loved it! Temporarily overcome by joy, she leaned back on the wall of pillows to take it all in. *Yes! Champagne would be wonderful!* She started to pour the small bottle of bubbly into a flat bottom champagne glass when she heard a clink. Something was sparkling amidst the bubbles. She put her finger into the glass and pulled out an exquisite diamond tennis bracelet. *Each diamond is big enough to be mounted for an engagement ring,* she thought as she counted thirty-four of them. It was the most beautiful thing she had ever seen! She put on her bracelet, grabbed her champagne, and ran naked to the perfumed water of the giant bathtub to luxuriate in her memories of lovemaking with Boots the night before. After a half an hour or so, she wrapped herself in the white robe laid out by the maid and went to the vanity to inspect all the wonderful toiletries displayed on a tray.

When she was made up and dressed and could no longer justify her stay, she pushed the button that was marked STAFF.

"Yes, Miss Brandi?"

"I'll be leaving shortly, can you arrange a taxi?"

"No need, Miss Raleigh, there is a car and driver at your disposal when you are ready."

Brandi looked around to take in the room one more time. The last thing she wanted to do was leave and it seemed to take all of her effort to walk toward the door. *Why was it so easy to become accustomed to nice things*, she wondered? At this moment the thought of returning to the squalor she called home was more than she could stand.

Right beside the door on a small table was a picture of Boots, tanned and smiling, standing on a golf course with a politician she had seen on TV. She felt her knees buckle slightly. She loved him. She knew she would always love him.

Chapter 6

Lion Terkel rolled off the exotic beauty and reached for a joint. The thrill of having sex at thirty thousand feet just never seemed to get old. Still, there was a niggling hint of discontent that continually threatened to clarify itself and he was now ready to give it an audience. He was becoming aware that he was finished with this woman and he was disappointed because just one week before, when they had left for this romantic trip to Paris, he had actually entertained the idea that she could be the one. All that togetherness had left him feeling lonely. Conversation felt contrived after a couple of days and the physical chemistry was wearing thin. And, to top it off, her eyes were just too close together. Another day of looking at them was becoming unbearable, never mind a lifetime. He simply could not cope with imperfection and he was determined never to settle for less than his ideal woman. Women never looked like their picture in a magazine. He should have known better than to try that again. Look how well it had worked in the past.

Facing the realization that he was truly alone again sent his mind spinning back to memories of Acelyn. Memories revived the rage that simmered just below the level of his conscious thoughts and rekindled that ache in the center of his being that had never gone away since she left twenty-eight years ago. Love and hate co-existed with equal passion in his twisted soul.

As he walked into the cabin of the plane, Lion threw on a long purple robe with a large crest on the back featuring a roaring lion with devil horns. The presence of one tear falling from the lion's eye made his patch unique in the club and denoted his exalted position as President of Lucifer's Pride Motorcycle Club. Dex, a small sophisticated man of about sixty with a brusque efficient manner and an upper class British accent put down the phone. Twenty years of working with Lion had given him a nose for trouble and his intense blue eyes registered trepidation.

"Bad news, Gov."

"Give it to me Dex," Lion said impatiently.

"Baldy called from Daytona. He said the warehouse was ransacked and they got it all. About thirty million in crystal meth and maybe fifteen in ecstasy." Lion threw his head back and laughed long and hard.

"Mickey?"

"Mickey's fine. Hadn't arrived on site yet but they got Harley." Lion gave an internal sigh of relief. Good cooks were the heart of the operation and Mickey was the best in his field.

"Get Boots on the phone," Lion demanded before he retired to the privacy of his dressing room. Lion, at six foot four, had a custom built shower with a bar that ran across the top. Shaking with rage, he grabbed the bar and started pumping his body up and down as the water ran through the long wavy black hair that fell to his shoulders. During his first stint in jail for drug trafficking when he was seventeen years old, he learned to use this exercise to release tension. Maybe it was a form of self-flagellation or maybe it was a way of attempting to regain strength when circumstances made him feel vulnerable. Whatever it was, it worked. Exhaustion overtook him and his inner rage receded enough that he was able to compose himself and face the world again.

Lion was a basket of contradictions that mesmerized a curious public. Partying was his trademark and he spent a small fortune entertaining associates, celebrities, and members of the club. Only a handful of people really knew the ruthless soul that had compensated for a loveless childhood by building an empire out of pure greed for power and control.

The loss of money was not what upset Lion; he had more money than someone could spend in a lifetime. But, the struggle for power and domination still ruled his life and this incident had thrown evidence of his vulnerability in his face. It was the loss of control that still drove Lion to prove his sovereignty in his world. His gut told him that this raid was the result of a very old beef between the Lucifer's Pride and their rivals of thirty years, the Purple Flames. This old vendetta had haunted his every waking moment for years and he would use his last breath to make sure he came out the ultimate winner.

Lion's personal goal had been to see Lucifer's Pride proliferate throughout the world, converting every worthy outlaw bike club to the Pride patch and, for the most part, he had been successful. As the Pride patch moved into new territory, local bike clubs were given the option to convert or remain independent. If they allied themselves with the strongest club in existence they prospered along with them; if they did not join eagerly they risked being in the bad graces of the Pride. A small number of clubs, enamoured with their autonomy, made the latter choice and soon met with death and destruction. And now, for most intents and purposes, the Pride ruled the underworld in any place that mattered throughout the world. The Purple Flames were the one exception to the patch over tradition. The official club policy was that every Flame was an enemy of every Pride and it would remain that way until Lion's last breath.

Like all outlaw bike gangs, The Pride's financial foundation was based on illegal activity, mainly the drug trade, even though they had branched out over the years into legitimate business—primarily for the purpose of money laundering. Members prided themselves on living a life that embraced a philosophy of personal freedom and hedonism that flouted the accepted rules of society. These philosophies still governed every member of Lucifer's Pride and always would. Lion's mission, as president, was simply to convince the public otherwise. The strategy had worked. Lion made sure the club kept a low profile—police scrutiny was kept to a minimum and business was booming. This same policy had spared the lives of every member of the Flames. Now with the attack on the warehouse, Lion's priorities had changed. Things were going to get dirty.

Dex indicated that Boots was on the line.

"We've got trouble brother. The warehouse was hit by a fuckin' tornado so the orders are going to be about three weeks late." Lion listened silently for a moment while Boots cursed.

"I hear ya. Mustard and I discussed it. After the party I'm calling an emergency church where I'll lay out our course of action." They were not about to get into details about business over the phone. Boots asked Lion if he was bringing Vita to the party.

"No, son, I'm coming alone," Lion said with exasperation in his voice. "One more down, three billion to go."

"What about you?" Lion asked.

"No kidding?" Lion seemed surprised. "And she's dancing tonight? That'll be a blast. I can't wait to meet her. See you in an hour."

Shane's new customized Road King Harley Davidson shone like a pearl as he pulled up to the curb. His decision to hook his lucky star to Lucifer's Pride Motorcycle Club was beginning to pay off in exactly the way he had hoped it would. He was even starting to cut into some Purple Flame territory in South Jersey. Selling the highest grade crystal meth in the world—made with the Pride's stamp of approval—was like taking candy from a baby. Years of being the heavy on the toughest range at Attica was proving to be the perfect prerequisite for his new job as drug supplier and money collector for the Pride.

There was a time, a generation or two before, when all you needed was a love for riding and a rebellious nature to be taken into the brotherhood of the club—no longer. Membership was now only an option for those who had the brains and the entrepreneurial spirit to make money for the organization and Shane was intent on making his mark. Tonight was going to be a personal celebration of his association with the club and it was also a chance to meet the leaders of the Pride in person.

Flood lights lit up the sky and tiny lights simulating stars floated over the exterior of the enormous building that housed the latest addition to The Dancing House chain of strip clubs started by Lion twenty-five years before. The grand opening of the club was being used as a cover for the real celebration which was the anniversary of thirty years since the inception of the Lucifer's Pride Motorcycle Club. There was a red carpet stretching from the curb to the front door where a handful of private Pride security, proudly flying club colours, stood to prevent any outsiders from crashing the party.

When James entered the club Snake yelled out, "Hey Popeye! Over here." Shane stood up to greet James and grabbed his friend's hand throwing his other arm around him in a hug. As their eyes met they gave each other a knowing look. The tale of James' handiwork was being acknowledged and memorialized. When a brother of

Snake's stature gave you a nickname it was a sign of respect and your future had been decided. Suddenly they knew that James was going to be promoted from Prospect to Full Patch at tomorrow's church meeting and Shane would be promoted to Prospect because of the bloody job they had done for the club just a week earlier.

Excitement was building as the crowd waited for their star members to show up and add glamour to the proceedings.

Dex deplaned first in order to give Lion and his entourage clearance to follow. A few photographers from the supermarket rags were there, as usual, to chronicle a lifestyle of hedonism and riches that few people could even imagine. Lion, dressed in a black suit with a jacket that brushed his knees, descended holding hands with Vita, the beautiful blonde model whose face was presently gracing the cover of Vogue magazine. Light bulbs flashed and Lion, saying nothing, put his hand across his face after giving the photographers enough time to snap some good pictures. Mustard, the retired Sergeant-at-Arms for the club, and Tiny, a trusted member from the old days, followed fifteen feet behind him. Andrew, his steward/valet and a couple of trusted Pride members acting as body guards on the trip were the last to step off the plane.

Lion and Vita jumped into the front of the stretch limo, while Dex, Mustard, and Tiny took their place in the rear section.

"Listen Honey, I'm going to drop you off at your place—I've got business tonight," Lion stated casually.

"But Lion, the club opening is tonight and I want to go. I think it will be fun."

Lion turned to Vita and gave her a cold stare.

"Look, Vita, it's a strip club, a boy's night out. I can't take you," he uttered flatly.

Vita had read about Lion's cold eyes and how he wore his famous round sunglasses day and night to avoid frightening people. As silly as that seemed when she read about it in STARLIGHT magazine, she felt a cold shutter go up the back of her neck and now wondered how she had failed to noticed that look in his eyes before.

"Will you call me tomorrow?" she asked as suspicion grazed her famous grapefruit coloured eyes.

"I'm going to be busy for the next little while . . . ."

"You're dropping me, you bastard! I am the top model in the world! How dare you treat me like some common tramp!" she shrieked.

Lion did not take kindly to someone correcting him or pointing out his faults. No one had ever given him anything in this world and he felt no obligation to anyone, for anything.

"Well, the two are not mutually exclusive Vita. Maybe you are the top model in the world, and a common tramp . . . ." Lion's words dropped liked stones.

"You prick!" Vita screamed as she jumped at Lion and started to throw a clenched fist at his face which he managed to block. The car came to an abrupt stop and Lion's men opened the door and dragged Vita kicking and punching out of the car. Mustard hailed a cab and threw her in the back while Tiny gave the taxi driver a hundred dollar bill and an address.

Twenty minutes later Lion pulled up to the curb beside the red carpet and, as planned, Boots' limousine pulled in behind him. Running With The Devil by Van Halen, played over the loud speaker in honour of Lion's arrival. The crowd cheered and called out their names as if they were movie stars arriving at a movie premier.

"Hey, Black Cat where's Vita?" someone yelled. Lion smiled and waved to the crowd stopping a couple of times to sign autographs along the red carpet.

James and Shane had been sitting with Snake riveted by his stories of his early years in the club.

"You haven't heard about the big contract? Shit I thought everyone knew about it even if they weren't in the Pride," Snake said with a smirk, relishing his role as mentor.

"What contract?" James asked eagerly.

"Thirty years ago Lion met Acelyn. She was a singer for a rock band at the time, long black hair, exotic looking and gorgeous. Lion was nuts about her and they were together for two years when the shit hit the fan."

"What happened?" James' eyes flashed with excitement at the hint of trouble.

"Lion would pester her to quit singing but she was stubborn and wanted a career. He was very possessive and he didn't like her being in clubs where she might meet other men. I saw her couple of times and she was unbelievable—would have been a big star. Well, one night she's doin' her thing—Lion's somewhere building his empire—and the leader of the Purple Flames, Jimmy Bourke, goes into the club where she's singing. He's not wearing a Patch and so, of course, he hits on her after the set and Lion's worst nightmare comes true. She falls in love with him and they ride off into the sunset together. Lion goes crazy lookin' for her. For about two months he drops the ball when it comes to business and is totally focused on finding her. Finally someone spots her with Jimmy on the street somewhere in Philly and tells Lion. Well, I guess she didn't know Lion too well after all. You don't fuck with Lion. Maybe she thought she was protected by the Flames and maybe she would have been but someone must have got to Jimmy—that's all I can figure. Lion found out that he was supposed to be at a certain place, at a certain time and . . . well . . . let's just say Jimmy made an error in trusting someone."

"What happened?"

"There was an ambush on an old dirt road in the countryside. He showed up alone."

"Well?" Shane asked impatiently.

"Jimmy disappeared after that night. The story goes that it was the only time that Boots and Lion got blood on their hands." Snake paused for effect and then continued the lesson, "First of all, you do not disrespect the Patch that way—Jimmy paid with his life for that. But I think most of it was about Lion getting revenge on Ace. Lion immediately put a contract on her head. It started out at ten thousand dollars but of course it grew as Lion became rich. Now the contract is worth a million bucks. He pays agencies to maintain a search but so far-nothing. Fucks around but hasn't had an Ole Lady since."

Shane shrugged, "Way too much fuss over some pussy, if you ask me."

Chapter 7

Brandy was sitting in front of the makeup mirrors backstage, a long cigarette in one hand and a drink in the other, waiting for the glue on her false eyelashes to dry. Monica came running into the room where the twelve or so dancers sat in various stages of undress, squealing with excitement.

"Oh my God! Boots and Lion just walked in! They're sitting right in front of the stage, in the centre banquette!" Monica was a boisterous redhead whose claim to fame was her enormous natural bust. She cupped her breasts in her hands and purred, "Hey, I heard Boots is a tits man and I think he came alone!"

Brandi repositioned her chin to a more regal angle and yelled, "He's with me, you moron!"

The room fell silent as the thought of Brandi having that much power settled into the minds of the other strippers. Monica, however, was undaunted as she strutted over to Brandi wearing only a tiny G-string. Putting her hands on her hips, she leaned into Brandi's personal space.

"Oh really?" she asked loud enough that every girl in the room could hear. "And what does his Ole Lady, FANCY, have to say about that?"

Without hesitation Brandi looked at her and screamed through clenched teeth, "Get your goddamned saggy tits out of my face and mind your own fuckin' business!" Monica gave Brandi a knowing smirk and left the room.

Brandi dabbed a little more lipstick on her full red lips, double checked her makeup from every angle, slowly got up from her chair, and walked down the hall. As she passed a special washroom reserved for handicapped persons she looked back to see if anyone was watching before she ducked in and gripped the vanity to steady her shaky legs. She barely recognized the girl in the mirror with the look of terror etched on her face.

Fancy! Who the fuck was Fancy? Brandi searched her mind to understand how she could have missed the simple fact that Boots had an Old Lady. *Maybe Boots had chosen not to tell her because she was nothing more to him than sex on the side.* She closed her eyes and felt a big lump in her stomach that seemed to be climbing up to her throat. In a second she was throwing up in the sink even though nothing was coming up. It felt as if she was trying to expel the idea that this other woman called Fancy existed. Her mind wandered back to their last time together and she remembered how he had gazed into her eyes as he made love to her. The thought that another woman had touched Boots after that was more than she could stand. Brandi took a deep breath and looked down at her watch. She was scheduled to go on at exactly ten o'clock as the feature dancer. She had only fifteen minutes to pull herself together.

Boots and Lion were having a great time mingling with the guys and catching up on all the news as they awaited the commencement of the entertainment. Lion's first foray into a legitimate business was a strip club called The Dancing House and as the years passed he expanded the chain throughout the USA. He still loved the atmosphere of fun and decadence that each one created.

One of the first bands that he hired for his clubs was a rock band called Soul's Gate. Lion admired the band's dedication to their art and the way their music brilliantly filled the room with a mood, sometimes upbeat, and sometimes dark and smouldering. Later, the band had topped the charts with three albums that gave their indescribable rock genius the recognition it deserved. A couple of years later their lead guitarist and music composer was tragically killed in a car accident and the band had permanently disbanded—until tonight. They had replaced the lead guitarist and agreed to play this gig in honour of Lion who had given them their start a generation earlier. Lion went over to shake their hands as the band was warming up for their next song which was a rendition of Body Sends Us/ Message Reaches Us for the feature dancer. When Brandi heard Boots mention this song as one of his favourites, she decided to use it for the opening number.

Brandi stood in the wings as the MC took the microphone.

"Well, my friends, they say a Harley is a vibrator with a kick stand. I am here to tell you that tonight we have the next best thing—our answer to Viagra—our feature dancer—the irresistible Brandi!"

The band started to play Body Sends Us and Brandi strutted out onto the stage wearing a black sequined mini dress, black fishnet stockings that reached the top of her thighs, black shoes with five inch spiked heels, and a white stole of artificial fur. She danced across the stage to showcase her long muscular legs which she knew to be Boots' fetish. Brandi smiled, tossed her long blonde hair back, and unzipped her dress to reveal a black bikini bottom and sparkly tassels that covered her nipples. She danced and gyrated and then adopted a sultry look as she planted herself right in front of the banquette where Lion and Boots sat with a few friends. She shoved her hand down the front of her tiny costume and threw her head back as she pushed it down her thighs to reveal a tiny sparkling G-string. After stepping out of the panties and throwing them toward Boots she sunk slowly opening her legs. Looking down and then back to Boots, she undid the tiny string to reveal all to Boots and anyone who cared to see. She put her hands on either side of her hips and rotated her pelvis as provocatively as she knew how—giving the most lewd demonstration of her anatomy she could provide. Glancing at Boots, she caught the most lascivious look she had ever seen in her life. As the song came to the end, she brought her hands to her lips and blew a kiss to Boots. He laughed and gave her a nod. She left the stage knowing she had his stamp of approval by the look of lust in his eyes. However, before she reached the door of the dressing room she was abruptly jolted back to reality by a big biker with large decorated arms and a hoarse voice.

"I have something for you—from Boots."

He unravelled an exquisite floor length sable mink and held it out so that she could put it on. She could not believe her eyes. The guy leaned over to her and whispered.

"He wants you to join him at the table wearing only the coat."

Brandi grabbed the coat and wrapped it around her body as if it were Boots himself. With a spring in her step she joined him at the banquette and he introduced her to Lion and a couple of other associates sitting with them. Boots opened her coat and grabbed her breast as he kissed her passionately. Brandi melted in his arms as his hand slipped down between her legs. Lion and the other two men ignored the two lovers and continued their conversation. Finally, Boots pulled himself away from Brandy giving her a loving look that sent chills up her spine.

The night was enchanting and she sipped her champagne as she wallowed in her victory. She pushed the thought of Fancy way back into the recesses of her mind. Nothing was going to ruin the high she was on tonight. Brandy turned to Boots and smiled seductively, "Did you like my dance?"

"Are you kidding? We were all sitting here with big boners—your body is a dangerous weapon. Maybe after the party we could go back to Nick's office with Sparky and Bull and have a little party—before we go back to my place. You know how I love to see your body in action. You can handle three of us can't you?" Boots' eyes flashed with mischief. A feeling of supreme confidence swept through Brandi like a spring wind. She had used her body to get what she wanted all of her life. She understood what Boots wanted and she could deliver.

"Mmmm . . . can't wait," she whispered.

As Boots ran his hand up and down Brandi's thigh, the lights dimmed to complete darkness and the room fell quiet.

A single violin pierced the silence and the spotlight slowly lit the centre stage to reveal a woman standing with her arms in the air holding layers of blue and green chiffon covered in tiny silver sparkles. She slowly started to spin to the music and as her arms came down—her face was revealed. Brandi knocked over her drink and stood up in stunned surprise. Boots stood up beside her to get a better look at this beauty moving like a ballerina across the stage. Fear struck her heart. *Sherry! Here?* Confusion and hatred made her head spin.

All the blood drained from Lion's face as he stood beside Boots watching this perfect woman losing herself in her dance to Rimsky-Korsakov's Sheherazade. Suddenly, he felt as if he could not breathe and he pulled at his shirt collar breaking open the top buttons. The rest of the audience watched in stunned silence.

After a minute or so of graceful movements, she revealed a tiny blue-green bikini top and G-string beneath the chiffon. She was very thin but perfectly proportioned with long shapely legs and a tousled mane of thick dark hair that fell down her back. Draping herself in chiffon with one arm, she removed the tiny string top and held it out for the audience to see. Looking out into the darkness, she naturally focused on the tall man in the front row. Lion looked into her big violet-blue eyes that sloped down just a little on the corners and saw that hint of vulnerability that made every man's heart yearn to be the one to possess her. She dropped the bikini top and brought both hands down to her sides revealing perfect breasts carved out of a well toned upper body. Lion felt his legs moving him toward the stage but he was not sure why. He was walking toward the stairs that led to the stage and then he was walking up the stairs—this beautiful dancer was drawing him like a magnet. On some level he knew that she was his and that he refused to share her with the others.

Once again she was draped in chiffon as she removed her G-string. As she held it out for the audience to see, and prepared to drop the chiffon, Lion reached her on stage. Before she was able to reveal her nudity, he swept her up into his arms and carried her offstage. The song finished shortly and the MC brought up the lights but dared not make a comment on the performance since no one was quite clear as to what had just transpired.

Time stood still as Sherry peered into the stranger's eyes and saw a look of such intensity that she was compelled to return his gaze. He was very strong and the embrace of his powerful arms made her feel completely safe and protected. The long moment ended as he dropped her down and a look of foreboding crossed her face once more.

"I feel like I want to say thank you but I must go back out there . . . ."

"You don't belong there," Lion said firmly.

The truth in those words brought tears to her eyes. "I know," she said as she dropped her eyes. "But I need the money desperately. I have to go back out there. My boss will be wondering what happened to me . . ."

"Don't worry about that—I'm his boss. Come into the office so we can talk." Lion was still shaking from the intensity of the last few moments. He opened the door to his office and invited Sherry to have a seat on the couch while he searched the closet to find something to cover her. Lion looked into her eyes in the better light of the room as he draped her with a blanket and caught his breath at the sweetness and beauty of her youth.

"Tell me how you ended up here," he said softly. Sherry dropped her eyes and hesitated. A feeling of helplessness engulfed her and before she knew it, her normal reticence gave way and she began to reveal her personal struggle to the complete stranger sitting before her.

"I was living with my mother and sister but they kicked me out of the house last week. I had to leave my niece behind with them and I know she won't be safe without me there to look after her. I've been staying with my friend Natasha but if I can get a place of my own I have a chance at getting custody," she said as she began to cry.

"Don't you have a husband or boyfriend who could give you a hand?" Lion asked.

"No, no. I'm all alone. Completely alone." Stated so plainly, it was almost as if she felt the gravity of her predicament for the first time.

Lion drew in his breath and a wave of relaxation passed over him as he took in this crucial piece of information.

"I'm going to make all of your problems go away," he said with conviction.

A flicker of recognition flashed across her mind but she could not place the handsome face in front of her.

"Who are you and why do you want to help me?"

"I'm Lion Terkel. I own this club and I like to help people when I can. It's as simple as that. Will you allow me to lend you a hand?" he asked earnestly.

"I'm usually stubborn when it comes to my independence," she said as her voice lowered. "But I'm not in a position to be proud right now—I have to think of my niece. I'll accept any help you are willing to give me and I'll worry about paying you back when I get back on my feet."

Lion suppressed an urge to smile.

"There will be no more talk of paying me back for anything. Karmic law says that you must accept all gifts with the same grace you accept the unfortunate incidents in your life, like the turn of events that brought you to my stage." Sherry sat quietly, enthralled by the powerful figure of Lion as he continued to speak in a reassuring voice.

"I can't leave here tonight because I have an important meeting after the show but I have people who work for me who will provide you with everything you need. It'll just take me a moment to set things up for you, so while I'm on the phone, feel free to just put your feet up on the couch and have a rest." Total exhaustion overtook Sherry as she looked into the eyes of this perfect stranger with complete trust, and said, "Thank you."

"Oh I forgot to ask you. What's your name?"

"Sheherezade. Sheherezade Ivey." Her eyes flashed with steely determination and then closed as she obeyed his voice and stretched out on the couch. Sherry was so exhausted from the tension of the past week that she fell asleep as soon as her head touched the pillow. Lion walked over to the desk and picked up the phone. He turned and examined every inch of the beautiful young woman as she slept peacefully.

"Dex," Lion whispered, "I want you to look after some things for me tonight . . . ."

Chapter 8

An hour or so later, Lion was on his way to the meeting when he passed Brandi exiting the boardroom looking rather tousled and sporting an evil grin. Boots, Sparky, and Bull were sitting around with drinks in their hands showing signs of exhaustion.

"Spreading things a bit thin, aren't we boys?" Lion said with a smirk.

Bikers arrived one by one until the large room was filled with about thirty of the highest ranking and most trusted members of the Pride. Lion stood before them and his eyes darkened, "Most of you have already heard that those pricks hit us in Florida and got a fair volume of meth and ecstasy. I don't give a shit about that but, God damn it, they killed Harley, a respected brother and the son of one of our oldest friends. Boots, you've been saying for a long time that we've got to get back into the game. You all know I've been doing my best to avoid this kind of a situation because it threatens all the work we have done to give the club a more, let's say *presentable* face, only so we can take care of business with the least possible amount of heat." The veins in Lions neck began to fill with blood as he continued, "Business is one thing but that does not mean that we will eat shit dished up by these lowly motherfuckers!" Lion yelled, "These fuckers are going to pay!"

Boots yelled, "Hey, Hey!" as he lifted his fist in the air. The room broke into a loud thunder of cheers. Boots stood up.

"They've had it too easy for too long! These pricks have to know who is running things and we're going to fuck their world!"

Lion looked out at the group, "Does anyone disagree with this plan of action?" These seasoned bikers knew that Lion, as leader, called the shots for the gang. They also knew that to speak at a time like this would be a sign of disrespect that would surely get them killed before they left the room.

Lion's voice lowered and became calm, "We are not going to fight a war; we are going to pick them off one by one like birds on a wire. I'm putting a bounty of $25,000 on every Purple Flame Patch on a warm body and then we'll see how long it takes to wallpaper the clubhouse." Lion took both hands and started to pound on the desk, "I want them dead! Dead! Dead! If one of the Pride falls we find out who was responsible and we wipe out their family." The members were quiet for a moment as the words sank in and then they started to hoot and holler and high five each other. Someone yelled from the back "Yeah! Black Cat is back!"

Sheherezade was awakened by a matronly middle-aged woman with glasses and a big smile. "Hello, Sheherezade, my name is Tina and I have been sent by Lion to look after you. I brought a change of clothing for you and there is a car waiting outside." A combination of exhaustion and trust in the kind stranger who had vowed to help her, melted her natural resistance, so she smiled back at the woman and followed her instructions. After changing into the soft pink leisure suit provided, she followed Tina to the car. A white stretch limo whisked them through city streets to downtown Manhattan. Sheherezade was shocked to find herself in a magnificent fully furnished condominium. Tina explained that one of Lion's corporations kept the suite ready for business associates. She showed her into the bedroom and told her to make herself comfortable. Sheherezade entered the ensuite bathroom and discovered a shower that could accommodate five people, a huge bathtub, an assortment of expensive toiletries and an exquisite pink peignoir set of fine lace and silk. She took a hot shower and scrubbed off the heavy makeup she had applied for her debut as a stripper and then collapsed on the bed. Tina knocked quietly on the door and presented her with a tray of hot tea, finger sandwiches and cakes. She announced that Lion's personal physician had arrived to give her a quick check-up because Lion was concerned about her level of stress. After the examination, Dr. Lindsay suggested that she allow him to give her sedation so that she could relax completely and have a good night sleep. *Was this a fanciful dream?* Sheherezade felt the sharp prick of the needle and as the tranquilizer coursed through her veins all her anxiety about Lila dipped into blackness for the first time since she left her in the little flat in Dover.

Sheherezade awoke to the smell of yellow roses that decorated the big window which displayed the bustle of New York City from the complete silence of the sound proof room. Tina poked her head in, "Good morning dear, are you ready for some brunch?" Sheherezade nodded and smiled, "Yes, please, if it's not too much trouble."

"Nothing is too much trouble! Lion told me to make sure you have everything your heart desires. I understand you have been under a lot of stress and the doctor has ordered rest. However, you have an appointment with one of Lion's lawyers at one o'clock, here in the suite. He'll help you sort out any legal problems you have concerning your niece and follow through until the matter is cleared up." Sheherezade covered her face with her hands and tears sprung from her eyes out of unmitigated relief. Tina put her hand on Sheherezade's shoulder, "You must have been through an ordeal but you are going to be fine."

After an hour long meeting with the lawyer, Sheherezade's mood shifted as the reality of the turn of events started to sink in. Just last week she was scrambling to find a job as a stripper in order to make quick money in tips. She knew the club where Brandi worked was hiring strippers so she put on some makeup and a sexy dress in order to look the part, told a little white lie about being experienced, and was hired on the spot. While researching her new name, she had discovered that Sheherezade was a heroine in a Persian legend which had inspired a classical symphonic composition by Rimsky-Korsakov. Upon hearing an old recording in a private sound booth at the library, she was completely enchanted by the music and felt she understood the great honour that had been bestowed upon her. Sentiment welled up in her chest and she wept for the empty void in her life that had taken the place of that promise. But, she told herself, there was no room in her life now for such thoughts. She had no choice but to muster all of her strength and forge ahead. Sheherezade was her namesake and she was determined to choreograph a dance befitting the music. If she had to be a stripper, she would do it in her own way and try to make her dance an exotic work of art rather than a lewd display of flesh.

Natasha had convinced her parents to allow Sherry to stay with her for a very short time until she was able to get some money together for an apartment of her own. Sheherezade had left Brandi no choice but to take Lila to their aunt Wendy's home while Regina was in jail. However, the day Regina was released from jail, Wendy brought Lila back home to Dover and within an hour Regina had left Lila alone in the apartment. Sherry had been keeping a close eye on the house, knowing that after a week in jail, Regina would be way overdue for a party. When she knocked on the door, Lila asked who it was, and there was a tearful reunion as Sherry explained her plan to Lila. When Lila was alone, Sherry would be with her and leave through the back door when someone came home. Lila fell asleep and Sherry stayed with her until Regina, Luke, and some losers from the bar, came back with a case of beer to finish off the party at the house. Sherry fretted about leaving Lila in the house with those people but she had to stay optimistic because her hands were tied until she had worked a couple of nights at The Dancing House and could use her tips to get a place that would be a suitable home for Lila.

Now, with the help of Lion's lawyer, the plan was foolproof. A private eye had been assigned to watch the house and the moment Lila was left alone the authorities would be called to pick her up. They would surely remove her from the home for neglect and as the next of kin with a clean record and a means of support for Lila, she would be given temporary custody. Sherry could relax now knowing that Lila was under constant supervision.

Sheherezade was sitting in the living room taking in the beauty of the elegant suite and ruminating on her sudden good fortune when Tina came in with a bowl of homemade chicken soup, pate, cheese and French bread.

"Now have a bite to eat dear so you can get your strength back. A couple of aestheticians are coming over from the Thunder Spa to do your nails and give you a massage and a facial so I will run a nice hot bath for you. Tina answered the phone.

"It is for you, my dear—it's Lion."

"Hello Lion, I want to thank you for everything but I don't know where to start . . . ."

"Well, I have an idea. Would you consider having dinner with me tonight?"

"I would love to!" she said, "I want to tell you what you have done for me and my niece."

"Wonderful! I'll see you about eight."

By eight o'clock Sheherezade was wearing a shimmering floor length gown of beige beads with long sleeves and a cowal neck that revealed her stunning figure. A personal shopper had been given Sheherezade's measurements and had brought over a complete wardrobe for her with matching accessories. Tina answered the door and Lion walked in to see Sheherezade approaching from the living room. He stood frozen to the spot in stunned silence. She looked like a different person. Gone was the scared helpless girl from the club last night—this was an elegant woman with a rare beauty and an air of confidence. He loved what he saw; she was the woman he imagined she could be. He knew she was *the one*. His woman. Perfection.

In an exclusive restaurant on the Upper East Side, Lion and Sheherezade shared delicious food in a private dining room that was designed to give the patrons the impression that they were alone, yet pampered by the waiting staff, in an old English mansion. As they lingered over coffee and brandy she discovered that she felt truly comfortable with a man for the first time in her life. As he shared some stories about his life her eyes fell on his full sensuous lips and drifted to his broad masculine shoulders. Lion exuded the essence of masculine strength and power but, at the same time, presented a gentle understanding side that melted her heart. Here was the man that she yearned to have in her life from the time she was a child, the protector that would love her, care about her, and shield her from the world of her mother and sister. "I feel like I'm in a dream," she said wistfully. "I think when I see Lila I will be able to believe that dream."

"It won't be long now," he said confidently knowing he would never trust something so important to fate. If Children's Services did not have the opportunity to pick up Lila later that evening, he had arranged to have a police raid find drugs in the house as soon as Regina was alone with the child the next day. He wanted Sheherezade free of worry so that she could enjoy her time with him.

"You can relax and just trust me," he smiled.

"That's the part that I'm having trouble with. I've never had anyone that I *could* trust in my life. I grew up without a father, and my mother and sister always took advantage of my good nature. Of course, it took me twenty years to appreciate the full extent of my predicament," she laughed.

"Yes, that's the disadvantage of psychological abuse . . . its insidious nature. Now I had the advantage of physical abuse. I knew where I stood for as long as I can remember," he mused with a sigh of resignation.

"Can you talk about it?"

"Oh, sure I am past it now. I never knew my mother and father—I grew up in foster homes. I just wasn't lucky enough to be adopted and I was moved around all my life from home to home. When I was dropped into a couple homes with people that I did like, it hurt even more when they moved me, so in a way I preferred to be in a home that I knew I was going to be glad to leave. When I was about fourteen, I met Boots and we became close friends. I guess we created our own family." Sheherezade looked into his handsome chiselled face and felt the strength that he had forged out of unthinkable pain and loneliness.

"Well, obviously you won. They didn't break your spirit—you are successful and happy."

"Well, I have been successful, and, if you believe my press, I'm having a lot of fun, but to tell you the truth personal happiness has eluded me. I never married. I've always been alone in any real sense."

"Well, I don't imagine you have a difficult time rounding up a date . . . ." she said to lighten the mood.

"No I can't say I haven't tried to find the right woman," he smiled. "I just haven't found her." Lion looked into her eyes at that moment and Sheherezade felt a powerful connection that was mesmerizing. She felt her chest heave and she wanted to feel his powerful arms around her again but instead she looked down demurely and said, "That is so sad. You deserve that kind of happiness."

Just then, Lion's cell phone went off and he smiled knowing that only one call was going to be forwarded to his cell after nine-thirty.

"Well, Sheherezade, you need your rest, and it is time we got you home to your niece."

"Oh, Lion did she get out?" She looked into his eyes hopefully.

"Yes, she's at the apartment waiting for you."

"Oh my God!" She said as she felt the emotion rise in her throat. She got up and threw her arms around Lion giving him a lingering hug.

"How can I ever thank you?"

Chapter 9

Lila's little face glowed with health and happiness as she watched the giant apes at the Bronx Zoo. Just seeing Lila in beautiful designer clothes instead of the home-made clothes she had reconstructed from Goodwill seconds filled Sheherezade's heart with a joy she had never experienced in her life.

It had been two days since she had met Lion and life could not be better. Lila had been ecstatic to be reunited with her aunt and to live in a nice safe place without her mother, grandmother, and a stream of ne'er do wells that were a constant in her daily life. Lion had taken the day off work in order to treat them to an outing at the zoo and an elegant dinner. Sheherezade felt herself tearing up as she watched Lila enjoying quality food that she had never tasted before. She felt intense gratitude toward Lion but she was also overwhelmed by another emotion that was filling her being in a way that she did not know was possible. Is this what love was? How could she have missed the message that explained how it would grip her by the throat and prevent her from thinking about anything but him? Lion. Powerful, intelligent, dangerous. She was not intimidated by him. She was familiar with that dark, forgotten place that held the memories of a brutal childhood. She yearned to help him forget his past and be there for him the way no one had ever been before.

When Tina took Lila into bed, Lion and Sheherezade shared a pot of mint tea and talked and laughed for another couple of hours. Finally, Lion announced that he had to work early in the morning and said good night. Inconsolable loneliness overtook her sensibilities and she tossed and turned wondering what to make of Lion Terkel, her feelings for him, and this totally bizarre arrangement.

The next day, Lion called Sheherezade and asked if he could come for a late visit when he finished his meetings. She told him that they would love to see him and that they would wait to have dinner with him at the apartment. Tina prepared a wonderful turkey dinner. Lion teased Lila and there was so much laughter and comfortable conversation that Sheherezade wished they were a real family and that this togetherness would never end. Shortly after Lila went to bed, Lion explained that he had to leave for Philadelphia that evening for an early morning meeting. Once again she wondered if his attention to them was simply one of obligation as the rescuer of two misplaced waifs on their own in the big city. She felt there had been chemistry between them from the beginning but she hesitated to express her true feelings in case she had misread the signals.

Lion called the next day to say that he had forgotten to tell her that he was going to be doing a special with Larry King that night. He said he would call her again after the show because the taping was about to start. At nine o'clock Sheherazade put Lila to bed and tuned into the show.

Lion was looking very serious in a white open collar and black suit jacket. Larry started by making comments about the media interest in his lifestyle and showed video footage of Lion and Boots arriving at the opening of his new club the week before. *Oh, I wish I did not have to be reminded of that night*, she thought.

"Lion Terkel, founder and leader of Lucifer's Pride Motorcycle Club speaks in a public forum for the first time ever, live tonight with Larry King . . . ."

Sheherezade waited anxiously for the commercial break to finish.

"Lion you have built an enormous financial empire as the leader of Lucifer's Pride Motorcycle Club and for some time now your life has been a subject of press scrutiny. You are known for your hedonistic lifestyle, the parties, the women, and your bad boy image. You get more attention from the press than most movie stars. Why is there so much interest in the way you live?"

Lion's demeanour was honest and sincere and he had a soft smile on his face as he did his best to answer the question.

"We value individual freedom and we don't live our lives the way other people expect us to or want us to and that makes us a target of both fear and envy. Most people have zero tolerance for someone who is not exactly like them. They can't understand people who refuse to buckle under society's pressure to conform when they themselves dedicate their lives to trying to live up to some imaginary standard of normal." Larry barely paused before he continued.

"The partying—your party lifestyle is well documented by the press."

"I entertain the way many CEO's of major corporations entertain business associates. I *am* in the hospitality business so naturally my clients and associates expect a certain standard of excellence. Besides, I'm not making any apologies. My philosophy—our philosophy of life—has always been to live for today and let tomorrow look after itself. That, of course, is what every guru has been espousing for thousands of years. Once again, people choose to criticize me for it but I believe the criticism is fuelled by envy. It's something that brings joy to my friends and associates and I guarantee that if my critics could just get their hands on an invitation they wouldn't pass up the opportunity to party with us."

"Donald Trump has been critical of your recent real estate transactions calling you unscrupulous in your dealings. How do you answer these allegations? Lion lowered his eyes and shook his head impatiently. "What Mr. Trump called unscrupulous, I simply call competitive. Maybe, I'm used to fighting for what I want so I just try a little harder than everyone else. It's easy to make a million dollars once you've graduated from Wharton School of Business. I would have attended Wharton but I couldn't afford the subway fare." He paused for a moment and his painful past registered fleetingly across his handsome features. "What I am saying is that I have no obligation to live up to Mr. Trump's expectations. In my experience, most criticism is thinly veiled jealousy."

Larry was his usual enthusiastic self, "Let's talk about your bad boy image. Are you involved in organized crime as your detractors claim?" Lion gave a little shrug, "I will admit that when I began my career some thirty years ago, all of my activities were not legal but that was a long time ago and things have changed. Now I admit that I have a very diverse business empire and, no—I'm not just selling ice cream. I own a chain of strip clubs and gambling establishments around this country and abroad, but while some people may not agree with these activities, they are legal businesses, and I pay my taxes like everyone else."

"What about accusations of your involvement with drugs, firearms, loan sharking, prostitution, and other activities traditionally associated with bike gangs? Are you denying that you, or members of the club, have ever used these illegal methods to make money?" Exasperation crossed Lion's face.

"I have only been associated with legitimate business for many, many, years. A motorcycle club is a brotherhood of men who enjoy individual freedom that includes riding their motorcycle. If some members indulge in illegal activities it certainly is not condoned or encouraged by the club, and I object to the notion that I am responsible for the behaviour of another human being. I believe in live and let live."

"You are one of America's most eligible bachelors. The tabloids followed your relationship with Vita. Are you still dating? America is interested," Larry placed his chin on his hand and tried to stifle a smirk knowing he had put Lion on the hot seat. Lion smiled broadly and suppressed an impulse to laugh.

"Well, Larry, Vita is a wonderful person but we're no longer together. I'm still single."

"Would you marry if the right woman came along? Or is marriage a convention that you eschew as well?"

"No, I would love to be married if the right woman came along. I would say that it is probably the only goal that I have not achieved." Shortly after the show ended Lion called Sheherezade.

"I saw the show and thought you were wonderful," she said.

"Thank you, that means a lot to me. I just wanted to let you know that I am flying to Florida tonight. I have to attend the funeral of a business associate so I won't be back until tomorrow evening.

"Oh, I am sorry to hear that . . ." Sheherezade said. "Will we see you tomorrow?"

"Well Sheher, I have a serious question for you."

"Yes?"

"I realize there is an age difference between us and I want you to know that there are no strings attached whatsoever to this question but would you like to go out on a date with me tomorrow night?"

Hope hit her like a lightening rod. "I would love to Lion," she answered, trying to maintain her decorum.

"Good, let Tina baby sit and we'll have a quiet dinner alone. I know a wonderful place. I'll pull some strings right now to get us a table, and I'll pick you up tomorrow at eight."

"Wonderful!"

"See you tomorrow . . . ."

The girls from Thunder Spa came over in the afternoon to pamper Sheherezade with a manicure, pedicure, massage and updo. They suggested she try their head to toe artificial suntan and then they went to work creating a glamorous evening look with makeup. When Lion walked into the entrance he saw Sheherezade approach in a long low-cut dress in her favourite shade of purple. He stood mesmerized by her breathtaking beauty and looked deep into her eyes.

"You are stunning—the most beautiful woman I have ever seen." She smiled coyly as he kissed her hand and wrapped her arm around his own.

"Let's have our first date, shall we?"

When they arrived at the restaurant they were seated in a very private cove which included a view of Manhattan at night from thirty stories in the sky. Lion ordered Martinis, Caesar salad and Chateaubriand for two. He had never let go of her hand and brought it up to his lips, giving her a light kiss.

"How is it that the most beautiful woman in the world was available on a Saturday night? If I'm not being too personal, I am curious as to how it is possible that you are all alone."

"Well, you have met my dear sister Brandi. Growing up with her complicated my opportunities in that respect."

"How so?"

"My sister had a well-deserved reputation for being loose and everyone expected me to be the same way so I was never sure what the motives were behind the invitations I received. After a while it just seemed to be too much bother, and with a job, school, and all my responsibilities at home, I just didn't have time anyway. My mother always encouraged us to exploit our sexuality from an early age. Brandi did her best to live up to mum's expectations but the rebel in me pushed me to go the other way. My mother and I never got along and I enjoyed a little bit of passive aggressive satisfaction in presenting myself as a nonsexual nerd." Sheherezade laughed, "That goes to show you how upside down my upbringing was that I remained a virgin just to piss off my mother."

"You're a virgin?" Lion could not believe he had heard her correctly.

"Yes," she said uneasily. Lion felt his chest fill with emotion. *She could be all his*, he thought.

"Well, I have good news for you," Lion attempted to lighten the mood. "Brandi is just not my type."

Sheherezade laughed. She looked over at his handsome angular face and impulsively grabbed him by the collar, pulling him toward her. She gave him a long sensual kiss. Lion took her into his arms and kissed her again with more passion. After a long moment he pulled away and searched her eyes with his own.

"I wanted to do this from the moment I laid eyes on you. You might as well know that I have been consumed by thoughts of being with you, falling in love with you, making love to you."

Sheherezade was breathless at the sincerity and drama of the moment. One tear fell as she looked at him and said, "I felt the same way." He kissed her and she felt those powerful arms around her once more. Suddenly, he released her and she sat before him silently, somewhat surprised at the change in his mood. A very serious expression crossed his brow as he slowly got down on one knee, "Sheherezade will you marry me?"

Sheherezade threw her arms around him and her lips brushed his ear.

"Yes, Lion, I will."

Chapter 10

Brandi was bored. It had been days since she had heard from Boots. As much as she resented the intrusion of her sister into her thoughts, she could not help but wonder where she went after pulling that stunt at the club. Was she with Lion? Did she somehow know Lion before that night? She had questioned Boots about it but he had pleaded ignorance. *Mum and I used to laugh about how uptight and backward she was,* she thought. *What got into her? And who does she suddenly think she is?* She knew she had been granted temporary custody of Lila and that meant she must have a place of her own somewhere. Not having Lila was a bit of relief for Brandi but losing her to Sherry nagged at her no matter how much she tried to avoid thinking about it. The mental picture of Boots staring at Sherry on that stage haunted her. *How she loathed her sister.*

Brandi intended to get very high as soon as possible in order to stamp out her foul mood. Nick looked up and smiled lasciviously at Brandi as she barged into his office.

"So Nick, where's your new star, my sister Sheherezade, who by the way, is really just plain old Sherry?"

"I don't know," Nick frowned. "I had her scheduled to work this week so I assume she didn't like the work and quit." Brandi shot Nick a look of exasperation, spun on her heels and marched out of the room in a huff.

Brandi entered the bar in the hope of scoring some coke before heading home when she saw a pair of icy blue eyes staring up at her from a table near the front of the stage.

"Hey beautiful, remember me?" The eyes conjured up a vague memory but she could not place them. When she noticed a shiny new tattoo of a lion with horns adorning his upper left arm she knew he must be a Full Patch member of the Pride. She was hoping her search for some coke could end right there and then.

"Was it at the clubhouse, and did I have a little too much champagne?" she giggled.

"Yep, we had some fun that night. Can I buy you a drink?" Nick had told James that Brandi was still turning tricks in the V.I.P. room and there did not seem to be any moratorium on sex with the infamous Brandi despite the fact that Boots still had an interest in her. However, James knew full well that, as a member of the Pride, she was off limits to him. Such disrespect for the Vice President's property was a major infraction of biker etiquette. At the moment, however, his lust was getting in the way of that essential logic.

"Sure, sexy! I could use a drink! Did you catch my set?"

"I've caught it many times since the first night I met you," he said as he gave her an unblinking gaze. She liked his cocky self-assurance. He talked with pride about making full Patch the week before and celebrating his new status by getting the club logo tattooed on his arm just yesterday. Brandi attempted to be friendly and engaging but thoughts of her sister continued to persist like a toothache that wouldn't go away.

"To tell you the truth, I was just going to find some coke to help take my mind off things," Brandi said.

"No problem, gorgeous. I've got my bike outside and it's a beautiful night. Do you want to go for a ride?"

"Oh fuck! I'd love to!"

Brandi followed James out, donned a helmet, and jumped onto his new Ultra Classic Electra Glide Harley. They rode west along the 280 highway and then pulled over at Troy Hills to park at the lake. Moon beams danced on the water and the air was redolent with wild flowers as James pulled a big baggie of white powder out of his jeans.

"You like meth?" James asked.

"I usually do coke. I've never tried it," Brandi answered.

"You're goin' to love it," he said. "Just let me get it fired up." Brandi inhaled deeply and felt the rush hit the back of her brain.

"Mmmm . . . that's nice . . . ." James took a hit and closed his eyes for a second. Brandi reached up and put her hand behind his neck drawing his lips to hers. James pushed his hand down her pants and reached his fingers between her legs.

"How do you like to fuck your women, James?" Brandi asked softly.

"Hard," he answered.

Brandi and James smoked meth and had sex on the picnic table until sunrise when he finally drove her to her mother's flat in Dover. Brandi jumped off the bike, threw her arms around James' neck and kissed him. Her brain was in a nice haze and all of her physical senses seemed to be enhanced.

"Thanks James, you made me feel sooo good . . ."

"You've got the sweetest little cunt I've ever had babe," James grinned.

After a long goodbye, Brandi ran into the house and flopped down on the couch. Her mind wandered into blissful nothingness. Sherry had drifted into a big black hole. *Maybe she was gone somewhere far away never to return again. Her obsessive thought about Sherry had stopped and now she could concentrate on Boots.* Just then her cell phone rang.

"Hey! How are you beautiful?"

"Boots! Where are you?"

"I'm still in Florida. We were at Harley's funeral. But listen sweetie, Friday is the yearly run and I was hoping I could convince my best girl to join me."

"Are you kidding? I'd love to!"

"Good. I'll have a car bring you to the city Friday morning. I can't wait to see you in the leather outfit I picked out for you. Gotta run, see you soon . . . ."

Chapter 11

Boots had arrived at the clubhouse early and was holding court with a crowd of bikers and their Old Ladies when Brandi arrived by limo. She was wearing the red leather outfit he had sent over which consisted of leather pants, a bomber jacket, and a pair of over the knee boots that the girls at the club called, 'come fuck me' boots. When she saw Boots her knees became weak. He was a deep bronze from the Florida sun and he was wearing only his Originals—the first leather vest he owned with the Pride Patch—which displayed his chiselled abdomen and muscular arms. Shiny black leather pants clung to his long muscular legs and fell over custom made black cowboy boots. He was sitting astride the most beautiful bike she had ever seen. The Lucifer's Pride logo, engraved into solid chrome, sparkled in the bright sunlight. She ran up to him and gave him a long sensuous kiss to mark her territory for all the other members to see.

Boots had made arrangements for about twenty bikes to follow him over to Newark and told everyone else that they would meet up at Tarrytown, the first planned stop of the trip. Brandi jumped on the back of the bike and they rode through the streets in a loose formation until they reached a one story building on the outskirts of the city. Parking the bike in front of an office window, he told Brandi to sit on his bike, strike a sexy pose, and watch for him to wave. The rest of the bikers and their Old Ladies waited under the sign that displayed the name of Dr. Lynn Bailey.

He recalled the day he had his physical with Dr. Lynn Bailey. That meeting culminated in a spontaneous jaunt in his private jet to a romantic dinner in Quebec City and a passionate love making session in the jet on the return trip. *She wasn't even a challenge*, he thought with contempt. *And now this arrogant bitch was about to get her comeuppance.*

Standing six foot five and sporting a perpetual tan that contrasted his light blue eyes, Mustard looked like a caricature of a biker. The business suit he wore as an executive of the organization was put away for the day and the Mustard of old was at his biker best for the ride to the lake. His signature long blond hair was entwined with braids and feathers and his biceps were defined with tattoos and bone armbands drawing stares wherever he went. It was a sight that once struck abject fear in anyone foolish enough to cross the Pride. As the first sergeant-at-arms for the club he was credited with the take no prisoner policy that guaranteed cooperation from any opposition to the will of the organization. Bull was as wide as he was tall with a long ZZ Top style beard. Both men now spent most of their time in their corner offices of a Manhattan high rise but they loved to put on the patch and morph into their alter egos whenever possible.

Acting as bodyguards, they walked into the doctor's office and stood at attention on either side of the doorway, arms crossed in front of them, before Boots sauntered in and walked up to the reception desk. Leaning over on his elbow, he gave Ashley, the receptionist, a big smile.

Fear registered in her eyes.

"Can I help you?" Boots looked over his shoulder and an expression of confusion registered on his face.

"Don't you recognize me?" he asked politely.

"Uh, no?" Ashley hoped that was the right answer but the whole situation was not making any sense.

"I'm here to see Lynn. Is she busy?"

"She's in the back. Can I tell her who is here to see her?"

"Well, maybe I should be a little insulted that I am that forgettable," he answered loudly as he turned to Mustard and Bull with an expression of indignation.

"Tell her that Boots, or rather Lou Falcone is here to see her. We just came back from a romantic trip a couple of days ago. Are you having trouble keeping track of all her men?" he asked with a little more agitation.

"No, no. I didn't mean that. I just . . . ."

"Please find her will you?"

"Yes, I'll be right back. OH!" She turned and bumped into Lynn who was coming into the reception area to investigate the source of the loud voices. Lynn looked up and saw Boots and smiled brightly before a look of horror gradually came over her face as she took in the entire scene.

"What is this?" she asked as she looked around the room vaguely and began to back up and shake her head from side to side at the same time. The desk blocked her path and she started to speak in a loud shaky voice.

"I'm not going with you. I didn't know you were . . . ."

"What?" Boots asked giving her an intimidating stare.

"B . . . B . . . Biker. You were bikers. I didn't know . . . I can't . . . I won't . . . go anywhere . . . ." her voice reached a fevered pitch.

"Well, Lynn, I hate to correct you on this small point of etiquette, but no one has invited you anywhere," Boots stated sarcastically.

"I came here to make an appointment. Now, let me get this straight. It wasn't for my girlfriend Brandi." He turned and waved at Brandi who was sitting with one high-heeled boot perched atop his bike displaying her cleavage to maximum advantage. Lynn watched in horror as Brandi waved and smiled back at Boots.

"Oh, that's right! I remember now. It was for my Old Lady—Fancy!"

Lynn felt a little light-headed and staggered backward. Ashley's expression reflected a new level of horror as she stood paralyzed with fear.

"Damn it! It's tough to get service in this place!" Boots exclaimed to Bull and Mustard who were trying to stifle their laughter.

"Funny, Fancy said the same thing. Shouldn't be a problem next time though, right Lynn?"

Lynn's face froze with fear.

"Yes. I mean NO! I mean it will not be a problem!"

"Oh, good! Glad to hear it. By the way, thanks for the good time. Not a bad piece of ass—all things considered," Boots winked. Lynn's legs collapsed and she found herself sitting on the floor defeated. Boots gave her a menacing glare, shook his head, and turned to leave followed by the other men. Outside, he gave the waiting members a nod and a big smile and they jumped on their bikes and headed toward Tarrytown to meet up with the rest of the club for the run to Indian Lake.

Sheherezade stepped out of the limo looking stunning in a white leather pant suit. The bomber jacket had a custom design on the back in bright colours that were a close facsimile of the Pride's logo. Although no woman was permitted to wear the patch because women were not allowed to be members of the club, her jacket came pretty close—an exception tolerated only because she was the Old Lady of the club President. She found Lion in the middle of a large crowd of bikers and gave him a big hug and kiss. The crowd broke out in applause as the rumour was being confirmed before their eyes that Lion finally had an official Old Lady. Sheherezade acknowledged them with a big smile and then marvelled over Lion's motorcycle which was truly a work of art and engineering.

"This will be fun," she whispered. "I have never even been on a motorcycle."

"I hope you can handle this bunch of ruffians; they don't always mind their P's and Q's," Lion said with trepidation.

"Don't worry, Lion, I have not lived a sheltered life and I have always been drawn to individualists with quirky personalities. I like to laugh at life and have fun despite the fact that my sister always made me out to be a real priss."

Sheherezade was seeing Lion in black leather for the first time and she decided she liked the new macho persona. She thanked him for the beautiful white leather suit and told him how much she admired the skilful artwork in creating the logo on her back. She stepped behind him to compare his logo to the one on her jacket and noticed that his logo had a tiny tear falling from the lion's eye.

"Why is your lion crying?" she asked.

Lion hesitated and then replied, "Whoever did the design took artistic licence and just put their own touch on the design, I guess."

His custom made black leather jacket sported the largest logo of a lion with horns. The lettering above the logo, called the top rocker, read Lucifer's Pride. The bottom rocker signified the state of their authority so where most of the member's patches read New York, his bottom rocker read President. On the front of his jacket was a 1% patch and on the shoulders were chevrons that denoted his Presidency.

"What does that 1% symbol mean on the front of your jacket?" she asked.

"That means that only 1% of the motorcycle owners in the country would want to be in our club," he replied.

"Oh, look, Sheher, here comes Boots and your sister, we can get started. Are you going to be alright having your sister here?"

"I'm going to do my best to ignore her and have fun," she smiled.

Brandi was having one of the best days of her life as she and Boots joined the parking lot full of bikes of every description. Suddenly the crowd parted and she spotted Lion kissing a girl in a white suit with long dark hair. Sherry! *Fuck, it can't be,* she thought. *This experience should be mine alone and I am being forced to share it with her. She never fit before; why was she here?* She could not let her sister ruin her day with Boots. *It won't be long before Lion finds out what a wet blanket she is and dumps her* she promised herself.

Boots waved to Lion and Brandi looked away for fear of having to make eye contact with her sister.

"I can't wait to get going!" Sheherezade said with enthusiasm as she put her arms under Lion's jacket and gave him a hug to flaunt her happiness in front of Brandi. Lion gave a fist of victory to the crowd and yelled, "Shiny side up!" as he and Sheherezade jumped on his bike to start the ride.

Four hundred Harley-Davidsons snaked their way north up the Taconic State Parkway on the west bank of the Hudson River. Motorcycle aficionados know that you can discern a Harley by the distinct roar of the engine. On this hot summer day the procession sounded like an approaching tornado—an unstoppable force of nature. Dex travelled as a scout a mile ahead of the bikes in an SUV in order to report back to Swami, the Ride Captain who rode as the very first person in the formation. Behind the Ride Captain, and a little to the right, rode Lion as President. Behind him sat Sheherezade, bursting with the joy of this perfect moment, hugging Lion and feeling the wind blow through her hair under her white helmet. A little to the left and behind them rode Mustard, the infamous, Sergeant-at-Arms for the Lucifer's Pride who stood shoulder to shoulder with Lion and Boots when they were fighting for their right to exist as a club in the 80's. Although he had officially retired as the club's Sergeant-at-Arms years ago, the position had remained vacant, and once a year he sat in this honorary position. His time was now spent working closely with Lion as a top executive of the world wide conglomerate. Behind Mustard and a little to the right rode Boots—his hair blowing in the wind and his white teeth flashing a big smile. Hugging him tightly and occasionally wrapping her legs around his waist to signal total ownership of her man, was Brandi. On and on in staggered rows, bikers with their Old Ladies in this, the most glorious moment of the biker's summer, enjoying the freedom, the weather, and the joy of their brotherhood.

Near the end James rode solo on his sparkling new black Harley, bursting with pride at his newly acquired status as an enforcer and hit-man for the club. Shane, now a Prospect, rode behind the Full Patch members with his Old Lady Jamie, her long red hair waving like a flag in the wind. It was a tradition for the New York and Philadelphia chapters to share this run at the first week in July and usually it was the one run of the year that Lion and Boots joined in. Club rules were strict and it was mandatory that all members attend compulsory runs, meetings, and outings. Lion and Boots and some of the original members who worked closely with them, were now exempt from protocol due to the responsibility of running a financial empire that had burgeoned from the original concept. All Full Patch members profited greatly from their efforts and gladly accepted these exceptions. A few trusted "friends" of the club and their Old Ladies were included by invitation only. These were guys who had worked faithfully for the club but, for various reasons, had not been given official club status. At the rear of the formation were a few biker mamas who rode their own hog. Snake was riding Back Door and following him were two Chase Vehicles.

Internal bickering was forgotten for the day. The run was a metaphor for the biker life: danger at every turn, sharing fun with the Old Lady, and dependence on the skill and strength of brother rebels. The procession turned onto Hwy 90, headed west, and then turned onto Hwy 30 to head north to Indian Lake. Soul's Gate filled the air with song from the stage set up by the lake, as bikes rolled through the gates of the two hundred acres of forest owned by the Pride on Indian Lake in the Adirondack Mountains of upper New York State.

>Stephen which is my name
>Watches his friends arrive
>On windy days like this

All wild and I love them so
A bird clown
Casts a grim shadow
Down on the ground
    We don't have a country
    We celebrate our happy home
    Where we gather
    My family is strong
    And with everything
    We don't have a country

Bring tears to the eyes
Attention audience
You and your long career
You and your fancy house
I'm going down to the beach
For a swim with my girl, ya
    We don't have a country
    We celebrate our happy home
    Where we gather
    My family is strong
    And with everything
    We don't have a country
    We don't have a country, baby

    The trip to the lake used to consist of camping in tents with sleeping bags for a couple days of partying. Over the years the facilities had been upgraded to reflect the club's new level of prosperity but many members still liked to maintain the tradition of roughing it in the woods. So while many members had an RV or mobile home parked at the camp, others still slept in the tent they packed on the back of their bike. There were permanent washrooms with showers typical of most camp grounds. Food and drinks were trucked to the kitchen /refrigeration building and set up beforehand. A giant open barbeque stood ready for a great quantity of chicken, ribs, and steaks to be cooked over an open fire. Cooks were already spreading out a feast of baked potatoes, salads, fruit pies and other desserts. Fridges were packed with cases of cold beer, wine, and hard liqueur and a bartender stood ready to serve up anyone's preference. Beside the lake, Soul's Gate provided the live music from a permanent stage.

Lion pulled up to a large RV parked on the campsite that had housed his humble tent for many years. Sheherezade was amazed to find all the luxuries of a small apartment in his little bachelor pad in the forest.

"It is not exactly roughing it Lion," she giggled.

"Well, if you want me to round up a little tent, I can," he laughed.

"No, I think this will do nicely, as long as you promise that some time just you and I will come back here and sleep under the stars together in that little tent."

"I'll put it in my wedding vows," he said with a sentimental note before he took her in his arms and kissed her.

"When I found this land I bought three hundred acres and kept the best one hundred acres for myself. I'm going to have a home built there for us. The next time we'll come up by ourselves and I'll show you our little bit of heaven."

Boots poked his head into the open door.

"Lion! Good ride man. God I always forget how much fun it is to get out on the road again," Boots said wistfully. "It reminds me of the old days and why we felt so strongly about starting the whole thing." Sheherezade turned around and looked over at Boots with her hair all tousled from the ride. For the first time he was given a better look at the beauty who had been doing the exotic strip tease that fateful night and a pang of envy hit his chest like a thunderbolt.

"Hey, how are you?" he asked weakly. "Lion's told me all about you but it's not quite the same as seeing you in person. Lion was right—you are stunning."

Sheherezade blushed as a big smile broke onto her face, "Nice to meet you Boots."

"Well let's get some champagne for the girls and get this party started!" Boots exclaimed.

There was a sandy beach for swimming and naked bodies of all sizes jumped into the water to get relief after the long sweaty ride in the heat. Brandi was still reeling from the knowledge that Sherry was with Lion, President of the Lucifer's Pride. Never in her wildest imagination would she have predicted that turn of events. Jealousy gripped her soul and gave her even more resolve to become the most important woman in Boots' life. She refused to let thoughts of Sherry derail her mission.

Brandi sauntered over to the barbeque tent wearing a tiny white bikini and then began a campaign of introductions to let everyone know that she was there with Boots. Seeing a few tables of women, she saw an opportunity to clarify her new social status as girlfriend of the Vice President.

"Hi, ladies! I'm Brandi. It's so great to meet everyone! I hope you will drop over after and have a drink with Boots and me in our trailer. I'm meeting so many new people today. I guess I just don't go down to the clubhouse that often," she said condescendingly.

Jackie, Fancy's close friend and the acknowledged social arbiter of the club, was holding court at a table in the middle of the action. Most of her cronies were Old Ladies that had been around for decades with the exception of a few new faces like Monica who had latched onto Nick at the club and who hoped to be accepted by the inner circle.

She looked up stone face at Brandi and replied, "That's why you haven't met us. We never go to the clubhouse."

"Well, I hope you can make it down to the club sometime so that I have the chance to buy you a drink," she said in an attempt to hold out an olive branch to this women who seemed a little too brazen.

"I don't think so," Jackie retorted.

Brandi was becoming miffed by this woman's lack of deference after she had explicitly indicated that she was here with Boots.

"What do you mean?" she asked, unable to disguise the impatience in her voice.

Jackie pronounced every word clearly to emphasize her meaning, "Ole Ladies are NOT allowed in the clubhouse."

The meaning of this statement took a moment to sink in. Jackie was pointing out Brandi's lack of status in the club. The fact that she could enter the clubhouse meant that she was not truly Boots' Old Lady. Brandi gave Jackie a look that would kill and stormed off to the trailer. As she walked away, she could hear snickering and she thought her head would blow off with anger. *Those skanky hoes! How dare they speak to me that way knowing that I am here with Boots? If they think they can fuck with me, they don't know who they are dealing with,* she fumed.

Chapter 12

As the music played some people swam while others ate and had a cold beer at picnic tables amidst the trees. A tall man with an intense demeanour and a long brown braid pulled up on his motorcycle with his Old Lady in tow. Members ran up to him to pat him on the back or shake his hand while the word of his arrival spread among the crowd and caused a stir. As he dismounted from his bike the crowd started to cheer, led by Lion and Boots. Sheherezade watched as Lion approached him and gave him a big hug. She asked Sissi, the beautiful buxom wife of Mustard, why this man was being greeted with such enthusiasm. Sissi told her that she honestly did not know and went on to explain that as the wife of a member you are often not privy to club business—you learned not to be too interested because it was considered none of your business. Sheherezade had to wonder what could possibly be a good reason for such secrecy and let the matter go, thinking she would give Lion a subtle prompt to tell her what the stir was about later to see if she, too, was excluded from the inner circle of club news.

Looking over the crowd Sheherezade thought she recognized a face but she could not place it so she asked Sissy who the fellow was that brought along his daughter. Sissy told her that the guy with the bandana and wearing the patch on his leather jacket was Dr. Lindsay, Lion's personal physician—the same man that had attended her that first night in the apartment. The young girl was, in fact, his girlfriend. Years ago there had been complaints against him for nefarious practices concerning anaesthetic and sexual assault on some of his patients. Despite the fact that the charges did not stick, he had trouble finding clients so Lion and Boots hired him full time to look after club members. He patched up wounds without reporting them, gave working girls abortions, treated sexually transmitted diseases, dispensed medication on demand, and performed any other service that the club required. He had a penchant for under aged girls and was known for his talent as a pornographer, but that, Sissy assured her, was before his association with the club. When Soul's Gate wrote their song Dr. Hotel years ago, Sissy told Sheherezade, the song had been inspired by the good doctor. Only the club members, however, were privy to that little tidbit of information.

> Doctor Hotel standing at the end of the hall
> You stare at him he'll run to his room
> Squat down and listen
> You've got young boys and little girls coming out of the darkness
> Your notebooks filled with horrible stuff
> You're carrying a briefcase full of fluff
> His expression says I'm crazy
> I've got no soul . . .
> Glancing behind himself the rest of the way home.

Sheherezade paused at the thought of his atrocious history and then reminded herself what Lion had said about taking responsibility for the actions of others. *Just because the doctor was a member of the club did not mean that Lion or Boots condoned his past behaviour. That would be like the President of the country taking responsibility for the actions of everyone that was a member of his party.*

Jackie introduced herself to Sherry with a big hug and then took her around to all the tables of women and made sure that she met everyone. She shared a few laughs over champagne and burgers with the ladies before Lion found her and suggested they go for a swim.

Shane was spreading his charm thick over a table of seasoned Pride and their Old Ladies. Jamie, the woman he moved in with after his release from prison, looked at him with admiration as he commanded everyone's attention with his stories. She, too, was captivated by his presence and completely under his spell. She guarded her turf with rabid ferocity and the more she got to know Shane, the more she suspected that she had reason to be on guard. Particularly, she resented the fact that he spent so much time at the clubhouse since he had made Prospect. He did his best to pacify her with his most creative stories of how hard he was working on the expansion of his territory and his growing authority. Most of it was true. The money was rolling in and he was so well liked by his new colleagues that he was on a meteoric rise up the social ladder within the club. That, however, did not account for the smell of cheap perfume that followed him around like a cloud. When she harped on her suspicions, he would just giggle to himself and ruminate about the fun he was having behind her back. When she became too annoying he would just give her a slap and that usually shut her up.

Jackie was letting loose and dishing the dirt with a table of the wives who had been with the club for years. She had been married to Dooney, a close friend of Lion's, who found himself in a financial bind some years back. He chose to make a little money on the side when he turned state's evidence against the club by supplying information about the drug operation. When he told Jackie what he had done, he informed her that they would be entering the witness protection program shortly and that she should discreetly pack up her stuff and say goodbye to her family. She agreed that it was a good idea and then immediately called Lion to tell him what Dooney had in mind before too much damage had been done. Dooney disappeared right after the next church meeting and Jackie became as close to being a member of the Pride as any woman would ever come. Shiny dark shoulder length hair and a gorgeous face attracted men like flies but it was her earthy sensuality that drove them wild. She liked sex more than they did and never lost interest in experimenting with every known variation on the theme.

Jackie's eyes fell on Shane for the first time.

"Who's that fine piece of meat over there, Monica?"

"He's a new Prospect. Very solid. He's earning a lot of respect from Snake and the guys for the work he's done for the club. He's going to be right up there before too long."

Jackie only took her eyes off his massive shoulders and biceps long enough to check out his cute dimples.

"He's mine."

The girls at the table looked at each other knowing that the hunky new red-headed Prospect was about to be hit by a train. When Jamie left to use the washroom, Jackie stood up to reveal a low cut T-shirt that unabashedly showed off her ample breasts. She walked up to the table where Shane was sitting, looked him up and down, and asked, "How about coming over for a drink?"

Shane loved spunk in a woman.

He gave her a big grin and looked at the other guys as if to say, 'Do you believe this?' "I'd love to honey but the Old Lady will have my balls hangin' by that tree before you can say castration."

"Oh fuck it—do it anyway," she replied quickly with an unblinking gaze.

He knew what she wanted and he was about to give it to her. He stood up and pitched her over his shoulder and headed toward the bush. When they were far enough back that they could not be seen, he put her down. His passionate kisses soon stifled her laughter. Her hands immediately went to his crotch to rub the growing bulge in his pants. Kneeling down, he unzipped her jeans and ran his tongue up and down her clitoris. He stopped only long enough to ask, "You ready for some cock, aren't you honey?"

"I was ready as soon as I saw you," she answered.

He grabbed her by the arm and pulled her down on top of him. They removed their jeans and made out on the soft blanket of leaves. He shoved his penis into her with ferocity and she returned his passion with her entire being. The other guys at the table were trying to suppress their laughter as Jamie became more and more concerned that Shane had disappeared from the festivities. Roach told her that he was up getting a drink at the bar and then someone else said that he just saw him at the washrooms. As they had fun at her expense, she became more and more agitated. When the guys heard Jackie's screams of enthusiasm from the bush they really started to lose it and the more Jamie looked around for Shane, the harder they laughed.

Shane and Jackie shared a smoke in the bush and made out for another fifteen minutes.

"You go first," Jackie said. "That way you won't get into trouble."

"I was just *in* trouble," he chuckled. "And that's where I always wanna be. When I go out there, you are going with me."

Jackie loved this guy's style. He grabbed her by the hand and they left the quiet of the forest. Jamie spotted them and was temporarily stunned. She got up from the picnic table in disbelief and ran at Shane screaming—her red hair flying. Shane dropped Jackie's hand to defend himself against the screaming shrew beating her fists against his head. The guys at his table and many of the other people sitting at the picnic tables were hysterical with laughter at the impromptu entertainment. Unfazed by his Old Lady, Shane picked her up, threw her over his shoulder, and headed toward the gate. When he got there, he put her down and once again she tried to lash out at his face. He grabbed her by the arm and twisted it behind her back.

"You fucked her right under my nose you bastard!" she screamed.

"Sure did and I'm going to go back and fuck her all night long, so get the hell out of my face." He issued his order with an expression that told her he was serious.

"You expect me to get home by myself from this God forsaken place?" she protested.

"I don't expect anything bitch. Just don't bother me anymore." He spat.

Shane walked back from the road and approached the table with a big smile on his face. Jackie ran up to him, threw her arms around his neck and began kissing him passionately. Jamie walked to the road and stuck out her thumb as the black sedan approached. She had been associated with the Pride long enough to know that a biker owned you as long as he said he did and a woman had little say in the matter.

At about eight-thirty as the sun was setting over the lake, Steve, the lead singer, took the microphone in between sets and told everyone that Lion had a special announcement to make.

Lion smiled and held his hands up to indicate to the crowd that they should hold their applause.

"I want to thank everyone for coming out for the ride. It has been just as much fun—no more fun—than any other run we have ever done together and there have been a few . . . ." Everyone applauded and yelled their enthusiastic agreement.

"Tonight I have something I want to share with you guys—the only family I have ever had. Something that means everything to me." He was a little choked with emotion and paused. Everyone was quiet with curiosity. "I met the woman of my dreams just one week ago. I think you have all had the pleasure of meeting her so I don't have to tell you how special she is. Anyway, she has said 'yes' and we are engaged to be married." The crowd went crazy screaming and yelling in support of their brother who they all knew had been torn apart all these years with the memory of a love he had been unable to replace. Lion invited Sheherezade onto the stage and the cheers came up even louder. At the table directly in front of the stage, Brandi's mouth fell open as she tried to maintain a grip on reality. *Could she be hearing that Sherry, the object of their scorn for so many years, was about to marry one of the richest men in America?* Jealousy rose in her chest as she searched her mind for some comforting piece of information that would make it seem alright. She could not come up with one. Regina used to say that Sherry would never get a man because she was so uptight she might as well be a eunuch, but all the rationalizations that once assuaged their fears were not working. Sherry had won the prize and Brandi felt, in a visceral way, that mental acrobatics were not going to erase the reality facing her. She didn't hear the rest of the announcement. Her mind began to swim and as soon as she could discreetly leave, she excused herself and walked across the field to the building that housed the washrooms and showers. Once in the washroom she pulled out the package of meth that James had given her and cooked it in the stall. She leaned back against the wall and felt the emotion falling away as the rush hit her head. *That fuckin' bitch.* The details were dropping away but she still felt the unmitigated hate in her chest. She knew she needed another hit in case she ran into Sherry living her fairy tale or Jackie and her vicious tribe of hostile bitches.

James had been following her every move and when she didn't appear after a reasonable time, he waited until the coast was clear and walked in. Seeing the closed stall he knocked.

"Hey babe, what's going on?"

Brandi opened the door. Tears of anger were running down her face along with her makeup.

"That fuckin' bitch. She is nothing. Nothing!" she screamed as her face contorted into an ugly mask of strained muscles.

"Shhh . . ." James whispered, "You're right, she's fuckin' zero compared to you babe." He took her in his arms as she cried in anger and frustration.

"Look honey, you can't go back looking like this. Don't give her the satisfaction of being the centre of attention while you sit there and watch. Why don't you walk out to the gate around the back and we'll get on my bike and get out of here."

"Are you fuckin' crazy?" she hissed into his face. "I came here with Boots and I'm leaving with Boots!" The suggestion that she concede the fight to her sister fired up her old feelings of competition for Sherry and set off a renewed sense of revenge. She might have lost this battle but she was not about to lose any ground in the war. She pushed James away and stomped off in the direction of the camper.

Back at the camp one of the members they called the Swami had been entertaining everyone with magic tricks and demonstrations of hypnosis that had everyone in stitches—particularly when he made Sissy forget her Old Man's name. Afterward some of the members were telling stories about Lion as a young man and Sheherezade was laughing so hard she could not remember when she had had more fun. The wives and girlfriends of the club members were friendly and warm and she was beginning to see how the club was like a family to Lion. It was comforting to have a group of people you could trust to be there for you—it was something she had never had in her life. Maybe they *were* a little different, but then some people would say the same thing about her. God knows her life had been bizarre; who was she to say what was normal? Lion pulled Sheherezade into him as he wrapped his long arms around her.

"What are you thinking?"

"I'm thinking I like your little family."

"I knew you would. We were meant to be." He looked into her big violet-blue eyes and his heart began to race.

"You ready to pack it in for the night?"

"It was a terrific day, but I think that's probably a good idea. Many of your friends are tired but they won't leave until we go first." Lion nodded in agreement.

"Listen everyone, it was a great day. We'll see you in the morning," he announced.

When they were alone Lion took her into his arms and they began to kiss passionately. The embrace of his powerful body made her limp with desire.

"Lion, make love to me. I want you so much . . ."

"Sheher, I like the idea of marrying a virgin . . . I'm going to wait until our wedding night to make love to you," he announced. She was surprised by the sensitivity of her macho biker boyfriend.

"Well Lion, I guess I can wait if you can."

"Well that's the problem . . . you could drive any man crazy with desire and I can't wait. Let's get married as soon as we can." He looked at her, waiting for a reaction. Sheherezade let out a squeal and threw her arms around him.

"Lion, you have made me the happiest woman on the planet and I can't imagine my world without you. Now if you are not going to put out tonight, please take yourself to the other bedroom," Sheherezade laughed.

Lion sighed, "I think that's a very good idea." He took her in his arms and kissed her goodnight and then used all of his willpower to pull himself away and keep his word.

Chapter 13

*L*ion dropped Sheherezade off at the condominium so that she could explain their new plans to Lila before the limo picked her up at four o'clock to take her to the airport.

"Meme, you're back!" Lila exclaimed as she ran into Sheherezade's arms. She could see the change in her niece since she came to live in their luxurious new digs just one week before. One week. The changes in their lives in that short time had been remarkable.

"Lila, I've got some exciting news! You, Lion, and I are going to be a family and we are going to live in his house in the country outside of Philadelphia. It's going to be fantastic! But first, Lion and I are going to get married and people usually go on a little holiday when they get married. Do you think you could stay with Tina for just a few days if I call you everyday to make sure everything is OK?"

Lila smiled, "I can stay with Tina. Will you hurry back?"

Sheherezade took her into her arms. "I will hurry back and then we will never be apart again. I love you and I will always look after you Lila. We are going to have a wonderful life with Lion."

"Meme?" Lila's little brow knit.

"Yes, Honey?"

"I don't think Lion likes me."

"Of course, he likes you. What makes you think he doesn't like you?"

"Well, he looks at me sometimes and he scares me with his eyes."

"Lion doesn't mean to scare you. He might seem a bit scary because you don't know him very well yet but I know that he likes you very much and you will see when we live together that he will be just like a daddy to you. You have nothing to worry about." When the car arrived for Sheherezade at four, Lila was happy and enthusiastic about being part of the new family that they were about to create.

As her car drove out onto the tarmac Sheherezade saw Lion's private Lear Jet with the Pride logo emblazoned across the side. Lion came down the stairs to greet her, picked her up, and kissed her. They laughed and talked for a moment while the staff ran up and down the stairs putting supplies on board the aircraft.

"What is all this luggage?" she asked as she looked at the large pile on the trolley.

"Well, I only have one suitcase so most of it must be yours," he said with a grin. "Your personal shopper has been the busiest person in New York City for the past twenty-four hours."

"Oh, Lion, what have you done? I don't need anything but you." She was not used to so much attention and she wondered if the floating guilt of having things she had not earned would ever go away.

"You are my woman now and you will have everything. And I mean everything. Better get used to it. Now let me show you our jet. You can redecorate it to match your eyes if you don't like it." Sheherezade saw what real luxury looked like as she stepped into the interior of the jet. The couches were warm orange leather and the table tops were polished bird's eye maple to match. Lion took her hand and showed her the bedroom and ensuite at the back of the plane. The linens were silky, sumptuous beige cotton with a discreet Pride logo custom woven into the fabric in the same colour. *Not quite like my hand-sewn creations,* she thought. The closet was filled with clothes and shoes for every possible occasion. The personal shopper had done an incredible job of interpreting Sheherezade's taste in style and color. She turned to Lion and tears started to fall.

"I can't believe this is happening, Lion. I can't help feeling I don't deserve you and all this good fortune." Lion held her in his arms until she was able to compose herself.

"I love you and I will always love you, nothing else matters Sheher," he whispered.

They chatted over champagne as the plane took off. Once they were in the air Lion turned to Sheherezade, "I have something to give you. Maybe you can guess." Sheherezade giggled coyly as she opened her eyes wide feigning innocence, "I can't imagine." He had managed to bring her out of herself and she felt the excitement return.

"Hold that thought, Lion! I want to make myself beautiful for you. I will be out in fifteen minutes!" she exclaimed.

Sheherezade returned to the bedroom and looked with awe at the array of designer clothing set out with matching accessories in the closet. Each article was exquisite and exactly what she would have chosen herself: sumptuous fabrics in monochromatic light shades. For this, her last evening with Lion before they were to be married, she had her sights set on the sexiest dress in the closet. Her eyes fell on a long lilac chiffon dress which she removed from the closet and lay on the bed. The top was sleeveless with a low décolleté front opening, cut almost to the form fitting waist. The skirt was a gossamer structure of long ruffles with an opening up the front that displayed the delicate silk under dress. She was pulling the under dress over her head and happened to look down at the masterpiece of lilac ruffles on the bed. She stopped. *All those other women. All those bodies he has made love to and here I am competing with every one of them. I must distinguish myself and make this time together memorable! Brandi's thinking was flawed,* she thought. *You cannot capture a man with your body; you have to use your mind. I am going to give him something they did not give him. Anticipation.*

She dropped the thin silk under dress, picked up the see-through chiffon and stepped into it. The top revealed some cleavage and her nipples could be seen clearly through the fabric. The front opening started at about mid thigh but it, too, was transparent enough to see the outline of her naked body. She stepped back to look at herself and smiled.

Lion stood up as she opened the door into the sitting area of the cabin. Looking her up and down, he swallowed hard. He was mesmerized by her perfect breasts as he took her hands in his. "My God, you are not going to make this easy are you?" She gave him an enigmatic smile, "No." She dropped her eyes and sat on the couch.

Lion poured the champagne. They clinked glasses as he said, "To us." He put the glass down and reached into his pocket for a small black velvet case.

"I hope you forgive me Sheherezade. You are the first person I have ever proposed to and I forgot that it went with a ring. I hope this makes up for my faux pas."

Sheherezade smiled at him as he opened the case. Her eyes widened as she peered at the largest diamond she had ever seen—or even imagined. As much as she wanted to say something apropos she was speechless. Lion held her left hand and got down on one knee to put it on her finger. Tears flowed down her cheek as she marvelled at the beauty of the perfect gem. Sheherezade slipped onto his knee and kissed him softly on the lips. "You are everything to me Lion. Thank you so much for such a stunning ring. I love it almost as much as I love you."

"I hope it will remind you how much I love you," he said as he nuzzled her neck.

"Oh, my God, you smell so good, and you are so deliciously feminine in that gorgeous dress . . ." He kissed her large sensuous lips and she returned his passion. He pulled back and looked at her nipples thrusting out against the chiffon. He brought his lips down to her breasts and started to caress her through the fabric. With quivering fingers, he started to move the garment to reveal her skin in order to press his lips to her flesh.

"Uh, uh, don't muss my dress," she said coyly. Lion's eyes flashed with passion and he stopped to breathe.

"I can't wait to lick every part of your body," he said with a distant look in his eye. "Well, I guess you could start with my toes," she replied seductively.

A spark of hope and surprise registered on his face. He let his eyes run down her body and noticed that he could see the outline of her labia under the chiffon. She took a sip of champagne as she slowly stretched out on the couch. He moved to her foot and took it in his hand, removing her shoe. He plunged his tongue between her perfect toes and moved it up the front of her foot all the while watching her face for a reaction. She closed her eyes and felt waves of passion surging through her body. Moving his hands upward he felt the sculpted muscle of her leg and caressed her calf with gentle kisses. As his open mouth moved up her inner thigh, she let out a soft sigh and to his surprise gave no resistance to his heated advancement up her leg. His tongue eagerly caressed her velvet skin as he opened her legs and looked at her perfect, hairless genitals. His mouth covered her labia and his tongue found her clitoris. Her soft moans drove his passion to a savage level and he circled his tongue around her vagina. She could feel his hands shaking as he squeezed her buttocks and held her body so tight that she could not move if she had wanted to. He abruptly let go of her and brought his lips to her lips.

"I have to make love to you now. I've changed my mind. I cannot wait any longer. You are driving me crazy," he pleaded with stark pain in his eyes. Sheherezade looked him in the eye and trying very hard to keep her tongue out of her cheek, replied, "No, Lion—I think you were right in the first place. I have decided. I want to be married as a virgin."

Lion was momentarily startled out of his frenzy. Not having what he wanted when he wanted it was a concept he had not dealt with in many years. Sheherezade smiled and whispered, "Stick out your tongue." Lion was mesmerized by the violet-blue eyes that commanded his soul and did as he was told. Demonstrating in graphic detail on her tongue she taunted him with salacious stories of what sexual desires she would satisfy after the ceremony. His hand moved to her genitals and she groaned as she tried to maintain the control she knew he no longer possessed. Lion had lost the blood in his face and wrapped her in his arms. "Why wait, Sheher? Let's make love now, please!" Sheherezade smiled and kissed him letting her tongue softly touch his tongue. "No."

Lion excused himself to do some pull ups in his shower with the cold water running.

When Sheherezade came out wearing a white vintage pantsuit by Balmain, Lion wrapped her in his arms as the plane landed and whispered, "Let's stay in tonight and cuddle." He gave her a bite on the earlobe.

"On our wedding night? You know that's bad luck!" she said with mock outrage.

"Wait a minute. Are you telling me, that I'm on my own tonight?" he asked with desperation.

"What else?" she replied with wide innocent eyes.

Lion's passion was consuming his rational thought but there was absolutely nothing he could do about her decision and he knew that he had to live through the torment she was dishing up until the next evening.

When he saw Dex and Andrew, he told Dex he needed a room for the night and headed for the Casino strip. Lion's cell phone rang.

"Hey, Boots! Are you in town yet man?"

"Ya, we just got in, what are you two up to tonight?"

"*We* aren't up to anything, she's a . . . well it's a long story and right now I can't even concentrate to tell you about it. She's driving me out of my mind. Did you bring Brandi down with you?" Lion asked.

"No, I know the sisters don't get along and there was no way I was going to rub her sister's wedding in her face but I can have her fly down if you need some female company. That girl is the sexiest piece of ass I have ever . . . ."

"No, no! I'm obsessed . . . I'm out of my mind crazy for Sheherezade and messing around with someone else just won't scratch the itch."

"Well, obviously she's nothing like her sister or you would have a smile on your face by now."

"No, she's not like her sister—she something else though. I have never wanted a woman so much in my life. I hate gambling but tonight I have this urge to lose some money. Just something to distract me so that I'm not pounding on her door at three am because right now I'm mighty tempted. I'm doing my best to maintain my masculine pride but I have to confess that at this point it's hanging by a thread."

"Sounds like you're pussy whipped already my brother—but it's your night and I'll try to have a good time without you. I'll see you at noon tomorrow. If you come to your senses—I mean change your mind, you have my cell number," Boots chuckled.

"Ya, Ya . . . I know I'll never live this down. But seriously, thanks for coming Boots. It means a lot to me to have you stand up for me tomorrow. You know how long it's been in coming and what it means for me to finally put the memories of Ace to rest."

Lion went to Caesar's Palace and found the biggest game of Baccarat in the house. Betting fifty thousand dollars at a time he did his best to find some release by losing money but was thwarted by win after win. By three o'clock he was up two and a half million dollars and in frustration he quit playing and went up to his suite. The sexual tension made him so hyper he doubted that he would be able to find sleep but he knew if he knocked on her door she would not answer. Finally he took a sleeping pill and lay on the bed with pictures of Sheherezade wearing the see through chiffon dress, stretched out on the couch in the jet, playing on his imagination. Thoughts of making love to her tormented him until the pill wiped the scenes away.

Chapter 14

A twisted distortion of a smile was frozen on Brandi's face on the trip back from the lake even though her jaw was clenched so tight she could not separate her teeth. What should have been the best weekend of her life turned out to be a series of humiliations that she was determined to avenge. She was even more disappointed when she realized the shiny white limousine waiting at Tarrytown was there to take her home. Her attempts to wrangle an invitation from Boots to spend the evening together had fallen on deaf ears. Chances were he was going to the wedding and she hated to think that there was the possibility that Boots would be with his Old Lady—Fancy—on such a special occasion.

Worse still, she was scheduled to dance at the club so she called Nick and told him she would not be able to make it. Nick was pissed that his feature dancer was a no show on a Saturday night but he knew better than to say anything to her about absenteeism now that it was becoming known that she was dating Boots—he certainly would not dare to interfere with the boss's fun. Brandi was not in the mood to put on a happy face and do the bump and grind. Even though she could hardly admit it to herself, she knew the real reason was that she did not want to face that bitch, Monica. She had been sitting at the table and took in the entire scene when Jackie had pointed out that she was not Boots' Old Lady. *They will see,* she thought. *When I am his Old Lady they will be kissing my ass and then life for them will never be the same.* Her jaw relaxed a little as she envisioned the future the way she was going to make happen.

Her mind wandered to a picture of Lion announcing his wedding to Sherry and she pushed it away—it was just too much to deal with right now. She told the driver to wait a moment after Boots left so she could try to catch James. As always, he had her in his sights, and pulled up to the car shortly after Boots pulled away. He jumped into the back of the limo with Brandi and she closed the window to the driver.

"You don't look so good, Babe. Not having a good day?" Brandi's dissatisfaction with her Boots' world lightened James's mood.

"Fuck no, I could use a hit. You have something left?"

"Sure, let's get out of here. Maybe go to a club and have something to eat."

"I just don't feel up to it tonight James. I'm not even going to work. The weekend was overwhelming and I just want to go home."

"OK, whatever you say, Babe." He passed her a bag of white powder. "Take care of yourself and call me as soon as you can—we'll have some fun. Don't let those skanky bitches get to you. They aren't worth it. Not one of them has your style."

Brandi hated to be so transparent; she didn't like the fact that James had seen through her mask of self assurance. If James had not been on the other end of a bag of meth she would have told him to go fuck himself. Mercifully, the drugs had erased the memory of the tantrum she threw in the bathroom at the picnic. Brandi closed the door of the car and waved the driver to take her home. She discreetly cooked up a little meth and smoked it. She hoped her mother was out. She just wanted to be alone.

"Hi Honey, how was the picnic?" Regina was sitting with a drink in one hand and a cigarette teetering between two long acrylic nails in the other, reading the newspaper. Dishes littered the kitchen counter, clothes covered every couch and chair, and a new smell permeated the tiny cluttered space. Brandi was not in the mood to share her humiliation. As deft as her mother was at minimizing Sherry's accomplishments, she knew that it wouldn't work this time. *On the other hand*, she asked herself, *why should she suffer alone?*

"You won't fuckin' believe this one mum."

"What?"

"Sherry and Lion are together. She came along on the run and then in the evening, Lion made an announcement that they were going to get married."

The blood drained from Regina's face as she took in the news in silence.

"You've got to be kidding," Regina's face froze with disbelief.

"What the fuck would he see in her? I mean she has some of my looks but she is about as amusing as a mannequin. It won't last long. A guy like that will get bored with her quick. Real quick."

"You had to see her though—so fuckin' full of herself. That night she made a fool of herself dancing at the club, she had the MC introduce her with the stage name SHEHEREZADE. Well now she has renamed herself Sheherezade because when Lion was making the announcement about their wedding it was Sheherezade this . . . and Sheherezade that . . . I don't know who the fuck she suddenly thinks she is but . . . . What's the matter, mum?"

Regina's face had dropped and her eyes started to dart around space looking for answers.

"Shit! I wonder if . . ."

"What?"

"Well, she must have found out somehow . . . she must have got a copy of her birth certificate. Shit! I hope this doesn't ruin anything . . ."

"What do you mean?" Brandi asked.

"I never told you guys the truth about Sherry's dad because I knew she would get a big head and it was big enough already."

"Well, you always said that her father was a john . . . a client, right mum?"

"Well, ya but he wasn't. We lived together for a short time—but he was a pain in the ass . . . just like her."

"So her name is really Sheherezade?" Brandi asked incredulously.

"He wanted to name her after his favourite symphony by Rimsky . . . someone or other. Sounds like her, right? He was paying for the hospital so I had no choice at the time. She must have found her birth certificate. God, she could never leave things alone. What a nut case! She would find a way to fuck this up. I've got to think about this. I'll tell you the whole story but don't breathe a word of it. I mean to NO ONE!"

Chapter 15

At noon Lion, Boots, Dex, and Andrew waited at Chapel of the Fountain, the small chapel upstairs from the casino in the Circus Circus Hotel. Patrons gasped at her beauty as Sheherezade made her way through the casino escorted by hotel staff and photographed by the paparazzi.

Lion took a deep breath as Sheherezade entered the chapel. Her hair was piled high on top and she wore a white veil with a hint of sparkle that hid the beauty of her face. The dress was a thin sheath of white silk that fell in a low cowl neck and clung to her thin body until it found a little flare at the bottom and touched the floor at the back. Her beautiful shoulders were exposed as the sleeves, attached only under the arms, hung in folds off the shoulder and then clung to her delicate limbs. Only a perfect set of pearl earrings and her magnificent engagement ring adorned her body. She was gorgeous beyond measure. Lion felt the tears well up in his eyes as his chest burst with proprietary pride.

Boots was deeply disturbed by the jealousy that had haunted him from his first meeting with Sheherezade. Today was no different. He was having difficulty reconciling the fact that he had never had her, and might never have her, knowing Lion's possessive nature. He did not want to envy Lion because he was like a brother to him but Lion was right—she was something else. There was an air of class and dignity about her that her sister did not possess and her beauty was undeniable.

Traditional vows were exchanged in front of the minister and both Lion and Sheherezade could not stifle their tears as they said, "I do." Only after Lion had placed the diamond eternity band on her finger, and she had placed his ring on his finger, did he lift up the veil to kiss her at the behest of the minister. Their eyes melted into each other and as he gave her a kiss their passion was palpable in the room. Boots looked away. Lion and Sheherezade thanked the wedding party, and then, taking each other's hand, the couple raced through the casino. Bulbs flashed and the crowd cheered. Lion and Sheherezade smiled, waved, and continued to run to the waiting limo that would whisk them to the jet. After a champagne toast on the jet and half an hour of being caught up in each other, Sheherezade looked puzzled.

"Just wondering . . . Where are we going?"

"Well my little vixen we are going to find the biggest, softest bed on the west coast and I am going to make you my wife."

"Mmmm . . . I can't wait. Where is this bed?"

"It is in the Presidential suite of the Fairmont Hotel in San Francisco. We'll be there in half an hour."

The plane landed and there was a limo waiting to whisk them to the hotel. It was a crystal clear California day and she marvelled over the stunning view of the bay and the Golden Gate Bridge on their way to the hotel. There had been so many "firsts" for her this week: the first time being away from home, the first ride on a plane, the first time being in love, and, soon, the first time making love with a man.

As they approached the Fairmont Hotel they saw Harley-Davidson motorcycles parked on the sidewalk. When they pulled into the wide driveway they saw the Honour Guard of two hundred bikers wearing the Pride colours standing shoulder to shoulder from the corner of the road to the entrance of the hotel on both sides. Boots had honoured Lion's request for privacy before his wedding but afterward he had released the good news to all chapters and the boys from California had come out in full force as a show of respect. Stepping from the limo, Lion put his fist to his chest to pay tribute to the honour guard. Together, the couple shook hands and accepted congratulations all the way to the front door.

The hotel was a picture of old world elegance; shiny marble glowed in the light of the chandeliers. To the left was a grand staircase that looked as if it had been plucked out of the movie Gone with The Wind. Sexual tension prompted Lion to forgo the elevator and carry Sheherezade all the way up the giant staircase. When they reached the suite Lion kicked open the front door and carried her across the threshold for good luck. Passing the gourmet lobster lunch that Andrew was organizing in the dining room, Lion grabbed a bottle of

Champagne cooling in an ice bucket as he carried her straight into the bedroom.

As promised the bed was the biggest and softest on the West Coast. Sheherezade took her time that afternoon making all of her sexual promises to Lion come true. By the time they reached the point where he was about to take her virginity, they were both delirious with passion. As he moved into her he looked into her face and whispered, "You're mine. You will always be mine." "Yes," she whispered. "Make me yours."

After breakfast in bed the next day, Lion announced that his brain was beginning to function once again and that he had forgotten to give her his wedding present.

"But Lion, I didn't get anything for you." Sheherezade felt a pang of guilt.

"Are you kidding? Nothing on earth or in heaven could have topped that," he said as lust flashed in his eyes once again.

"But I have an idea. If you really want to give me something that would mean a lot to me."

"Anything."

"OK, before we leave California, I have a friend in L.A. who is a terrific ink slinger. I would love you to have my logo tattooed on your body somewhere, any where."

Sheherezade laughed, "No problem. I'll get my brand but I think I'll put it where only you can see it—if that's alright."

He handed her a fancy red envelope with gold trim. Opening it she saw a key and some legal papers. She opened one piece of paper and found a picture of a red Maserati Granturismo convertible.

"For me?" she was incredulous.

"I wanted to show you the coastline and I thought you would look cute in it." She threw her arms around his neck and thanked him profusely.

"Where is it?"

"Downstairs waiting for us to take it for a spin—but you haven't seen the other part of the gift." She opened the other piece of paper and read that she had a bank account in New York City. On the bottom it said: Balance: $10,000,000.00.

"Ten million dollars? Last week I didn't have a bank account!" She was stunned by the vastness of the concept and couldn't suppress a fit of laughter.

"Some spending money for my wife," Lion smiled. "Just in case I don't fulfill your every desire, you'll have your own money to buy whatever you like. C'mon we're going on a little road trip up the coast. I hope you can drive."

Time fell away as they drove up Highway 1 which hugged the coastline of the Pacific Ocean. They were lost in each other and the experience of this perfect day, enjoying their togetherness on God's beautiful earth.

"We are nearly there." Lion looked lovingly at Sheherezade to prepare her for the trance to be broken.

"I've got a surprise for you. We're going to be meeting the yacht. I thought it would be the best place to find total privacy and solitude for a few days."

"Oh Lion, that sounds glorious. You own a yacht?"

"Yes, *we* own a 260' yacht that sleeps twelve guests, six staff and a few crew. Jeff, who pilots my plane, also captains the ship for me. I've flown Marshall, my chef and Coral, my housekeeper out from the house in Philadelphia to look after us. Of course, Dex and Andrew will be there but I've told them to make sure we have privacy." Lion pulled the Maserati into the Forest Cove Inn which was situated next to a dock and a speedboat that would whisk them out to sea. As Lion spoke to a few of the honour guard that pulled in behind them, Sheherezade went to the front desk to find a washroom. There she saw a paper lying on the coffee table in the lobby. Her eyes picked up the headline which read, 'Biker Clubhouse Blown up—eight killed'. She read on to see if they were affiliated with Lion and found out that it was, in fact, the clubhouse owned by The Purple Flames in Florida that had blown up. She made a mental note to ask Lion if he knew any one from that club.

When she joined Lion, they said their goodbyes to everyone and descended the long staircase to the water to find Dex waiting at the helm of the speedboat.

"Congratulations!" Dex shouted. "You ran out of the chapel in such a hurry I didn't have a chance to wish you well before you left."

"Thanks, Dex. Sorry, we left in a hurry. We were a little wrapped up in the excitement of the whole thing. Everything on schedule?"

"Well, we have a report from security that there is a helicopter on its way and the Paparazzi are right behind you, so I'm glad you showed up when you did." They jumped into the speedboat and watched as the San Francisco chapter members kept a horde of reporters and photographers at bay.

The boat skipped over the rough water to the magnificent white ship parked a couple miles out at sea. Approaching the side, she looked up and saw her name, SHEHEREZADE, in black letters under the bow. Looking over at Lion, she tried to hold back the tears and he smiled at seeing how touched she was by his gesture.

As they pulled up to the side of the yacht the staff was waiting to welcome them on board and they said a quick greeting before the sound of the approaching helicopter drove them below deck.

"I want you to meet Coral," Lion said enthusiastically. I rented a room from her when I was about eighteen and I never forgot how nice she had been to me so after a few years—when I was doing a little bit better—I went back for her and she has been the closest thing to a mother I have ever had. She's the housekeeper at my estate in Ottsville but she also travels around with me if I am here, or staying at the apartment in New York for any length of time. I hope you come to care for her the way I do—she is extremely loyal to me." Sheherezade was impressed by the gentle woman with a severe hair style reminiscent of Edith Head and soft blue eyes who immediately started to fuss over Lion like a mother hen.

Lion took Sheherezade for a tour starting with their master bedroom which was on the second level in the bow of the ship. The bed faced two large windows meeting at a ninety degree angle in the front. To the rear of the bedroom was a large ensuite bathroom that featured a magnificent Jacuzzi tub with solid gold faucets and custom made linen embroidered with the name Sheherezade in gold lettering.

She turned to Lion in amazement and asked, "How were you able to have all this done before our wedding?"

"Well, I get what I want and I wanted to please you," Lion replied. Sheherezade was shocked at how much she had to learn about her new husband—his drive, his attention to detail, and his incredible sensitivity.

"Dinner is being served on deck, let's change and enjoy the sunset, shall we?"

"I would love nothing more, my husband," Sheherezade said tenderly. She showered and found another stunning gossamer gown in pink which fit her like a glove. *I will never take this luxury for granted,* she said to herself. She checked on Lila and then went up to the top deck to find Lion dressed in a casual suit and waiting at an elegant dining table at the rear of the ship. Andrew served aperitifs and Lion and Sheherezade toasted to the bliss they had found in each other's eyes. The scent of fresh flowers and the sea filled the air as seagulls swooped around the ship. Andrew served a gourmet meal of pate de fois gras, surf and turf, salad, and chocolate orange torte with raspberry coulis for dessert. They moved to a comfortable couch on deck to sip coffee and liqueurs and watch the sun set as the ship sailed south. Coral came up on deck and gave a little, "Ehemm," as a warning signal.

"Lion, Boots gave me instructions to wait until you two were relaxing after dinner to give you this—his wedding gift to both of you." Coral handed them a large envelope and a box. Lion looked at Sheherezade and said, "It's your colour it must be for you." Sheherezade removed the exquisite purple silk wrapping and gold bow. Inside was a mauve onyx box with a lid. Opening it she found an exotic purple perfume bottle with her name artistically painted across it in gold leaf. The accompanying card explained, "I wanted to give you something that would be as unique as you are so I had this perfume custom made for you in Tunisia. I hope you like it. The name of the perfume is SHEHEREZADE. P.S. I shipped a case to the estate."

"Lion! My own signature perfume! What a thoughtful gift!" Sheherezade pulled the wand out and applied a little to her wrist. The mixture of jasmine with citrus and other scents was the most glorious smell she had ever experienced. "Oh, I love it! What do you think of it Lion?" she asked as she held out her wrist for him to sniff.

"I think I could live with that scent for the next fifty years or so," he said lovingly.

Lion picked up the large envelope and broke the gold seal. "I wonder what Boots is up to here. I never expected a wedding gift." His look of surprised delight told Sheherezade that he was very touched by his friend's gesture. He took out a series of pictures: the Mediterranean Sea, an exterior shot of a grand villa, a few interior shots of the villa, and exterior shots of the pool and grounds. There was a deed at the bottom of the stack of paper and a personally written letter from Boots:

> *This is your new villa in Tunisia. Wishing you all the happiness you deserve in your new life together.*
>
> *Your neighbour and brother,*
> **Boots**

"Lion, this place is fantastic! Look at that pool, right next to the white beach!"

"Wow, it looks terrific," Lion enthused. "Boots has been going on about the beauty of the place for years and he always wanted me to see his villa there but I just never had the chance. Now he'll finally have his way. We'll have to call him after and thank him." As the sun painted the perfect backdrop for their honeymoon, they sipped Cointreau and counted their many blessings.

Sheherezade looked at Lion and deeply wanted to express the love and gratitude she felt for him.

"Lion, these last three days have been more magical than I could have thought possible—you have taken my life from abject misery to the heights of joy. You've made me happy—so happy, when just last week I wondered if I would ever find peace in this life."

"And it will always be this way," Lion whispered.

Chapter 16

Snake and Butch sat in Snake's Cadillac parked in South Jersey and passed a joint as they scanned the neighbourhood for any members of the Purple Flames. The bounty Lion put on the Flame's patch had created a very popular reality game for members of the Pride looking for some excitement.

"Wicked stuff, eh? One more for the road?" Snake asked.

"Why the fuck not? Can't find those pricks on the street anymore—they've all found a hole to crawl into. Must be scared shitless after the clubhouse went boom last week."

"Any word that the Flames realize what went down?" Snake wondered.

"Not yet, they are still assuming that Skunk blew up with their clubhouse. Fuck, he's turned into a folk hero. Did you see that greeting he got when he arrived with the Old Lady at the picnic? That job is gonna pay big time. Wait till they find out their new prospect was a Pride prospect. They will be looking at each other wondering who they can trust and without trust there is no club," Butch smirked knowingly.

"Too bad he didn't get in earlier and tell us about the plan to raid the warehouse."

"The price of doin' business, brother."

"Do you think any of those fuckers know where Ace is hiding out? Just think—we could have two contracts in one and the contract on Ace is worth a million." Snake slurred as he felt the full effect of the drug. After sitting in the car for half an hour, they both relaxed into their stone and began to lose interest in the search that seemed to be going no where.

"Thursday night . . . there's sure to be some good entertainment at the clubhouse tonight . . . might as well get rolling. Ready to go?" Snake asked as he started the car.

"Holy fuck, man!" Butch was starring at the entrance of the club. Exiting was a heavy biker dressed in jeans and a leather jacket with a couple other guys deferentially following a couple feet behind.

"A herd of Flames just ready to be picked off!" He instinctively put his hand on the Berretta under his jacket.

Snake's nostrils flared as he recognized his old nemesis, Potchi. Potchi had been around since the beginning and had standing in the club. Twenty years before Snake had faced Potchi in a street fight that had never been avenged or forgotten. A number of the Pride had been sliced up badly and the savage nature of the injuries had resulted in the bad blood that existed for years between the two clubs. Snake had a tattoo designed to wind around his neck to cover some of the battle scars inflicted by Potchi that night. Here was the opportunity that Snake had dreamed of for years. Snake's eyes were dark with hatred and Butch knew they were in a fight to the finish despite the fact that they were outnumbered.

"Let's do it!" Snake said calmly as he pulled the car out slowly and started down the street following the small posse that walked toward a parking lot filled with motorcycles. Butch rolled down the window and kept his eyes on his target.

Just as they were approaching closely, a woman holding her child's hand came from the other direction and walked past, blocking the view of their quarry. Snake brought the car to a near stop and lowered his gun to take aim. There was a flash of steel and the sound of bullets rang off the buildings. Two of the five bikers went down like bowling pins and Butch continued to shoot. One guy ran toward the parking lot but the other two men were on the ground and obviously injured.

Snake stopped the car by the curb. Both men got out and took a safe position on the far side of the car in order to assess the situation. Potchi had pulled a gun and was shooting from a supine position on the sidewalk. The other guy was on his side and struggling to draw a gun from his jacket. Butch got a good aim at the Flame struggling for his gun and shot him through the head. Potchi fired back and a bullet hit Snake in his left arm. A searing pain moved up the entire left side of his body but adrenaline kicked in and allowed him to focus on his task.

"You motherfucker," he yelled, as he came out from behind the car to finish the job, even if it meant dying in the process.

Potchi took another shot and it entered Snakes abdomen as he continued to walk toward his target. Butch now came out from behind the safety of the car and walked toward Potchi as well. Even though one of their shots had entered Potchi's chest and he was rapidly losing strength, he used every ounce of what he had left to hold the gun on Snake as he approached. When Snake was within range, Potchi fired. Nothing happened. The gun was empty. Realizing he was free and clear, Snake ran at Potchi and kicked him hard in the ribs. Butch ran up and grabbed Snake and said, "C'mon man, let's take him." Recognition registered on Snake's face and the pair grabbed Potchi under the arms and dragged him over to the car, throwing him in the trunk.

Snake realized that he had been seriously injured but hatred drove him to finish what they had started. Butch had come out of it completely unscathed and he looked over at Snake and asked, "Were you hit bad man?"

"Bad enough, but I'm still going to take care of business," he said with conviction.

He pulled the car onto a deserted country lane and continued to drive to the end. Butch spoke up with urgency in his voice in order to grab Snake's attention, "I know you want him, man, but remember, he might be able to give us a million dollars worth of information."

"OK, OK, I hear you bro . . . let's do it." They parked the car and opened the trunk. Potchi was lying there staring at them and not saying a word. Butch reached in and pulled him out of the car, tossing him to the ground. They could smell fear in the air.

"Where's Ace?" Snake snarled. The pain in his side made his eyes deadly serious. Potchi did not answer. He just spat in their general direction. Snake flashed a switchblade in front of his face and looked him in the eye, "You are going to tell us now or later."

Potchi's loyalty to Jimmy and Ace helped him to hold out until later, but finally the words came out involuntarily, "France."

"Where in France, you mother fuckin' goof?" Snake made a telephone cut from his ear to his mouth. Potchi was semi-conscious at that point and never knew that he had given up the town of Cannes before he died at the side of the road.

"Popeye, I need you man, a little clean up . . . ." Snake gave James the directions to the body as Butch sped towards Lion's estate near Ottsville, Pennsylvania, where Dr. Lindsay was waiting at his on site operating room to patch up a righteous warrior.

Chapter 17

"How the fuck are you?" Jackie smiled as she walked into Fancy's enormous condominium on the Upper East Side of New York City.

"I'm great, c'mon in. The girls from the spa are coming over in half an hour to make us beautiful. Erma is serving lunch in a few minutes. Let's have a drink—I can't wait to hear all the gossip from Indian Lake!"

"Well, it was the best camping trip ever. Why the fuck weren't you there? You're missing out on so much fun woman!"

"Oh, you know me, I'm not about to jump on a hog and pitch a tent the way you do. I hate camping and I hate motorcycles. My hair gets all messy."

"Spending a night in a luxury RV isn't what I would call roughing it, Fancy."

"Well, I don't like it. Anyway, I was having my own fun with Vance at the villa on Cat Island. I don't imagine a weekend of camping on some God forsaken lake is going to top that!" Fancy's sense of drama made all of her conversations take on an urgency that confused strangers and emotionally drained her friends.

"Well I thought it topped that." Jackie replied with mock sarcasm. "I met the best hunk of man I have ever laid eyes on and took him home with me!"

"Really? Who is he?"

"He's a new Prospect but he's already in with the top guys and he's earning respect. Big time. I asked him to have a drink with me so he picked his Ole Lady's ass up and kicked her out of the park and spent the rest of the picnic fuckin' me," she laughed, her eyes sparkling at the thought of her conquest.

"You little minx!" Fancy squealed, "And you're still together?"

"I'm not letting this one go Fancy. He's built like a truck, he has brains, he's good lookin', he takes care of business, and he doesn't take shit—even from me. And best of all he has a continual hard-on and you know me—I can't get enough. He moved into my house the night we got back."

"Wow! I almost wish I had gone to that stupid camp to see that," Fancy said sincerely.

"Well, Fancy, other things went on; things that I know you would not approve," Jackie eased her way into the conversation that she had been dreading, knowing Fancy's propensity for emotional paroxysms.

"What?" Fancy commanded to know.

"Boots was there of course, and he brought a date."

"Oh, he has his amusements and I have mine. I don't get worked up about that anymore. I know where he stands and vice versa. No big deal," Fancy replied with a shrug of her shoulders as she breathed a bit easier.

"Well, I know that's how it has been but I think this one is different. I got the impression that she actually thinks she is moving in on your territory. I can't put my finger on it; it's just in her attitude. And to take her to the lake—you have to admit—he's pushing the line. I can understand how she would be getting ideas . . . ." Jackie had Fancy's attention now and her competitive spirit was kicking in.

"How old is she and what does she look like?" she asked as she studied Jackie waiting for a response.

"Oh, the usual young bimbo." Jackie tried to shrug off the question knowing Fancy as she did.

"Jackie! Tell me! I am waiting!" Fancy's voice rose imperiously.

"OK, she's about twenty-two and she's gorgeous. Long blond hair, great legs. What do you expect? She's a stripper at Lion's new club."

Fancy started to bite her lower lip and waited for Jackie to continue.

"She was bopping around there like the newly crowned Queen, coming up to the tables and asking people to join her and Boots for a drink. So you know me—I had to set her straight. I fuckin' let her know that she wasn't Boots' Ole Lady. She gave me an evil look and stomped off in a huff. It was pretty funny. She's a real cocky little bitch and I think you should put her in her place. Besides, it would be so funny to watch. You've got to come to the Hog Day Picnic.

Please come! We all want to see the look on her face. It would be hysterical." Fancy did not allow Jackie to see how perturbed she was by the account of the events. She just casually said that she would give it some thought and asked Jackie what else happened at the picnic.

"Well, Lion announced that he was getting married."

"God! What next?" Fancy's eyes widened. "That Vita he was flying around the world with?"

"No, actually she's a younger sister of Brandi, the girl that Boots brought to the lake." Fancy face registered concern as she contemplated the sexual power of these two sisters who were obviously formidable enough to have an affect on both men.

"Well, I think I'm going to the Hog Day Picnic!" she said pointedly. A look of revulsion crossed her face.

"Fuck I hate hogs!"

As soon as Jackie left, Fancy picked up the phone to call Boots. *That bastard. Was he forgetting who he was fucking with?* She thought for a moment and then realized that for something as important as this she was better off seeing him in person. She always got better results when she could throw a loud tantrum. He hated yelling.

She stormed into the reception area of his office hoping he was there. Today, she was in luck. She glared at the receptionist and yelled, "Now!" as she continued to march in the direction of the large double doors to his office.

"Fancy, how are you doin'?" Boots searched his mind for the reason that he was in Fancy's bad books.

"We have to talk!"

"What's the matter, Fancy? You look upset."

"This fuckin' Brandi is the matter. We had an agreement!"

"Oh fuck, you're not going to get bent out of shape over some bimbo, Fancy."

"Some bimbo who is trying to pass herself off as your Ole Lady. And maybe she is your Ole Lady now! Is she Boots?" Her voice rose. "Is she Boots?" she screamed as the vein popped in her forehead.

"Fancy, don't get worked up over a piece of ass I took to the lake. You know . . . ." Boots did not have a chance to finish before Fancy started to scream over him.

"Because if she's going to be your Ole Lady them I'm going to remember where a certain body is buried!"

Boots turned white and tried to concentrate on what approach to take with Fancy. He was well aware that she could be a loose cannon, and it was that knowledge that had led him to make that cursed agreement with her twenty-eight years before.

"Fancy, maybe I shouldn't have taken her to the lake but we've been doing our own thing for a long time now. I didn't think you cared who I was with at this point."

"Oh, Boots don't give yourself so much credit. I don't give a fuck who you spend your time with, but flaunting this little bitch in public all the time is a sign of disrespect to me. God! Do you think I'm going to sit still while you prance around with some little tart half my age and make me look like a sucker sitting on the sidelines? I should just call off this agreement and see who comes out the winner. I will Boots!" She shook her head as hysteria, real or otherwise, set in.

Boots panicked, knowing that she was quite capable of doing something stupid that she would regret later. He had seen her cut off her nose to spite her face before because of her uncontrollable temper.

"Fancy, listen to me. I will do anything to make this up to you. You know I had no intention of disrespecting you and our agreement. I like it the way it is. Just tell me what it is you want."

"I want," she said slowly, "Everyone to know that I am still your Ole Lady and that this little bitch is just your whore."

"Done." Boots said exhaling deeply with relief that the crisis had passed. "How? You name it."

"Take me to Hog Day Picnic. Treat me with the respect that I deserve as your Ole Lady and put her in one of the trailers."

"No problem, sweetie." He leaned forward to kiss her but she turned away from him—he had not delivered yet. She left Boots' office knowing that she had won.

Boots sat at his desk staring into space. How could that one decision have such a profound affect on his life? *Fuck,* he thought, *you can't even leave witnesses when they're on your side.* His mind drifted back to the hot summer night when Fancy gave them Jimmy. He never understood why she would go out of her way to help Lion get Jimmy but it certainly had paid off for her. She had lived in grand style for twenty-eight years just for keeping her mouth shut about what she had witnessed that night. Boots shook his head. He had blood on his hands over some guy he barely knew and had no beef with at the time. Lion hated Jimmy; he had stolen his Old Lady. But what was in it for him? Boots did not have a reflective nature except when it came to regrets and this was the biggy.

Boots was starting to obsess about his problem with Fancy. He needed a distraction that would release him from this introspection which invariably led to tormenting thoughts about whether or not he was happy. *What was happiness?* All his life he had studied others who seemed to be happy and then he would strive to get whatever it was he thought was making them happy. It seemed to work for a while but then he would lose interest. He would latch onto someone else's dream, fulfill it for himself and then once again, the empty feeling would return. Now at the age of fifty-three he had everything. Deep down he knew that happiness, as others experienced it, escaped him but he could still feel small thrills and he spent more and more of his time chasing those thrills to make up for a deep longing that he had never satisfied and never understood. Boots fantasized about Brandi having sex with Bull, and as the energy filled his body, he knew he was onto a good idea. He dialled Brandi's cell phone.

"Hi, sweetie, how are you doin'? Miss you too, big time. No, I haven't been around. I went to Lion's wedding to your sister. I knew you wouldn't want to go so I went alone, partied with the boys down there, and just got back this morning. I've got a surprise planned for us at my place tonight. I'm sending the car for you right now. Have a nice day at the spa and I will see you tonight about eight for dinner. Later babe." Boots mood lifted and thoughts of Fancy were kept at bay.

"Hi Mitsy, how are you honey? Everything running smoothly? Great, I want to put in an order for tonight . . . ."

Chapter 18

Brandi whisked past the doorman with all the self-possession of Jackie O. She looked stunning in a low-cut clingy white gown with rhinestone shoes that had been delivered to the spa for her evening with Boots. They shared a sumptuous dinner of fettuccini carbonara and swordfish with tiramisu for desert. Boots glanced discreetly at his watch. The door bell rang and Brandi looked a little miffed at the intrusion.

"It's probably nothing," Boots said as he leaned over and kissed her.

Vivienne could be heard talking before she discreetly announced, "Your guests are here Mr. Falcone . . ." Boots looked over at Brandi and gave her a mischievous smile. Brandi sat frozen to the chair as two attractive, well dressed women entered the dining room. Boots was watching Brandi as he made the introductions.

"Good evening girls, I'm Boots. Mitsy didn't tell me your names." They identified themselves as Sarah and Jennifer.

"Great, nice to meet you, this is my girlfriend Brandi. She's a little too much woman for me so I thought it might be fun to bring in reinforcements. Do you think you can handle her?" he glanced over at Brandi lasciviously. They looked at Brandi and giggled. "Oh, I think so." the blonde purred. "Great, have Vivienne show you where the shower and robes are and we will meet you in the bedroom." Brandi sat in stunned silence. *She didn't do pussy. She was no dyke and she had never had an urge to see what she was missing. The idea of a ménage a trios with two other women was revolting to her. Her mind raced but she quickly came to the conclusion that there was no way out. This is what Boots wanted and she could not disappoint him. Get on with it and get it over with,* she told herself.

She had an urge to run to the bathroom and do a hit but she was afraid to chance it. Boots slipped his hand down the front of Brandi's dress as he pushed his tongue into her ear.

"What do you think of my surprise, babe?" She reminded herself that he was not with her because of a mutual interest in antique coins.

"Wow, Boots, you know how to make life interesting, don't you? You know what would be nice tonight?" she asked casually.

"What have you got on your dirty little mind?"

"No," she giggled. "Some coke would be nice. You know—arouse the senses."

"I didn't know you like coke," Boots said. "You should have told me before." He went into the drawer, pulled out a big bag and laid down some lines on the dining room table. Before long they both had a nice buzz. As Boots took her in his arms and pressed his body close to hers, she could feel his body shake with excitement. Euphoria swept through her along with another dimension of sexual arousal. Her mind was hazy now and the coke was giving her the edge she needed to get through this experience. She hated the thought of a woman touching her. Brandi leaned over and did another couple of lines and prepared to give the performance of her life.

After the girls left and she had Boots to herself, Boots brought out some more coke. Before long all the memories of the interlopers went away and they shared a special night of laughter and intimacy. Brandi could feel her power over Boots growing. *If this is what I have to do to keep him, this is what I will do,* she thought. Her concerns about Fancy disappeared. *He wants me,* she told herself. *Not some old cunt . . .*

Brandi woke feeling a little shaky. Lately she had developed a habit of doing a pipe as soon as she rolled out of bed and this morning it would be impossible. When she looked over she was surprised to see Boots still in bed beside her. Coffee and a cigarette settled her nerves down a bit as they cuddled and ate breakfast in bed like any other typical couple.

"You enjoyed yourself last night with the girls, didn't you?" Boots asked enthusiastically.

"Well, yes, but what made it good for me, was watching it turn you on, Boots," she whispered seductively.

"Ya, I have to admit I love to watch you in action with other people. You get right into it and really enjoy yourself. You're one of a kind, sweetie. Which reminds me, the Hog Day Picnic is coming up and everyone shows up from chapters all over the Eastern Sea board. We have games and prizes and food. Some people bring tents. There's music and an open bar. Everyone let's loose. Oh, ya, we always set up trailers and supply girls for the boys to have some fun. You know—in for a quickie and out. Well, I was thinking of having a Big Hog contest this year. The girls would decide who has the biggest dick and I would put up a new Harley as a prize. Might be fun. I was hoping you would judge the contest and give away the prize."

"Ooo, that sounds like fun . . . watching for the big one!" Brandi giggled.

"Well, you know, I didn't mean watch. I meant you would be taking care of the guys," he said calmly. Brandi sat in stunned silence as she absorbed the enormity of his request.

"You mean you want me to blow a bunch of guys all day long?"

"Well, there will be about five trailers all together but you can help out in one of them and then you can get up on stage and give away the prize." He leaned over and whispered in her ear, "Afterward, you can tell me all about it." *Dykes, now this,* she thought. She was becoming very close to losing it on Boots. Her jaw clenched.

"Is Fancy, going to be there?" she looked into his eyes to monitor his reaction to the question.

"Oh you've heard about her have you?"

"Yep, will she be going?" she pressed.

"Uh, I think she said she *was* going to go this year," Boots replied while trying his best to sound vague.

"Well, how is it that she gets to be your Old Lady? What has she got that I don't have? We're good together aren't we?" Brandi looked at Boots imploringly.

Boots had never shared the details of his personal life with anyone and he squirmed under the pressure.

"Listen, she means nothing to me anymore. It's just a title. You are my Ole Lady in every way that matters. You know that," he lowered his eyes for emphasis so that he would not have to return her gaze.

"Well why is she's still in the picture then? When does the title pass to me?" Brandi inquired while attempting to keep the impatience out of her voice.

"Look, sweetie, I have an arrangement with Fancy—something I don't have the power to change. I can't discuss the reasons, but I am sorry to say, she has the title for life."

Brandi knew she had hit a brick wall.

Brandi took a sip of coffee so that Boots would not see her chin quiver.

That will be the day I'm in a shed giving blow jobs to drunken bikers while Fancy is sitting there with Boots getting all of the glory. Fuck Fancy and Fuck Boots.

She needed a hit.

Chapter 19

When they entered the gates of the Lion's Den, Lion's estate near the town of Ottsville in Pennsylvania, Sheherezade's mouth fell open at the opulence of the grounds. A mile long road wound its way through mature trees and past two manicured ponds where white swans languished in the sun. As the mansion became visible she realized it looked like a modernized version of a castle. Beige stone covered the three story structure that was dotted with big bay windows and walkouts to grand balconies. They pulled into the car port which was attached to an enormous carriage house and saw Lila and Tina waiting beneath. Sheherezade leaped out of the car to greet Lila with a big kiss and hug. Bugsy jumped up at her, vying with Lila for attention.

"I want to show you my bedroom, Meme! It's really big and I have my own bathroom. Here everyone sleeps in a room all alone."

"Yes, we're both going to have some culture shock." She shot Lion a furtive glance and tried to stifle a giggle.

Lion gave her the grand tour with Lila in tow. As they stepped onto the balcony from the second floor master suite, Sheherezade took in the view of the pool and her eyes opened wide in disbelief. As impressed as she was with the mansion, she was in complete awe at the sight of the pool and spa. Whenever Sheherezade had a little extra cash she used to take Lila to the gym for a swim; it was a love they shared as often as possible. Unfortunately being poor meant there wasn't much time for that kind of thing. She was amazed by the luxury that was now a part of her life.

"Lila isn't it beautiful?"

"Meme I didn't go in yet. I waited for you!" Lila instinctively knew what a joy it would be to her aunt. Lion turned to Lila, "Are you sure your aunt isn't a dolphin? I think I better check for fins the way she is looking at that pool."

"We love to swim! Do you like to swim, Lion?" Lila asked.

"Not really. Cats don't like water you know . . ." He looked at Lila and she laughed at his joke.

"I like to cool down in the water but I can't swim."

"Meme is teaching me to swim and she can teach you too, Lion."

"When I bought this land they told me there was a small private lake in the back somewhere; a rare meromictic lake formed by glaciers eons ago. I had the house built two years ago and I never had the time to go looking for it. The property used to be a farm and there is a well-worn path to the lake that starts down by the guest house."

"Oh Lion, you're kidding! A lake! Can we walk down after lunch and see it?"

"Of course! Let's check it out," he smiled.

After lunch Lion, Sheherezade, Lila, and Bugsy, followed the old path that they found near one of the two guest houses. Before long the terrain changed and they entered a thick forest. The pines growing out of the unusual rock formations were so tall that the forest became dark. Moss hung from the branches and covered many of the rocks that jutted up as if giant hands had squeezed the ground together. After walking for about ten minutes, sunlight began to stream through the trees creating an enchanting atmosphere of untouched beauty. An ancient glacier had cracked the earth like a nut and created a natural lake fed by springs. Lila ran down to the edge and threw her arms up in the air with excitement screaming, "Look Meme!"

The shoreline was a series of rocks that met the water in some places and rose to a height of twenty feet off the water in other areas. There was no sign of a lake floor. Looking into the water from the rocky shore, there was a sheer drop down into the ancient chasm. Sheherezade felt such emotion for this peaceful sanctuary that she just knew she was home.

There was a path that followed the shore and it allowed them to search out all the best rocks for jumping into the lake. At the highest rock ledge, Sheherezade found a beautiful wild rose bush in full bloom. She picked a flower and told Lila that it was her favourite flower in the whole world, not only because it was pretty and smelled lovely, but because it was strong and could grow to be beautiful anywhere in the wild.

"Lila, let's make this Wild Rose our secret password. Whenever, or if ever, I have to send you a message and I want you to know, for sure, that it is from me I will use the Wild Rose as a secret signal. Do you understand, sweetie?"

"I understand, Meme. I won't forget." Lion reached the top of the rock where they were standing and seeing the joy in Sheherezade's face, said, "I have a great idea."

"What Lion?"

"You're right, it is beautiful down here. I am going to have some surveying done to find the best location for a cottage. It will be my gift to my two favourite ladies."

They sat by the water enjoying the natural beauty until they began to get hungry and decided to head back to the main house. Lila was going to have a little nap before dinner and Lion had some calls to make so Sheherezade went up to her new bedroom to take a long, luxurious bath. She picked up the newspaper and took it upstairs. On page two was a story that read, LITTLE BOY KILLED IN BIKER CROSSFIRE. It told the story of two members of Lucifer's Pride and five members of the Purple Flames who were involved in a shoot out late the night before, outside of Finales night club. A woman walking down the street with her five year old son had been struck with a bullet but was expected to live. Her son had been critically injured and died later that night in the hospital. The article said that police believed that the Pride were escalating the war between the clubs which included the explosion at the Purple Flame's clubhouse in Florida that killed eight of their members just the week before. *Did that mean that Lion was responsible for the boy's death?*

Coral directed Sheherezade to Lion's office and she ran in with tears still glistening on her face. Lion looked a little surprised and ended his phone conversation.

"What's the matter, honey?"

"I just read about the little boy that was killed last night; he was the same age as Lila."

"I know it was a horrible accident," he said ruefully.

"Well, you are the leader of the club. Isn't there something you can do to make sure the members don't get into these vendettas and disputes?"

"I wish that were possible. These are grown men with their own reasons for doing what they do. I'm just the leader of the motorcycle club that they belong to and I can't control their behaviour. I never wanted to involve you in the politics of the club but after this incident I can see that I have no choice. The Purple Flames are a savage bunch of bastards and they are starting a campaign of terror against our members. As the President I'm their prime target and that means that anyone I care about is going to be a target as well. Now I have state of the art security at the estate here, but I want you to travel with a couple of body guards whenever you go outside the gates."

"Oh, Lion what about you, will you be careful?"

"I'm used to dealing with it; you don't have to worry about me. But there is something else I am worried about and I hate to bring it up."

"What?" The expression on Lion's face was scaring her.

"Well, it's Lila. I think she could be a target. I think it might be for the best, just for a little while, if Lila went off to school somewhere in another country. I think we could both sleep better at night knowing that she is away from the danger. It would only be until things settle down—I promise."

Sheherezade sat down on the couch and put her head in her hands. *How could this be happening?* She thought they could finally live together in peace and happiness. After a couple of moments she looked up at Lion with trust in her eyes and said, "You know the situation best, Lion. If you think she would be safer somewhere else then I will take her away from here until the danger is over. When? When should we go?"

"As soon as possible," Lion said sadly.

After a wonderful evening of dinner and swimming, Sheherezade was tucking Lila into her bed.

"Meme, I love it here. We can swim and go down to the lake and you're always home with me. Can we swim all day tomorrow?"

Sheherezade was afraid she was going to break her niece's heart.

"I know honey, I love it here too and we are going to be spending so much time together swimming at the pool and playing down at our lake but that is going to have to wait for a little while. Lion has some men that don't like him and he is afraid they might want to take you from us. Lion and I are determined to make sure you're safe because we love you more than anything else in the world. We think it would be best if we take you away from this house just for a little while and as soon as we think you will be safe, you'll come back. Do you understand, my darling?"

Lila's soulful eyes met Sheherezade's eyes, "I told you that Lion didn't like me Meme."

As the plane touched down at Toronto International Airport, Sheherezade was thinking of her conversation with Lion. She insisted that only she should know the whereabouts of Lila's new school. She had even kept the details from Lion citing the same argument and in the end he had no choice but to agree to her terms. She had taken the limo to the nearest town to make arrangements via pay phone for Lila to attend a very old patrician school in an elegant part of Toronto, Canada. Lila would have every advantage living there and it would be close enough to visit, if there came a time when a visit did not endanger Lila's safety.

Sheherezade could not help but notice how Lila was accepting her fate with total equanimity. She recognized the maturity that she herself possessed at that age—forged out of an experience of life where disappointment and neglect were a daily occurrence. As she kissed Lila good-bye she thought of the mother who could never kiss her little boy again and she felt lucky that she had the resources to keep Lila safe. Lila looked into Sheherezade's eyes for one final promise of reassurance, "You won't forget about me will you Meme?"

Sheherezade clutched her to her breast and then looked into the eyes that expressed both hope and resignation. "Lila, never worry about that. I love you and love *never* forgets."

When Sheherezade arrived home Coral told her that Lion had to go to New York unexpectedly and that he would call her later on in the evening. She changed into some jeans and, after having some lunch, she decided to roam around the mansion and explore every nook and cranny of the estate. She found an enormous wine cellar in the basement, a games room, and a magnificent indoor pool with a high vaulted ceiling and a big fire place at one end. She walked over to the smaller of the two guest houses that were hidden by trees and was startled to find that the front door was open. *Why wouldn't it be*, she thought? The compound of over a thousand acres was guarded day and night.

The sunken living room had three stone walls and one wall was almost entirely made of glass. There was an opening to a big kitchen with its own fireplace built into the wall that could be used as a wood burning stove. The three bedrooms were on another level and spread out amongst the trees. Every room had a big window on at least one wall which gave the impression that the occupant was sleeping outdoors. Sheherezade could not help but think that this guest house was three or four times bigger than most family dwellings on her street. Resting on a haystack by the stables, she thought back to her little room on Prospect Street in Dover and she could picture her mother sitting at the kitchen table and chairs that were artefacts of the 1950's. She felt a little twinge of guilt. Here she was living a lifestyle the average person would never glimpse and her mother was sitting in a tiny flat that she could barely afford. She had a sudden epiphany. She had money! She could finally give her mother everything she always wished her mother could have.

Sheherezade went into the library and took a deep breath as she dialled her mother's cell phone. Regina answered using her cheerful, optimistic voice that was reserved for non-family members.

"Hi mum! It's me, Sherry."

"Yep."

"Well, I don't know if you heard, but I wanted to let you know that I got married."

"Yep, I heard."

"Anyway, Lion gave me a lot of money, as a wedding present, and I was thinking that I could afford to move you into a place of your own. If you find a condo you like I'll make arrangements to buy it for you."

"I hate condos."

"Well, I just thought that a condo would be best for you because that would mean you wouldn't have to worry about cutting the grass or anything like that but it doesn't make any difference to me . . . pick out a house."

"No, I'm OK here."

"Well, I know you're OK but I can make your life a little more comfortable now, if you'll let me." There was a slight hesitation on the other end of the phone.

"Not everyone is as materialistic as you are Sherry. If I wanted a big house I could have found some rich sucker to marry but that just didn't do it for me. If it turns your crank then I hope you got what you wanted."

Sheherezade shook her head and closed her eyes with defeat.

"Well, actually I married Lion because I fell in love with him. I had no idea how rich he was at the time and it wouldn't have made any difference to me if he didn't have a dime. But now I have some money and if I can do anything for you, or buy you something you want, just let me know because I would love to help out."

"No, don't want anything. Brandy has a good job and her boyfriend is one of the richest men in America too, so if you want to flaunt your money call someone else OK? Take care." CLICK.

O.K. So some things never change, she thought. *Mum's passive aggression is as healthy as ever. Some day I will learn.*

Chapter 20

Lion and Boots had spared no expense to make the Pride clubhouse on the outskirts of New York City the quintessential motorcycle club headquarters. A prospect at the main gate screened all visitors. Once inside the perimeter gate, two staircases led to a huge wooden door that opened into the main building. All windows and doors were reinforced and wired to a security system that could be activated to maintain complete privacy. Past a grand foyer, the main floor had two large rooms. The first room resembled a typical sports bar featuring a thirty foot bar lined with stools and equipped with beer taps. The opposite side of the room was filled with banquettes. In between were tables and chairs and a large dance floor that was the focus of a magnificent sound system. The walls were flanked with three huge flat screen TVs. At the far end of the room was a door that led to a smaller lounge that had four regulation size pool tables and another bar. At the back of the room was a kitchen manned by professional cooks that provided meals and snacks on a twenty-four hour basis for members and guests. A staircase ran from the front bar to the second floor which housed eight bedrooms, two executive suites and a large office. The third floor housed the control room for the security system, police scanners, cameras, and a watchtower with windows that allowed a 360 degree view of the compound.

The bar was packed with members who were there to pay their respects to Snake who had been out of commission for a little over a week after being patched up by Dr. Lindsay. He was being hailed as the newest hero for picking off four Purple Flames in the dramatic street fight a week before. The information regarding the whereabouts of Acelyn was another matter. Lion told Snake to keep the information quiet to prevent her from being tipped off by someone's indiscretion. Times were such that no one could be trusted.

James pulled into the parking lot on his newly customized Night Rod Special and strolled through the front door dressed head to toe in black leather. He was making a name for himself within the organization as one of the most ruthless and trusted members in the New York Chapter. Tall, dark, with light blue eyes that mesmerized women, he was one of the most eligible bachelors in the club. It was a bit of a mystery to everyone why James never found a woman to fill the sentimental position of Old Lady. Little did they know that he had a secret obsession and her name was Brandi. Despite the fact that she worked as a stripper and turned the odd discreet trick in the VIP room of the club, she was recognized as Boots' property. As a full patch member of the Pride, it would be seen as a sign of disrespect for James to show an interest in the Vice President's woman. The consequences of a contravention of biker ethics such as that would certainly lead to his demise as a biker and perhaps as a breathing human being.

He came up behind Snake and gave him a slap on the back

"I hope the doc patched up those holes real good. We don't want beer all over the floor," James teased.

"Hey, my man, Popeye!" Snake gave James a kiss on the cheek.

"What's goin' on tonight?" James asked.

"Butch and I were on our way here that night to party but we got sidetracked for a while so we're back and ready to let loose. We're gonna need some split tail James. We're due for a splash and after more than a week I'm ready."

James grinned, "Give me half an hour to round 'em up. You're gonna owe me a brew."

James signalled a couple of girls who worked the street for him to go upstairs to the rooms. When he gave the same signal to a very pretty blonde sitting in the corner banquette she sat staring back at him with a look of confusion. As he informed her that she was to stay in one of the bedrooms and give the boys what they asked for, a look of sheer terror crossed her face and she explained that she just dropped by the clubhouse as a guest of a friend and was about to leave. Grabbing her by the arm, he walked her up the stairs and took her into the empty bedroom.

"Look bitch, if you're in this clubhouse you do what you're told to do." He pulled his hand back and gave her a hard backhand across the face.

"Is there any part of that you don't understand?"

The girl paused for a moment, mentally weighing her options, "No, I understand."

James walked back downstairs.

"OK boys, party is starting. Rooms are full of lovely ladies waiting to please. He picked up a pitcher of beer and poured himself a big stein.

"Here's to Snake and his work for the club." The guys went wild cheering for Snake and he flexed his muscles as a show of his renewed strength before starting up the stairs to find a woman. Shane was right behind him. While the bartender cranked up House of the Rising Sun, and lowered the lights, a couple of the girls began to put on a strip tease show for the boys. Moral was high and everyone was in a raucous and celebratory mood. The half naked girls were kissing and fondling each other and the guys were cheering them on. As they stripped down to G-strings Boomer went over to one of the girls, grabbed her, and stuck his tongue down her throat. He pushed her down over one of the tables and pulled his pants down, entering her from behind. The guys at the bar were cheering him on and everyone was laughing at his beer belly which seemed to be getting in the way of his lewd intentions. Subjugation of the enemy had brought a renewed pride to the club; feelings of brotherhood were magnified in the face of a common enemy.

Suddenly the alarm started to blare: MEEP MEEP MEEP. The Prospect at the gate had given as much warning as was possible and the person in the watchtower picked up the microphone. RAID! PIGS AT THE FRONT DOOR! The warnings continued as members ran to the bathroom to flush drugs and Boomer tried to pull up his pants. Girls were throwing on their clothes and everyone was cursing loudly as they tried to get their bearings. Loud banging echoed through the club as the cops pounded the front door, attempting to break down the reinforced steel with special equipment created just for that purpose.

When the police entered, members were expecting the usual shakedown which meant a thorough search for drugs and weapons, but the cops were unusually calm and focused. They approached Butch and arrested him for the murder of one of the Flames. He was handcuffed and escorted out to the cruiser. The club had been under surveillance and the police knew that Snake was on the premises so they began a systematic search of the club to find him. Shane was aware of the police raid but he was not about to tell the cute little blonde to stop what she was doing, so when the cop opened the bedroom door, he told him to go away. The cop did not appreciate the attitude so he yelled back into the room, "Miss, are you there of your own free will?" Shane was aghast when she took her mouth off of him and through a sudden barrage of tears, yelled back, "No!"

"Fuck, you must be kiddin' honey. You should get an Oscar for that performance. From where I was standing you had real talent!" he smirked.

The cop entered the room and took the girl by the arm to escort her downstairs. "Pull your pants on buddy—you're coming downtown." Shane was left standing there with an erection and a big problem. He wasn't worried about the legal charges; the problem was the hell he was going to catch from the Old Lady. *He laughed to himself as he thought of what a feisty piece of work Jackie was.*

Another cop had found Snake naked with a girl in another room.

"Get up Walter you are under arrest for the murder of Nickolas (Smokey) Wilson, Mark (Animal) West, and Jason (Yogi) Talbot. He pulled on his clothes and two cops handcuffed his hands behind his back before leading him down the stairs. When they were gone, the front door was left open as everyone stood around in stunned silence.

"Someone call Lion."

A pall hung in the air as paranoia set into the crowd of partiers at the clubhouse. Everyone understood that bikers do not speak to police. Snake and Butch were solid, trusted members of the club but still, everyone in the room knew that their arrest would have repercussions for everyone there in one way or another.

Chapter 21

*B*randi was pulling off her false lashes as Monica came bouncing topless into the dressing room after having just finished her set. Brandi had managed to avoid her since the bike run to the lake and she intended to treat her like a spider on the wall for as long as she worked at the club.

"What a raunchy crowd tonight! I made a bundle on that last dance. Hey Angey, give me a toke will you?" Angey passed her roach over to Monica as she dropped into a tub chair and threw her legs over the edge. Brandy waited for the shoe to drop.

"Hey Monica, are you going to the Hog Day Picnic at Lion's Estate?" Angey asked casually.

"Oh, ya, of course. I'm going with Nick. It's been a long standing tradition that all the Ole Ladies have their own picnic beside the pond away from the guys and all their silly games. This year Sheherezade should be there and I hear Boots' Ole Lady, Fancy, is going to be there too." She glanced over at Angey and gave here a wink, indicating that this was information she was fabricating in order to press Brandi's buttons.

"Oh, I can't wait either. It's supposed to be the best shindig of the summer. Lion throws quite a bash." Angey enthused.

Those bitches are so transparent, Brandy thought. *Monica planned that conversation just to get under my skin.* Brandy steadily packed up her stuff and left the room. Her head was swimming with the dilemma confronting her. *If Fancy shows up at the picnic, I'll never live it down,* she fretted. *Never. Sherry reigning over the picnic like the queen! I will not be giving blow jobs in a shed!* Her cell phone rang.

"Ya, Brandy, the landlord is asking me for the rent. You gonna be home tonight?" Regina asked flatly.

"Ya, I'll be home later on. How much do you need?"

"It's five hundred."
"OK, I'll pay him tomorrow."
"Bye."

Brandi took the three hundred dollars from the half drunk overweight man that smelled of cigars. His preening, self-satisfaction at having a beautiful young girl service him made her want to punch him in the face but she smiled and took the money.

"Call me next time you're in town, honey," she cooed. Brandi had managed to stay high since her last night with Boots and the two girls at his apartment but today the reality of that nightmare was hitting her hard. She loved Boots but she had to face the fact that their time together always seemed to be about his sexual gratification. She could no longer believe that her sexual power over him would be the only magic she needed to achieve her goal. She wanted to be his woman. She had given herself to him and done her best to satisfy his every desire. Revulsion seized her gut. *She had been with other women.* The memories had clarity in her sober mind that she could not escape. She felt cheap. Used. She could not help but wonder if Fancy would do that for him and if she had done those things to earn her title. Boots had given her beautiful things but they didn't pay the rent. She thought back to her room in her mother's dirty little flat and the revulsion she felt for the trick she had just turned to pay for another month in that place. She closed her eyes and tears of anger ran down her face. Brandi's mind wandered to the big estate that Sheherezade now called home. Nice clean sheets. Breakfast in bed. Servants looking after her every whim. She wondered where Fancy lived and if Boots was with her. It had been over a week since she had heard from him and she knew he was not the type of man to be celibate when they were apart. She had managed to keep the anger and desperation at bay but now all the thoughts she knew she would have to face eventually were showing up uninvited to her reluctant psyche. Brandi needed a hit to make her stomach ache go away so she could think of a plan. There had to be a way to make it all work. She had to find out why Boots insisted that Fancy had the title of his Old Lady for life. She had to find a way to take her place. Sheherezade was living large and here she was with nothing. That was about to change. She would show them all.

She tried James again.

"Hi James, how are you honey?"

"Hi beautiful! I'm glad you called—it's been a bad fuckin' day."

"Why, what happened?"

"Are you at the club? I'll come and pick you up and I can tell you about it."

"Ya, Come and get me. I'll meet you around the block in the usual place."

James pulled up to the curb and Brandi jumped on the back of his Harley. James took her over to his apartment where they poured themselves a drink and lit up a bowl of meth. They relaxed and ordered some Chinese food while they did another bowl. James told Brandi about the raid on the clubhouse and Brandi told James that she was being harassed by the bitches at work without getting into the details of her humiliation about not being Boots' Old Lady. The meth was not making the memory of that repulsive trick go away. Or Sherry playing with Lila on the lawn of her mansion in the countryside. Or Fancy languishing in a huge marble bath in her opulent condo.

"James have you got any works in the apartment? I thought I might like to try to mainline it once. It's supposed to be a nice buzz."

"Sure babe," James said as he pulled out a couple of packaged needles from a drawer. "Just let me find a vein for you in a place that won't show when you're wearing a G-string." James tied off her ankle and found a suitable vein between her toes. As he shot the meth into her vein Brandi relaxed into the chair and a broad smile crossed her face.

"Feeling better, babe?"

"Awesome James. Thanks. Hon, what do you know about Fancy McFarlane? Do the guys ever talk?"

"Ya, I've heard rumours. Rumours that I wouldn't want to get back to Boots. She was there from the beginning with Boots and Lion and Lion's girlfriend Acelyn. The way the guys tell it, she was the biggest slut you could hope to meet. She would throw herself at every guy she took a liking to, and if they'd have her—they could. Now the other members of the Pride did their best to stay out of her way because if you rejected Fancy McFarlane she would turn on you like a rattlesnake and she loved to stir up shit. They were terrified that she would make trouble for them with Boots. But—and this is the part that would stir up major shit if Boots ever found out—she was fuckin' some of the Purple Flames who thought that it was as funny as hell that they were doin' the Vice's Ole Lady."

"God! What a pig," Brandi huffed. "Personally, I think Boots has the right to know he has been dissed like that. What happened to Acelyn, Lion's girlfriend?"

"You haven't heard that story?"

"No, babe, you are the only Patch I hang with. I don't dish dirt with the girls—that's for damn sure."

"Well, Acelyn was a singer and she met Jimmy Bourke, leader of the Purple Flames, in a club where she was performing. There was something about Jimmy that drove women crazy—he was supposed to be a real sexy guy—I don't know. Anyway, Ace went to the other side and that wasn't cool because there was already bad blood between the clubs. Lion found out—went nuts. Three months later Jimmy and Ace were seen together. Maybe they thought it was going to fly with Lion and he'd get over it. I don't know all the details. Anyway, Lion and Boots got Jimmy out to some field and they did him. Ace must have figured she would be next because she disappeared. Lion has a contract on her head for a million dollars but hasn't found her yet."

"How did they get him out to that field?"

"No one has figured that out."

She thought back to what Boots had told her about Fancy. *We have an arrangement. It is something I don't have the power to change.* If he did not have the power then Fancy had the power and the question was why. Why did she have power over Boots? She must have something on him and whatever it was it had to be something that happened a long time ago. Maybe it was murder.

Chapter 22

A couple of dishevelled guys with long hair dressed in leather jackets and well-worn jeans sat at the booth of a diner in the heart of the Bronx.

"Pretty good night," Lenny said in hush tones over a breakfast special at twelve noon.

"One of our better ones. I spoke to Tilly this morning and he tells me the little fish isn't talking but the big one is turning State's evidence. He knows he's looking at forever for the little boy." Sandy looked down into his black coffee, closed his eyes and chuckled. "The boy's mother made a positive identification because of that big fuckin' snake crawling up his neck. You've got to love it. Their tattoos allow us to sort them according to kingdom, phylum, family, and species. God help us when someone joins their team that's smart enough to figure that out." Both men laughed as they dug into their food.

"More coffee?" the waitress smiled down sweetly.

"So what is he giving up?"

"Only the biggest motherfucker of them all."

"Are you telling me he is turning over on Lion?"

"Yep, the Black Cat. Isn't it sweet?"

"When is it going down?"

"Soon . . . real soon."

"Can I take those plates for yous guys?" the waitress asked as she bent over and flashed a bit of cleavage.

"Among other things, he's singing about the murder of Elise O'Neil. We knew it was James Barrett and Shane Rawlings who did the hit because we had a witness. The DA felt we needed to firm up the case before making an arrest, but now Snake is giving us corroborating evidence that will have those boys playin' with themselves, or each other, for a very long time." Sandy laughed as he lit a cigarette.

"Brave woman," Lenny's eyes explored space as he let out a heavy sigh.

"Oh, don't worry, as soon as she came forward she was given protective custody. But you're right; she's exceptional. She packed up two teenage daughters and a baby to get these guys. Seems she was up that night with a sick baby when she happened to look out her window and saw those two scumbags creeping down the street."

"Unbe-fuckin'leivable."

"Tell me."

"Thanks, fellas. Here's your bill."

"Thanks honey," Lenny said grabbing the bill. "My turn." Sandy thanked Lenny, walked out the front door, surveyed the street and roared off on his Harley-Davidson motorcycle.

The waitress went to the backdoor and stepped outside to light a cigarette. As she took a large drag on her Marlborough she pulled out her cell phone.

"Hi baby, I've got something for you. Information. Those two undercover cops that come in once in a while dressed like bikers. I don't want to talk over the phone. Oh, it sure is worth the trip. See you in fifteen minutes. Love ya."

Chapter 23

"Oh shit!" Brandy said when she awoke in James' bed at two o'clock. I told my mother I would be home today to pay the rent."

"Oh, fuck it babe, it's Sunday. Let's spend the day together," James said as he lit a cigarette.

"Love to, hon." Brandy recalled the nice high she had the night before and could not wait to do it again. "But I still have to go home, so if you can drop me off at my car, I'll drive back after I give the rent money to my mother."

As Brandy turned onto Hwy 280 to Dover her cell phone rang.

"Hey, Gorgeous, how are you doin'?"

"Boots, I am great but I miss you. When am I going to see you?"

"Well I was thinking, tonight. I have tickets to the theatre and reservations at a very hoity-toity restaurant that would require you to look spectacular as usual."

Brandy's heart leapt, "Oh that sounds wonderful, honey! What time?"

"Well, how about if I send the car early so you can spend some time being pampered at the spa?"

"Fantastic! Just what I needed!"

"O.K. the car is on its way and you enjoy. See you about seven at my place."

"Honey, work on my buttocks will you—got some kinks there," Brandi instructed the masseuse. She loved to languish in the spa where she was always treated as if she were Boots' queen. The meth she smoked before she left home had made all those bad thoughts about her last date with Boots go away. The lights were dimmed and soft music played in the background as Brandi drifted into a semi-trance state where all was perfect.

"So you are the whore of the month. I can see he's losing his taste in women. There was a time when he was a little more discriminating." Brandi wondered how her perfect dream state was changing so abruptly into a nightmare. She gave her head a shake and as she came out of her reverie a woman's voice brought her attention to the doorway of the room where she saw the silhouette of a pair of long legs in very high heels and a cascade of blonde curls.

"Excuse me? Are you speaking to me?" she squinted into the light.

"I was in the Spa and one of the girls told me that Boots' whore was here so I thought I would straighten you out on a few points because I know Boots doesn't care enough to take the time to do it."

Brandy's brain was working now and it finally dawned on her that before her stood none other than Fancy herself. Brandy took a deep breath and clenched her teeth at the sight of the enemy as she dismissed the masseuse with the wave of her hand.

"You will have to excuse me, but who are you?" Brandi asked sweetly.

"Don't fuck with me you little bitch, you know exactly who I am. I'm Boots' Ole Lady. Something you pretend to be—but will never be." Brandi's eyes narrowed and her nostrils flared slightly before she started to speak.

"It seems to me that it's you who are pretending. You have been replaced by someone younger and more attractive and you're pretending that you still have what it takes, when obviously you don't." Brandy gave her a contemptuous glance and put her head down on the table as if to dismiss her.

Fancy had to resist grabbing her by the hair and knocking her off the table for such insolence but she had to suppress her anger in order to set her straight.

"Jackie told me you were thick but I can see that I will have to explain how things actually work in our little world. Look, what you are not getting is that Boots has his amusements. You are his sex toy—just one of many. But understand, when I say, 'Boots let's be together,' he drops all you little whores and spends his time with me. Now, since you *are* so thick, I can see that I will have to demonstrate my point. The club has the Hog Day Picnic coming up and I am going to tell Boots that I want to go. You will find me sitting by the pond eating finger sandwiches with all the other Old Ladies of the club members and if you insist on coming to the picnic, you'll find yourself on the other side with all the mamas and cheap whores the boys keep around for amusement. You're a cheap whore and you'll *always* be just a cheap whore."

Brandy could feel a black anger engulfing her head but she refused to give Fancy the satisfaction of letting her know that she was hitting a nerve. She sat up slowly on the massage table and calmly addressed Fancy as if she were speaking to an inferior. "I don't know who you are lady but I *can* tell you this. Boots is quite a man and he can have any woman he wants and I know he wouldn't want an old hag like you when he can have a beautiful cunt like mine." Brandy took off the sheet that was draped over her back and stood up with her fingertips holding the blanket behind her as a frame for her beautiful body. Fancy could not prevent her eyes from scanning the form in front of her. Livid with anger, she screamed, "You're just a whore! A common fuckin' street whore!" Fancy hoped everyone heard. She turned on her heels and marched out of the spa.

Brandy closed the door to the room so she would not be disturbed. She flung herself on the massage table and tried to catch her breath as her chest pounded with anger. The image of Fancy's face twisted in loathing was burnt into mind and her words echoed through Brandi's brain. *Street whore. Cheap whore.* There was a time when she hoped she would never hear that word again. Memories of standing on the corner flashed before her eyes. The tenderloin. She would never forget that corner and the smell of the garbage she stepped over while strutting her young body up and down that part of the strip that was her own. Fancy had triggered a painful memory of the johns that would take pleasure in calling her a whore to her face knowing she would say nothing because she was there to please.

Pictures of her mother's radiant face laughing under the street light bubbled up from her subconscious. Regina seemed to revel in the power she yielded at having something that another human being was willing to pay for. She enjoyed the game. Her mother had fun being a hooker. She had seen it in her face. *She didn't know,* Brandi thought. She didn't realize how traumatic it had been for her at fourteen to be taken out onto that street corner. She had heard her mother's stories about being poor and having no other way to feed herself and her daughter, but she knew the truth. It was not about the money; it was the game. *I never enjoyed the game the way she did. I just hated every minute of every day of those two years.*

She remembered how she had envied Sherry who had been left with a neighbour when they moved that time. Regina had been determined to move out of the apartment she was sharing with one of her boyfriends and Mrs. Dennis had kindly offered to allow Sherry to stay with her and her daughter—Sherry's best friend—until they got settled. Somehow, that stretched into two years. Shortly after they moved Regina convinced Brandi to join her on the street. *Convinced. What fourteen year old makes a decision of their own volition when the parent is suggesting they do something? I did what my mother wanted me to do. It was not my choice; it was her choice. Why was I chosen to be the whore? Why not Sherry?* Resentment engulfed her body and tears ran down her face before she suddenly caught her breath and bolted upright. Brandi looked around and realized that she had been sitting in the dark lost in these deep thoughts; thoughts she had placed in a dark corner of her mind for almost six years. The pain was too sharp so she pushed the thoughts away once more, deciding instead to focus her hatred onto Fancy.

Boots looked dashing in a tuxedo as he met the limousine in front of his coop on Fifth Avenue. He jumped in and gave Brandi a big kiss.

"You look fabulous sweetie, but you've lost some weight. Your tits don't quite fill out that dress the way they used to," he teased.

Brandi feigned surprise, even though she could see how gaunt her face had become every time she looked into a mirror.

"Really! I guess I need a good meal!" she laughed.

They ate by candlelight at the best window table of an elegant restaurant in Soho. Boots cuddled Brandi as they laughed their way through The Producers on Broadway. After the show Boots suggested they go back to his place and have some quiet time together. Boots opened a bottle of Champagne and laid out a couple of lines of coke on the side table beside the hors d'oeuvres, pastries and fresh fruit which Vivienne had left for them.

"You seem a bit quiet, tonight Brandi," Boots said softly as he pushed a hair out of her face.

"Just thinking how wonderful it is to have an evening like this with you. I wish we could be together more often," Brandi added as she looked up at him longingly.

"We will babe, don't look so sad." Brandi wanted to take him in her arms and beg him to make that evil bitch, Fancy, go away but she knew it wouldn't work. She also knew that if she pushed him too much she would be replaced fast enough with a girl who did not come with emotional baggage. Boots cuddled her on the couch and asked her about her life before they met. For once, it seemed to Brandi that they were a normal couple just getting to know each other better.

"I think I can cheer you up," he said as he got up and went into his study.

"What are you up to, Boots?" Brandi chuckled as a feeling of dread swept through her like a cold wind. Boots walked back into the room and she looked at him quizzically. Taking her hand, he pulled her up into his arms. "I'm sorry for being so absent lately. You know we have had some real problems with the club and I have had a lot on my plate. I hope this makes up for it, somewhat." Boots handed Brandi a small velvet box. When she opened the box she let out a squeal and threw her arms around him.

"What kind is it?"

"I don't know . . . I just told them it had to match your hair."

"No, tell me!"

"It is the newest Mercedes SL 550 Roadster. I hope you like it . . . ."

"Where is it?"

"Downstairs in my parking space. Don't tell me you want to see it now." She gave him a playful punch and took his hand pulling him to the door. After they took it for a ride around the streets of New York City laughing and enjoying each other's company for about an hour they returned to the apartment. Boots took her into the bedroom and they kissed passionately while they had a glass of champagne and lounged on the bed. After he had made love to her, Brandi wrapped her arms around him and held him as tight as she possibly could.

"I am so madly in love with you Boots."

"I feel the same way, sweetie," Boots whispered. "I have such a good time with you. I want to see more of you."

"Well, I think you have seen every part of me there is to see," Brandi teased.

"No, you know what I mean. More nights like this where we just kind of hang out."

"I would love that!" Brandi could feel hope flowing into her heart.

"Well, we'll make a point to do this more often but this week I'm swamped. I don't think I can even squeeze in one night with my favourite girl. The next time I see you might have to be at the picnic next week. I can count on you to man one of the trailers, right?" Brandy was taken aback by this subject that seemed to pop up out of nowhere. His eyes were dark with intensity and on some level she knew that the topic was not up for discussion. She could not help but suspect that the evening had been orchestrated to ensure an affirmative answer to this one question. Her mind wandered dangerously back to her encounter with Fancy. Why was he being so persistent about having her work a shed at the picnic? It wasn't like she was the only woman associated with the club who knew how to give a blow job—in fact many of them were professionals. But Boots wanted *her* to do it. Why? *Why do you want to whore me out just like my mother did when I was fourteen,* she wondered.

"Of course, Boots," she whispered. "Anything for you."

Chapter 24

"You dumb son of a bitch, didn't you hear the sirens going off?" Jackie tried to keep a straight face as she confronted Shane.

"Well, I don't remember them going off. Fuck, if I heard them I wouldn't be having this conversation, now would I?" Shane grovelled a bit to appease Jackie because he was not sure how much trouble he was in.

"You prick! How dare you fuck around on me with some skanky tramp in room number two?" Jackie hauled off and clocked Shane in the side of the head. He put his arm up to block her, but not soon enough.

"It was just a blow job, Honey. I didn't fuck anybody. You know I wouldn't do that. I love you. I'm crazy about you."

"You better not, you son of a bitch, or I'll cut off your nuts and fry 'em up for dinner."

"I'll serve them to you on a platter myself if it ever happens."

He held her hands behind her back so she could not get away while he kissed her neck.

"Come on, how about sugar, babe?" Jackie laughed and tried to untangle herself but was unable to move.

"What about the charge?" Jackie asked.

"I'm going to have one of my guys have a talk with the slut and make it all go away. Don't worry about a thing."

"Fuck, what's this?" Jackie looked out the window and watched three police cars pull into the driveway.

"Holy fuck!" Shane ranted, "It was just a goddamned blow job!"

Shane stepped into the living room and allowed Jackie to answer the door.

A detective and two officers stepped into the foyer.

"What is it?" Jackie asked blandly.

"We want to speak to Shane. Is he here?" one officer asked.

Shane walked into the foyer and looked at the officer who spoke to Jackie without saying a word. The officers threw him against the wall to conduct a frisk search of his body to look for weapons. When they were finished the detective spoke to Shane as the officers grabbed his arms and put them behind his back in order to apply handcuffs.

"Shane Rawlings, you are under arrest for the murder of Elise O'Neil . . . ." Shane spun around and looked at Jackie. An involuntary sound escaped Jackie's mouth that sounded like the muffled scream of a wounded animal. She ran over to Shane and kissed him before the officers had a chance to grab him by the arm and escort him to the cruiser. Snake was talking.

"Make a call, babe," Shane said casually.

Dex had called to say that Lion was dealing with a small emergency and would be staying in the city for a least one night. Alone, Sheherezade decided to enjoy the peace and solitude of the evening. After lingering over a delicious dinner of grilled fish and vegetables served by the pool, she played in the warm water and lounged in the hot tub. But, as much as she revelled in her new life, she ached to share it with Lila. Tina came out to the pool with fresh strawberries and cream served with the ice wine she had bought back from Toronto. She phoned Lila and spoke for a long time about her first day at school. When she hung up she felt good about the decision they had made to protect her. Lila was happy and that meant more to Sheherezade than anything else in the world.

When the sun went down she perused the DVD/ video library in the home theatre and screened the movie, Indiscreet, starring Cary Grant and Ingrid Bergman. She stretched out on a big suede couch that was more like a giant pillow and lost herself in the romance. Marshall came in to deliver an Irish coffee before going home to the staff residence that was nestled in the woods just down the lane from the main house.

Solitude gave her time to think. She was haunted by the mystery of Terrance Ivey, the man named as her father on her birth certificate. *I have money,* she thought, *I'll hire a private detective agency. They could probably track him down in no time. But, they wouldn't be able to piece together the whole story. Karen! She was there. She would know. Maybe she would be loyal to Regina and hesitate to talk. On the other hand,* she thought, *I bet that loyalty isn't deeper than a mickey of scotch.* She giggled to herself. *Maybe I do have some of my mother's genes—the evil ones.*

In the morning Tina announced that Dex was waiting to see her in the library.

"I have some bad news."

"Is Lion alright?"

"Oh yes, of course, but he has been arrested and Monday will be the earliest that Randall can have him released on bail."

"Why was he arrested?" she gasped.

"The club member who was involved in the street shooting the other day was charged with the murder of the five year old boy who was killed. In order to get a lighter sentence he has made some false accusations against Lion and right now the District Attorney is entertaining his nonsense. I doubt it will ever go to trial because Lion has done nothing wrong. Lion wanted me to tell you not to worry. Just relax, enjoy yourself, and expect a huge shopping spree when he gets back." Sheherezade thanked Dex and decide to take Bugsy for a walk and digest this twist of events. When she couldn't find him she approached Coral who was working in the kitchen.

"Coral, I can't find Bugsy. Have you seen him?"

"Oh, I was supposed to tell you when you came back from your trip with Lila, dear. When Lion was alone with the dog he realized that his allergies were really being aggravated so he took him over to Dr. Lindsay's place. Marcia, the housekeeper, is a dog lover and she'll take good care of him. You can take the land buggy or drive over any time and visit him.

"Oh, poor Bugsy!" Sheherezade said with concern.

"He'll be fine. I remember when Lion told Acelyn that he couldn't have her dog around. She was so upset. She'd had that dog for eight years. The girl that took the dog in said that when Lion and Acelyn broke up the dog went missing from her backyard. She always suspected that Ace came for him."

"Why didn't she just ask her?" Sheherezade looked puzzled.

Coral's eyes dropped as she realized she had said too much, "Oh, Acelyn left the area. She had a career."

"Really, what did she do?" Sheherezade asked innocently.

"Oh, she sang a bit."

"I wonder if I've heard of her. What was her last name, Coral?"

"Acelyn Azhar."

Sensing her uneasiness, Sheherezade changed the subject.

"Coral, could I have dinner brought into the library? I am going to do some reading. Thanks." Sheherezade settled into the leather chair at the big oak desk and signed into the computer. Acelyn Azhar. SEARCH.

Chapter 25

"We have a problem and since it was created by you, we expect you to clean it up." Lion's eyes were riveted on Shane and James sitting across the table from him and Boots in an isolated motel on the outskirts of Jersey.

"It's that motherfuckin' Snake. He's singin' like a canary and we have to find a way to do him," James spat with rage. Shane cringed at the outburst and jumped into the conversation to maintain focus.

"We appreciate what you did for us. A cool million for bail is not chump change. We owe you—big time."

"A bit more than a million, brother, but it's pennies on the dollar. You were taking care of club business and the club takes care of our own. But now we have to make this go away," Lion explained.

"A friend of the club has an Old Lady who works in a restaurant frequented by two undercover cops. She heard them say there was a witness to the hit on Elise O'Neil. Now with Snake—that Motherfucker—backing up her story, they are putting a bow on their case against you guys. Of course, Snake told them a portion of intake rolls to the top and that gives them a licence to finger me as the mastermind. If you guys go down for this, I go down for Conspiracy to Murder as well. We got to take care of it." Lion was trying to appear calm but the thought of Snake's disloyalty made his blood boil.

Boots poured himself a coke and leaned back in his chair, "You know—it happens. These kinds of jobs go wrong but now you've got to fix it for your own sake and to set an example to other people who think they can testify against anyone in the club."

Lion nodded in agreement.

"Now Elise O'Neil's brother isn't talking and we don't have to worry about him. Apparently he learned his lesson. He hasn't borrowed any more money from the organization," Lion laughed. "The problem is the witness—this woman who can identify you two. We have a name of a woman who works in the witness protection program in California from a friend of the club. It is a good source. We know this woman can access the information you need. Once you have the witness's new location, we need a hit on the entire family. There's the witness—the mother—two teenage daughters, and a kid about two. Take them all . . . we have to set an example." Lion looked at the men before him for any apparent reaction. James lit a cigarette and his eyes sparkled with excitement.

"This is a big job and we have confidence in both of you. We've heard good things. You've earned respect," Boots added.

"You'll leave tonight by helicopter from the club and it will take you to a private air field. You'll have thirty people who will say you didn't leave the clubhouse for two, three days—whatever it takes. Good luck." Shane sensed that the meeting was over, stood up, and shook hands with both men. "You can count on us. The club has been very good to me and I intend to see that this all goes away, and soon." James and Shane walked out the door into the bright sunlight.

Lion turned to Boots, "That motherfucker, Snake . . . who would have guessed he'd turn? That's the name of the game now, breaking down the witness protection program. It took us thirty years, but the network is almost full proof at this point. If we can get it right this time it won't be a problem in the future," Lion's confidence returned as he allowed his impeccable sense of rational deduction to calm his emotions.

"Don't worry brother. They won't get us this time either." Boots leaned back in his chair and laughed.

"I believed you thirty years ago and I still believe you, brother." They grabbed each other's hand and gave each other a hug.

"Better get going, I haven't seen my new wife in almost a week. I've got some spinning to do," he rolled his eyes and grinned at Boots. "What's going on with you in the romance department?"

"Well, Fancy is putting some pressure on me because I've been seeing quite a bit of Brandi. She's insisting on going to the picnic and of course, I can't say no. You know what a loose cannon she can be. I've been on eggshells with her for thirty fuckin' years. I know we never would have gotten Jimmy without her. She managed to get him out there that night and God only knows how she did it. But when your problem went away, mine was just getting started. Anyway, she earned the title, I send the checks, and I only have to see her a couple of times a year. I think I've calmed her down and I think I have Brandi under control, so everything should be fine." Boots eyebrows arched and his eyes lit up.

"Fuck, you have to check out my new hardbelly. Nineteen. Gorgeous. She dances down at my club in Atlanta. I had her screaming for her mother last night. Hey, how about staying in town one more night and going out with us? I could have her bring a friend and we can have some fun."

"Not for me anymore, Bro. I did some shopping after Ace but now I only want to be with Sheherezade. I can't imagine ever desiring another woman. She's my soulmate. Sheherezade says it's because I'm a Scorpio." Lion said wistfully.

"No, it is because your head is up your Uranus," Boots chuckled. "When you come to your senses let me know so we can have some fun, you schmuck."

Sheherezade had been up most of the night digesting the information she had found on the computer. Coral's reticence on the subject of Acelyn had piqued her curiosity about her relationship to Lion. On a website highlighting bands of the 90's Sheherezade discovered an old photo of Acelyn. She was surprised to find that she had a tattoo on her ankle that matched the tattoo on her own behind. *Well,* she thought, *he marks his women. He must have thought she was a keeper.*

Next she went to the news websites to see if there was anything being written about Lion's arrest. The story was plastered everywhere. LION TERKEL CHARGED WITH CONSPIRACY TO MURDER ELISE O'NEIL. Snake had turned state's evidence against Lion and was giving up inside information. Snake claimed that Lion ordered the killing of Elise O'Neil which was carried out by two members of the Pride in order to teach her brother a lesson for not paying back a loan on time. Snake had also accused Lion of putting a price on the head of every member of the Purple Flames which was the reason behind the escalation of the biker war. Sheherezade sat in stunned silence. *That would make Lion responsible for the death of the little boy.* A child's life for what? Money, power, territory? It did not make sense that Lion could be motivated by such things. He was a very rich business man. He did not have to kill someone for not paying back a loan. It didn't add up. On the other hand, he was a biker. Could the stereotype be true? She was very confused so she started to surf sights that could give her more information about outlaw bikers in general.

One sight explained the significance of the 1% sign that was proudly displayed on the front of all of the member's vests. Years ago, the article said, the President of the American Motorcycle Association had responded to all the bad publicity that a notorious bike gang was generating by saying that 99% of bikers are law abiding citizens and only 1% were outlaw bikers. Sheherezade had remembered asking Lion what the 1% meant, and although she could not quite remember how he had explained it, she realized that she had been given the white washed version of its true meaning. They were plainly advertising that they were criminals and proud of it. She sat quietly in a state of shock at the idea that Lion had lied to her. Whatever his rationale had been, she did not appreciate being fed some watered down version of the truth as if she were a child.

Another site showed a number of tattoos that members of different clubs used to signify certain achievements, much like the Boy Scouts with their badges. They had tattoos that signified their affiliations, sexual exploits, and special assignments executed for the club. She saw a picture of a tear drop tattooed on a man's eye which reminded her so much of the logo on Lion's leather jacket. The article went on to explain that it sometimes symbolized a murder that had been committed on behalf of a gang affiliation.

It couldn't be! She ran up the stairs to search Lion's enormous closet. Coral had everything in perfect order. Pulling out his leather jackets one by one, she could see that the logo was identical on each one. They all had a lion's head with horns and one tiny tear falling from the lion's left eye. Lion's explanation for the tear had been that it was just the result of creative license taken by the person who made the jacket. Another lie.

He would be home soon. *She could not let her imagination run away with her.*

Chapter 26

The security at the gate always announced Lion's arrival home. When he saw Coral standing alone at the front entrance to greet him, he felt a dark foreboding. "Where is she?"

"She's up in the bedroom." Lion's steady glare told Coral that he wanted more information. "Since she heard about your arrest she has been having meals sent to the library or to the bedroom—she won't even speak to Tina." Lion took the stairs three at a time but when he tried to enter the bedroom the door was locked.

"Sheherezade, it's me—open up!" She opened the door and looked at Lion blankly; her eyes were red and swollen from crying. He moved toward her to take her in her arms but she turned around and walked to the window to stare at the sky.

"Tell me you do not believe this nonsense that they are writing about me! Sheher, they have been doing this to me for thirty years! If they actually had anything on me, I wouldn't be standing here, would I? If I was the monster they make me out to be, why am I not doing life in jail?" Lion's voice sounded so desperate that it tugged at her heart strings and fanned the flames of doubt that she already had for the things she had read. She wanted to run into Lion's arms and console him but she told herself that she had to be vigilant in finding out the truth for the sake of Lila.

"Lion, you promised us a life together and then you have me send my niece away because she is not safe. Now I find out the reason she is not safe is because you are escalating a biker war by putting bounties on your enemies. Why should I stay? If I leave I can have my niece with me and I don't have to worry about her being a target."

"Sheher, don't say you are going to leave me, I can't bear the thought. And I can promise you I will never do anything that will make you want to leave me. I haven't put any bounties on anyone. This Snake character took it upon himself to knock off a few members because he was pissed off that the explosion at our warehouse in Florida killed a member's son, Harley. His father has been with the club from the inception. He was a good friend and a lot of the guys are pissed off. They have minds of their own—I wish I could control them all but I can't."

"What about the accusation that this woman was killed to punish some guy who owed you money? Why would Snake make something like that up? Don't tell me that it's in his best interest to get on the wrong side of you and thousands of other associates of the club who are loyal to you . . ."

"Honey, he's not worried about pissing me off . . . he's only worried about saving his own hide. By accidentally killing that boy he will most certainly go away for the rest of his life and selling me out is the price he is more than willing to pay to be set free. And trust me, if he gets up on that stand and shovels enough shit to put me away they will have him sipping Margaritas on a Caribbean Island faster than I can say GUILTY. You are all I have Sheher. Say you believe in me and we can get through this together. You'll see that they have nothing on me."

"Lion, I cannot and will not live without Lila. I let her go away to school only as a temporary solution and I'm certainly not going to wait for two bike gangs to get along before I bring her home. I want to make a great life for all three of us together but I will leave my life with you to be with her."

"Sheher, this is temporary and everything has already started to calm down. Give me just a bit more time to make sure that we have nothing to worry about in that regard," Lion pleaded. Sheherezade was silent and then she approached him to look him square in the eye.

"That is only one part of it. If I ever find out that you are lying to me about any of it, I will leave. I could not live with the fact that you are ordering the murder of people whether they are other bikers or civilians. I could not love someone who could do something like that—I would not know that person."

"Then you will never leave me. No one could accuse me of being a Boy Scout, but I do not go around killing people." All of the tension of arguing was too much for Sheherezade and she started to cry. Lion gave her a hug and she fell into his arms.

"I am sorry, I love you, but when you are not here I do not know what to believe," she said as she looked into his eyes for some confirmation that she should accept what he was saying.

"You will see, honey. Everything will work itself out soon."

The man with freshly cropped red hair, dressed conservatively in kaki pants and golf shirt, glanced at the woman standing in front of him hitting a bucket of balls. *Nice ass,* he thought. Dragging his golf clubs he walked by her and then suddenly twisted his ankle causing him to fall into her, knocking her over. He got up quickly and limped over to her, reaching his hand out to help her get back on her feet.

"Oh, my God, I'm so sorry. Are you alright?" She looked up to see a handsome well-built man standing before her with a concerned look on his face.

"Yes, I'm OK. What happened?" she asked.

"I think I stepped on a golf ball. I should have been more careful. I'm so sorry . . . ."

"I was just leaving anyway," she smiled. "I'm fine." He helped her gather up her purse and empty bucket and they started to walk towards the clubhouse.

"Well, the least I can do is buy you a drink. Would you permit me to ease some of my guilt?" He smiled widely and his dimples gave him an innocent quality that erased all of the woman's defences.

"That would be nice. It is hot today isn't it?" she commented coyly.

"It's certainly hot enough for me. I just got in from New York and it's already starting to become cooler there at night. I'm really not a fan of this perpetual heat." As he pulled her chair out for her in the clubhouse bar he gave his head a shake.

"Sorry if I am staring, I just can't get over what beautiful eyes you have." He made it sound as if it was a problem he had to overcome rather than a compliment.

"What will you have? Do you like champagne?"

"That would be lovely!"

"Oh, I'm sorry, knocking you over really wasn't a proper introduction was it? I am Roger Killen."

She laughed, "I'm Charissa Van Veen. Nice to meet you."

Roger looked up and smiled at the waitress as he ordered their best champagne. He then turned to his new acquaintance and gave her his full attention until the waitress returned with the wine. Twisting the bottle in the ice bucket, Roger looked up at the waitress with concern and said, "Let's give it a moment to cool." Charissa thought the attention the waitress paid to Roger was blatantly flirtatious and she felt a twinge of possessiveness.

"So you're a golfer," Roger smiled. "I would love to invite you to a game while I'm out here but you would probably laugh at my ineptitude. The business has been expanding so fast in the last few years that I haven't had much time to keep up my game," Roger said humbly.

"What do you do Roger?"

"I'm in pharmaceuticals and we're expanding the distribution of our products to California. My company has been growing in leaps and bounds and I can hardly keep up with it. But I'm single so I don't mind the travel," he shrugged. His muscles flexed as he twisted the top off the bottle of champagne. Charissa felt her stomach tighten. Roger was an irresistible mixture of alpha male and boyish innocence. He apologized again for knocking her over but by then she was beginning to think of it as a very serendipitous happenstance.

Roger and Charissa seemed to have a lot in common as their conversation touched on their family backgrounds, their education and their interests. After an hour and a half neither one wanted their afternoon to end so they eventually moved into the dining room and shared a bottle of Merlot over steak dinners. Charissa told Roger that she should think about going home since she had to work in the morning, so he paid the bill and took her hand as they walked to her car.

When they reached her car he took her into his arms. "Well, I'm flying up to San Francisco tomorrow morning but when I get back, on Friday, I would love it if you would join me for dinner and dancing. I'm flying home on Sunday morning."

"That would be wonderful." Her eyes flashed with excitement and he leaned down and kissed her passionately on the lips. Charissa kissed him back and then reached up and put her arms around his neck.

"That is going to be a long wait. I really had a wonderful time tonight."

"I did too," Roger sighed. "I can't remember the last time I met someone who I felt I had known all of my life. Let's keep in touch this week. I'll have to take your number. I dropped my cell phone today and it won't be fixed until Saturday. She wrote her phone number on a book of matches from the club and handed it back. He took it eagerly and gave her a big smile.

Charissa looked into his baby face and made her decision. "Roger would you like to come over for a drink? I would like to spend some more time with you. We have so little time until you have to go back East."

"Love to," he whispered as he pushed his tongue into her mouth and held her tight.

Roger followed Charissa in his car to a residential part of town. They pulled into a quiet cul de sac and he followed her into the small house with an array of stones where grass would have traditionally grown in the East. The immaculate interior bore the stamp of a person living alone with a lot of time on their hands. Charissa entered the kitchen and took a bottle of wine down from a wine rack above the fridge. Her hands felt a little shaky as she twisted the corkscrew into the bottle. Roger moved in close putting his arms around her waist as he asked her if he could help. He adeptly removed the cork and poured two glasses of dense wine the colour of blood.

"Let's have a toast to one of the best days of my life," he beamed. Charissa lifted her glass to him and stared into his big blue eyes giving him the signal he had been waiting for. He put his glass down and wrapped his massive arms around her as he kissed her intensely. Charissa felt a shiver of pleasure as he pressed his hardness into her hips and she abandoned all cares of maintaining first date decorum. She grabbed him by the hand and led him into her tidy bedroom.

Charissa's head was reeling. After a marriage and a number of affairs, she had to admit that she had never, ever, experienced the pleasure that she felt making love to Roger for the past hour and half. The sheer solid stature of his body gave him a masculine aura that was intoxicating. But that alone could not explain the animal sexuality that permeated his love making. He had a large penis that made her quake when she had an orgasm. It was like nothing she had ever experienced with another man. *She would never, ever, get enough of him,* she told herself.

"Wow, Charissa, I'm sorry to keep you up so late. I know you have to work in the morning but I find you so exciting that I can't seem to control my passion. You are one sexy woman!" He took her in his arms and nuzzled her neck. She looked lovingly into his eyes and whispered, "I'm not worried about tomorrow. Stay tonight. I'd love to wake up with you in the morning."

"Damn it!" Roger suddenly seemed to be jarred out of their shared intimacy. "I forgot I have to go back to my sister's house tonight. I told her I would be there and I can't let her down. She's been going through a hard time and her nerves are just shot. I haven't even called her tonight—I got so caught up in meeting you. You're going to think I am a cad for saying I have to leave but I want to tell you that I would love nothing more than to spend the night cuddling with you. These are special circumstances. I know I can trust you, so I want to explain. My sister is in the witness protection program out here. She's a single mum with three kids. She turned in some low-life biker who killed her neighbour, Elise O'Neil—maybe you heard about the case—and she is all alone in an unfamiliar place trying to start a new life. Part of the reason I moved the expansion into this area is so that I can spend more time with her and the kids until she can make a life for herself here. So I hope you understand when I tell you I have to go. On Friday I will make sure she is not expecting me home so that we can spend the night together if you want to." Charissa looked into his eyes, "I want that more than anything."

She was aching for him to make love to her again but she could see that he felt a great responsibility to his sister and knew she shouldn't detain him any longer.

"I understand, Roger, don't give it another thought. That is very courageous of your sister and very kind of you to give her your support. I'll make us breakfast in bed on Saturday and maybe I can give you some golf tips in the afternoon." She gave him a final hug and threw her housecoat on as he got dressed. Charissa walked him to the door and they lingered in a passionate embrace before they could break away from each other. Roger waved to her before he got into his car and raced down the quiet street.

Charissa walked back into the bedroom and went over to Roger's side of the bed to fix the covers. She felt something hit her foot and looked down to see a black wallet. She picked it up realizing that it must have fallen out of his pants. Opening it she saw a platinum American Express card, a driver's licence, and about three thousand dollars in cash. Shoved into the cash pocket was the match book bearing her phone number. As she walked to the phone to call him, she remembered that his cell phone was broken until Saturday. Unless he noticed that he had dropped his wallet and came back to get it tonight there was going to be a major problem. She had to go to work in the morning, and since she had not mentioned where she worked, he would have no way of contacting her after eight am. He would need his wallet to get on an airplane to go to San Francisco. The knot in her stomach told her that she felt partly responsible for this little fiasco.

The next day Charissa arrived early to work and went to the computer to find the name and address of the family that had been relocated to Los Angeles in the last couple of weeks. She was quite familiar with the case of Elise O'Neil, who had been killed for no apparent reason at the beginning of the summer. Her security password allowed her to find the name and address of Roger's sister in a nice suburb not far from the golf course.

Charissa was driving slowly looking for numbers on the houses when she finally spotted #3, Belmont Crescent and pulled into the driveway. Surprisingly, Roger pulled in right behind her and got out of his car.

"You sweetheart, I hope you came to give me something," he said as he gave her a hug and a conservative kiss on the lips. She produced his wallet and grinned, "I knew you wouldn't get too far without this."

"You saved my life, sweetie. Thanks."

"Well I couldn't have you walking around without my phone number, could I?" she asked playfully. "See you Friday?"

"I'm going to have a big surprise for you, sugar," he grinned.

Shane watched Charissa drive off in the opposite direction as his SUV idled in the driveway. James emerged from the back of the vehicle dressed in black. He slung a bag of golf clubs over his shoulder and walked toward the house.

Chapter 27

"Imagine, Miss Big shot offering to buy me a condo," Regina huffed to Karen, Fred, and Luke as they sat around the kitchen table having more than a few drinks.

"I told her. I hate condos. I like it right where I am. If I wanted to marry some rich guy I would have done it years ago. Right Karen? If she only knew, eh Karen? She's got nothing on me. I've been there and done that. But she thinks she knows it all—always did. She'll find out. I always said that girl would end up in a big pile of shit. You just wait."

"How's Brandi?" Fred asked. "Still dancing at the club?"

"Oh ya, she's their big, hot star. That girl makes so much money! But I haven't told you the best. She's dating the Vice President of the Pride and you should see the gifts that he's given her. Diamonds, a mink coat, and last week a car. A Mercedes. Now that one can handle herself. She's just like her mother. She doesn't take shit from no one."

"I'd like to see her dance sometime," Fred smiled to reveal a mouthful of bad teeth.

"Sure, why don't we go tonight? Are you up for some fun tonight Luke?"

While James was out of town on an assignment Brandi had been going straight back to his apartment after work. She would order dinner in and then, with the help of a syringe, she would find a nice quiet space in her head where Fancy, Sheherezade, and Jackie didn't exist. She was shocked back into reality when her mother showed up unannounced at the club with her entourage for her evening performance. James arrived home in a very ebullient mood that same evening and went directly to the club to see Brandi. When he came upon their little gathering, he decided to play host. By the time Brandi had put on her makeup, dressed, and walked out to the banquets in front of the stage where Regina and her party sat with James, the group had had a bit to drink and by the look of her mother's glassy eyes, a bit more. Regina turned to Brandi and chuckled, "Get a load of this. I got a call from Her Highness. She offered to buy me a condo or a house—whatever I want. She said Lion gave her a big pile of money to spend however she sees fit." Brandi sensed that her mother was angry about the call and needed to talk about it as a method of catharsis.

"Did you take the offer?"

"Are you kidding? I don't want a house and I sure as hell wouldn't give her the satisfaction of buying me anything. But she's worked it out. Apparently she is sitting on her ass in a big fancy estate just looking for ways to spend her money." Brandi knew that the only time her mother would humble herself enough to flatter Sherry was to deliver a personal attack. Regina was riled by Sherry's new position of power and it was her way of spurring Brandi to try to overshadow her. Brandi knew the drill but it was becoming more and more difficult to compete.

"Oh, I couldn't sit in some big house doing nothing all day, anyway. I need action. I would be bored out of my mind," Brandi countered.

"Well, you would think Boots would at least get you out of here." Regina's words cut deep into her heart and Brandi was left speechless. After years of abuse she accepted it in the same way a baby accepts milk from its mother. She dissembled and chatted with the others in the group as if the remark had been water off her back.

It was time for her set so she left the group. Her heart was pounding with anger and frustration. She slipped into the washroom for handicapped persons and did a hit of meth. She was tired of playing second fiddle to Fancy and Sherry and having everyone rub it in her face. *Anger welled up in her chest as she looked up at the tile peeling off the ceiling. They all think I'm nothing. They think they can just grind me into the ground. No more,* she vowed. She walked out of that washroom with the conviction that she would no longer be humiliated by anyone.

Up on stage, Brandi smiled at James as she stripped off her long red satin dress with matching gloves. *Men wanted her. She was beautiful.* Brandi looked down at Luke and Fred and threw them her bikini bottom as she stripped down to just one tiny red rhinestone G-string. James was filled with pride as Brandi teased and tempted the audience. Her eyes locked on Luke who returned her gaze. She licked her red lips provocatively as she pumped her hips to the music. Regina did not react but the vein in her forehead began to bulge and throb.

After her second set Brandi came out to talk to the group as they were getting ready to leave. The guys were generous with accolades for her performance and Brandi glowed in the face of their praise. She loved the fact that her mother was reticent. Nothing set her mother off more than another confident female—that was *her* identity and she hated any competition. *That's for the Boots comment,* she thought smugly.

"You guys go back without me. I'll drive back in about half an hour after I take off this makeup and have a shower."

Karen and Fred said goodbye at the door and James drove back to Dover with Regina and Luke. At the house, Regina took beer out of the fridge for everyone and James laid out lines of coke on the table. James regaled them with the story of the raid on the clubhouse and how Boomer was caught with his pants down by half the police force of New York City. Regina told ribald stories of her career as a hooker as they put more coke up their noses. Luke went to the bathroom and Regina took the opportunity to sit on James's lap and tell him exactly what she would like to do to him. When Luke walked in on the intimate scene, Regina turned to Luke and laughed. Luke grabbed her by the hand and said, "I think it is time we took this little lady into the bedroom, don't you?" James gave his enthusiastic consent and they went into the bedroom where both men began stripping Regina while she giggled like a teenager. Once they were all naked Regina showed off her talents honed on the mean streets of New York.

Brandi entered the front door quietly and saw James standing naked as he looked into the open fridge. Before she could grasp what had transpired, Regina sauntered into the kitchen naked, and being quite aware that Brandi was standing in the doorway, casually stroked James' buttocks as he perused the contents of the fridge. She looked back to see Brandi's reaction but Brandi stood frozen to the spot in silence. Brandi knew her mother had won but the exact details of her victory were unclear.

Brandi's infinite forgiveness of her mother's many foibles hung on one fine thread of knowledge that in the end they were allies; a belief that ultimately she would be spared from the cruelty and selfishness imposed on the rest of the world by her mother for the concessions and sacrifices she had made to please her. She had forgone any attempt at worldly accomplishments and she had sublimated any opinions of her own in order to align herself with her mother's view of the world in return for love, or what she liked to think was motherly love. In the back of her mind she knew that her job at the club challenged that agreement and only the money it produced was keeping her within the golden circle. However, the reality of Brandi's beauty on that stage and the affect it had on the others, including Luke, had been too much for Regina. Brandi had broken their agreement and Regina had deemed it necessary to put her back in her place. She had used the ultimate weapon. Her love.

Brandi knew she had been reprimanded and it burned her heart like a hot poker. Ordinarily she would have reigned in the behaviour that she knew was offending her mother in order to be accepted back into the fold. Not today. Today she was not in the mood and she knew that she would never be in the mood again. Without a word, she turned and walked into the dark night.

Fancy remembered that the housekeeper had stepped out to do some errands so she walked over to the buzzer and answered it herself. The doorman announced that the girl from Thunder Spa was downstairs. *Stupid bitch, what is she doing here today? I told them to come early on Saturday so that I would look great for the picnic,* she groused.

Peering through the peep hole in the door, she saw the brim of a Thunder Spa ball cap and knew this girl was not one of the regulars. Being new, she must have thought she was following the usual schedule which meant standing appointments for Friday mornings. She allowed the girl into the foyer and lambasted her for her stupidity.

"You've got the wrong day. I changed my standing appointment this week to Saturday morning. Didn't you talk to the manager before you came?" Fancy scowled with condescension.

"Oh, sorry," the girl answered quietly with her head bowed in submission.

"Never mind now. You can give me a massage while you're here. The massage table is in the room next to the bedroom. You can set up and I'll be right in," Fancy said dismissively as she pointed in the general direction of her bedroom and went to pour herself another glass of white wine.

Chapter 28

As Sheherezade enjoyed a morning swim and Coral served a breakfast of yogurt, fruit salad, egg whites, and freshly baked croissants, Lion found the article he had been searching for in the newspaper. The headlines read, "PUZZLING MURDER OF SUBURBAN FAMILY." A family had been killed in a quiet little suburb on the outskirts of L.A. The three children had been shot and the mother had been beaten to death with a golf club. The paper reported that there were no suspects for what seemed to be a random killing in the course of a robbery. Lion leaned back into the cushioned chair and closed his eyes as he puckered his lips and blew a long exhale into the fresh morning air. Relief passed over his face.

"Will you be joining me for breakfast?" Sheherezade asked as she sipped her coffee.

"Absolutely! I'm famished. Coral bring some bacon . . . and some real eggs will you? I refuse to be completely pussy whipped by this gorgeous creature." Coral tousled Lion's hair with affection and walked off in the direction of the kitchen.

"I'm going up to Jersey for the day," Sheherezade announced.

Lion looked intrigued, "What's in Jersey?"

"I'm going up to Madison to meet with my dear aunt Karen so I can pump her for information about my birth certificate. I've developed a strategy and today is the day I intend to execute my plan. It should be interesting."

"Do you want me to tag along?"

"No, but thanks honey. I want to get her alone. There's a better chance she'll tell me what she knows. That is if she can remember that far back. For the past twenty-five years she has dedicated her every waking moment to killing every brain cell she ever had."

"Hmm, might be a real treasure hunt," he laughed.

"Well, take the limo. It's about a two hour ride. I'll send another car with it."

"You worry too much, but thanks."

"What was all the commotion about this morning?" Sheherezade asked.

"Well, if you would get out of bed in the morning you wouldn't have to ask," Lion replied with mock sarcasm.

"And if you didn't keep me up all night, I might be able to do that!" she laughed as she put her arms around his neck and sat on his knee.

"Once every summer the club throws a wingding on the back forty of the property here called the Hog Day Picnic. It's a lot of testosterone silliness that would not interest you in the least."

"Really, like what?"

"Well, we have a rice burner that we're going to ride without oil until the engine has a melt down and then we're going to hoist it into the sky on a gigantic crane and drop it so it blows up good. What would Freud say about that Sheher?" Lion teased knowing that she had filled many shelves in the library with psychology books of every description.

"Well, that would depend on what a rice burner *is*," she retorted.

"It's a Japanese motorcycle. The boys don't like anything on two wheels that isn't a Harley. Come to think of it, many of the boys don't like anything that isn't a Harley, period. I can assure you, it is no place for a lady like yourself. We have macho games and stupid contests and a big barbecue. We set up tents and serve food and play music. Club members and friends of the club are invited and usually a few thousand show up."

"Do any of the Old Ladies go?"

"Old Ladies?" Lion laughed at her use of the biker vernacular. "I hate to break the news to you Sheher, but you are just not going to make it as a true biker chick. Try as you might, you just have too much class. I'll tell you what . . . you can be my wife and my Ole Lady and my girlfriend. How's that? For most of the guys in the club that requires three different women. But, no, I am going to 86 you from the festivities—that's biker for I don't want you to go to the picnic. I won't have thousands of drunken guys drooling over my beautiful wife. You can find something to do. Invite your friend Natasha over and have a girl's day catching up on things. Some of the partiers bring tents so they don't have to drive home. I might bring a few of my executives back to the house later for a drink—just so you know."

"Well it sounds like my kind of fun," she said teasingly, "but I will do as I'm told this once and invite Natasha over to see the digs. I think I'll invite her to stay overnight. Can I put her up in one of the guest houses?" Lion kissed Sheherezade.

"Darlin', you are *my* Ole Lady," he said facetiously. "That gives you licence to do just about anything in this world your little heart desires."

Chapter 29

"I'll take it if you can complete the transaction in the next fifteen minutes. I brought cash," Sheherezade said to the salesman who was showing her the polished new gold Buick.

"No problem young lady," the salesman replied eagerly. "We can even put a bow on it if you'd like." The next stop was the liquor store. Her body guards loaded the ten cases of alcohol into the SUV while she slipped next door to a Chinese restaurant and bought enough takeout to feed an army.

As she pulled into the driveway of the tiny house with the derelict yard she said a prayer that aunt Karen was having a coherent day. The limo was a nice touch, so were the three carat diamonds she had in her ears and the enormous engagement ring on her finger. She knew the fear and reverence rich people stirred in the hearts of poor people—she had been there herself. And, she was prepared to use whatever ammunition she could muster to reach the truth about her origins.

Sheherezade knocked on the door. After a couple of minutes Fred appeared and squinted against the sunlight to see who had disturbed his slumber.

"Oh fuck, Sherry! How are you?"

"I'm great uncle Fred, how are you?" She smiled at him as if she were delighted to be in his presence. It was a talent she had honed for two decades living with a mother who dragged home reprobates of every description on a regular basis.

"Great! What are you doing here?"

"Don't worry, I just came by for a visit and to bring you a gift." Fred stepped back eagerly and asked her to come inside.

"Karen is just in taking a nap," he said pointing in the direction of the bedroom. Sheherezade knew that meant that she had not yet managed to get out of bed.

"Listen, I don't know if mum told you I got married. Anyway, I came into some money and you guys were so good to me when I was a kid that I just want to give you a bit of cash to say thanks." She knew Fred was not going to get hung up on the logic of what she was saying when he was about to have some money shoved into his hot hands.

"Gee, Sherry that would be fuckin' fantastic." Sheherezade pulled out five thousand dollars in cash and handed it to Fred. Oh, ya, I also bought you guys a new car—the gold one parked out front." He peered out of the door and saw a black limousine, a black SUV, and a shiny, new gold Buick.

"Holy fuck, Sherry! You did that for us? Wow! I can't believe it!"

"Well, I hope you enjoy it. Why don't you take it for a spin? I would really like to spend some time alone with aunt Karen this afternoon. Would you mind giving us gals some time to chew the rag?" She knew that he would be itching to get to the nearest bar as soon as he saw the greenbacks, and he would be gone for a week long toot to celebrate his windfall. *There is nothing more predictable than an alcoholic*, she thought.

"Oh sure, honey, I'll go tell her you're here and I'll leave yous ladies to catch up."

Fred went into the bedroom and Sheherezade could hear muffled conversation. In a couple of minutes they came out of the room grinning from ear to ear.

"Hi, Sherry, how are you doin'?" Karen clothes looked like she had pulled them out of a hamper and she had last night's makeup on but it was now in a different place from where it had started out. Fred understood the conditions delicately issued in return for the gifts and he was out of the door like a bolt of lightening before Sheherezade had a chance to change her mind.

"I'm doing great, aunt Karen. I was hoping we could spend some time together this afternoon, talking about old times." Sheherezade recognized the look of fear which meant that aunt Karen needed a drink and that this visiting session would interfere with her plan.

"Oh, I brought you guys some booze," she said casually as if she had just remembered an insignificant detail. She waved at the driver to bring in the cases of alcohol and food. She could see a new sparkle in Karen's eyes as she started to lick her lips nervously in anticipation of a good drunk.

"Oh, we usually drink beer but we also drink just about anything." Karen tried her best to put on airs but they always fell short.

"I should have thought of that," Sheherezade said with annoyance. "Mark run out and buy us ten cases of beer will you? Karen just tell him what variety you would like." Sheherezade talked about her honeymoon and anything else that came into her mind until aunt Karen had put back two big tumblers of Scotch. When her head became just a bit heavy and appeared to take some effort to hold in a vertical position, she knew it was safe to proceed to the topic of her birth.

"Karen, did you ever meet my father, Terrance Ivey?"

"Oh, sure! I mean did your mother tell you about him?" Karen looked a bit uncertain of the territory.

"Mmhm, she gave me her version. But, it's hard to get the real story from her because she likes to rewrite history and give it a spin to make it more interesting. And you know, aunt Karen, I really respect your opinion. I would like your take on the whole thing. Mum always claimed she didn't have feelings for him. What do you think?" Sheherezade knew that the probability that anyone had ever asked Karen's opinion about anything was negligible and she hoped that this spur to her ego would loosen her tongue.

Karen took a long swig and paused to give her answer some weight.

"She *did* have a thing for him because I remember when she moved in with him. They had a real cute apartment; I remember because I would go over there to babysit Brandi when she wanted to go out. He hated that. He'd be so pissed off when he came home and found me there that after a while I would just tell her. I ain't babysittin' cause I have to deal with him when he gets home and I ain't doin' it no more."

"Would he be coming home from work?"

"No, he was going to school in the day time. That school for music—Julie . . . ."

"Juilliard?"

"Ya, I think that was it—some fancy school. He was in a jazz band at night and played in a club on the weekends. That's where your mother met him. She was crazy about him when they first met. He looked like a movie star—a Robert Redford type." Sheherezade was excited about the progress she was making and got up to pour Karen a cold beer that the guys brought in.

"Do you remember how long they lived together aunt Karen?"

"No I don't remember but it wasn't too long before they started having problems because she was asking me to babysit more often and I would still go over once in a while."

"Why did they break up? Now, I have mum's version and I want to see if your version matches."

"She always said that he was a lot of fun to begin with and then he started to nag her about everything."

"Like what?"

"Well, you know your mum liked to party and he wanted her to settle down a bit. Then she got pregnant with you and he really tried to keep her from having any fun whatsoever. Well, your mum did what she wanted and she wasn't about to take no shit from some guy. She liked to have a drink, and he would be constantly on her back about it. At least that's what she told me. And then his mother got involved. Fuck, she hated that old lady." Karen's eyeballs rolled back and then her head snapped into a vertical position again.

"Ya, mum told me she was a real bitch," Sheherezade fibbed. "Did you ever get to meet her?"

"Yep, in the hospital. Your mum told me about the big fight they had at the end. About the old lady offering to give her, or them, an estate in the Hamptons if she would stop partying and settle down." Karen gave out a deep guttural laugh that turned into a cough as she reached for another cigarette.

"She told her to go fuck herself and her money and left him—just like that."

"Mum doesn't like to be told what to do!" Sheherezade said in an effort to maintain momentum.

"Yep, she told her to fuck herself." Karen repeated with even more satisfaction.

"Well, she was pregnant and all alone. I am surprised she didn't give me up."

"She tried to abort you. Her mother helped her. I don't know how they did it but it didn't work," she stated as a matter of fact. Sheherezade nodded knowingly. It was a story her mother seemed to take pride in rehashing at regular intervals.

Karen continued, "She gave up one kid and she said she didn't want to do that again. Despite everything she's a good mother. I always gave her that."

"Oh, sure it was hard on her to give up the other one. A little girl wasn't it?" Sheherezade was doing her best not to show any sign of surprise at the fact that she had a sibling she was not aware she had.

"No, a boy. The cutest little thing."

"How old would he be now, aunt Karen?"

"Well, let's see . . . he was a year older than Brandi. He would be about twenty-three now."

"Did they give him up before they went to California?"

"They gave him to Reggie's mother when they went west and then when her mother didn't hear from Reggie, she gave him up. She couldn't look after him."

"Oh, why not?" Sheherezade waited for the litany of excuses that she knew were coming.

"Well, you know babies are a lot of work and she wasn't getting any younger."

"I think she was only eighteen years older than mum so she couldn't have been that old—maybe forty." Sheherezade tried to keep the disgust from seeping into her voice.

"Well, I think her mother's old man didn't like kids or something. That's what Reggie told me. Anyway, Reggie was crazy about Billy and after he was shanked in prison she said that she wished she still had his son. Fuck, she talked about him a lot. Sounded like he could keep her in line. I think she needed that." Karen was doing better drinking beer; the hard liquor made her too drowsy.

"If mum walked out, how is it that his name ended up on my birth certificate aunt Karen? That just doesn't seem like mum's style."

"She didn't have any money. She was staying with me and when she thought she was getting close, she said she was going to squeeze the old lady for a private hospital," Karen laughed.

"She told her that if she wanted to see the baby she could pay for it. They picked her up in a limo and I went with her. We dropped

Brandi off with her mother and we laughed our heads off all the way to the hospital. You could order food! Whoever heard of that in a hospital? She didn't have you until the third day. Terry was there the whole time too. He nearly fainted every time your mother had a contraction."

"It's odd that my father and grandmother didn't stay in touch. They seemed to be so interested in me as a baby."

"They tried to stay in touch but your mother was not going to have any part of it. She moved without telling them, and she made me come with her so there was no trail. She used to say that that rich bitch was used to getting what she wanted but it wouldn't work with her. And the old lady never found you. You have to give her that."

"Oh, I'll give her that. Mum always had lots of motivation when it came to hurting other people. It's just too bad she never used any of her energy to do good things like making sure I had a father in my life," she said smiling sweetly at Karen. Karen squinted as she tried to process what Sheherezade had said.

"So where did my name come from? She told me she couldn't remember," Sheherezade continued.

"Terrance named you. He wanted to name you after his favourite song. Reggie just laughed at him. I could see that he really wasn't her type. Sort of stuffy. You know, we used to call them 'straight' in the 90's. Maybe they are nerds now, I don't know. Anyway, he did the paperwork because she was in bad shape for a few days and he was paying the bill, so he put his name on the birth certificate." Karen gave another guttural laugh, "She hated that name so much. She wanted to call you Jane. She said you were going to be a plain Jane—just like him."

Karen had always come out with insensitive remarks such as this and Sheherezade was never quite sure if she meant to be hurtful or if she was too stupid to realize other people had feelings. She had accepted insults all her life from her mother without so much as a word of objection and she vowed when she left that she would never do that again as long as she lived whether or not they were intentional.

She turned to Karen, "I'm so glad I found out my real name. I guess my father was more aware of my potential than mum. I mean look at me. Wearing diamonds, driving around in a limousine, and married to one of the wealthiest men in the United States. The name Jane just doesn't quiet fit does it?" Karen's drunken face twitched but no answer came. The mystery was solved. Sheherezade chuckled to herself. *I should have known a truly nice person wouldn't have anything to do with my mother.*

Chapter 30

The next day Sheherezade was up early to greet Natasha with hugs when the limousine arrived from Dover. She took Natasha into the kitchen to meet Coral who suddenly seemed to be frozen to the floor, and somewhat slack jawed during the introduction. Upon touring the main house, the guest house, and the grounds, Natasha could not believe how Sherry's lifestyle had changed in the course of a few weeks. On the other hand, it seemed to fit Sherry so well; she seemed to belong in a place like this.

They had some sparkling white wine with lunch by the pool and giggled like two school girls. Natasha was a little curious about Sherry's notorious husband whose name had been splashed across the news headlines recently.

"Sher, what do you make of the accusations against Lion recently? Just tell me if it is none of my business."

"I know they accuse Lion of a lot of things but being on the inside, I'm presented with another side that, so far, has answered all of my questions. If I believed Lion was the monster they make him out to be, believe me, I would not be sitting here. But, he has been nothing but the perfect husband—kind, loving, generous. Until I have some reason to believe that my perception is incorrect, I have no reason to think otherwise."

Natasha hesitated, then asked gently, "Did you see the story yesterday about the mother and three children who were murdered in California?"

"No, who were they?" Sheherezade looked concerned.

"They were, or rather she was, the witness to the murder of Elise O'Neil. The family was in hiding as part of the Witness Protection Program because the mother was set to testify against two of the

Lucifer Pride members. This guy Snake claims that the murder of Elise O'Neil was ordered by Lion as retribution for not paying a debt owed to the club. Of course, without the witness, there is no longer a case against the two bikers and therefore no more links to Lion. Quite a coincidence. They make it sound so sinister. I'm sure you know best . . . ."

"That's horrendous. No, I didn't hear anything about it. I'll have to look into it." Sheherezade was deeply disturbed by the coincidences that seemed to piling up like bodies in a Greek tragedy but she hid her concern, knowing that Natasha would only worry.

It was beginning to get warm so Sheherezade suggested they go for a swim. Natasha sprinted down to the quest house to change. Just then Lion walked in and said he came home to grab his sunglasses.

"Oh Lion, just wait a minute and meet Natasha!" Sheherezade begged.

"I can't honey, I'm giving away prizes at some of the contests and I have to get back." Just then Natasha came running up to the mansion in her bathing suit and robe. Coral walked out to the patio from the kitchen and slapped her hand to her mouth when she saw Lion standing on the deck. Lion's face turned an ashen grey.

"Sheherezade, come inside. I have to speak to you!" His voice took on an edge that she had not heard before. "What Lion? What is it?"

"Natasha is black."

"Yes, she is. So?"

"I can't have her here! You can't have her here!" Lion's eyes darkened and took on an unfamiliar intensity.

"Why not?" Sheherezade was doing her best to understand what Lion was trying to get at.

"I can't have a black person here."

"Why not?" Lion was becoming frustrated. He was angry that he was being forced to have this discussion with Sheherezade. He knew his worlds were colliding and he was helpless to avoid it this time.

"It's just club policy. We are a homogeneous group—most clubs are. Blacks are not part of our group. That is just the way it is Sher. She can't stay. Make up an excuse and put her back in the limo. I have other members wandering around the property today. You can visit on her turf but she cannot be here." Sheherezade could not believe the words coming out of Lion's mouth and she stood in stunned silence trying to come to grips with what he was saying. She did not like this person standing before her. Racism was one of those traits she could not understand nor forgive. Nothing could be more superficial than judging someone for their appearance. However, her first concern was for Natasha. She would not allow her friend to be hurt.

"OK Lion, I will ask her to leave. I will tell her we are having a family emergency of some kind but we will talk about this later. I simply cannot believe that you are capable of being so primitive, and I am extremely disappointed." Lion reached out to take her in his arms but she pulled away.

"Oh, Sheher, I didn't make up the policy but I am the President and I can't be the odd man out."

"Seems to me that as President you make the rules," she said coldly as she stomped out of the room. Sheherezade walked out to the pool where Natasha was standing, looking a little confused by the sudden disappearance of her hosts. Sheherezade went up to her and gave her a hug.

"Honey, I have to put you in the limo and send you home. The club is having a yearly picnic on the other side of the property and security has had some information that there is a possibility of a bomb threat from another gang. I cannot put you in harm's way so I am going to insist that you jump into the limo and come back on another weekend when we can relax and not worry about a bunch of crazy bikers trying to blow us up." Natasha looked surprised but agreed that it might be for the best.

In a few minutes Sheherezade walked Natasha to the car which she noticed had been pulled up to the side of the house instead of the front where the limo usually waited. "I feel so bad that this had to happen but we will do it again soon, I promise. I want to give you something and I don't want any guff from you either." She handed Natasha a wallet stuffed with thousand dollar bills. Natasha was familiar enough with that determined look that periodically crossed Sherry's face to know that there was no point in putting up an argument. As the limousine pulled away, a look of resolve was etched on Sheherezade's face. Her willingness to accept what Lion said at face value was over. She had a feeling there were pieces missing in the puzzle and she was going to start her search for the truth today. She ran up to her room and looked through her closet for something green.

Chapter 31

Sheherezade was careful that no one saw her walk to the guesthouse before she started running toward the distant roar of loud motors. Crossing ancient stone fences and jogging across fields of wild straw, she followed the sounds that beckoned her in the distance.

After fifteen minutes of stomping through virgin forests and yet more fields, the noises took on some clarity and she could hear voices through a microphone and the sound of music. She was glad to find that she had the cover of a forest that went right up to the edge of the field where the stage was positioned. In front of the stage there was a large area used as a dirt track that provided an arena for various motorcycle competitions. Just as Lion had described, there was a giant crane that they used to hoist a motorcycle about sixty feet into the air. Everyone went wild cheering as it smashed into a pile of tiny shards of metal.

Through her binoculars she could see a big white tent by a manicured pond that served as shade for a huge buffet and outdoor bingo game. She wondered why Lion had not allowed her to be part of that group of women who seemed to be having a very civilized good time. She decided to stake a place close to the stage where Lion and Boots were announcing winners and giving out prizes.

Boots turned to Lion and shook his head.

"Shit, I don't understand it. Brandi was supposed to be working one of the trailers and she hasn't shown up yet."

"You need some girls because I will just let one of the guys know...."

"No, that's not it. We have any number of girls to do it but Fancy made me promise to have Brandi pulling the train in one of the trailers today, just to make the point that she didn't belong with the Ole Ladies on the other side. I know it's bullshit but you know Fancy. It's her way or all hell breaks loose and, to tell you the truth, she has me worried. I'm afraid of what she might do if things don't go the way she wants them to go today," Boots cursed under his breath.

"You and all your women," Lion laughed. "Who has there head up their ass now?"

Sheherezade watched as a few thousand people partied in the main section where the games were taking place. Most of the women wore provocative shorts with very low cut tops and many were topless. There was a giant tent set up to dispense beer and refreshments and the party goers were considerably more raucous than those attending the lawn party on the other side. Behind the racing track, she could see five small trailers that appeared to be attracting men who were just hanging about the door of each one as if they were waiting to get in. Sometimes when they came out they gave the other guys a high five and she was curious to know what was going on inside.

At three o'clock Boots got a signal from security and he stepped down from the stage to meet a man holding a walkie talkie.

"Brandi just arrived, boss. She's driving a white Mercedes."

"OK, man. Thanks." Boots watched as she got out of her car dressed to the nines in a flowing pink dress with a matching floppy hat. She looked as if she were about to spend the day at the Ascot races rather than in a trailer giving blow jobs to drunken bikers. To his shock and amazement, she did not walk toward the stage but, instead, glided down to the tent where the Old Ladies were having a tea party by the pond. His jaw tightened as he became aware that she intended to defy his wishes. *Damn it,* he thought, *when Fancy sees this she is going to lose it and I am going to be wearing it.* He spotted Shane in the crowd and called him over. Shane and Boots shook hands.

"Listen Shane I have a little situation I want you to handle for me. Go down to the ladies tent and tell Brandi to get the hell over here."

"Sure boss," Shane smiled.

Brandi threw her head back and walked into the Old Ladies enclosure with an air of angry arrogance. She searched the crowd for

Jackie and when she had her eyes in a lock, she lowered her eyelids to negate her image and lifted her nose up into the air as if to say, 'I told you so'. Jackie's upper lip curled back and she was so livid she had a mind to go over to her and deck her. But considering Brandi's apparent new status, she thought better of it.

Where the fuck was Fancy? She was going to rip a strip off her for allowing this bitch to walk around thinking her shit didn't stink.

Brandi put a fixed smile on her face and scanned the area before approaching a table filled with drinks and helping herself to a glass of champagne. *Oh, this is perfect,* she thought. *No Fancy and no sign of Sherry either.*

Shane made his way quickly through the crowd and tapped her on the shoulder.

"Excuse me Brandi, Boots wants to see you right away." She realized she might have to face the music but that was fine, the damage had been done. She had won. There was nothing Boots could do to take away her moment of victory now.

"Sure, where is he?" she asked innocently.

"Just up here. Follow me." Brandi walked up the small hill toward the stage waving at some of the people she knew as if she were queen of the parade. Boots was watching the performance from beside the stage and could not get over the balls this girl had to defy his specific request.

"Brandi! You finally showed up. Where the fuck were you?" Boots asked gravely. Brandi could tell by the tone of his voice that he was not pleased with her rearrangement of the plans that he had so carefully spelled out the last time they were together.

"Hi, honey." She went over to give him a kiss but he pulled away and looked at her hard.

"Well I should have called you but I was in bed all morning taking pain medication for cramps. I just couldn't come out any earlier and I knew you didn't really need me—there are plenty of girls." Both Boots and Brandi knew there was a deeper meaning to the situation but neither one of them was prepared to admit it. Boots hated confrontations; they were not his style. However, anyone who crossed him was going to pay. Boots decided to collect at a later date. It appeared that Fancy had chosen not to come to the picnic and so far there was no fur flying.

"Can I still give away the Biggest Hog prize?"

"Ya, sure baby. It is about time we did that. Come on up on stage." Boots turned to Ziggy and told him to find out who the girls had chosen as the winner of the Biggest Hog contest. After a few minutes about ten girls who were working the trailers came up to the stage and Boots talked to them for a few minutes to see if they had arrived at a consensus.

"OK, everyone, we are about to announce the winner of the Biggest Hog contest and give away this brand new Fool's Paradise—a Night Train—to the deserving winner. Boots lowered his voice and looked lasciviously at the ten worn out women who had been working the trailers for the day.

"Let's hear it for Daisy, Lisa, Ashley, Petra, Sam . . . ." The crowd went wild cheering and whistling.

"You all know the beautiful Brandi—Queen of the Dancing House." The crowd cheered and whistled again. Brandi smiled and took the microphone.

"Hey, is everybody having fun?" the crowd cheered.

"Anybody interested in taking home this Big Hog tonight?"

The crowd went crazy cheering the brand new black Harley mounted and ready to be driven away.

"You guys know what it takes to win the Big Hog! Now let's find out if any one of you has it! The girls have been making some comparisons today and now it is time to hear from the experts." Brandi walked over to the girls and made a joke of whispering to each girl and then pointing to different guys and making gestures. Sometimes she would hold up her little finger, put her hand over her mouth and giggle and sometimes she would take her hand and touch her elbow to indicate a potential winner.

"OK, the Biggest Hog is . . . Boots! Oh, I'm sorry honey, I forgot you weren't in the contest." Everyone laughed and cheered. Boots whispered in her ear.

"It seems we have a consolation prize for the longest lasting erection." Brandi feigned confusion. "It's a five thousand dollar bar tab at the clubhouse put up by Boots and it goes to . . . Boomer! For his performance at the police raid on the clubhouse!" The already intoxicated crowd hooted and hollered for Boomer to take a bow. He jumped up on the stage and gave Boots a big grin and a royal wave.

"Next we have the real winner and it is . . . Frenchy! Come on up Frenchy! I'd really like to meet you! I mean come up and get your new hog!" Frenchy was pretty smashed but he managed to get to the new Harley and give it a big hug and kiss. Brandi gave everyone a royal wave and made her way off the stage and down the path to her car. She knew better than to press her luck. Everything had gone just the way she hoped it would and she wanted to avoid any further confrontations with Boots.

Sheherezade sat on an old log contemplating what she had just witnessed. The trailers were occupied by women who provided sexual gratification for the men and they had been busy little bees all day. The thought nauseated her. *How could they treat women that way?* This was Lion's world and it had been his world for a long time. She knew he owned strip bars but he always seemed to be so removed from the sordid details. Here he was up close and personal with the disgusting rituals of the tribe. His tribe. A shiver went down her back. *Wasn't this the kind of sordid lifestyle she thought she was escaping when she married him? It was beginning to feel like a recurring nightmare. It was a world that Brandi understood and flourished in; she had seen that with her own eyes. But Lion had been honest when he said that she did not belong. Why, then, had he invited me in,* she wondered.

Over fences and through bushes, Sheherezade raced back to the house with tears streaming down her face. When she reached the guest house, she took her pace down to a casual stroll and walked up to the back patio. In ten minutes she had her makeup done and was ready to receive her guests. She was determined to confront his world head on and let the chips fall where they may.

Coral had set out a buffet that sat warming in the dining room. Sheherezade had some dinner and a glass of wine and waited. Thoughts and feelings buzzed around her head like a swarm of gnats. She had another glass of wine and waited. As she walked back from taking her plate to the kitchen, she heard a faint murmur of voices coming through the door.

"Wow, Lion. What an honour! Sergeant-at Arms. I was shocked! I still can't believe it. Thanks, man."

"The crowd went crazy! Did you hear them?" Lion asked. "Anyway, Boots and I waited to give it to someone who really deserved it—someone solid. I think the Florida hit is pretty hard to top. Aside from the bonus we decided to make the job a paying position. Two hundred grand a year. You are going to be working closely on top level projects from now on. No more wet work. Welcome aboard, Skunk."

"Fantastic! I can't thank you enough, man."

"No heat at all from the job, either?" Lion mused.

"Na, I think they like them dead as much as we do . . . ." the tall swarthy man with the ponytail laughed.

Sheherezade had heard the conversation from the kitchen, but she had stepped further back into the room so that Lion and the other man would not suspect that she had been listening. She felt like she had been struck with a bullet to the chest. Seeing the darkly tanned man with the ponytail excited a vision of his arrival at Indian Lake, and she remembered Lion and Boots greeting him like a conquering hero. The ride took place before she read about the hit in the paper. *They all knew,* she thought. *They knew he blew up the clubhouse and killed eight Purple Flame members and Lion was rewarding him for it!* Her heart was pounding with indignation and anger. All of her suspicions were true! Lion had tried to prevent her from seeing the ugly underbelly of his world but it was not working. There would be no going back to the Pollyanna view of life she had been dished up by Lion and all his conspirators.

Boots came in with Mustard, Dex, The Swami, Shane, and the tall handsome guy with the haunting blue eyes.

"Can I take some drink orders?" she smiled as she met the men in the dining room. She could see the guys relax when she threw herself into the role of subservient biker wife. As she passed James, she saw a tattoo on his left arm that looked almost the same as hers. The difference was that his lion had tears. *Lion's logo had one tear but this tattoo had lots of tears.* At that moment she knew. She recognized his face from the newspaper; he was James Barrett, the man accused of killing Elise O'Neil. Her conversation with Natasha took on another layer of meaning. Now that the witness to the murder of Elise O'Neil had been snuffed out, James Barrett had received a get out of jail free card. When she came back, she positioned herself next to James who had his T-shirt sleeves rolled up to proudly display his tattoo.

"Wow," she exclaimed, "What a beautiful tattoo!" I have one almost the same on my . . . well, I'm not supposed to tell," she giggled.

James puffed up a bit, feeling very macho beside this beautiful woman who was giving him attention.

"The only difference is those tiny tear drops. But of course, I've never killed anyone. And let me see, you have about ten. Oh, what do you know? Four of them are freshly tattooed. Does that mean you just made a fresh kill?" She leaned in and whispered enigmatically, "They can't talk now, can they?"

James gave her a look that she would never forget. Part of it was confusion. He was not sure if she was asking a serious question. As Lion's wife he didn't know how much she knew about the inner workings of the club. But aside from that, she felt like she was looking into the eyes of pure evil.

A couple of the other guys heard some of the conversation, and Lion heard enough to stop speaking and turn his attention to her. Grabbing her by the wrist, he dragged her into the foyer to the foot of the winding staircase. He hesitated for a moment as his eyes turned dark. And then, without saying a word, he slapped her across the face knocking her to the ground.

"Go upstairs now and stay there," he commanded.

She looked into those cold dark eyes. Those eyes that scared Lila. Instinctual fear gave her the strength to pick herself up and run up the stairs to the bedroom.

"There's something fuckin' wrong. I can feel it." Jackie was having a drink and talking to a group of old friends as the lights positioned artfully around the manmade ponds came on and one of Lion's staff started lighting the torches near the tent. The music was blaring on the other side of the field as the raucous party continued unabated.

"She always answers her cell phone and I've been trying her number all day. It's just not like her. She told me she would be here and she was pumped about putting Brandi in her place. I've got to find out what the fuck is going on. Where's Shane?" she asked impatiently.

"I think I saw him leave with Lion, they were going up to the house," Sissy said with a concerned look. Jackie called Shane on his cell phone and he told her he would pick her up soon as the meeting was finished.

The doorman recognized Jackie, so when she insisted that she wanted to check on Fancy he escorted Jackie and Shane to the suite. Jackie asked if any of the staff had been there today and he told them that they did not typically work on the weekends, except when Ms. McFarlane was entertaining. In fact, he said, he had not seen the housekeeper or Ms. McFarlane the day before either.

"Fancy! Hey Fancy!" Jackie walked into the kitchen and discovered a warm bottle of white wine sitting half full on the counter. Fancy was fastidious and Jackie knew that something was amiss or the wine would have been put away. A look of panic passed over her face and Shane reacted quickly knowing that he could trust Jackie's instincts. They took off in different directions as the doorman waited in the vestibule.

"Shane! Oh my God! Shane! The bedroom!" Shane came into the alcove where Jackie was standing and he was taken aback by the wine coloured stain on the white carpet that framed the pale naked body of Fancy. Her breasts were sliced into ribbons of flesh that dangled to the floor and her face was mangled beyond recognition with the exception of her eyes which were fixed to the ceiling. Jackie started to shake and cry, as Shane buried her face in his chest. The doorman came into the bedroom when he heard the screaming and called the building security and police. Shane looked at Jackie, "I better call Lion."

Chapter 32

Violet Ivey said a prayer as she sat in the large wood panelled office of her attorney, Walter Hammond. One tear escaped from her deep violet-blue eyes and ran down her porcelain cheek before she could find the tissues in her purse. *Terrance, if only you could be here with me,* she thought. *Sheherezade was born twenty-one years ago today and we both waited so long for this day to come, in the hope that we would find her and finally be reunited.*

When Regina disappeared with their child leaving no trace, it seemed she took Terrance's youthful dreams with her. He had quit Julliard, switched to a degree in business and apprenticed with his father to become the CEO of the family business conglomerate. As each of her birthdays passed, Terrance became more and more solemn, sublimating his anger and sadness into his work. Just when Violet had given up all hope of him ever finding happiness, he met a wonderful girl and they had planned to marry. Only one month before the wedding, they had been on their way to Florida in the company jet when it had crashed in a freak storm killing everyone on board. Now, she was here alone hoping that by some miracle, her granddaughter would show up to the building that bore her name to claim her inheritance on her twenty-first birthday.

But, she had to prepare herself for the worst. All the searching, for all those years, had turned up nothing and the chance was remote that Sheherezade would find her way to these offices today. Still, she had one small flame of hope that never, ever went out. And now, with John and Terrance gone, all she had was that little flame to warm her heart when she felt all alone in the world.

She thought back to that day, twenty years ago when she had planted the seed that she hoped would bear fruit today. Terrance was still living with the dream that Regina would settle down and appreciate what they had as a family. He was becoming concerned that despite the fact that she knew she was pregnant, she was going out many nights, drinking, and he suspected, taking drugs. Maybe when she had the baby, he confided to his mother, she would change. Violet could not be that hopeful; she had looked into those icy blue eyes and knew she was dealing with someone Terrance, with his innocent nature, could never understand.

She did not blame Terrance for his misjudgement in getting involved with Regina; she was stunningly beautiful and could be extremely charming when she chose to be. She had witnessed the extent of her charms when she came to dinner at their home and did her best to impress her husband, John. With her brash spunk, she interrogated John as if she were writing his life story. She was inappropriately familiar and spent the entire evening teasing him about being stuffy. While John and Terrance interpreted her behaviour as a quirky kind of charisma, Violet understood it for what it was: thinly disguised disdain for the status John had reached in life and everything the family held dear.

Violet had married into the wealth of the Ivey family but she had grown up dirt poor. Although she had been breathing the rarefied air of privilege for some time, she remembered the feelings of fear, despair, anger, and resentment that poverty could engender. Being born to privilege meant that Terrance could not understand Regina's reactions to his world and Violet felt an obligation to do what she could to help Regina adjust. So, on a cool New York October day, Violet told her driver to come back in an hour and she walked up the two flights of stairs to the apartment on a day when she knew Terrance would be at school. Regina had been surprised to see Violet in this part of town, and she quickly gave her the impression she did not like it. She did not try to win the favour of other women, and, despite the age difference, Violet knew she was perceived as competition by Regina.

Violet talked about how small apartments could be stifling and how she was thinking how wonderful it would be for Terrance and Reggie and their little family to move to the house in the Hampton's that the family ordinarily used for only a couple weeks in the summer. Regina coldly stated that she hated the Hamptons. She was not about to allow Violet to be her benefactress because that would be admitting that she was in a position of weakness. In her eyes she was the best—the most powerful, the most intelligent, and the most beautiful—and she hated anyone who did not validate that opinion. Anyone who had the audacity to offer her help became the object of her scorn.

Violet thought she had better try a different tack. She told Regina that Terrance thought that perhaps she was getting bored with him and wanted her freedom. She went on to explain that the family would be willing to take custody of the child and in return she would be given financial support for the rest of her life and, of course, unlimited access to the child.

But Violet had underestimated Regina's resentment for the wealth and power of the family, as well as her determination to prove that it held no power over her. She told Violet that she did not need their money and they were not going to get her kid either. It was obvious that Regina saw the situation as a personal power struggle that she intended to win. The best interests of the child were never considered, nor were the feelings of Terrance, who was desperate to be in his child's life. In Regina's world nothing mattered but her own wishes and the power they held. Violet was afraid that any further discussion might provoke her further so she told her that she was excited about the birth and that they would make all the arrangements when she was getting close. She did her best to smile sincerely, and left feeling discouraged and completely helpless.

Regina left Terrance shortly after that meeting and Violet felt a twinge of guilt because she knew it was Regina's way of snubbing her offers as well. In four months, hope returned for both Terrance and his parents when Regina contacted them saying she was about to give birth. They soon found out that it was just another manipulation that would allow Regina to show contempt for them and everything they stood for.

When the baby was born, Violet waited for Terrance to leave the room before she came in to see if, as Terrance had hoped, motherhood had changed Regina's attitude at all, and if they could try one last time to work out an agreement of some sort.

After greeting Regina warmly, Violet told her that she could always count on the family for financial support and that they hoped that she would find somewhere to live that would be close enough that they could visit their granddaughter often. Regina's jaw tightened and she screamed that being rich did not give Violet the right to tell her what she could and couldn't do and that she planned to live anywhere she goddamned decided to live. If that was not what the family wanted, it was too fucking bad.

Violet realized that there was no reasoning with her—her view of life was too skewed. Custody of the child was going to be a life long battle and there was a real possibility that she would take the baby and leave given the first opportunity. Instinctively she knew that no amount of Ivey money was going to keep Regina from doing exactly what she wanted to do. Knowing what pain she was about to inflict on her son, Violet lost her temper and lashed out at Regina. She told her that she was a narcissist who needed constant adoration and validation of her belief in her own superiority and that these obsessions would have to be satisfied in some other—no doubt peculiar, manner. She told her that she was living out some fantasy of a competition in her mind that was at cross purposes to her own daughter's best interests. The family could offer Sheherezade the best schools, the best care, and a loving family and she was turning it all down for the sole purpose of asserting her will. She told her that her decisions were based on a selfishness that was beyond any selfishness she could imagine any mother would possess.

But, Violet said, there would come a day when Sheherezade would realize that everything Regina touched turned to poison. Sheherezade would see what contempt she had for traditional values; that it was her nature to rebel against all authority. Any conformity to traditional values belied her belief that she was unique, special, a leader not a follower. She told Regina that she would never know what it means to love, that if anyone in her life was not constantly validating her huge ego, they were thrown away, the way she was throwing away Terrance and the family that was willing to accept her with open arms. Tears fell from her eyes as she explained that Sheherezade would be her father's daughter and that there would come a time when she would belong to her real family—to people that could love her the way a family should.

Regina's cool blue eyes narrowed. She said that Violet simply could not tolerate anyone who was unwilling to kiss her ass because she had money. She pointed out that an unwillingness to spend every evening watching television with her boring son was not evidence that she was self absorbed. No one could tell her how to live her life and if she and Terrance did not like it then it was just to fucking bad. She would not be controlled by the Ivey money.

Violet started to grasp at straws. She told Regina that when Sheherezade was twenty-one she would inherit some of the family money in the form of a trust fund. Although Regina had a look of insolence on her face, Violet could sense that this information sparked her interest. Regina's eyes were hungry with entitlement. Anything that belonged to her daughter was automatically hers without violating the delicate balance of power she guarded with such ferocity. Violet felt she took the bait and today she would find out if her instinct had been correct. She had given Regina the address of the very building in downtown Manhattan where their lawyers would still be located in twenty-one years and here she was counting on the greed and selfishness of the most narcissistic human being she had ever met.

Violet's mind snapped back into the present as the door opened and Walter came into the room looking as pale as a ghost.

"You were right. Mother and daughter are on their way up."

Violet's heart pounded as she sat with Walter at one end of the long table with the details of the trust spread before them. The door opened and Violet recognized Regina in a tight white floral dress that was cut low to showcase her bosom. Despite the years of abuse to her body, Violet was surprised to see her still looking youthful and attractive.

Violet felt a lump come up her throat that threatened to choke off her air as she saw the young girl wearing an elegant grey suit with a matching broad rimmed hat walk in behind Regina. She smiled at her beautiful granddaughter and she saw her look back at her from under the shadow of her hat. There was no smile in return. Violet's feelings were crushed; she had a moment of deep despair when her granddaughter did not come over and give her a hug as she had envisioned for so many years. She looked at Sheherezade to search for some resemblance to Terrance. She had always expected to see him in her eyes but he was not there. Indeed, she had green eyes that, aside from the colour, reminded her a lot of Regina—very unlike the kind, deep violet-blue eyes of her son.

She lowered her head and tried to organize her thoughts. All was not lost. Maybe in time, when they got to know each other, they could build a relationship. She took a deep breath and raised her head smiling at both Sheherezade and Regina. She picked up a small paper weight and set it on one of the two identical leather bound binders that sat before them.

"It is wonderful to see you both. I have looked forward to this day for such a long time and I hope this is a fresh start for all of us as a family. Sheherezade, I can't tell you how much it means to me to finally see you after all these years. I just wish your father could have been here, but he was killed in a plane crash four years ago. He loved you with all his heart and he never gave up hope that he would someday be reunited with you. There are not words to convey how much it would have meant to him to be here. So, for now, I just want to say thank you for coming, and thank you, Regina, for bringing her here today. This is the happiest day of my life, and truly a dream come true for me. Happy birthday, Sheherezade. I hope this will be one of the best days of your life." Violet gave them a warm smile and waited eagerly for her granddaughter to say something. Both Regina and Sheherezade stared out the window and kept their silence.

Walter, sensing some tension, began to go ahead with the business at hand. "Sheherezade, it is the wishes of your grandparents, Violet and John Ivey, and your late father, Terrance Ivey, to bequest to you a trust fund on your twenty-first birthday and we are here today to explain what that will entail. Your grandmother, as the trustee has set out the terms of the trust."

"Jesus Christ!" Regina muttered under her breath loud enough for Violet to get the general drift of her dismay. Walter continued. Upon your grandfather's death, you inherited $25,000,000.00 which was transferred to the trust. There was an audible gasp from Sheherezade as she turned to her mother with a shocked look on her face that gave way to a huge smile and an involuntary giggle. Walter pretended not to hear and continued, "Your father specified that his entire estate be put into your trust to be dispensed at your grandmother's discretion if you were ever found before your grandmother's death. The trust includes an estate in Connecticut and a winter home in Palm Beach. Furnishings, jewellery, a yacht, some boats, five automobiles, and also cash holdings in the amount of $68,000,000.00." There was an audible gasp from Sheherezade one more time, but Regina maintained a stoic façade of smug satisfaction.

"Now, your grandmother has laid out the terms of dispensation as follows: Today you will receive a sum of $1,000,000.00 and then every six months after that you will receive $500,000.00. You will have access to the remainder of the money and holdings at which time she sees fit." Regina's mouth twisted into a knot and she stared back at Violet as her breathing became heavy. Sheherezade looked over at her mother but did not quite understand her objection. Regina leaned over and whispered that Violet was not letting them have all the money but had chosen to dole it out in half a million dollar sums every six months.

"An account has been set up for you with your grandmother's bank and the money is now yours." He gave Sheherezade the bank book that would allow her to take out the money at her discretion. Regina picked up the book and opened it to see the amount in black and white and then rose to leave. Sheherezade followed her cue and they turned on their heels and promptly left the room. Violet felt panic as she saw her hopes of becoming acquainted with her granddaughter slipping through her fingers. She jumped up from the chair and raced out the door, passing the receptionist to reach them before they left the outer office.

"Regina! Would you both join me for some lunch back at my home today? I have a car waiting for us downstairs . . . ."

"You won't even hand over what is rightfully ours and you expect us to break bread with you! You are still trying to control us! Who the fuck do you think you are?" Regina was turning red and her voice was getting louder.

"I am not trying to control you Regina. It is not your money. Try not to forget that. The million dollar stipend is for my granddaughter and that is an adequate sum for her to live on at this time in her life." Violet smiled at Sheherezade and hoped she was getting through to her on some level.

"You can pretend anything you want but we both know you are hanging onto that money so that she will kiss your ass for it and I can tell you right now that your plan is not going to work. You were wrong. She did not turn out to be a boring wimp like your son—she has balls like me. This girl has spunk like you wouldn't believe and she is not going to be controlled by you!" Violet just looked at Regina and shook her head. She was still in some internal struggle with authority that had no relevance with the situation at hand. Regina's face was contorted with hatred as she pulled open the heavy wooden door to leave the office. Violet instinctively reached out to touch Sheherezade to get her attention before she left with her mother. Just as she came close to reaching her, Sheherezade recoiled to avoid contact and her nostrils flared.

"Cunt," she hissed under her breath as she abruptly turned her back on her grandmother and left the office.

Chapter 33

Sheherezade spent her birthday alone in her room crying, totally isolated in her beautiful estate. Her nerves had been unravelling since the night of the Hog Picnic and an inner tremor prevented her from thinking clearly. She was trying to wrap her mind around the fact that the Lion she loved was just a façade for the real Lion, the Lion that ordered hits on civilians to protect his evil empire; the Lion whose lust for vengeance had resulted in the death of an innocent little boy; the Lion whose world was a twisted distortion of accepted morals and ethics. The images of the picnic and the events at the house flashed through her mind and tormented her sensibilities. The man that struck her that day was not the man she loved or could love. And her beloved Lila . . . so far away. How could she ever bring her back knowing what she now knew? Her eyes were swollen from crying and she felt sick to her stomach. Meditation had always been her final solace when she had a problem but right now she could not sit long enough to calm her mind. Finally, she came to the conclusion that she must get away, far away from Lion, to have any hope of sorting out her feelings.

A thought struck her and she reached for her cell phone.

"Dex, I want to go to our villa in Tunisia," she said trying to keep her voice steady.

"Of course, Sheherezade. I will make the arrangements and call you back with the details." *That was easy,* she thought. Dex called her back within an hour and set out the itinerary for her trip down to the meals she that would be served aboard their jet. Now she understood why Lion always spoke so highly of Dex's ability to organize his life.

Sheherezade was having trouble concentrating so she asked Tina to come upstairs and prepare her for a week stay in Tunisia. As Tina packed, they talked and she offered to accompany her on the trip but

Sheherezade said that she needed to be alone and Tina, sensing there was more to the story, was careful not to pry into her personal life. In an hour the car was humming along the highway to the airport where the private jet awaited her arrival.

When she arrived at the tarmac she was greeted by Andrew and Jeff. After boarding she noticed two other men sitting at the back of the plane. When she asked who they were Andrew replied that Lion had sent body guards and insisted that they stay with her at all times. She nodded and went into the bedroom where she collapsed into the big comfortable bed and fell into a deep sleep for the first time in forty-eight hours.

Sheherezade awoke just as the plane began its descent into the city of Tunis. Andrew served eggs Benedict that smelled delicious but her stomach was still in some kind of nervous rebellion so she went into the bathroom and threw up after eating. Sleep had calmed the relentless tremor but she needed more solitude before she could think clearly. There was a car waiting when she cleared customs and she was driven through the bright Tunisian sun to the villa on the outskirts of Cartage that she had received as a wedding present from Boots just a short time before. The housekeeper was a shy Tunisian woman about her age named Nejiba who spoke fairly good English. After giving her a tour of the home, Nejiba asked if she could make her some lunch and Sheherezade thanked her saying that she would love to try some traditional fare beside the pool.

Sheherezade stretched out on the chaise longue and inhaled the air infused with the scent of the glorious flowers that seemed to grow everywhere; a smell that reminded her so much of the perfume Boots had created for her as a wedding gift. She was completely enchanted by this ancient place with all its natural beauty and long history in the ancient world. On the other side of the pool she could see the green blue waters of the Mediterranean and she imagined the people that had passed through the historical city of Cartage over thousands of years. She had the strangest feeling that she had been one of them and that she was home.

Nejiba brought out a small feast which consisted of an appetizer made with soft egg and ground meat wrapped in phylo pastry, a big plate of couscous, Tunisian wine, almond pastries, and a pot of fresh mint tea. After consuming most of the delicious food, she asked Nejiba for a towel, took off her clothes, and jumped into the sumptuous pool. *No,* she told herself, *she would not think. Not yet.* She swam and sunned herself and then snuggled into the huge draped bed in the master suite where the sound of the incoming tide lulled her into a deep sleep. When Sheherezade awoke she felt a little more like herself. *Now,* she thought, *I am going to sort this out.*

It was dark when she walked out to the pool and then beyond to explore the white sandy beach. The tide lapped the shore in a mesmerizing rhythm and the smell of the night air was so delightful that it was difficult not to be caught up in the moment, to forget all of the problems that weighed her down like a giant anchor. She walked slowly along the shore listening to the waves as they licked her toes. Her plan had been to go over every detail of what she knew and did not know about her life with Lion, but that plan did not seem right anymore. She wanted to listen to the waves and allow her mind to be quiet. She wanted to hear the Sea's voice; she knew that the answers to everything were there in that immutable sound. In the distance someone played a flute as the lights glittered along the shore.

Suddenly, she became aware that she was walking past Boots' villa when she recognized the pool and giant outdoor fireplace from the pictures. Just then she saw him walking in her general direction, naked, with a thin blonde girl clinging to him. The bright lights of the villa shrouded the beach in darkness so they could not see her. *Well, Brandi,* she thought, *you are not the only amusement on the menu.* She continued to walk and enjoy the night air. By the time she came to a natural stone wall that separated the beach and delineated the property line she had made her decision. Maybe she would never know the extent of everything Lion had done in his life and what he condoned through his control of the club, but she was convinced that she did not want a life of trying to find out.

And she knew. As much as she had loved Lion, they were not going to fit. The Lion she fell in love with and adored was not the real Lion. She wished she could run into his arms and have him protect her from the harsh world that she knew all too well—the world she would have to face without him. If she returned, however, she would always be right where she was now—living with the feeling that she was part of something that was brushed with evil. *A cockroach life.* It would be like taking a step back into her old life; the one she vowed to escape. Any compromises she might be tempted to make in order to hang onto the security of this life of luxury could never be justified in light of her goal to give Lila a normal childhood. Sheherezade was determined to purge evil from Lila's life and that meant leaving Lion. As she walked back to the villa, she felt a great weight lift from her chest. She finally felt that she could stop thinking and appreciate the night air and the warm Mediterranean Sea that sparkled as far as she could see.

Sheherezade spent a couple of days enjoying the villa that she knew she would never see again. Upon reading the news on her laptop she was struck dumb by a story in the New York Post. Long time companion of Lou Falcone, Fancy McFarlane, had been found dead in her New York penthouse, a victim of homicide. The article rehashed some of the highlights of the recent gang war as a possible motive for the crime.

Lila! Maybe what Lion had warned her about was coming true—the Purple Flames were picking off family members of the Lucifer's Pride. Shaking with fear, Sheherezade called the estate and asked Tina to find Jackie's phone number in the rolodex in Lion's office. Jackie would have the inside scoop and chances were she would assume Sheherezade was still on the inside circle.

"Jackie, it's Sheherezade. I'm in Tunisia and I just read the story about Fancy. What a tragedy! I haven't been able to get in touch with Lion. You must be devastated . . . ."

"Sheher, it was horrendous. I knew something was wrong when she did not show up at the picnic, so Shane and I went over there and we found her in her bedroom. She was all sliced up. Oh my God!"

"Was it the Purple Flames? I am terrified they will target my niece!"

"No, don't worry about that! Haven't you talked to Lion?"

"No, you cannot get a phone connection out of this country. It sounds like the operators are having a party on the line."

"Well, Lion talked to the detective—you know he was one of ours—and he had him tell the press that it was the work of the Purple Flames."

"What do you mean, he was one of ours?"

"You know, one of the cops on the payroll. Lion wanted the Purple Flames to look bad but there was no evidence that they had anything to do with it. You don't have to worry about your niece or yourself. Bikers only hunt each other."

"Well, if the Flames didn't do it, do they know who did?'

Jackie paused, "They don't . . . I do . . ."

"Jackie, you can tell me. You know I would never say anything to anyone."

"I know, I know . . . When we were at the picnic Brandi came prancing into the Ole Lady's tent as cocky as ever. How the fuck would she have the guts to do that unless she knew that Fancy was not going to be there? Fancy would have taken a strip off her that she would never live down. Brandi did it . . . I know she did."

Surely, it could not be possible. Sheherezade was so shocked by the accusation that she could barely compose herself to say good bye.

"Hello? No, sorry, he is sleeping. This is Leo—his father—can I take a message? Well, he is under a doctor's care right now . . . yes . . . he took it very hard. We don't know when he'll be back but certainly it won't be too soon. Thanks for understanding . . . yes, I will . . . Bye."

"Who was that?" Marta asked.

"Dave's sergeant. Just wondering how he was doing. A very understanding fellow. He said to let him know when there is a tentative date for Dave to go back to work." Concern passed over Marta's face.

"I saw that woman . . . Mrs. Varley, who lives up by the graveyard. She told me she sees Dave's car parked there at all times of the day and night. He's spending too much time up there . . . it's just not natural, Leo."

"It's just going to take time, Marta. He'll be fine," Leo replied.

"But, he's not even functioning, Leo. I just worry he might hurt himself. Elise was everything to him. It's nine o'clock and he's still sleeping. I would like to have breakfast," Marta sniffed.

"Yes, I don't want to wait. I'll call him . . . David, are you getting up? Your mother wants to get breakfast going . . . ."

"Yep, I'm coming . . ." When David came down he walked to the glass doors and peered out at the lake that lapped the shore just one hundred feet away. Beauty did not touch his sensibilities anymore; he was immune to all outside stimuli.

"I'm starving, Marta," Leo said sternly. Marta bristled.

"Well, the bacon isn't done yet, Leo! Unless you want to eat it as is. Some people actually like to eat their bacon a bit limp, you know." She looked over at David to see if her statement had produced a reaction but he continued to stare out of the window at the sky.

"How are you feeling today, dear?" Marta asked her son as she gave her husband a furtive glance that indicated she was concerned.

"I'm O.K."

"Did you sleep well last night?" Marta inquired.

"No, not too well. Those pills make my heart pound. I'm going to stop taking them."

"Oh, I don't know. See the doctor first. O.K.? Will you do that?"

"Yea, mum, I will."

Marta put the plates on the table and poured the coffee. David picked up the cup, took a sip, and gazed out at the lake again.

"Well, Leo, how about getting the barbeque ready so we can cook up some steaks tonight?"

"Sure Marta, we've got some T-bones in the freezer; I'll marinate them. Sound good David? Will you be home for dinner?" Leo asked. It took a minute for David to break his concentration on the cloudless sky before he was able to focus on the question before him.

"Ya, I think I'll go check on the house . . . I'll be back for dinner." David's silver hair caught the sun as he looked down at the masterpiece of cooking artistry that lay before him.

"Aren't you eating, dear?" Marta asked.

"No," he said looking away. David's eyes perused the stylish townhouse, a paradigm of colour coordination, order, and cleanliness that failed to offer him any comfort.

"I'm going to go," he said as he got up and walked to the door.

Chapter 34

All the way from the airport to the estate, Sheherezade weighed the possibility that Brandi could be capable of such a heinous act as murder. Could she be that consumed with jealousy and hate?

Sheherezade had decided she must move out of the estate immediately to make a clean break. For now she had decided she would stay at their coop on the Upper East Side until the arrangements could be made for a separation. She was thankful she did not run into Tina. Any explanation she tried to muster might tip Lion off to her state of mind and she had some things to do before the showdown.

Sheherezade left the grounds followed by two of Lion's bodyguards in a black SUV. She took the private road that led to Dr. Lindsay's house to pick up Bugsy. There were cars in the driveway but no one came to the door when she rang. After a few minutes she heard laughter so she walked around to the back of the house to find Bugsy. A naked young woman bounced on the diving board while Dr. Lindsay and a few young men, also naked, lounged by the pool watching. Just then Bugsy spotted Sheherezade and let out a little howl as he ran toward her. She gave Dr. Lindsay a look of disdain as she turned and walked to her car with Bugsy in tow. Thoughts and questions rushed into her suspicious mind and she became aware that she was tired of always having them occupy her conscious thoughts. *No more Dr. Hotel and his Cockroach life.* She was glad to be leaving this environment that required a steady stream of excuses and justifications just to make it through a day.

The apartment had no sign of life. She knew that unless Coral was there, Lion preferred to stay at the suite in the clubhouse so he didn't have to be alone. When she entered the bedroom she had a sinking feeling as she remembered touching moments she shared with Lion in the oversized bed of the luxurious room. She pushed the temperature control button on the shower and relaxed as the sprays massaged every inch of her body. The heat lights warmed her body as she stepped out of the shower and wrapped herself in a warm towel. She went to the casual section of her closet that lined every wall in her dressing room and pulled out a designer suit consisting of soft slacks and matching top in a violet color that the personal shopper had added to her wardrobe. The lights from across the park mesmerized her momentarily. Anguish flooded her senses. Last week she would have put on her pajamas, made some popcorn, and curled up in bed with a movie on the five foot screen while she waited for Lion to come home. The romance. The luxury. It had all been a fantasy and it was time to get real.

She put some food and water down for Bugsy and made her way to the parking garage. She stopped for some take-out and then wound her way through the streets to the Dancing House where she waited for Brandy at the dancers exit. Before she apprised Lion of her decision to leave him, she wanted to speak to Brandi. Despite all of their differences she felt that she had to know if indeed her sister was responsible for the death of Fancy. If she could just look into her eyes and ask her if she had anything to do with it, she would know.

Brandi had just finished her last set and she was relishing the news that she was about to drop on everyone in the dressing room. Best of all, Monica was working, and she knew that Monica had a direct pipeline to that bitch, Jackie. The room was thick with the smell of weed signalling the end of the day's work.

"Well, girls, it has been a slice but I'm out of here!" She put her arms up in the air and pumped her hips in a victory dance.

"Where are you going?" one of the younger girls asked plaintively.

"My family came into a huge fortune and my Ole Man wants me all to himself anyway." She glared at Monica to make sure she heard the Old Man comment. There was no Fancy anymore, so she was claiming the title despite the fact that it had not been officially bestowed upon her.

"I hope you like cats," Monica chuckled under her breath.

"Did you say something, bitch?" Brandi put her hands on her hips and glared at Monica.

"I said I hope you like cats. I hear Boots has a new kitten. A cute, young, blonde, kitten." Brandi felt her chest tighten but she was too unnerved to think of a rebuttal for Monica.

As she turned around and walked down the hall she heard a few meows echoing from the dressing room. She nipped into the handicap washroom and looked at the face of horror starring back from the mirror. *A kitten?! Oh God, she had to see Boots.* She pulled a big bag of meth out of her purse and eyed the beautiful virgin vein on the inside of her arm.

Sheherezade honked her horn when Brandi exited the back door of the club.

"What the fuck do you want?"

"Get in. I have to talk to you." Brandi hesitated but could not resist the temptation to tell Sherry her big news.

"This better be good."

Sheherezade got a fix on her sister's eyes and noticed that they were glassy and freshly bloodshot, a sign that she had just used and was very high.

"There's a very strange rumour going around that you murdered Fancy McFarlane."

Desperation passed over Brandi's face and then anger bubbled up as her brows hardened into a frown.

"You have really reached rock bottom now, haven't you? You've heard the news and you're jealous. You have to try to ruin my day by making shit up. Well, it just won't work! This time there is nothing you can do to fuck it up for me."

"What are you talking about Brandi? Jealous of what?" Sheherezade was beginning to think that she would have to find another time to have this conversation because she suspected Brandi was too high to be coherent.

"The money! Moron. The money!"

"What money?"

"A sugar daddy mum had many years ago has left mum a fortune. She gets a big check every six months for life. I came back to the club tonight to quit."

Sheherezade was stunned by the news and was just about to ask more questions regarding the source of this windfall when she noticed the presence of a blue uniform beside the car.

"Step out and put your hands on the car, Miss . . . ." Someone opened the other door and was barking orders at Brandi. Sheherezade was instructed to stand beside Brandi by the curb while they searched the car and their purses. A short young cop broke into a big smile as he pulled a baggy out of Brandi's purse filled with a white powder.

After the booking, Sheherezade called Dex to let him know that she was being taken to a detention centre. The police told her that the earliest she would be able to have a bail hearing would be Monday morning so she would be spending the weekend in jail.

Brandi and Sheherezade waited for hours in a dirty holding cell with a couple of other girls that looked like they had just been picked up off the street for hooking. Three Correctional Officers in charge of the Admission and Discharge area were doing paper work in the strip room.

"Do you know who they are?" the pretty blonde asked the others.

"Who?" the rookie Correctional Officer asked wide eyed.

"They are Brandi Raleigh and her sister Sheherezade Terkel."

"I think I've heard the names somewhere . . . ."

"They are the Old Ladies of the grand poobas of the Evil Underworld. Brandi is the girlfriend of Lou Falcone better known as Boots, Vice President of the Pride, and the darker haired girl is the wife of Lion Terkel, the President of the Pride. The cops said she took off a diamond the size of a nickel and handed it to one of her bodyguards before they drove her Maserati home for her. And, guess what was in her purse. Thirty thousand in cash and her own brand of perfume called **SHEHEREZADE**. Whoever said that crime doesn't pay? We have to be careful to do everything by the book or they'll be all over us. They have serious money behind them."

"Is Regina Raleigh related to these girls?" the tough red head wondered out loud.

"Ya, that's their mother. A real fuckin' bitch. Turned out Brandi when she was about fourteen. Mother and daughter are cut from the same cloth. I had Brandi when she was a young offender and she was a real handful. Obnoxious, attention-seeking, arrogant. Just like mom." Kate handed the keys to the rookie, "Here you might as well jump in with both feet. Go bring in the charming one."

"Hi Brandi, remember me from juvy? Kate? I think I was your prime worker on one of your bits." The pretty blonde tried her best to make a connection that would snap her out of her tirade.

"You fuckers all look the same to me. You eat too many fuckin' donuts. Look, do you know who I am? My boyfriend is Boots, head of the Lucifer's Pride. Even you must know who that is," she spat.

"Well, that's not really an issue right now Brandi. We just want to ask you some questions, take your finger prints, do a strip search, have you take a shower, and then you can go to the unit."

"I told you, I'm not stripping. If you want to see this body you have to pay. I don't give anything away."

"That's not what I heard," Kate muttered to Joyce. Joyce turned away and disguised a laugh with a cough.

"What? What did you say?" Brandi screamed.

"Oh, you're just dying to see this body aren't you. You're just a bunch of dykes who work in a place like this to get a free peek . . . so go fuck yourselves!" Kate turned to Joyce, "Call Godzilla, I'm not dealing with this tonight. Where did she go anyway?"

"She had to go down to the I-MAT unit to deal with a Rembrandt." Megan looked confused so Joyce explained that she was referring to an inmate that did artwork on the wall with their own feces.

Joyce phoned I-MAT to tell Godzilla they needed her in Admissions & Discharge as she started to record the items in Brandi's purse. Soon a loud voice echoed down the hall just before the heavy metal door clanged shut.

"Well Brandi! How the fuck are you?" Godzilla asked as she came into the strip room. "We had your mother in here about a month ago. I guess she was doin' her Christmas shoplifting a little fuckin' early." Carol stood five foot eleven but appeared much larger because of her rotund middle section. Large bulging eyes stayed deadpan as the language that would make a sailor blush, flowed from the large hole in her face that never seemed to close. The respect she commanded from inmates was not based on the fact that she was a Lieutenant in the prison, but rather on some basic instinct that told them she was their kindred spirit. The other staff called her Godzilla, but not to her face.

"Carol, I'm not going to strip tonight because I won't be staying long. I want to get out of here!" Brandi was in such a state of pain from withdrawal that she was losing any connection she had with the reality of the situation.

"We got to do it babe. Don't get ugly with me. Just fuckin' do it," Carol retorted sagely as she rolled her enormous protruding eyes.

"Oh God, why can't they all be philosophers like they were in the Shawshank Redemption?" Kate moaned with exasperation. Brandi continued to hurl insults at the officers as she stripped down naked.

"OK Brandi, you know the drill. Open your mouth, turn around, bend over, squat down and cough." Godzilla instructed.

Brandi waved her naked behind at them and pointed to the tattoo of the unicorn on her right cheek.

"See this. It's like me. One of a kind. Unique. I don't have to work at some stupid job like you stiffs. My mother just inherited a fortune so enjoy it while you can. Bunch of fuckin' losers!" Kate stepped forward and looked Brandi in the eye.

"I know how special you are. I have an entire unit full of scrotes like you with a unicorn tattoo on their ass, honey." Brandi had a mind to give her a good one across the head for that comment but she had spent enough time in jail to know that it would guarantee that she remained in jail even longer.

"Fuck you, bitch!"

"Shut the fuck up, Brandi or I'll put you in a babydoll and let you spend the weekend with a fuckin' Poocasso for a roommate. How would you like to smell that all weekend?" Godzilla smirked. Brandi knew the threat was serious so she clamped up temporarily. Godzilla took her across the hall to the shower and gave her clothes to wear on the unit.

"If only they could grasp how little we care," Kate mused. "They all have problems with authority so they play out the same scenario over and over, and they never seem to realize that they're the only ones playing. We are just a bunch of grunts trying to do our job." Joyce nodded in agreement.

When Sheherezade walked into the strip room Godzilla was struck by her style and beauty and noticed the slight resemblance to Brandi, "Oh, your sister is Evil!"

"I know, I know . . . but I'm really nothing like her," Sheherezade said apologetically. Joyce, Kate, and Godzilla started to giggle but Megan did not get the joke.

"No," Godzilla laughed, "That's her nickname—Evil. I think she's had it since she was a juvenile and she seems to have grown into it nicely." Sheherezade had to laugh at her mistake and they all had a bout of giggles. Knowing Brandi made it funny.

"OK, then," Sheherezade said, "I am Trying To Be Good—Evil's sister."

"See it isn't a genetic condition, at least not all the time." Kate offered. They all chuckled as they started the paperwork.

"So you're Lion's Ole Lady?" Godzilla commented.

"Well, I was . . . but we will be separating shortly."

"Be careful, you know what happened when his last Ole Lady tried that."

"No, what happened?" Godzilla looked over at Kate with disbelief and then decided quickly that she better not reveal any information for her own safety.

"Na, I must be thinking of someone else . . . ."

Sheherezade was given two thin sheets and a grey wool blanket and was escorted to a six by ten foot cell containing bunk beds and a stainless steel toilet. Her roommate was a small chubby girl with a Friar Tuck hair cut named Marie who rocked silently on the upper bunk. Sheherezade sat on the metal bed stunned by the turn of events that had landed her in jail, of all places. She was deep in the bowels of Lion's world and she felt ashamed that decisions she made had led her to this place. It was taking all the self control she could muster to keep from breaking down in tears right on the spot.

Godzilla's comment had not been lost on her. She knew that she had been given a juicy nugget of information the officer could not take back. Knowing that some other girlfriend had a problem when she left Lion frightened her. She was realizing more and more that she did not know Lion as well as she should have before committing to him the way she had. The door clicked and a guard opened it.

"Your people have asked me to pass a message along. They are doing everything they can to get you out of here so you have nothing to worry about. You have both staff and inmates watching your back. This is for you." The officer dropped a pillow case filled with canteen items of every description. There was a carton of cigarettes, a real toothbrush and toothpaste, makeup, chocolate bars, chips, and an assortment of fresh fruit. The metal door clamped shut but Lion's presence lingered in the tiny room. An involuntary shutter provoked a bout of vomiting into the stainless steel toilet. Marie, who was still rocking quietly, did not seem to notice.

Sheherezade became aware of a rising commotion in the common area and she realized that what felt like the middle of the night, was the bustle of breakfast being served. After everyone had been ushered out into the common area, Brandi sat at the end of the table, looking even worse than she had the night before. Dark circles under her eyes had appeared overnight and her hands were shaking as she tried to bring the cup of coffee to her mouth.

A pale girl with long stringy brown hair walked up to the table, surreptitiously holding a small cup filled with brown liquid. She looked around cautiously and then quietly asked Sheherezade if she wanted some methadone. Sheherezade was somewhat confused, so she turned to Julia, the girl who had befriended her the night before, to ask for an explanation. Julia explained that out of respect for her position as the wife of Lion, the girl had saved her morning dose of methadone so that she could have it. Sheherezade was trying to understand. "I'm surprised they allow her to walk around the unit with such powerful medication," she whispered discreetly.

"Oh, they don't. They make her drink it at the nursing station and then she made it come back up in her cell so you could have it," Julia explained. Pictures of the process danced through Sheherezade's head and she had to fight the urge to run to the bathroom and throw up. Being the stranger in a strange land that she was, she knew her best course of action was to accept everything with as much equanimity as she could muster.

"Thanks honey, but I don't need it. You use it," Sheherezade said softly. Brandi had figured out what was going on at the end of the table.

"Give it to me!" she hissed with haughty entitlement. The cup was passed under the table and Brandi downed the liquid in one gulp, following it with a swig of the foul coffee. Sheherezade looked away, swallowed hard, and tried to think of lemons.

Chapter 35

Only the glow of the city lights eased the darkness of the living room where Lion sat drenched in sweat. No amount of jogging seemed to have any affect on the mood that settled into his psyche like an old friend. Anger was bubbling up from a dark, forgotten place and Lion was losing the battle to contain it. Dex had noticed that he had not been himself since the night of the picnic and had surmised that it had something to do with the death of Fancy and the threat of his old rivals, the Purple Flames. Lion did not take any failure well and if the Purple Flames were responsible for Fancy's death, they were hitting very close to home.

In truth, Lion had not given the death of Fancy a second thought. They knew immediately by the murder scene that it was not a job done by any biker. The theory proposed by Jackie, that it was the work of one of Boots' other girlfriends, was probably a good one. Boots did not appear to be upset about her death either. On the contrary, he felt relief at having their secret buried and Lion shared those sentiments.

No, Lion's problem was Sheherezade. Everything had been perfect until she began to intrude on club business. He was faced with a dilemma. What was he supposed to do, tell her she was right about her suspicions? That he had to make life and death decisions in his line of work? He knew what her reaction to that would be, and losing her was not an option. He would not allow history to repeat itself.

Her trip to Tunisia had been a relief to him because it gave him the hope that she was mulling things over and would come around to his way of thinking. The club business had nothing to do with his marriage; he wanted to keep them separate. Once she came to the same conclusion everything would be fine.

His intention was to go to her that Friday night after attending Fancy's funeral and try to work things out. When he arrived at the coop Dex called him on his cell and told him that Sheherezade and Brandi had been charged with drug possession and would be spending the weekend in a detention centre. Lion understood that the authorities were retaliating for the twenty odd Purple Flames that had been picked off for bounty and the hit made on the family in the Witness Protection Program but right now he was having trouble thinking clearly. Did they know that by taking her away they were hitting the one nerve that made his world black?

He tried to reassure himself that she would be back before long, but the feelings—the loss of control—that triggered emotional memories of being small and unloved bubbled up again and filled him with a white heat that he could only try to exercise away. Nothing belonged to him as a child. They weren't his toys; they weren't his homes; and they weren't his parents. Now, when he got something of his own, the boundaries were solid walls. He had built an empire to protect the things that were his and they had snatched her away. And, they would pay. Lion bent down to pet Bugsy who was whining for attention. Sheherezade was his and he refused to share her—even with a dog.

Dex knew that Lion remained in the New York apartment because the body guards had told him that he went in on Friday night and had not left. When he would not answer his calls, Dex became concerned about his state of mind and phoned Coral at the estate. He suggested she have someone drive her up to New York, making it look like it was her idea. If anyone could help his state of mind it would be Coral.

Suddenly, Lion was struck by an idea and he reached for his cell. James arrived within fifteen minutes.

"James, I have a job for you."

"Anything, boss."

"We've had nothing but trouble with the prisons lately. Guards whining that the Pride gets special treatment: extra conjugal visits, unlimited phone calls, special food, drugs. You know, the usual. These fuckers even went on strike about a month ago to force the management to do something about it. It's getting out of hand. To top it off, they pinched my wife on Friday and for that, they *will* pay. They have to know that we will retaliate when they do things to piss me off. I want you to pick off a Correctional Officer—one from the joint holding my Ole Lady. As soon as possible".

"No problem, boss."

Brandi came back from the visit with her lawyer with her eyes lit up like light bulbs and a big smile on her face.

"Did they search you?" a girl with a well-worn face asked intently.

"Ya, but I had it hooped where the sun don't shine. I knew Boots would come through for me," she preened, knowing full well it was James who had sent in the drugs with the lawyer.

Sheherezade lay on her cot overwhelmed by all the unknowns she was about to face when she was released. Was there real danger in declaring her independence from Lion? Here she was in his world. The Underworld. A place where Lion was King and, apparently, she was Queen. Frustration set in as she contemplated the mountain of information there was to be had about Lion in this prison—information she could not leave without. This could be her only chance to hear the truth.

She decided that her only recourse was to speak to a guard. She also knew that she had to be careful because some of the staff were on Lion's payroll and a mistake could be costly. She had a growing awareness that Lion could be dangerous when things did not go his way. Instinctively she felt Kate in Admission and Discharge was someone she could trust and she prayed that she was on duty.

Her request to see Officer Kate on a personal matter was granted. She explained to Kate that she had been married a week after meeting Lion and now that she was about to leave him she was becoming aware that he had another, more dangerous side. The problem was that, in her position, she couldn't get any information and she had no one to turn to for help.

Kate hesitated, "I really don't want to piss off Lion Terkel." Sheherezade frowned. She could appreciate the woman's position but her desperation made her persistent.

"Look, I know my family is strange but I'm not like them. I'm about to leave Lion and I would like to know what I'm dealing with . . . The other guard alluded to the fact that things did not go well for Lion's old girlfriend when she left him. I have to know what happened. I'm in the same position. As soon as I'm released, I'm going to tell him that I want a separation. I would never repeat what you tell me, I swear. It would mean so much to me, and I don't have anyone else I can trust . . . ."

Years of listening to jailhouse lies told her that *this* girl was telling the truth.

"OK, what do you want to know?"

Everyone waiting for visits could not help but sneak a peak at the beautiful woman with the upsweep hairdo dressed in high heels and a full length mink coat.

"I'm here to visit my daughter, Brandi Raleigh. She could be using her common-law's name: Falcone. And that's THE Boots Falcone." Regina huffed and rolled her eyes at what she deemed to be the incompetence of the staff as she and Luke cooled their heels in the small anteroom waiting for the visits to start.

"Hi mum, Luke, how's it going?" Brandi smiled as she entered the visiting room.

"Well, we're OK, but what the fuck happened to you?" Regina giggled.

"Oh, shit, I had some stuff on me and I was leaving the club to have a little party. You know, it was my last night. Well, Sherry was sitting there waiting for me and I got into her car. The cops are all over the Pride because they're kickin' ass. Boots sent a message right away saying he was taking care of everything. I'll be out of here in no time and am I going to party!"

"So, she's in with you?"

"Oh ya, the queen bee . . ."

"Did she say anything to you, about her birthday or . . . ."

"No, she has her head up her ass as usual," Brandi laughed.

"You should have seen these morons staring at me on the way in. I bet they never saw a mink like this, eh Luke? Bunch of fuckin' losers," she uttered the epithets while she looked over at the Correctional Officer with a red pony tail monitoring the visits.

"Watch your language, Ms. Raleigh, or you will be asked to leave the visit," the C.O. reprimanded.

"Big fuckin' deal," Regina said with disgust. "Unlike you, I have better things to do with my life than to sit around a jail anyway," she said as she stood up.

"Remember, behave yourself!" she admonished Brandi with dramatic flourish. "And take my advice and don't eat the food . . . you wouldn't want to look like that," she sneered as she pointed to the guard. The C.O. glared back with contempt. Brandi giggled to herself as they left the visiting room and she waited to be strip searched. When the C.O. came out she shook her head at Brandi, "You and your mother have sooo much class."

"Shut up bitch. I'm not stripping either. I'm sick of you dykes getting a cheap thrill."

"Honey, if I were gay, which I am not, there would certainly be no thrill at looking at some emaciated meth freak with bad skin. But I will certainly remember you and your mother, and I'll see you the next time you're both in."

"Well, don't hold your breath because my mother and I are rich. Rich!" She spoke slowly and clearly the way her mother did when she was doing her best to be very irritating. The C.O blinked her eyes slowly and stared her directly in the eye. "It doesn't matter how much money you have Brandi, people like you always fuck up. Always. You have what we call the Reverse Midas touch—whatever you touch turns to shit."

Sheherezade gave Kate a hug before they left the A&D area and thanked her for telling her what she knew about Lion's history. Kate hesitated and held onto her, "Maybe I should tell you . . ."

"What?" She asked as a feeling of impending doom washed over her.

"The health centre was going to call you over later. You're pregnant."

A baby! She loved it so much already! She had never planned to have children but knowing that it was growing inside her filled her with such love that she knew abortion was out of the question. She had plans to make. After hearing Kate's rendition of how everyone suspected Lion and Boots were responsible for Jimmy's death, she was convinced that she knew the meaning of that one solitary tear on Lion's patch. It was for murdering Jimmy, the leader of the Purple Flames.

Naiveté might have contributed to her present situation, but she had more than enough evidence to know that this was not the life she wanted for herself and it certainly was not the life she had planned for Lila and a baby. More than ever, she was convinced that she had to make a clean break. As soon as she could see Lion, she would tell him that she was leaving. If he had any feelings for her he would respect her choice and support her and their child. Lion was the father; nothing was going to change that now and she would not impose the heartbreak of not having a father on any child. At the same time, his world was darker than she could have ever imagined and she hoped that, even though they were not together, he would give it up and change his lifestyle at some point for the sake of their child.

Knowing this might be her last chance, Sheherezade walked over to the table where Brandi was holding court and asked her if they could speak privately. The other girls scattered like cockroaches, and Brandi looked around angrily realizing her friends had not waited for her consent.

"What the fuck, now?" Brandi winced. Sheherezade looked at Brandi without makeup in the unforgiving prison lighting and noticed that she had a few open red sores on her cheeks and chin. Her hair looked dry and she was emaciated and dehydrated. Suddenly she realized that Brandi's drug habit was taking a serious toll on her physical health and it was happening at a frightening rate.

"I'm pregnant. I just found out from the nurse."

"Congratulations. Anything else?" Brandi clenched her jaw and refused to make eye contact.

"I'm leaving Lion. I had no idea what I was getting into when I married into a motorcycle club and, now that I know, I want out."

"Dah, might have guessed he wouldn't be up to your standards. No one is really good enough, are they?"

"Brandi, don't be sarcastic. I'm talking about how they use women and treat them like property. I'm talking about racism, violence, and even murder. They're dangerous people and they generate suffering. I've admitted my mistake and I want to help you get away from them as well."

"Unlike you, I don't have any complaints. Boots treats me like a Queen. If you can't have it, then you don't want me to have it. Is that it?"

"Brandi, listen to me! You told me mum came into some money. You don't need Boots anymore. Get away from the Pride. I'm worried about you. You look like you've been hitting the drugs hard. You're so thin . . . ."

"Shut the fuck up. You don't know what you're talking about. I don't need your advice, and I'm not leaving Boots. I'm his Ole Lady!" she hissed at her sister.

"Yes. There's a convenient vacancy there all of a sudden. Isn't there?" Sheherezade looked directly into Brandi's green eyes. Brandi looked away and then her face contorted with fierce determination.

"You can't stand the fact that I'm happy. Mum said you would never hang onto Lion."

"Brandi! There's no competition! I'm worried about you. Why can't you get that through your head? Boots is not the kind of man who treats women with respect. I just think you should get away from him before he hurts you."

"I know how to make my man happy. Just because you're a stiff . . . ." Sheherezade had avoided bringing out the big gun but she could see she was not getting through to Brandi.

"I saw him with someone else when I was in Tunisia, at our villa. He was swimming naked in his pool with a thin, young, blonde . . . ."

Brandi jumped up from her seat and swung at Sheherezade, hitting her in the side of the head with a closed fist. Sheherezade fell off the metal chair that was bolted to the floor and landed on her side. Two Correctional Officers and ten inmates immediately ran over to break up the fight. As the Correctional Officers each grabbed an arm and escorted Brandi through the door, her hair was hanging over her face and she was screaming back at Sheherezade.

"You lying bitch! You're jealous! Just jealous!" Her voice echoed down the hall that led to the segregation area.

Kate was thinking about the discussion she had with Sheherezade. It was so rare to find someone passing through the jail system that truly did not seem to belong there, but she felt that she had met the exception. She could not forget what Sheherezade had said about her mother being so thrilled that her sister had been dating a biker. With role models like that it was little wonder the girls she saw going through the system had trouble making their lives work. Strangely enough though, this girl seemed to be coming through it with a normal set of values. She could feel it.

As Kate pulled out of the prison parking lot, she wondered to herself if she had made a mistake in telling her everything she knew about the murder of Jimmy, Lion's jealousy and possessiveness, and the rumours of a million dollar contract on Acelyn's head. Would there be any chance that in a pillow moment Sheherezade would tell Lion what she had said? She would never have thought she would ever go out on a limb for an inmate like that; it flew in the face of everything she had learned being in the prison system for so long.

A car pulled up to pass her on the quiet street. She looked over at the car and saw a dark, handsome young man with haunting blue eyes. A flash of light from the street light bounced off the metal. A bullet struck Kate in the temple. Her car swerved off the road and hit a tree, bringing it to a full stop. The black Impala disappeared into the black of the night with the headlights turned off.

Chapter 36

The Lucifer's Pride helicopter touched down at the clubhouse about five o'clock and Lion sprinted toward his lair. He was in a better mood; in fact, he was almost giddy. Sheherezade had been released from jail right on schedule and she was back at the apartment. Now he could concentrate on business.

When he walked through the large wooden double door, he was greeted like the conquering king returning home from battle. Rounds were being bought at the bar, and the mood was festive. The Black Cat never disappointed his pride. His psyche mirrored their psyches and they loved him as their guru of evil.

The mantra of every biker is freedom: freedom in how they dress, freedom in sexual mores, freedom in every aspect of life. But, as Kate explained to Sheherezade, a true individualist claims those rights as their own, and has no need to flout them to the rest of society. Individualists do not join clubs; people looking for support for their cause join clubs. And the cause being supported and celebrated by every outlaw bike gang is rebellion against authority. A rebel must have something to rebel against.

She told her that the criminal mind wants to control others, and the outlaw bike gang was a manifestation of that goal. Some criminals felt more powerful when their con was their secret, and some criminals felt more personal power when it was represented by a patch on their jacket. They were like two branches of the same religion. The important thing to remember was that they were not ordinary people. They did not value financial security, love, family ties, friendship, or personal growth and therefore it was necessary to find a lifestyle that supported their skewed view of life.

Sheherezade wondered how anyone having the work ethic required to build an empire could have a criminal mind. Kate told her about her observation of the people she had seen pass through the jail over the years. Very few could hold jobs but their problem was not an aversion to work. The problem was that in a typical job their boss represented an authority figure. It was not long before they felt resentment for that authority and their rebellion led to them to quit or be fired. If, however, they could feel that they were outsmarting the authorities by participating in criminal activity, you could see real enterprise. Lion's empire was built on illegal activities, and he was no exception to the rule.

But Kate was no longer around to sort out the subtleties of the criminal mind. She was dead. The joy on the face of everyone in the club that evening, spawned by the murder of an authority figure, revealed the true nature of their brotherhood. A feeling of power wrapped around them like a warm blanket, and everyone was in the mood for a party.

Lion made the compulsory rounds of greetings to everyone and then climbed the stairs to the upper level where the security tower was located. He dismissed the Prospect that had been assigned to monitor the security system so that he could be alone in this, his favourite place in the entire world. Windows banked each wall so that Lion could purvey 360 degrees of the clubhouse grounds. Here he was King of his empire and as he sat in the big leather chair alone, he took a deep breath and felt power course through his body. Never had he been so content in his own skin.

He had found his perfect woman and she was his. He had immense wealth, and he was surrounded by close friends and loyal subjects. His enemies were a small and distant threat that he had managed to control. And now, his dream of retaliation on Ace was about to unfold. His people located a club in Cannes, France where Acelyn was scheduled to perform. The thorn that had been pushed into his foot three decades ago would soon be removed. Only a niggling fear dared to upset his perfect world and that was the court case he was facing for the conspiracy to murder charge.

Boots arrived at the clubhouse with Shane by his side. Since they had gotten to know each other better at the Hog Day picnic they had become good friends. Boots preferred the company of men and Shane was someone with whom he had a lot in common. Shane had delegated his street work to a trusted buddy from the pen and had started an informal apprenticeship with Boots. Shane kept life interesting for Boots so he could be exactly where he wanted to be—learning from the best. Lion was a little surprised to see Shane come into this top level meeting with Boots but he trusted Boot's judgement. No one was less trusting than Boots.

The intercom buzzed and the front gate announced that Mickey, the cook, had entered the complex and was on his way up for his appointment with Lion. Mickey had been working for the organization for twenty-five years but wasn't one to socialize with the boys in the club. His personal style had not kept pace with the times. Long flowing hair brushed his shoulders and he was invariably wearing sandals regardless of the temperature. In the early years he had lived in a small dilapidated trailer on an acre of land near Naples Florida. Lion had personally delivered the bags of money to him for the first few years so he knew that the man must have enough paper money to fill a trailer by now. However, he was the type of person who lived in his own little world and never seemed that interested in the money. Lion believed that if they did not pay him at all, he probably would not have even noticed.

Being the scientific genius that he was, he could have landed any job he wanted right out of college but instead he dedicated himself to making the best drugs possible for the underbelly of society. It was not long before they recognized how important he would be to the organization and signed him to an exclusive contract. Boots and Lion had encouraged him to party with them through the years as a sort of reward for all his hard work on behalf of the organization but he seemed totally disconnected to other people. They were surprised to find that his motivation never seemed to flag; if he had a lab to work in, he appeared to be totally satisfied with life.

Mickey came into the security tower with a big smile for his old friends Lion and Boots. A few lines and a few grey hairs denoted the passage of time, but basically he had not shaken his boyish, unsophisticated demeanour.

"Hey Mickey, old buddy, I was so relieved to hear those pricks didn't get you when they blew up Harley a couple of months ago,"

Lion said grabbing his hand and wrapping his other arm around him in a hug.

"Yep, nearly went boom," Mickey nodded and grinned.

"Are we back on track, Mick?"

"Oh ya, we're making all orders. No problem. Business is good. Real good," he giggled.

"So what's new with you? Got a woman yet?" Lion pried.

"Nope. Just minding my own business basically." *Loquacious he's not,* Lion thought.

"Mickey, Boots and I want to give you a bonus. What can we do for you? Name it."

Mickey laughed, "Gee, I don't need anything, Lion. I just bought an RV."

"An RV?" Lion looked at him, and then over at Boots with amused disbelief.

"Mickey you must have enough money to buy Libya by now. Go wild man. Life is short," Lion laughed.

"Oh, I have a new designer drug I'm developing," Mickey's face lit up.

"I've been doing trials and I've had a few bad batches but I think I am getting closer."

"Had a few rats die, Mick?" Boots asked.

"No, I tested them on the street. Couldn't get the rats to smoke those little pipes," he snorted with laughter. "A few dead junkies . . . but that's not a problem. They can't trace it back to us. They can only test cadavers for known substances and since it's my own formula it doesn't show up in standard tests. Once I hone the formula it will take them a couple of years to identify the new drug and then they have to go through the process of making it an illegal substance."

"How far are you from the real thing?" Boots wondered.

"Dunno yet. Might have a few more dead junkies before that happens, but it's going to be real good. We'll have it on the market for a long time before they decipher this formula." He started to bob up and down and laugh hard. Lion threw his head back and laughed with him knowing that, as quirky as he was, he was always right.

"Maybe if we get you laid tonight, it will clear your mind and speed up the process, eh bud?" Boots joked.

"Maybe." Mickey bobbed up and down even more and continued to laugh.

Boots turned to Lion and they grabbed each other's hands.

"Fuckin' perfect move. We got them thinkin' twice now before they go after any one of us," Boots said smugly, referring to the hit on the Correctional Officer earlier.

"I know I like these bolder tactics. They're creating a more solid base of power. Should have done it a long time ago. I know . . . you wanted to and I resisted. You can kick my ass around the block before I do it myself," Lion said with annoyance.

"Doesn't matter, either way the Purple Flame patch is about to become a collector's item," Boots snarled.

"Yep, everything is coming together and just to put a cherry on it, I got a call from France and they say they have a close lead on Ace, thanks to Snake, that piece of shit. The trail is hot and as soon as she surfaces they'll have her."

"Fuckin'eh!" Boots remarked.

Dex walked into the room looking agitated, "Shit, Lion, I'm being bombarded by everyone with a microphone and some of the heavy hitters: Nancy Grace, O'Reilly, Piers Morgan. What do you want to do?" Lion looked up to the ceiling as he shook his head. "No! It won't do us any good to make comments about the trial. Just give them the same old bullshit—an inept police force looking for a scapegoat, yadda, yadda . . . and for Christ's sake find them a diversion. Find some goddamned orphans . . . organize a run for kids . . . I don't care, just any photo op of the Patch so that they have film to run when they start reporting on the trial. The less they see of my face the better right now." Dex nodded in agreement, "OK, Lion, I'll think of something."

"Hey, Randall! What do you know?" Lion yelled as the club's lawyer walked through the door. "What's going on with the trial?"

Randall stood and shook his head for a moment to quiet the mood in the room before he spoke.

"They moved it up. They're afraid we'll get to Snake, so they're giving you a speedy trial. It seems three hundred and fifty potential jurors had to be excused for a variety of reasons. Most of them were struck by a sudden case of the plague when they realized that the trial involved members of the Lucifer's Pride. We've been left with the twelve least imaginative people in all of New York City, and the trial is going ahead next week."

"Delay it," Lion said firmly.

"I think it is best to go ahead. Without a witness, James and Shane are off the hook for the O'Neil murder so there's no trail to you. They're not going to take the word of a child killer with a snake crawling up his neck that you forced him to kill someone. The longer we delay it, the greater chance they have of gathering evidence for their side and I just do not see any reason to put on the brakes. My case is not going to get any better."

"O.K. son you know best," Lion remarked calmly.

"Can you get that pretty little wife of yours to come out for the trial?" Randall asked. "Maybe shed a few tears with those big baby blues for the sake of the club?"

"If you think it will help," Lion responded.

"Absolutely. How could someone who's married to an innocent angel like that be guilty of conspiracy to murder?" Randall smiled.

"If it doesn't work, what am I looking at?" Lion asked. Randall held up his open palm. "You are looking at that for at least twenty-five years."

"A fuck it! Let's go party," Lion grinned. No one would have guessed that he wanted to get off the topic before the white heat of vengeance swallowed him up.

"Nick is bringing over some fresh meat from the club. Maybe Randall can make up a few legal release forms just in case Shane wants to get lucky," Boots joked.

"Most fun that bitch ever had!" Shane boasted as they walked down to the second level.

Chapter 37

*D*ex had informed Sheherezade that Lion had a late meeting and would be spending the night at the clubhouse so when she returned to the apartment she was surprised by the sudden appearance of Coral who had gone to a lot of effort to prepare a home cooked meal for her return. Coral attempted to coax her into a conversation over some food in the kitchen but Sheherezade declined and asked her to make up a tray for her to have alone in the bedroom. She wanted to think.

The events of the weekend had been overwhelming but hearing of Kate's death was beyond the pale. The officers had been absolutely despondent as she was processed through Admission and Discharge of the prison and she sensed that they believed Lucifer's Pride was responsible. But, why would Lion do such a thing? Could it be simple retaliation for her incarceration? She could not even begin to understand his motivation but she was beginning to lose the naiveté that allowed her to dismiss such incidents as mere coincidence. It was a lopsided world but it was becoming more predictable and she felt in her heart that, indeed, Lion had a hand in the murder.

The guilt felt like a sac of rocks tied around her neck and when she was finally alone she cried for that dear girl who did her best to help her only to have her life snuffed out for no reason at all, or at least no good reason. Most of the death and destruction associated with the Pride seemed to have a lot to do with Lion's pride and not much else. When an ordinary person is slighted in some way, they have a drink, or write in a diary. When Lion was slighted, people died. She was still hoping and praying that Kate's death was not related to her incarceration. She could not bear to live with the guilt of that reality. After a few hours of just lying on the bed and thinking about her jail experience she was struck by a thought—she had not seen Bugsy. She walked into the living room and called his name but he didn't come. She walked into the kitchen where Coral was tidying up.

"Coral, where's Bugsy?"

"Oh, Lion thought he would be more comfortable at the estate so he sent him back with security," Coral answered, doing her best to make the gesture sound innocuous.

Sheherezade bit her tongue and made her way back to the bedroom. *Coral the watcher.* She was beginning to feel resentment for Coral whose life seemed to be dedicated to the indefatigable defence and protection of Lion. The long tentacles of Lion's control were suffocating her and she felt as if she were ready to explode.

He had surmised her intentions to stay at the apartment in the city. *How dare he decide for me that I am moving back to the estate like I am some wayward child? He may rule Lucifer's Pride but he will never rule me!* Rage overtook her better judgement and she decided that her showdown with Lion could not wait. She grabbed her purse and was relieved to find the keys to her car in the small drawer of the antique table in the foyer. Without a word, she slipped out the front door, jumped into her car and took off toward the clubhouse.

She set the navigator for Dundas Street and headed to the outskirts of the city. The radio played an old song and for a moment driving anonymously through the unfamiliar streets gave her a sense of freedom she had not felt in some time. She was not someone's sister, someone's daughter, or someone's wife. *I'm going to have this feeling again,* she told herself. *I just have to get through this disaster and I will be alright. I have to be alright for Lila, for the baby, and for myself.*

As she approached the front gate she was surprised to discover that the clubhouse was a huge complex with a stone wall that ran around the entire perimeter. The Prospect at the front gate bent over, looked into the car at Sheherezade, and quickly waved her through after recognizing her as Lion's Old Lady from the picnic. Club policy did not allow Old Ladies to step foot onto clubhouse property but he was not about to stop the wife of the President. Butterflies hit her stomach as she walked up one side of the double staircase that led to the front door of the club. She knew she would not be welcome in this place.

The heavy door creaked open and she peered into the large empty bar room. From beyond she could hear music and the sounds of people having a drunken good time. She walked up to the door that opened into the next room and saw a bank of some fifteen bar stools and there, in the middle, was Lion sitting next to Boots, laughing. They seemed to be fixated on some action taking place on the other side of the room.

Sheherezade took a step to the right to see what everyone was staring at, and the other side of the room opened up to her field of vision. There were women and men draped all over the pool tables in every possible sexual position that an imagination could invent. Before she could close her eyes she saw Rick, Lion's business manager, having sexual intercourse with a girl she remembered from the picnic. A wave of dizziness struck her and she felt like she was falling over before she caught the bar chair to steady her balance. Moving quickly, she sprinted down the length of the room and exited out the big doors.

Sheherezade took off into the night not knowing where she was going or why. Tears flowed down her face as she cried for the little girl who had to face so much of that ugliness growing up and knew it all too well. How could she be going through this torment again when she had always done her best? Always been kind? Always tried to help the people around her that she loved? *I just wanted a nice life*, she thought. *How was my dream distorted into a nightmare of orgies, racism, murder, violence, and alienation from my niece?* She wiped her tears away with the back of her hand and pulled over to a wooded area just before the highway.

She stood under the pines and took a deep breath of the fresh air. It was a big sky full of stars and she realized that it was a new day falling on the earth. A day where she did not belong to Lion or anyone else. A falling star soared across the sky and disappeared into nothingness. *A wish* . . . she thought . . . *no* . . . *a promise* . . . *to live life my way.* Nothing was going to stop her.

Chapter 38

Sheherezade got up with the sun and enjoyed a swim and a Jacuzzi before the staff came up to the main house. She felt like a warrior preparing herself for battle; a battle that she could not afford to lose.

The past month had been a rollercoaster of emotions for her and she knew that if she dwelt on what she had with Lion just a month ago, she would be an emotional wreck. Why agonize over a fantasy of perfect love? She had to reconcile herself to the fact that he was not the man she believed him to be in the beginning. Maybe she should have waited to get to know him better but, on the other hand, he was the master con. If she had discovered his true nature at a later time would it have made any difference? The end of their relationship was inevitable and she had the rest of her life to sort out how much of the fiasco was her fault. Beating herself up about it was not going to fix anything. It was imperative that she cut her losses and extricate herself from the situation as soon as possible. The wild card was Lion. Would he accept her decision?

Lion awoke feeling rested after his night of partying with Boots and the boys. Shortly after Sheherezade saw him sitting at the bar, he had excused himself and went upstairs to relax in the executive suite. He wanted solitude to savour his impending victory over Ace. Now he wondered if today would be the day that he would get the call. The cat and mouse game had lasted twenty-eight years and he could not wait to taste victory. That helpless little boy that had been beaten and abused was being buried deeper and deeper in some dark, forgotten place. People would respect him and those who did not would pay. Closing his eyes, he imagined the peace that would descend upon his psyche when it was over.

Coral was waiting in the limousine when Lion left the clubhouse for the ride back to the estate. Coral had called Dex in a panic that morning when she realized that Sheherezade had not slept in her bed, fearing that Lion would be livid that she had not kept a closer eye on her. Dex determined that Sheherezade had driven the Maserati back to the estate the night before so he arranged for Coral to drive back with Lion, knowing Lion's intentions to meet with her and get their relationship back on track.

Coral had made a portable breakfast for herself and Lion for their trip back to the estate. Lion was sipping coffee, when he turned on the radio to catch up on the news of the past few days. After a few minutes into the news broadcast the announcer said that there had been a double murder at Indian Lake and the bodies had been discovered late Sunday night. The bodies had been identified as former World Class Wrestler and executive, Jerry Ridsdale, better known as Mustard, and his wife Sissy. Their bodies had been burned beyond recognition. The cause of death was still under investigation, although it appeared to be a professional hit.

Blood had been draining from Lion's face at the first mention of Indian Lake. His fingers entwined his hair and he screamed for the driver to stop the car. He was like a caged animal trying to get out of its cage. As soon as the driver pulled over on Route 12, Lion ran out about twenty feet from the car and then, realizing the futility of his actions, fell on his knees and covered his head with his arms crying out in pain. That pain, along with the knowledge that it could have been an act of retaliation from the Flames, was calling up the white anger—a white anger that immobilized him. It was twenty minutes or so before Coral had the nerve to go over and attempt to comfort him. She convinced him that it was best that they get him home as soon as possible, for his own safety, and she guided him back to the car. Lion's eyes turned dark and he stared into space for the remainder of the drive, tears falling in silence. When they reached the estate Lion told Coral to clear all of the staff out of the main house until further notice. He wanted privacy.

Sheherezade heard Lion coming into the house but did not move from her place in the library. He went up to the bedroom and saw a number of suitcases packed and ready by the doorway. Panic gripped him as he realized that she was planning to go somewhere.

"Sheherezade! Where are you?" Lion came bounding into the library; all blood had drained from his face.

"What are the suitcases for?"

"I'm leaving, Lion." Lion was momentarily shocked by the resolute look on her face.

"Leaving? Going where?"

"I'm leaving to live by myself. Well . . . with Lila and . . . I found out that I'm pregnant . . . so with the baby." Lion took a step back and looked away. He grit his teeth together and his heart started to beat with such force that he could barely breathe.

He turned toward her and his eyes were dark chasms of fire. "You are not going anywhere!" he screamed. Sheherezade was shocked by his intensity but knew she had to face her new reality.

"You can't tell me what I can and cannot do!" She screamed back at him as she stared into the blackness of his blue eyes.

"I can tell anyone what to do! I am Lion Terkel, president of Lucifer's Pride. Have you forgotten?" His calm quiet voice was more menacing than his screams but she had no choice but to persist in her quest for emancipation.

"Lion, there is no point in forcing me to stay with you when I don't love you anymore. I was naïve to think you were this businessman who put all his biker ways behind him. I have been enlightened in the last couple of weeks. I can't condone it and I don't want to live with it. It's too much like the life I was trying to escape when I married you."

"You are my wife and you have nothing to do with my business. The fact that I am president of a motorcycle club should not affect our relationship in any way."

Sheherezade's eyes closed and resignation registered on her delicate features.

"How can I pretend that you are not involved in all this criminal and immoral behaviour when I see you in the thick of it on a daily basis, Lion? That's just not realistic," Sheherezade stated emphatically.

"Look, Sheher, you have a family. I know you don't get along with them, but you have someone. For most of my life, I only had the club. It means a lot to me and I'm not going to give it up. But that has nothing to do with our relationship."

"I can't separate you from what you do. You are what you do and who you associate with. You said it, you are the leader of the Lucifer's Pride and you're also everything the members do, whether they are taking direct orders from you or not. As leader you give your tacit approval for all their actions. Save the speech about not being responsible for other people for the press. I'm holding you responsible and I don't want any part of it." Her eyes flashed with determination.

"God damn it! You live like a queen here," Lion yelled. "You have everything any woman could possibly want!"

He stood in front of her and stared down at her with such intensity that she considered running as fast as she could to get away from him but she knew that would not solve anything and she had to stand her ground.

"I want a life I'm not ashamed of!" Sheherezade screamed returning his gaze.

"That tear on your jacket is for killing, Jimmy. Isn't it? Why did he have to die, Lion? For your pride? Other men have a little bit too much to drink when their girlfriend runs off with another man but your answer to the problem was to kill him! That's what I cannot live with. Your character." Lion slapped her hard across the face, knocking her back until she caught her fall with the corner of the desk.

"You don't understand the entire situation," he screamed. "You can't judge me unless you live in my world." Lion was breathing heavy and the white heat of his anger was engulfing his being.

"Yes, your world. I have lived in your world for the past month. I've seen my best friend become a victim of racism. I've seen an innocent family murdered because they happened to see two of your thugs murder some poor innocent woman. I've seen how your organization treats woman—putting them in trailers to service the boys. I went to the clubhouse last night and saw you and Boots at the orgy, probably celebrating the murder of the Correctional Officer who, by the way, was a wonderful person. My sister has been treated like a cheap whore by your friend Boots! Drugs! Racism! Murder! Weak men who want power! I *have* lived in your world and I don't want to live in it anymore!" she screamed.

Lion slapped her again across the face again, knocking her to the ground. He leaned over and yelled at her face, "You are my wife and you're not going anywhere. Now shut up!" He closed his eyes and shook with anger. Sheherezade started to get up as she screamed back at him.

"I will not live with you and I would never, ever allow my baby to grow up surrounded by evil!" Lion moved toward her, fixed his black eyes on her, and kicked her shoulder knocking her flat onto the floor.

"There is not going to be any baby!" Lion yelled. He lifted his foot and brought it down with intense force squarely on her abdomen. Sheherezade screamed, rolled over on her side, and passed out. Lion stood shaking for a moment and then a wave of serenity seemed to pass over him as he stood staring down at his wife. He walked calmly to the phone at the desk, "Ya, get over here and bring the car. Sheherezade has fallen and I think she's losing her baby."

Within a few of minutes Dr. Lindsay came into the library followed by two teenage boys carrying a stretcher. When Sheherezade appeared to be regaining consciousness, Dr. Lindsay gave her a needle that relaxed her to the point that she was unaware of her surroundings. She was lifted onto the stretcher and placed in the ambulance car painted a discreet grey which transported her to the small private hospital attached to the doctor's house. Lion gave them enough time to reach their destination and then picked up the phone.

"Ya, doc, make sure that there is no baby."

Chapter 39

Brandi lay on the bed covered from head to toe in mud with the exception of her left ring finger which sported a giant diamond ring. Boots had sent the car early so that she could be pampered at the Thunder Spa and, as usual, a bottle of Champagne sat chilling in the silver cooler. Upon closer inspection she found the most spectacular diamond ring she had ever seen tied to the neck with a pink bow. She closed her eyes and came very close to saying a prayer. Could it be an engagement ring? She wondered why Boots had not presented it to her himself, but she refused to get too hung up on the details when she was so relieved that he had contacted her at all after defying his instructions at the Hog Day Picnic.

She breathed a sigh of relief. Everything seemed to be working out the way she had originally planned. Fancy was gone and she would be taking her rightful place as Old Lady of the Vice President of the Lucifer's Pride. She had thought about what Sherry had said about seeing Boots with another woman and decided that it just did not make sense. Who could believe that she was wandering around the beach by herself in some foreign country and just happened to run into Boots? There was a greater chance that she just could not keep Lion amused and hated the thought of anyone else being happy. She had to giggle to herself. *That bitch had that coming for a long time.*

She looked at herself without makeup in the direct light of the makeup mirror. Her skin looked pale and she had a few reddish open sores. She knew they were the result of using too much meth but she had been under stress and she had been spending too much time with James. *Now that Boots was back in the picture all that would change,* she told herself. She planned to cut back after tonight.

Brandi signed for all the treatments she received and left the salon looking like a movie star in a sexy white low-cut dress, her long blonde hair hanging in soft waves to her waist. As she stepped out of the car at the entrance of Boots' coop, she felt as if she were stepping out from under the dark cloud that had been following her around since she could remember.

Upstairs, Vivienne answered the door and Boots charged over to escort her into the living room.

"Wow, you look ravishing sweetie," Boots enthused as he perused the goods.

"Come here you," she whispered as she hugged him and wrapped one of her legs around him pulling him close to her.

"I love the ring. I have never, ever seen anything like it! Boots, I can't tell you what it means to me . . . ." Brandi started to kiss Boots and shove her tongue into his mouth. He stiffened as if he was trying to extricate himself from her grip.

"I'm glad you liked it," he whispered as if to change the subject. Brandi was confused by his reaction but shrugged it off and tried to maintain a light mood.

"Oh, I'm famished! We're eating late tonight," she said cheerfully. "It smells wonderful! What are we having?" Boots hesitated a bit and then responded.

"Sure, Vivienne could make you up a plate. I'll tell her . . . ." Brandi sat down and pulled a long white cigarette out of a gold case.

"Well, aren't you eating, honey?" Brandi was beginning to think something was amiss but she could not put her finger on it.

"No, I . . . uh, ate . . . ." Boots started to look uncomfortable and then bolted toward the hall to the bedrooms. Before he could reach the entrance a young blonde girl of about twenty came through the arched entrance into the living room dressed in a red see-through negligee. A look of apprehension came over Boots as he stopped in his tracks and took a deep breath.

"Oh, hi! I'm Kitten," the girl cooed as she walked toward Boots and wrapped a jewelled arm around his neck while staring down at Brandi.

"Kitten, I would like you to meet Brandi. She was the star at the Dancing House until recently and . . . ." Brandi stood up and stared at the girl as if she had seen a ghost; her nostrils flared as she glared back at Boots.

"You son of a bitch! I was supposed to be the entertainment tonight! You weren't even going to invite me to dinner!"

"Brandi! We were hoping you would join us for some fun. What's wrong with that? If you don't feel like it, that's OK, I'll have the car take you home." Brandi was shaking with anger, humiliation, and hurt.

"Don't feel like it?!!! Are you fucking crazy? You thought I would touch that little skank? No, you can have her all to yourself Boots." She lifted her cigarette into the air and dropped it onto the carpet before turning on her heel and leaving quickly through the door. Boots leaped over to the cigarette and picked it up, but not before it left a black mark on the expensive broadloom.

"Fuck!" Boots said under his breath.

Chapter 40

Sheherezade awoke to the gentle fluttering of the curtains in the pretty room and saw the sun dancing on the pond outside the open window. Tina was sitting beside the bed and smiled when she saw her stir.

"There's my girl. How are you feeling, dear?" Sheherezade's mind raced to her last memory and then she took a breath and started screaming.

"My baby! He tried to kill my baby! Oh my God, what kind of a monster would do such a thing?!" Tina suspected that she was a bit delirious but just as she turned to call for Dr. Lindsay, she saw him coming into the room with a big syringe.

"Take it easy, Sheherezade. You need your rest and I am going to give you something that will help you relax," he said as he popped the needle into the muscle in her arm.

"He's sent Dr. Hotel to keep me drugged so I can't talk!" she started to scream at Dr. Lindsay until her voice got lost in the haze of warm fuzz clouding her mind.

"She has been through a trauma . . . she's bound to be a little disoriented. We'll just keep her quiet for a while," Dr. Lindsay said in a reassuring voice. Sheherezade reached out with the little bit of strength she had left and gripped the doctor's wrist.

"My baby . . . ?" Her eyes reached his and he knew what she wanted to ask but could not find the strength.

"I am sorry, Sheherezade. You lost the baby. Just rest now and we'll take you home in a day or two." Tears welled up in her big violet-blue eyes as she stared into space. Tina could not tell if her silence meant she was thinking or if she was just spaced out from the drugs. She went over to the bed and gave her a hug.

"You are going to be fine, dear. You can have another child. Sometimes these things are just not meant to be and nature takes care of it." She believed what she said because she had no idea that Lion was the force of nature that had destroyed the child.

When Sheherezade awoke the next morning she wanted to scream from the rafters that Lion had killed her baby but she knew that would just get her another syringe in the arm, so she remained quiet and ate as much as she could in order to regain her strength. The events of the last two days had only given her a more steely resolve to leave Lion as soon as possible. *She would not give up hope. Lila needed her strength.*

On the second day of her stay, Sheherezade got up and walked around as much as she could. Her legs were still a bit shaky but the grogginess was going away. She noticed that her diamond ring had been removed from her finger and it was not with the rest of her things in the bedside table. Jackie appeared at the door with a large bouquet of pink roses which she placed in a vase on the window sill before giving Sheherezade a hug.

"How are you doin'? So sorry to hear about your accident, Sher. Lion told me that you lost the baby and I had to see you." As much as Sheherezade yearned for some company, she suspected that Jackie had been sent by Lion to give her clarity on the ways of their world.

"Thanks for dropping by. Sorry I don't feel like talking today."

"When Lion told me about the accident, I had a feeling there was more to it," Jackie said haltingly. Tears started to fall as the truth of the statement sent Sheherezade's mind reeling back to that horrible day.

"As soon as I'm strong enough I'm going to leave him," Sheherezade stated flatly.

"Whooah, Sheherezade! You do not leave a biker. They own you until they decide they don't want you. Now we are talking about Lion—head of Lucifer's Pride. This is a man that cannot lose face in front of the guys or the world, whatever . . . I wish I could help you with an alternative plan but there is no column B in a situation like this. It's their way or their way and to disobey Lion is not an option."

"Or what, I will end up like Acelyn, or worse, Jimmy?"

"In a word, yes." Jackie's eyes were fixed intently on her to convey the seriousness of her belief. Sheherezade put her head down on her knees and started to cry uncontrollably.

"My niece needs me. How am I supposed to raise her in an environment like this?" she asked rhetorically.

"I haven't met her. Is she at the house?" Jackie asked with a puzzled look on her face.

"No, she's away at school but I want to bring her back, to be with me."

Jackie's eyes filled with tears of understanding. "Lion was always so adamant that Ace didn't have children. Hell, he wouldn't even let her have a dog. He's possessive that way; he wants his woman all to himself. But, it was different with you, Sheher. He was willing to have a baby with you. You changed him." Jackie smiled at the positive note she had managed to introduce into the conversation. Sheherezade sat quietly for a moment as she related this new information to her situation. As she had begun to suspect, Lila had been right. Lion had erased her from their life while making it appear as if he were doing her a favour. True to form, even poor Bugsy had been shipped off to another home. Anger overrode her very rational fears until she felt she would explode.

"I didn't change him—he killed my baby!" Sheherezade blurted out bitterly.

"Oh no," Jackie reached out and took Sheherezade's hand. A tear of sympathy ran down her cheek but she had no solution and no suggestions.

"Now is not the time to come up against Lion. The guys were saying how much tension he is under with the trial next week and then there's the memorial which is being held off until after the trial. When Lion is pushed into a corner he comes out fighting. Give him some time . . . I'm sure things will get better."

"Memorial? Whose memorial?" Sheherezade asked.

"Mustard and Sissy were murdered up at Indian Lake. Retaliation by the Flames. Lion and everyone else heard about it over the radio the day of your accident. Of course, he was like a brother to Lion and Boots. He was with them from the very beginning of the club and he saved their lives a few times. It was a big blow. Things are bound to get worse, now."

"Murder, death, vengeance. It will never end!" Sheherezade wailed. "They feed off it like fire feeds off oxygen. If they didn't enjoy it, they would find another lifestyle. I just know that I can't live with it and I won't."

"I hear you, but for God's sake, let things settle down. You are going to have to be at Lion's trial next week and then maybe, in time, things will change." Jackie tried to sound optimistic but deep down she knew the true hopelessness of the situation.

Optimism crept into Sheherezade's heart. *Yes! The trial. Maybe with a little luck they will put him away for a long, long time.*

Chapter 41

Brandi felt a little out of her element as she passed the gold letters on the polished black skyscraper that spelled out Thunder Corporation. As determined as she was to get what she thought she deserved, she could not help but feel the power of this man she was up against. By the time she found the reception desk outside of his office, the butterflies were so overwhelming that she wondered if she had the guts to go through with her plan.

"I am here to see Mr. Falcone."

When the secretary announced the arrival of Miss Raleigh, Boots was not completely surprised. He was half expecting a showdown sometime today and, in a way, he was relishing the confrontation. The end always came in a predictable sequence of events and when he set them straight he always had a renewed sense of freedom and power. It was part of the game.

A new relationship had its charm. He loved to bedazzle women. He loved the seduction and the experience of making love to an unfamiliar body. As soon as routine set in he became bored. The true finale, however, hailed its arrival when a woman had expectations of him. Brandi had stepped over that line last night. She had expected to be treated as if she were his girlfriend, to control who he could and could not see, and to hold him responsible for making her feel angry at his behaviour. Most men buckled at this juncture in a relationship. They gave in to the woman's demands in order to keep the peace. Boots did not have to buckle. Brandi was just one of millions of women, and he could have any one of them. He loved the surprised look on a woman's face when she realized that she had no power over him and all of her expectations, dreams, and hopes, along with her sense of entitlement to any part of his life, disappeared before her like a ring of smoke. His entire life had been dedicated to making that delicious moment possible.

His mind brushed upon images of Brandi up on that stage and in his bed. A yearning hit his chest that he was not prepared to feel. He was uncomfortable with feelings that threatened his self control. To be captivated by desire meant weakness. Desire never got in the way of tossing a woman aside like yesterday's bread before, and he was not about to succumb to it now. Those legs. That hair. Those green eyes that looked at him with such yearning. When he felt love, he felt hate and he was beginning to hate Brandi.

"Brandi, how are you doing?" Brandi walked up to the desk and stood before him.

"Not too well after last night, Boots," she said sadly. The sunlight from the wall of windows behind him caught her beauty and he fought the urge to take her in his arms.

"Yeah, you shouldn't have run off like that . . . ."

"I thought you loved me . . . you told me that you loved me." Brandi said softly, holding his gaze.

"You're a big girl Brandi. You know men say a lot of things . . ." Boots responded casually.

"I thought you were the kind of man who didn't have to lie . . . the kind of man who was so powerful he could always state his truth. I thought that if you didn't want me you would just tell me instead of pretending to love me." Boots did not like to intellectualize and he was beginning to feel like he was snared in a trap.

"Brandi, I do what I want, OK? If I want to call you, I call you. But I'd be lying if I said you were the only woman in my life."

The stark words stung Brandi even though it was a formula she could have easily surmised on her own.

"I know you're a free spirit Boots. I'm the same way . . . but I thought we had something special. I thought that ring meant something. Was I wrong?" Brandi persisted. Boots recalled the treasure-trove of jewellery he had distributed from Fancy's collection. *Maybe that was a mistake but what else was he supposed to do with all of those God damned diamonds?*

"I don't know what you're getting at Brandi. I haven't said that I don't want to see you anymore. I invited you over just last night . . . ."

"Well, I was hoping that now that Fancy is no longer here, you would make me your Ole Lady and give me special status in your life. I'm not saying I would have to know what you are doing all the time, or who you are with, but it would be nice if we could live together, wouldn't it?"

"Well, Brandi, I don't want to live with anyone." An edge entered Boots' voice.

"OK, then could I have the title of your Ole Lady and the respect that goes with it? It would mean a lot to me," Brandi pleaded.

"I'm not really looking for an Ole Lady, either . . . ."

"Boots, people are laughing behind my back because they see you with that little tramp, Kitten, and it's humiliating. If you gave me the respect of being your Ole Lady you could do what you want and . . . ."

"I can do what I want now," he stated coldly. Boots fixed his eyes on Brandi's face, holding his breath for his moment of victory.

The memory of Kitten in her red negligee flashed through Brandi's mind and she knew she would not and could not tolerate any more humiliation. She perched herself on the desk and crossed her legs as a small smirk grazed her lips.

"Well, no . . . you can't," Brandi said slowly and softly.

"What do you mean, I can't?" Boots asked as fury darkened his eyes and his voice lowered.

"I mean that I know where the body is buried, Boots. Fancy took me into her confidence before she died and so, you see, you're going to have to treat me the same way you treated Fancy. The life style. The title. The respect." Brandi returned Boots glare with cocky ferocity and took satisfaction in having the upper hand for the first time since the day they met. Boots slowly leaned back in his big leather chair as a tiny bead of sweat popped up on his temple.

"Are you confessing to murder, Brandi?"

"No . . . are you?" In a split second, Boots realized she held all the cards and quickly conceded.

"OK, Brandi. Take Fancy's apartment. Her things are still in it. Keep them or throw them out, whatever you like. I'll make the same deal with you that I made with Fancy. You have the title of my Ole Lady and I have a bit of freedom. Now get out of here. I have work to do." Brandi was somewhat shocked at how quickly Boots had accepted the new arrangement. She gave him a hug and a peck on the cheek and made a hasty exit before he had a chance to reconsider.

Boot's pupils narrowed to two small pinpoints and the engorged vein on his forehead marked his growing vexation as he stared at the closing door. Fancy's death had been such a blessing, a stroke of luck, and now here he was again, dancing to the same tune. That taste of freedom had been so sweet and now it was being snatched away by another cunning bitch. Underestimating Brandi had been his mistake. He would not make that mistake again. He pressed the intercom on his desk.

"Get Mickey for me."

Chapter 42

Coral approached Sheherezade in the evening and asked her if she could help her get any clothing ready for the trial the next day. It was not hard for Sheherezade to figure out that it was Lion's way of telling her that she was expected to give a command performance in court daily. As much as she felt like resting for a couple more days after her ordeal, she got ready and put a bit more blush on than usual to try to look healthy. Rebellion would not help her cause; she had to bide her time. Riding in the limousine all the way to New York without one word of exchange between her and Lion had been very intense and she was relieved to be sitting beside Dex in the courtroom where the trial would be held. A gallery of reporters, paparazzi, and spectators took their turns staring at Sheherezade as she sat with her eyes fixed on the judge's bench waiting for things to get under way.

Sheherezade became more and more ashamed as she listened to the prosecution set out the many offences for which Lion was being accused. If only she had been enlightened in this way before she married Lion the entire fiasco of her marriage would never have occurred. At the end of the court day they left the courtroom to a barrage of flashbulbs on the way to the limousine and drove back to the New York apartment. Sheherezade had her dinner alone in the bedroom and then collapsed exhausted and dejected from the day's humiliation.

Another designer suit meant it was another day playing the loyal wife of an innocent man. Sheherezade felt more and more hopeful as the prosecution laid out an impressive case that told the story of a loan sharking operation that was effective because of the outrageous interest charged for borrowed money and because of the force that would be used, if necessary, to collect the loans. Snake was brought in and talked for the best part of a day about the biker operation and, most importantly, the strong leadership of her biker husband. He testified that Lion had directly ordered the death of Elise O'Neil to serve as a warning for her brother to pay the loan he took out to support his compulsive gambling. He also told the story of how Lion put a bounty on the head of each Purple Flame member and ordered their deaths as retribution for blowing up their drug warehouse and for providing sanctuary for his ex-girlfriend, Acelyn Azhar.

Snake confessed that he had murdered at least two of the three Flames that were killed on that same fateful night when the five year old boy had been caught in the crossfire.

The prosecution continually referred to the witness who had been found murdered in her home. There were no fingers pointed directly at members of the Lucifer's Pride but the implication was clear. Sheherezade was thrilled with every fact that the prosecution presented that showed the depraved morality of the bike gang and, in particular, her husband. By the end of the week the faint dream of Lion being put away for a long time had blossomed into a full fledged hope as it seemed clear that the prosecution had a very good case against him.

On Monday the defence started their case. *Damn Lion and all of his money*. His lawyer was the best brain money could buy and he was punching holes in many of the facts that sounded iron-clad when they were presented by the prosecution. Each day Sheherezade ate her dinner alone in her room and remained silent in the limousine ride to the court house and back again in the evening.

By the end of the day on Thursday the prosecution had presented their rebuttal and she wondered how she would ever wait for the decision to come in. Due to safety concerns and also the possibility of jury tampering, the jury would stay sequestered until they rendered their decision. Sheherezade held her breath knowing that winning her freedom depended on Lion losing his.

Chapter 43

Early Monday morning Brandi went over to the luxury condominium building where she would begin to live the life she had always believed she deserved. She and James had been celebrating her victory all weekend so Brandi had not slept the night before in anticipation of getting the key and moving into her new home. All the meth they had put back over the weekend was making her feel edgy and she told herself that she would cut back now that she had finally achieved her dream.

As she stepped into the large foyer she realized that she had absolutely no memory of being in the apartment before. Her recollection of many things was becoming sketchy from the drug abuse but this day she decided it was because she had blocked out the gory scene of Fancy's demise. Another person might have been haunted by the location where they committed past evil deeds but Brandi felt only the pride of victory as she stepped into her new penthouse in the heart of Manhattan.

A double set of French doors opened into a grand living room with large windows on the opposite side of the room which framed a panoramic view of the New York skyline. Colourful original oil paintings decorated every wall and the furniture and wall coverings reflected their colour scheme. There were large sofas in the centre of the room with a grand fire place on one wall. The modern eclectic style was uncluttered and immaculate.

Brandi walked through the living room and discovered a formal dining room that also featured a floor to ceiling view of the city. On the other side of the dining room was a kitchen that was big enough to accommodate a restaurant. Peeking into the cupboards she found that they were completely stocked with dry goods. Only the perishables from the enormous fridge had been cleaned out; frozen food still remained in the freezer section. She walked out into the hallway off the kitchen and followed it to the first room on the right which was another large comfortable sitting room with a giant screen TV on one side and a window that opened to the kitchen on one end. The room had a built in bookcase that covered the entire wall. There were nooks for interesting items Fancy had collected from travel and other knickknacks she had collected over the course of her life. Knowing that she did not own one memento from her own life, Brandi felt a touch of jealousy for the life Fancy had led until she told herself that it was now hers. All hers. At the far end of the apartment was an exercise room that was obviously Fancy's pride and joy. One wall was covered entirely in windows and the other walls were mirrored. She had the best equipment money could buy in every assortment invented. Brandi giggled at her obvious obsession.

She went across the hall and realized that this was the room where it had happened that day. To one side was the enormous master bathroom with a giant tub that looked out over the city and right beside it was the dressing room which was easily the size of a large bedroom in itself. Brandi was overwhelmed by the clothing that covered every bit of closet space and shelves. Hundreds of shoes were arranged in an organized colour scheme behind one mirrored door. She immediately tried a pair on to discover they were her size. She pushed back another mirrored door and found fur and leather coats in every variety under the sun. Beside the vanity, she found a bank of drawers filled with designer jewellery in every colour and for every occasion, along with a large quantity of makeup in every shade and description. There was a beautiful pink chaise longue in the middle of the room. She threw herself onto it, pulled up the soft blanket that was folded neatly at one end, and gazed out at the clouds floating by. *I did it,* she thought. *I have it all.*

At that moment she heard the door bell ring and she jumped up to see who it could be. A small, women with curly salt and pepper hair and an arm full of groceries introduced herself as Erma. She informed Brandi that she worked from Monday to Friday and had been asked to stay on as housekeeper by Boots. Brandi immediately asked Erma to prepare her breakfast and serve it to her in the bedroom.

When Erma left to prepare her meal, Brandi searched several drawers until she found what she was looking for: a lace negligee that was made of silk as light as a feather. Peeling back the soft beige cotton sheets, she hopped into the king size bed that was fit for a princess. The remote control closed the curtains and produced a giant television that rose out of the wooden box at the end of the bed. Brandi could not remember the last time she ate but it seemed like a long time ago.

Soon the smell of fresh coffee permeated the apartment and Erma arrived with an enormous breakfast of yogurt, sausages, eggs, and coffee which she placed on the serving unit beside the bed. Erma presented Brandi with an envelope sent from Mr. Falcone that had been left with the security downstairs. As soon as she left, Brandi ripped open the seal and found a large pile of thousand dollar bills wrapped in a note. It read:

Dear Brandi,

Here's a few bucks to help you run the household. Let me know if you need anything for the apartment. See you soon, sweetie.

Boots

Closing her eyes she told herself she would always cherish this moment of triumph. Her plan had worked just as she thought it would. She did a hit of valium on one of the few good veins she had left and peace fell on the beautiful penthouse in the city that never sleeps.

Chapter 44

Shane made full Patch faster than any other Prospect in the history of the Lucifer's Pride franchise. There had been a huge turn out for the ceremony at the last church meeting when he was bestowed the honour by none other than Boots himself, who had become his mentor and closest friend. His forte was in delegating the distribution and expansion of his territory to his trusted associates from the inside and then focusing his time and energy on networking and the promotion of Shane Rawlings.

In the daytime Shane and Boots wore business suits as Boots gave Shane the layout of the land in his world of business. In the evenings they could be seen in leather pants and a patch. Boots loved to get out into the streets with Shane; it was like reliving the old days of working the streets and kicking ass. He found exhilaration in seeing the fear in the faces of the men and women working the streets when the patch crossed their paths.

After an evening of taking care of business Boots and Shane dropped into a small local bar in Shane's territory and, over a couple of beers, Boots put his plan in motion.

"Does Jackie ever mention Fancy?" Boots asked.

"Ya, she's convinced that Brandi did her. She says that it had to be someone who hated Fancy because she was sliced up so much and I think she's right. The wounds were to the face and breasts. Jealousy. You know what they're like. Of course, Jackie has always said it was Brandi. She had the most to gain by her death. As soon as she showed up at the picnic, Jackie knew something was wrong. Everyone who knew Fancy knew the fur would be flying if she had been there—including Brandi."

"Ya, even I was sweating that day thinking Fancy was going to be after my ass when Brandi swooped into the Old Ladies' tent dressed like a whore going to the fair. She must have known she was already dead. I think Jackie is right. Brandi did it." Boots paused and looked into space as if this were the first time that the idea had occurred to him.

"I can't let it go. Fancy was my official Ole Lady. I'm going to have to deal with it or everyone is going to think I'm getting soft." Shane nodded in agreement and took another chug of beer.

"Want me to arrange it?" Shane asked nonchalantly.

"Na, I have a better idea. I hear Brandi has a little meth habit. Find out where she gets her dope."

"That's easy . . . Popeye supplies her," Shane said casually.

"Popeye? You mean . . . they have a thing going?" Boot's face registered shock. The idea of Brandi keeping another man on the side had never occurred to him.

"Oh, ya. Have for some time." Boots lips pursed and he started to nod his head gently up and down as this tidbit of information sunk in.

"How long?"

"He's had a hard on from the first night he met her at the clubhouse—same night you met her. As far as I know it just carried on from there," Shane said. "Popeye has it bad for her but whether or not it is mutual . . . I don't know." Boots sat still for a moment to absorb this new information. Finding out that she had a steady boyfriend, who was also a Full Patch, made him choke with anger. And jealousy. He felt he had been played. The revelation that he had not been her whole world did not sit well. On top of everything else, it occurred to him that Popeye could have been privy to the information that Brandi was using to blackmail him.

In the next instant he put his arms under the table and stood up, tossing it eight feet across the room. Grabbing his helmet, he made a speedy exit out of the bar.

All week Brandi and James had lounged around the condo indulging in an unparalleled binge of top grade Pride meth. Brandi was holding a secret vigil for the phone call from Boots that never came, and the drugs helped to make the plain reality of his disinterest recede into a hazy mixture of rationalization and hope. Everyday they would turn on the news to follow Lion's trial in order to see if they could spot Sherry on TV but little else brought them out of their fuzzy euphoria. After all the evidence was presented, most of the talking heads were speculating that Lion would be convicted and Brandi was becoming a bit testy at the thought of Sherry having it all while Lion sat in jail.

"That bitch, Sherry, would love that wouldn't she? Big house, all that money, and poor Lion, who only earned it all, cooling his heels in jail for a quarter of a century."

"Yep, could happen babe. Better behave herself though. Lion will be keeping an eye on her."

"Oh fuck, she's so cold and stuck up I'm surprised any man was ever good enough in the first place."

"Wow, she's nothing like you or your mother is she?" James chuckled. That comment hit a nerve with Brandi and she changed the subject.

"Did you have a tough childhood James?"

"Not really, my parents were both school teachers . . . we went on a lot of vacations. It was OK. But I got out of there as soon as possible. I couldn't handle all the rules."

"Did you have brothers and sisters?"

"After they got me they had a daughter of their own, but I don't have any contact with her. She's about five years younger than me."

"You were adopted?"

"Yep."

"Do you know anything about your real parents?"

"Oh yeah, it was an open adoption. Part of the agreement my adoptive parents made was that my real mother's family could have contact with me. They insisted on it but then they never came to see me."

"Did you know anything about your real parents?"

"Oh ya, they said my mother was a drug addict, that's why she gave me up. And my father was murdered in Chino. Like father like son, I guess." Brandi looked over at James and wondered at the coincidence of what she had just heard.

"My dad was murdered in Chino too—in 1989."

"Ya that would be the same year my father was murdered."

"What was his name?" Brandi asked.

"William Anderson," James responded.

"That was my father's name!" Brandi said with a note of irritation. "No, there is no way. I would have known if my mother had another kid . . ." Her voice trailed off and she looked at James as if she were seeing him for the first time. *Those eyes. Those icy blue eyes.* A look of concern passed over James face as he slumped back into the big chair. The room was completely silent for about five minutes until James said, "Call your mother."

Brandi picked up the phone and dialled her mother's new number. She could hear the sounds of a party in the background as her mother's cheerful voice came over the line.

"Hello?"

"Hi, mum. You busy?"

"Just having a few drinks Brandi. What's going on?"

"Boots gave me a big penthouse with a housekeeper and the whole works, you have to come and see it."

The light cheerful lilt dissolved from her mother's voice as she replied, "Yep. Did you call for something?" Brandi could tell that her mother was far more than drunk and was having a difficult time focusing on the conversation. She began laughing and Brandi was afraid she would hang up.

"Ya, mum, a crazy question. Did you and daddy have a son before you had me?" Regina laughed and talked to someone in the background.

"Oh, Freddy is getting a little randy here, I better go . . . ."

"Mum wait! Did you and daddy have a son before you had me? Tell me!"

"Didn't I tell you? Ya, a boy. Had my looks. When Billy was murdered I wished I had kept his son."

"Why didn't you go see him? You had an open adoption didn't you?" Brandi asked coldly.

"Oh, I don't know. That was a long time ago. I have to go . . . ."

"Wait. What was his birthday, do you remember?"

"I forget. Oh, wait. I had him on your grandmother's birthday . . . Uh . . . July 17, 1989."

"OK, Bye." Brandi turned to James who was listening with concern as she spoke to her mother.

"When is your birthday, James?"

"July, 17th . . . ."

James could tell by the horror in Brandi's eyes that the unfathomable coincidence was true. Regina was his mother and Brandi was his full sister. Regina's self-absorbed, cold heart had created a twisted abomination of human interaction that was a violation of natural law beyond repair.

Brandi crumbled onto the floor next to the sofa and began to weep. She was filled with anger that she had pushed down all of her life. She knew clearly, for the first time, that her anger was for the one person she had always excused, denied, and defended, as the source: her mother. Regina whom she loved, Regina, the only parent she had ever known, was the source of pain. She acknowledged that she was a cold, heartless monster who was incapable of loving another human being. There were no thoughts of giving up James so that he could have a better life; he was simply excess baggage that she had carelessly burdened her mother with at a time when she wanted to find adventure by going out west with her equally callous boyfriend, Billy. Regina had no more feeling for that little boy than she did for her girls. They had been used or abused according to her needs and then discarded whenever she could bilk some attention out of another source.

James sat for a moment letting the enormity of the situation sink in and then he sat next to Brandi who was still sobbing uncontrollably. After a few moments she seemed to notice his presence and let out a deep wail, throwing her arms around him, and pulling him close. There they remained for a long time holding each other gently, not as lovers but, for the first time, as brother and sister.

Sheherezade was reading in her room when she heard the phone ring. There was a bit of commotion out in the living room and Coral knocked on her door.

"They have reached a verdict. Can I help you get ready, dear?"

"No, thanks, I'll be ready in ten minutes." Sheherezade was used to interpreting Lion's commands which were relayed through Coral in this more euphemistic format. Sheherezade's stomach began churning with anticipation. A verdict coming in this quickly was usually a good sign for the prosecution. *Dare she hope?* Her heart started to pound in her chest. There was a good possibility she could be free in just a matter of an hour or so. The closing arguments had ended at approximately two o'clock in the afternoon and the venerable Judge Yagers addressed the jury before they started their deliberations. No one, however, dreamed that they would reach a verdict the same day that the trial ended. Lion had been agitated all week, but now, on their ride into the city, he seemed to be inordinately calm. Perhaps it was the sign of the warrior going into battle, she surmised.

Sheherezade watched closely as the lawyers for the prosecution took their seats at the front of the courtroom. She closed her eyes and said a prayer when she saw the smiles of hope on their faces. The jury was coming back into the jury box and for the first time she let her eyes drift to the expressions on their faces. They were all doing their best not to reveal any emotion as they took their seats. The last juror was a small blonde woman in her early twenties dressed conservatively in a dark suit. As she entered the room, Sheherezade was surprised to see her scan the courtroom until she had a fix on her; the woman pinned her with her gaze and gave Sheherezade a big smile.

Sheherezade closed her eyes and dropped her head to think. She knew this was a signal and she had to figure out what it meant. *It would tell her if she was a free woman.* Her mind was racing and she could not sort out the thoughts that would help her interpret the sign. She raised her eyes and looked over at the blonde juror who was still looking at her and smiling as someone was reading the verdict: not guilty.

A black cloud descended on her mind as people around her were reacting to those two small words. The walk to the car was a blur. Dex took her by the arm and rushed her past the throng of reporters who screamed questions at her. They locked the door and waited for twenty minutes as Lion faced the press condemning a police force that tried to pin any and every unsolved crime on their favourite scapegoat, the Lucifer's Pride Motorcycle Club.

Sheherezade went directly to her room, got into the bed and pulled the covers up over her head. All of her hope was lost. Lion had been her saviour and now he had become her destroyer. *How many years would it take before she could leave Lion's world without hurting his pride?* The decision to be with him was made with so much hope and trust. What she once believed to be the road to paradise had turned out to be the highway to hell.

Chapter 45

At noon the next day the ringing of a cell phone broke the silence of the bedroom where James and Brandi lay sleeping. It had been a long night of quiet thought and the unsettled mood remained as Brandi watched James reach for the phone.

"No, I have been sort of busy this week."

"Get the fuck out. No I didn't hear."

"Son of a bitch!"

"Oh, ya. Where it is and what time do I have to be there?"

"OK. Yep."

"No! I wasn't watching the TV last night."

"Right on. OK, I'll watch out for you."

"OK bro. Couple of hours."

"What was that about?" Brandi asked.

"We've been out of the loop . . . Mustard and his wife were murdered at Indian Lake and the memorial is today. Purple Flames. I have to be part of the honour guard," James replied.

"Oh James! I really didn't want to be alone today!"

"I know babe but you know I have no choice."

"Ya, I know."

"Oh ya, some news you might enjoy. Lion was found Not Guilty."

"No shit! Good for him. He deserves to have a life. Right on!"

"He's giving out bonuses just for the hell of it. 50 G's."

Brandi attempted to smile but her cheeks felt too heavy.

"Come back as soon as it's over OK?"

"You know it babe," James winked.

Brandi picked up the intercom phone and told Erma to bring them some food as she lay back on the bed, lit a cigarette, and sank into deep contemplation while James got ready for the memorial.

Lion insisted that Mustard's memorial reflect the revered position he held in the club and he assigned Dex to make the arrangements for a service that would be a grand affair never to be forgotten by the Pride or the Flames. It would be designed to strike fear in the hearts of Mustard's assassins; the honour guard would be a show of the force that would have to be reckoned with in the future onslaught of retaliation.

Sheherezade had received her instruction from Lion via Coral the evening before in the usual manner. She would be attending the memorial for Mustard and Sissy the next day with Lion. As she put on the light navy suit she could not help but feel like she was watching herself go through the motions of everyday life from a distance. *Maybe that comes from not feeling you are in control of your own life,* she surmised. She put on the matching navy hat and pulled down the veil that covered the hollow expression in her violet-blue eyes. *Maybe in between the hours and days that I have to endure with Lion I will have moments of peace,* she thought. She saw herself swimming with Lila in the lake and playing games with her in front of the fire. *Even if I can't have the life I want,* she thought, *maybe I can eventually make a good life for Lila.* A knock at her bedroom door broke her mood and she braced herself for the afternoon charade of loving biker wife.

The service was being held in a large funeral home in downtown Manhattan. The overpowering smell of sickeningly sweet flowers made her queasy as she took her place in the front row beside Lion and Boots. She was mystified by Brandi's absence. Wasn't this just the perfect occasion for her to flaunt her new status as Boot's Old Lady? She could not help but think that perhaps something had gone seriously wrong with Brandi's plan or she would be standing here today next to Boots. She thought back to the evening she saw Boots romping with another woman by his pool in Tunisia and felt a pang of pity for Brandi and her hopes and dreams that were being crushed by this callous, self-absorbed man.

When the service ended, Lion, Boots, and many friends and associates of Mustard gathered in the anteroom where lunch was being served. Sheherezade excused herself to go to the washroom and as she walked down the hall she realized that there were no bodyguards following her. To her left, she could look down another hall and see a door that led directly to the street. A thought crossed her mind as she entered the washroom. *What if she just left? If Ace got away, why couldn't she? Money,* she thought. *I need money.* She washed her hands and started down the hall. There was no one in sight. When she came to the door to the outside her heart started to pound. She looked back to see if anyone was watching and then stepped outside into the bright sunlight. Looking around she started to run toward the busiest side of the street in search of a Chase Manhattan bank. Her heart was pounding hard as she glanced back again to see if anyone was following her. Before long she slipped into the parade of bodies that walked the street on a busy Friday afternoon. Just two blocks up, she saw the bank and sprinted up to join a queue for a teller. *No,* she thought, *I can get faster service.* She walked up to a customer service representative on the side and requested privacy because she planned to withdraw a substantial amount of money. The teller asked her name and then asked Sheherezade to follow her to a small room where someone would be right in to help her. In a couple minutes a small man with rimless glasses and a pale face came in and asked how he could help her.

"I would like to take my money out of the bank. I am going to be leaving the country." She tried to stay calm and not show the fear that was making her heart pound and her hands shake. She shoved the bank book toward him and his eyes widened as he saw the amount listed at the top of the page. He quickly turned to the computer and punched up the account number and studied the screen.

"I am sorry, Mrs. Terkel. The money was withdrawn from this account and closed eleven days ago by your husband. Perhaps he invested it for you and just forgot to tell you." Sheherezade smiled and tried to speak but she felt like she would choke.

"Maybe," she offered. "Thank you, sir," she whispered.

She saw herself stand up and leave the bank. She began walking down the street in a somnambulistic trance until her mind came back to her. There was no escaping. Without money, she was trapped. Panic set in and she started to make her way back to the funeral home. *No one had to know she had tried to get away.* Her feet started to pound the sidewalk until she reached the side door and entered the building windblown and breathless. A body guard she recognized from the estate was walking quickly toward the door until he looked up, saw her and slowed down. She realized he had probably been sent to find her so she smiled broadly and patted her hair.

"Wow, it is windy out there. That fresh air was nice." She walked briskly past him and entered the room where the wake continued. Pouring herself a coffee, she did her best to compose herself. When she noticed Jackie in the crowd, she walked over calmly to say hello and chat about recent events.

After about a half an hour people were beginning to leave the funeral home to go to their cars for the long procession out of the city to the graveyard where Mustard and Sissy had been buried. Lion and Sheherezade were in one of ten or fifteen black stretch limousines at the front of a procession of hundreds and hundreds of motorcycles. Every patch member had a crew of their own associates, many of whom also rode bikes, and on this windy, sunny day, many of them turned out to pay their respects to their righteous brother, Mustard, the honoured Sergeant-at-Arms of Lucifer's Pride for over thirty years.

Once everyone arrived at the graveyard the patch members stood shoulder to shoulder in circles around the lovely green spot beneath the giant maple tree where Mustard and Sissy had been laid to rest. Another grave lay open waiting as the sound of a distant engine broke the quietude. Swami rode to the site on Mustard's legendary Harley where a crane was waiting to lower the bike along with a sterling silver box containing his patch, into the grave beside them. Many of his brother's were seen wiping a wayward tear. Lion was stoic but when Sheherezade caught sight of his eyes through her veil a cold chill went up her neck . . . and she knew. *There would be hell to pay for this.* Everyone would just have to hold their breath to see where and when the axe would fall.

When the service ended Sheherezade turned and walked directly back to the limousine while some of the guys stood around talking. Shane came up behind James and they grabbed hands while giving each other a short hug.

"Too fuckin' bad man. He was as solid as they come."

James nodded, "Ya, those fuckers are going to pay for this one."

"Right fuckin'on," Shane said, gently shaking his head. "Hey, I have your money. Come on over to my bike and I'll give it to you." The pair walked over to Shane's motorcycle and he reached into his side saddle.

"Here, fifty big ones for you from Lion—just for a party. Oh, I have something for you from Boots too. This is something new

Mickey cooked up and it's supposed to be dynamite, so make sure you have a night off when you get into this bit of magic," Shane grinned. James eyes lit up as he looked at the small package of white powder.

"Fuckin' eh. I'll give it a whirl." James smiled as he gave Shane a pat on the back and left him to return to Brandi.

"We're partyin' tonight babe. Lion's throwing a wingding at the clubhouse. Fifty thousand dollar bonuses for everyone to celebrate his victory," Shane grinned as he took Jackie in his arms.

"Nice . . . of course I wish I had the bonus that is being dropped into Judge Yager's Swiss bank account," Jackie giggled.

"Maybe things will settle down a bit now."

"I've known him for thirty years, I can guarantee you that Lion is just getting started," Jackie sighed.

"Confidential information, babe—I thought you might be interested. Boots has decided that Brandi is going down for murdering Fancy. Says he can't leave unfinished business. It would make him look like he's getting soft."

"When?"

"Soon."

"Na, I'm not buying it," Jackie said shaking her head. "Only you and I suspected Brandi because we saw how Fancy's body was sliced up. And besides, Boots didn't give a fuck about Fancy. I'm sure he's glad to have her out of the way. There must be another reason . . . ." Shane knew that years of living among the club members had refined Jackie's instincts and her insights into their motivation were impeccable.

"Maybe, he just has one too many women," Shane opined.

"Be closer to the truth, if you ask me," Jackie laughed as she took another swig of beer.

"Well, at least if Brandi did kill Fancy so that she could have Boots, her scheme didn't work. Fancy will be avenged and that should give you some satisfaction," Shane deduced.

"Well, Fancy and I became friends over the years but we didn't start out that way. Sometimes I think about the way she died and I have to wonder if it wasn't her due because of what she did years ago." Shane was intrigued by Jackie's sentimental mood.

"What the hell did she do?" he asked.

"She gave up Jimmy, to Lion."

"The leader of the Purple Flames that ran off with Lion's Ole Lady, right?"

"Ya. You had to know Fancy. When she was young, she was a looker but that wasn't enough for her. Every guy had to want her or she wasn't happy. Boots didn't have a clue what was going on around him at the time, and as far as I know he never really found out. Fuck, he met his match with Fancy," Jackie laughed.

"Ya, I heard she spread it around a bit."

"Well that's an understatement but with Fancy is wasn't so much about the sex as it was that she liked to think she could control men or have power over them. Rejection was something she couldn't handle. If a guy wanted to find out what a viper she could be, all he had to say was, 'No'."

"So, are you saying that Jimmy said 'No'?" Shane asked.

"She knew Lion was desperate to get his hands on Jimmy and Ace. What Lion and Boots didn't know is that Fancy had a real thing for Jimmy. Jimmy was sexy and smart. There wasn't a girl with a pulse who didn't fall in love with him as soon as they met him. Fancy had never been able to get anywhere with him and believe me she had been working on it! When Jimmy met Ace by accident and they got together, Fancy went into a spin. Green wasn't a pretty colour on Fancy; she was so jealous of Ace that she became obsessed with her. All she talked about at the time was the fact that they ran off together and how cruel it was of Ace to do such a thing. That, coming from the Queen of screwing around, was hilarious. And, anyone who knew Lion knew that he was so possessive that he was impossible to live with, but she loved to stir up shit and keep everyone fired up."

"She gave him over somehow?"

"I'm not sure how she found out where they were. She was banging a couple of the Flames so maybe it was pillow talk. She would do whatever it took to get the information—she was driven. She called Jimmy and told him she had information that would save their lives. Jimmy went to the meeting with Fancy not knowing that her agenda was something altogether different. She was going to give him one last chance to come to his senses. Her hope was that he would ditch Ace and choose her. But instead, he told her that he was in love for the first time in his life and that they were going to get married and quit the club."

"Let me guess, Fancy didn't take that too well?"

"No, sure didn't. She had a friend of hers make a phone call to Boots and Lion at precisely ten o'clock and give them the location of her meeting with Jimmy. If he had agreed to be her man she would have left with him before the call was made and his life would have been spared. But, as it turned out, Jimmy was pressing her to give him the information that she said she had while Boots and Lion were on their way. And, like I said, she could be vicious when she was rejected. She stayed to watch while Boots and Lion did their very best to find out the whereabouts of Ace. Jimmy was strong; he never gave her up. I don't know who was more disappointed Lion or Fancy. Even with Jimmy dead, Fancy wasn't satisfied. Ace had won the prize and it burned a hole in her heart. She wanted Jimmy so much and she knew Ace had his mind and heart forever. Fancy was never the same after that. We became friends over time, but in the back of my mind I knew that she was hoping that Lion would find Ace and finish the job."

"Were you friends with Ace?"

"Ya."

Chapter 46

Sheherezade was relieved when Dex came up to the limo and told her that she might as well go back to the estate because Lion was going to be held up by business in town for a day or two. She threw off her shoes and decided to do something she rarely did; she opened the bar in the car to see if there was something alcoholic to drink. The bar was stocked with every kind of liquor that had been invented, and there was a fresh bucket of ice awaiting this very mood. *Maybe, I should have guessed,* she thought. She grabbed a crystal glass, added a couple of ice cubes, and poured herself a double scotch. The drive home was quiet and it felt like she had just stopped banging her head against the wall. Upon arrival the staff congratulated her on Lion's acquittal and she put on a happy face to assuage any suspicion. Marshall had made a gourmet dinner and she told him she would change and then have her dinner on the terrace by the pool.

An ice bucket chilled a bottle of Riesling and a candle flickered on the table set for one. Sheherezade thanked Tina as she poured the cold wine and served her a large pasta bowl of spaghetti carbonara. As she savoured Marshall's creation she looked at the glorious sunset draped in pinks and mauves and thought of the contradictions in her life. There was the superficial beauty of this magnificent estate and then there was the ugliness of the business that made it all possible. A month ago she had what she thought was a fairytale marriage but behind closed doors the relationship had crumbled into a twisted fusion of neglect, hate, and abuse. Decisions she made to develop a closer relationship to her niece had resulted in her being farther away than ever. Going to the authorities would not guarantee her protection. She had seen first hand how the Pride infiltrated the police, the prisons, the court system, and even the Witness Protection

Program. Here she was enveloped in luxury and wealth and her biggest problem was money. Her account had been closed out the day she lost the baby. If she had money she could get away; without it she told herself, she had no hope.

The camouflaged lights set strategically through the grounds came on automatically with the encroaching darkness. Tina presented her with another course consisting of sole with lemon sauce. In the back of her mind she knew she must eat as much as she could in order to regain her strength. As she bit into the fish a thought struck her like a bolt of lightening. *Mum has money.* The adrenaline rush left her gasping for breath. Her mother inheriting money was such an implausible turn of events that she had pushed the story back into the recesses of her mind. Now she was entertaining a faint hope that it was true.

There was only one way to find out. She dropped her fork and ran into the library. *What would she say?* She sat for a moment collecting her thoughts. Five minutes passed before Sheherezade placed her hand on the phone and dialled the number.

"Hello," Regina answered cheerfully.

"Hi, mum. How are you?" Sheherezade asked warily.

"Yep. I'm busy. What do you need?" Regina's voice switched from cheerful to taciturn in an instant.

"I have a favour to ask of you, mum. I hope you can help me. Lion and I are having problems," her voice began to break. "I was pregnant and he stomped on me and I lost the baby." Her voice trailed off but there was complete silence on the other end. "He's keeping me captive here on the estate and I don't have any money. Brandi told me that you inherited some money. A lot of money."

"That's right," Regina said smugly.

"I was hoping that you could lend me just enough for air fare out of the country—away from Lion and all his club members. I could get a job and pay you back." There was a pregnant pause before Regina spoke.

"I always knew you would land in a pile of shit," Regina huffed with disgust.

"It wasn't my fault, mum! Before we were married he was the kindest, warmest person you could ever want to meet but once I saw what the bike gang was all about, and I let him know that I knew . . . ."

"Sherry, the same thing is going to happen wherever you go. You think that you can go around judging people and they're going to put up with it. They're not. You have to stop looking down your nose at people. You create your own problems and I refuse to bail you out. I don't blame Lion. You are impossible to live with," Regina droned on in her nasal voice.

"Mum, it would only be a couple of thousand dollars and I promise I would pay you back. I have never broken a promise, and I always keep my word."

"I don't know what to believe. You are all over the place. You always lived in a dream world."

"What are you saying? You won't lend me just two thousand dollars? I'm telling you I'm desperate, and you won't do that for me after all I've done for you over the years?"

"No, I won't . . . I think it's about time you learned a valuable lesson," Regina stated flatly.

"What lesson? How to live with a psychopathic biker?" Sheherezade snapped back bitterly.

"You picked him, now you want me to pay for your mistake," Regina retorted.

"And you are just so sick of picking up after me, are you? I've never asked you for a damn thing in my entire life! All these years I was so careful not to be a burden. You didn't even notice I was there unless I was making your life easier in some way. What kind of mother is able to help her own child but absolutely refuses? I don't know what is wrong with me, I keep expecting you to be human but you never measure up. Sorry to interrupt your party. It won't happen again!" Sheherezade slammed down the phone and sobbed. She should have known that she was on her own in the same way she had always been.

Chapter 47

James arrived at the penthouse to find Brandi busy in the kitchen.

"You're cooking?" he asked rhetorically as shock registered on his face.

"Yep, maid's day off. Funny how easy it is to get used to eating," she quipped. Some of the gloom of yesterday's revelation seemed to have lifted.

"What are we having?" James asked.

"We're having salad, mashed potatoes, Tenderloin steaks, and corn on the cob," Brandi replied proudly.

"Wow, you aren't going to knit me socks after dinner are you babe?" James smirked.

"No, but I have made a decision that is going to change things around here," she replied seriously.

"What?" James looked puzzled.

"I'm going to take some of the money that Boots gave me and I'm going to rehab on Monday. Want to come with me? Maybe they have a sibling rate," she closed her eyes and smiled at her own sarcasm.

"Rehab? Why now?"

"Well, I feel like shit and, for the first time in my life, I have everything to live for now." She did not tell James that after a week of rethinking her last meeting with Boots she had finally realized that she was chasing an impossible dream. Trying to make him care would only lead to heart break. Some of the attraction had been his lifestyle and now she had a beautiful home and money to live, without having to strip naked or give blow jobs in the back of some smarmy club. Also, facing the reality of her mother's true nature had lightened her heart in a way she would never have imagined. The truth had set her free. Just realizing that she could be different from her mother was an epiphany that had somehow given her hope.

"I'd have to think about it, babe . . . Hey, that reminds me, Shane gave me some new concoction of Mickey's that is supposed to be dynamite. How about a little celebration before you go off to rehab Monday?"

"Sounds good!"

Brandi and James had dinner at the bistro table for two in front of the floor length window off the kitchen. *How could she not have noticed that she had been looking into her mother's eyes all of this time? James had been there for her. She could count on him. They would never be lovers again but she felt good about finding a lost brother.*

"We'll hit just a little in case it is strong," James suggested. He retrieved the white powder from the pocket of his leather jacket and they sat at the table cooking up enough white powder for both of them. James eased the syringe into his arm and allowed the liquid to flow into his vein. His eyes rolled back and his arms fell to his sides.

"So, any good?" Brandi asked.

"Fuckin' lightning babe," James responded with his eyes still closed. Brandi took her turn and after a couple of minutes of silence a broad smile touched her lips.

"I think you guys better figure out a way to patent this stuff, you'll make a fortune," she said slowly.

After a few minutes they got up and walked to the big sofa in the living room to look out at the lights of the city. Brandi pulled her legs up under her as she sipped her cognac.

"Did I ever tell you I had a kid James?"

"No, you never mentioned it. How old?"

"A little girl, five. She looks more like Sherry than me."

"Where is she?" James asked.

"Sherry has her. I guess she thought I was partying too much to look after her. Maybe I was, but I hope if I get through rehab, she can at least come and visit me sometimes . . . here . . . now that I have a place for her," Brandi said wistfully.

"Sure, why not?" James replied as he got up and walked to the window.

"What's the matter, babe?" Brandi asked as she saw a concerned look cross his face.

"Oh, nothing, I did a bit more of this shit than you. It's strong that's all. It'll wear off shortly." Brandi went over and took his hand in hers.

"Thanks for being there for me, James. I just want you to know that anything I had with Boots is over. I'm not going to take any more bullshit from him. I don't have to—I got what I wanted," Brandi said throwing her head back haughtily. James looked into her eyes and tightened his grip on her hand.

"I am proud of you babe. I'm proud to have you as a sister." James fist came up and he started to pump his fingers.

"Something wrong James?"

"Fuck, my hand is going numb."

'Probably just good shit, hon," Brandi offered. She felt a small tremble in her core and tried to ignore the sensation. James was shaking his arm and beginning to pace up and down in front of the floor to ceiling window.

"Fuck, babe it's getting worse. It's moving right up to my elbow".

"I'm starting to feel sick to my stomach. I think I'm having a bad reaction too," Brandi whimpered.

A look of terror passed over James face.

"It can't be bad shit—Shane gave it to me himself," James protested. Brandi was feeling waves of cold passing up and down her spine and she began seeing tiny lights dancing across her field of vision. A thought crossed her mind that she did not care to share with James. Shane had become Boots right hand. *Would it be possible? Would he be capable of being so heartless?* James was now shaking both arms as he paced up and down the room.

"Are you feeling cold?" he asked Brandi.

"Yes. Cold and light headed . . . I think it's getting worse." Brandi coughed. James grabbed his stomach and ran to the kitchen sink where he brought up dinner. Brandi got up from the couch with the intention of doing the same but her food shot out of her mouth onto the carpet. She fell to her knees as her body contorted to accommodate convulsions that continued long after dinner had been expelled. Brandi started to cry as she began to believe the worst.

"James, I think Shane gave you bad shit. It was from Boots. He wants to kill me," she gasped.

"No, don't say that babe. Why would he want to kill you?"

"James, I killed Fancy. Boots knows that I made her tell me everything about the night that he and Lion killed Jimmy. I blackmailed him to get the apartment. I should have known what he was capable of . . . ." she started to wail.

James knew in his bones that she was right. He tried to stay calm.

"We better get to the hospital. I'm going to call an ambulance." As he talked to an operator Brandi became disoriented. James grabbed Brandi's purse and the door key and buzzed the doorman to ask for assistance as he felt himself becoming incapacitated.

In a haze of red lights and loud sirens Brandi and James made their way through the streets of Manhattan to the emergency room where they were immediately taken to the intensive care unit.

Mickey's new designer drug, predictably, did not show up on any of the drug scans administered by the attending physician. The doctor could see that the central nervous system was deteriorating in both patients but he had no idea what could be done for them. Holly was the nurse assigned to Brandi that evening in the ICU. She was a veteran nurse of twenty-two years who had never seen anyone in the same condition as the beautiful blonde girl in the bed in front of her. She had been doing her best to keep Brandi comfortable by applying cold rags to her forehead as she muttered away about Boots, James, and Sherry. After the doctor told her that the girl's condition was deteriorating rapidly, she looked frantically through Brandi's purse for a contact number. Finally she found something that gave a next of kin as a Regina Raleigh, her mother.

"Mrs. Raleigh?"

"Yes."

"I am a nurse at Roosevelt Hospital and we have just admitted your daughter Brandi. I'm calling to inform you that she was admitted for a drug overdose and she is in very poor condition. Would you be able to come to the hospital right away to see her?"

Regina was entertaining Luke, Karen, Freddy and a new couple they had just met at the local bar a few hours earlier. She had been drinking most of the evening but was not about to admit that she was not in complete control of her faculties to some nurse or even to herself.

"What's her condition?"

"She's in grave condition. I think that you should come to the hospital right away," Holly repeated gently. Regina was annoyed by the inconvenience and she was particularly irked at having some nurse telling her what she should do.

"Well, she is very strong; she has my constitution. I think with a bit of rest she will be fine. Just fine," she said in her most condescending voice. Holly bristled at this woman who did no seem to be willing to acknowledge her daughter's condition for some reason.

"No, Mrs. Raleigh, maybe you did not understand what I was saying to you. If you are at all able to come to the hospital, I would advise you to do so because your daughter is floating in and out of consciousness and this may be your last chance to speak to her. The doctor does not think that she will live through the night. She's in grave condition and she is deteriorating rapidly." Holly could hear laughter in the background as if there was a raucous party going on at the other end of the line. She waited for a response from Regina who seemed to be distracted from their conversation.

"Look, I can't make it out there tonight but I will get out there some time tomorrow to see how she is doing." Holly was flabbergasted by this woman who did not seem concerned about her daughter who was fighting for her life. She realized that she was wasting her time talking to her and decided to go back to her patient to give her what comfort she could in case she regained consciousness.

Brandi appeared to be in a semi delirium and continued to talk about people and events in a nonsensical stream of consciousness. The delirium was digging up long forgotten memories she had of when she was a child in a similar condition from measles, mumps, and tonsillitis. Her mind was thrown back to a time when she was a little girl tossing and thrashing around her bed, groaning and calling out for her mother to come and see her in her room. She could hear Regina calling back to her in an impatient tone that she would be there in a moment. After a few minutes she would work up the strength to holler one more time, begging for her mother to come and check on her. All the horrible feelings of despair that she felt as a child were jumping out of the nooks and crannies of her brain, along with the fever that raged in her head. Where had they been hiding all these years? Images of her mother sitting in a haze of blue smoke at the kitchen table filled her with pain as she realized how uncaring she had been for her as a little girl, sick and begging for her attention.

Next she had a memory of her sister coming into her room with a bowl of hot soup and feeding it to her by spoonfuls as she did her best to lift her head to take the soup into her mouth. She saw her sister sitting with her and placing cold cloths on her forehead, holding her hand and bringing her aspirin for her fever. Sherry. Sherry cared. Sherry had always cared and looked after her whenever she was sick. Why had she never wanted to admit that? The fever was helping her access thoughts deep in her subconscious and suddenly she knew why she would never admit that she loved her sister. Her mother would never have approved and she wanted the love of her mother. She had chosen her mother's love over her sister's and that was a mistake. The truth hit her like an arrow in the heart.

Brandi became aware of her surroundings in the quiet ward of the hospital as she looked up and saw the kind face of woman holding her hand.

"Brandi, I'm Holly. How are you feeling dear?" Brandi remembered what had happened back in the apartment and knew she had to act quickly.

"Call my sister for me," she said pleadingly while pointing to her phone number.

"Yes, of course," Holly answered. She dialled the number and in a moment Tina had informed Sheherezade that the phone call was for her.

"Sheherezade, it's Brandi. I'm dying. Can you come?" Brandi cried softly.

"Of course! Where are you?" Sheherezade screamed anxiously. Brandi handed the phone to the nurse and asked her to give her the details as she lay back to conserve her energy.

The Intensive Care Unit was quiet and peaceful as Sheherezade scanned the beds for her sister. Brandi raised a hand to signal her presence at the other end of the room. Sheherezade ran to her bed and hugged her tight as tears began to flow down her cheeks.

"What is it Brandi, why are you here? What happened?" Sheherezade demanded. Brandi grabbed her hand.

"I don't think I have much time so I want you to listen. I'm sorry for everything. I love you and you're the best sister anyone could hope to have—I just wish it had not taken me all these years to admit it. If I had more time I would make it up to you. And I would make it up to Lila too. I know you will take care of her. I don't even have to ask you. You will be a great mother to her." Sheherezade started to shake her head to deny everything that Brandi was saying. Brandi looked at her pleadingly.

"Sheherezade, listen to me . . . I can't prove it but I believe Boots gave us the bad drugs because he wanted me dead. I was with James; he is our brother, my full brother who was born one year before me. Mum gave him up. I know now that mum didn't care about us. I guess I knew it all along but when that is all you have . . . . I planned to go to rehab on Monday. We were just going to party this last weekend. Please tell Lila, I wanted to get clean and have her visit. Maybe you don't believe me but you would have seen. I told James before we took the drugs . . . ." Sheherezade could see that Brandi had tremors and was doing her best to maintain consciousness.

"I always loved you Brandi and it wasn't our fault that we had a hard life with mum. I never held it against you and I will explain it all to Lila. But you're going to get better and you can tell her yourself . . . ."

"Sheherezade, I want you to know what I did. She pulled her sister toward her ear and she whispered for some time before collapsing back into the bed with exhaustion. Her eyes cleared for a moment and she poured every ounce of strength she had into a sudden urgent message that came out in a slurred version of what she had intended.

"Mum has your money. Make her to give it to you . . . ."

Sheherezade cradled Brandi in her arms and talked softly to her, reassuring her that she would get stronger and they would all have a good life together. After a few minutes Sheherezade broke down and wept hard. She realized that Brandi had stopped breathing and that nothing more could be done for her. After fifteen minutes she composed herself enough to call Dex and ask him to make arrangements for her sister at the hospital. Holly came up to Sheherezade and told her that her brother James had also passed away. She told Holly that someone would be coming to the hospital to take care of things and she summoned the driver to take her back to the estate.

More tragedy. More than she could bear.

Chapter 48

The most tortured night of Sheherezade's life was punctuated by a glorious sunrise that gave promise where there was none. Brandi was gone, along with a long lost brother; both lives expendable to an evil twisted empire of greed, violence, and pride. Meals were delivered to her room so that she could be alone. She wanted to make it clear to Lion that this tragedy was not an opportunity that he could use to try to ingratiate himself back into her emotional good graces. If he had any idea of the loathing that she harboured for him, Boots, and the entire organization, he would have set her free and cut his losses. However, she knew his pride would not allow that and so she would bide her time for that one moment when her life would be hers again.

Alone in her room, she went over the events of Brandi's last day. She had heard it said many times that people often have a clarity of vision for their life just before they die and it seemed so true in Brandi's case. Sheherezade felt a genuine change had taken place in her and she just wished she could have come to know the Brandi that was emerging stronger, more focused, and emotionally independent from Regina.

She thought back to the kindness of the nurse who had called her and stayed with Brandi until she reached the hospital and she decided that she must call her and thank her for being there for her sister. After several connections she finally reached the ward where Holly was working.

"Hello, Holly, this is Sheherezade, I was in your ward last night with my sister Brandi . . . ."

"Oh, yes, of course. How are you doing?"

"Well, it's a horrible shock. I am still numb but I wanted to thank you for being so kind to her."

"I did what I could. I just wish I could have convinced your mother to come."

"You spoke to my mother last night?"

"Yes, I found the number in your sister's purse and called her when Brandi first arrived."

"Did you know how serious her condition was at the time?" Sheherezade asked.

"Yes, but I had a hard time getting through to your mother. It was quite frustrating, but I did my best to explain that Brandi was in grave condition and that this could be her last chance to speak to her daughter because the doctor's did not believe she would make it through the night. I don't think she believed me. She seemed to be entertaining at the time. She just said that Brandi was strong and that she would visit her the next day."

"I understand exactly what you are saying. My mother only believes what is convenient for her to believe. If she had guests she would be distracted enough that she wouldn't want to bother," Sheherezade explained bitterly.

"I am so glad you were there for your sister."

"I want to thank you for calling me and for being so kind to her. It meant the world to me."

"Well, I did what I could . . . ."

"Thanks again, Holly. Good bye." Sheherezade hung up the phone and sat speechless at the desk. *Regina was having a party and could not be bothered to make the trip in to the hospital,* she thought. *Why does this still surprise me,* she asked herself. Disgust touched Sheherezade's bones but she would not waste her time stewing about the actions of her mother—that was giving her far more attention than she deserved.

Dex planned a beautiful funeral in the one day he had to make the arrangements. Sheherezade had not mentioned a word to Lion but ritual was an important aspect of his life and he was ready in a black suit when the limo pulled up to the house. As they entered the funeral home she was greeted by the staff and taken to the room where both coffins lay draped in flowers. When Regina, entered with Luke, Karen, and Freddy she gave Sheherezade a commanding wave to join them.

"Why are there two?"

"Two?" Sheherezade looked puzzled.

"Two coffins!" Regina huffed with exasperation while making a grimace with her mouth.

"Maybe Dex didn't know the whole story when he contacted you. Brandi was with James Barrett in her apartment at the time and he also died from the drug. What Brandi had just recently discovered was that James was the first born child that you and Billy gave up as a baby. By some weird set of circumstances he was a Lucifer's Pride member and they dated not knowing that they were brother and sister."

Rage and indignation passed Regina's face at having been exposed for her misdeeds. Her teeth clenched but she was lost for words. Turning away, she took a seat in the pews at a distance from the front rows.

The service was very touching and emotionally draining. Everyone joined the procession to the gravesite and both coffins were quickly poised to be lowered side by side into the cold ground. The day was bright and warm and the birds sang in the tall trees that surrounded the small plot of earth where her sister was to be placed. *If only those birds would stop singing as if everything in the world were perfect,* she lamented. Sheherezade closed her eyes and listened with hope to the words of the reverend but she was snapped back into the present by the soft roar of a distant motorcycle. Through the small grove of trees she saw a lone biker on a big chrome Harley. Although he was far enough away that she could not positively identify the rider she knew that it was Boots. *What on earth was he doing here? Was he revelling in his handy work or was he haunted by feelings that he could not face?* She would never know.

Many people were leaving but Sheherezade wanted to have a private moment alone at the gravesite so she remained behind to say a prayer for the sister that she loved so much despite their differences. When the gentle breeze was the only sound around her she closed her eyes to say a final goodbye to Brandi and James. A branch behind her snapped and she turned around to see Regina coming at her with a look of hate radiating from her icy blue eyes. She was not about to let Sheherezade have the last word on the subject or allow her the satisfaction of feeling any moral superiority.

"You! You just think you know everything, don't you?" Sheherezade looked at Regina and decided she was going to speak her truth instead of taking a passive stance as she had all of her life. Out of respect or necessity she had always tiptoed around her mother's gigantic ego and pretended that her mother's twisted view of life was one that she shared.

"I know that you wouldn't leave the party on Saturday night to be with your daughter who was dying." Defiance flashed in Sheherezade's eyes as she glowered at Regina.

"You little bitch, who the fuck do you think you are?" Regina hissed.

"The question is who do you think you are that you are so busy getting hammered, you can't be with your own daughter when she is on her death bed?" Sheherezade spat back.

Regina was shocked and enraged at the defiance that was emerging from her normally compliant, submissive daughter. She put her teeth together and curled her lips back as she spoke slowly and clearly to show condescension, "The nurse told me that I couldn't possibly get there in time because she was already unconscious, you idiot!"

"That's a lie! When I spoke to her the next day she told me exactly what she told you. She said that this might be your last chance to see your daughter alive and possibly speak to her. But even if it was going to be too late, you should have got off your ass and gone to the hospital. Your daughter was all alone! What kind of a mother can't put down her drink long enough to go to her daughter's deathbed?!" Sheherezade screamed.

"You should see yourself! Your face is all contorted and twisted!" Regina half grinned as if she had found a real rebuttal to the accusations. Sheherezade ignored her blathering and continued, "You abandoned James as a child because you just couldn't be bothered to raise him and now, because you didn't want anyone to know how heartless you were, Brandi ended up dating her own brother! But that isn't the best is it mum? You had to compete with your own daughter and ended up seducing your own son! You are disgusting!" she said in the same slow, clear voice her mother used when she wanted to be irritating.

Regina was furious that Sheherezade had uncovered the truth and she was being criticized for it. She had spent her entire life telling herself that she was perfect and beyond reproach. Today her attempt at rewriting history was not working.

"No wonder Lion is dropping you. You are going to be on the street and penniless because you don't have the brains to survive the way I did!" Regina fumed.

"Since when does it take brains to spread your legs?" Sheherezade asked flatly. Regina's nostrils flared and her face contorted in anger.

"You'll end up in a big pile of shit and when you do, don't come begging for money again. I've done all I will ever do for you."

"Well, that was exactly nothing as I remember it. And don't worry, I learned my lesson very well. You don't care about anyone but yourself. You're not capable of love, or kindness, and you certainly would never put yourself out to ever help anyone. The funny thing is that Brandi also came to the same conclusion at the very end of her life. No, I will never ask you for anything again. In fact, you can just pretend that the attempted abortion of me was a great success!" Sheherezade put her hand up in front of Regina's face and walked briskly to the waiting limousine. Regina stood in the same place, stunned, as Sheherezade's car pulled away.

Chapter 49

Sheherezade poured herself a strong drink in the car and then stretched out on the seat and closed her eyes. She was exhausted by the confrontation and the entire ordeal of the funeral, and hoped she could sleep all the way home to the estate. Her eyes opened as they pulled up to the front entrance. She ignored Lion, who had been silent all the way home, and walked toward the winding staircase that led to the sanctuary of her suite. The house seemed to be eerily quiet and she wondered if the staff had been given the afternoon off.

Sheherezade was sitting at the table by the window in her bedroom reading her Bible when she heard the bedroom door open.

"Lion, I am not in the mood."

"I want this to end," he said firmly.

"What?"

"You are my wife and you will start acting like my wife," he stared at her with eyes that pierced her heart.

"You cannot tell me how to feel or behave and it would be only acting, so you might as well allow me to leave," she responded trying her best to appear calm and in control of her emotions.

"You are not going to leave me," he stated still pinning her with a fixed stare.

"OK, Lion but I want to bring Lila back. I want her to live with us."

"You can visit her a couple of times a year but I don't want a kid. I never wanted kids. I can't have her living with us," he announced unceremoniously. Sheherezade could feel her temper rising and she was helpless to reign it in.

"She comes back or I leave!" she screamed as loud as she could muster. Lion could not tolerate this defiance and he felt a white anger rising in him that told him he was losing control over something that mattered more to him than anything else in the world. He grabbed Sheherezade by the arms and pushed her to the bed pinning her under his weight.

"Don't you ever say that again! You will never leave me. Do you understand?" his voice was low, quiet and intense. "You don't seem to appreciate that I'm the leader of Lucifer's Pride. If you ever try to leave me, I will hunt you down, and when I find you, I will kill you. Now before you do anything stupid, think about that." Lion pulled up her nightgown and held her arms above her head as he unfastened his jeans. She knew better than to challenge his strength. After satisfying himself he pulled his hand back and slapped her across the face with all of his force. He stood over her for a moment glaring down as if he were anticipating a reaction before he strode out of the room.

Sheherezade turned over on the bed and sobbed until her ribs began to hurt. Crying made her feel better but she was running out of tears. Her only thought was for Lila and what kind of a life she would have now that Brandi was gone and she was unable to be with her except for a couple of visits a year. She knew she could not live with that arrangement; a life without Lila was not the life she was willing to accept. Lucifer's Pride had created a hell for her with no doors. Something had to change.

At eight o'clock, Tina finally called to ask her where she would like her dinner to be served. Sheherezade thought better of asking where everyone had been and simply asked that her dinner be sent up to her suite.

Tina arranged her dinner at the table by the window as Sheherezade sat staring at the beautiful orange and pink sunset beyond the large maple in the yard. *How dare it look so beautiful when life was so hopeless?* She was becoming aware of the pain she felt in her jaw where Lion had decked her to make his point and she hoped Tina hadn't noticed the swelling on her face. Tina assumed that Sheherezade was dealing with grief over her sister's death, gave her a gentle hug, and left her alone without saying a word. Tears fell making a hollow sound which drew her attention to a brown envelope that had been sent up with the tray. From the address on the front Sheherezade could see that it was from the agency she had hired to uncover information about the man who had put his name on her birth certificate.

She put the envelope down and tears continued to stream down her face. Every nerve in her body was raw and exposed making the thought of more uncertainty or, perhaps, disappointing news, utterly unbearable. *Maybe not knowing was better.* The brown envelope lay there looking intriguingly full. *Should she take the chance? No, not today,* she thought, *as another tear dropped onto the paper. I cannot take one more bit of disappointment or my heart will break.* Lila would be waiting by the phone, and even though she had no intention of telling her about Brandi's death over the phone, she knew she could not keep her voice steady enough to make the call. She was willing to use her last breath to be with Lila but how could she fight one of the most powerful organizations in the world? She closed her eyes and the word HOPELESS was etched into her psyche. True, she had always been alone but she had always felt strong in her resolve to make things work in her life. Today she felt defeated, small and weak. Memories of her childhood pushed their way into her mind. Again she was the helpless little girl whose mother didn't notice if she had clean clothes or care if she was happy. *Somewhere . . . . Somewhere, she had a father. She did not know him and he did not know her but just the same, she had a father,* she told herself. *Dad,* she heard herself saying. *Dad . . . wherever you are . . . I am your daughter . . . help me . . . I need you. Wherever you are . . . I love you . . . please help me . . . .*

She wept silently as her mind wandered through a black cloud of despair and hopelessness. The orange and pink sunset melted into dark blue and grey clouds. She had lost all concept of time when music from her cell phone brought her back to reality and her presence in the room. She reached over to the bedside table and answered it.

"Hello?" A low, melodic female voice spoke, "Sheherezade, it's Ace. We're going to get you out of there. Can you be ready in half an hour?"

"Ace? Lion's old girlfriend?" Sheherezade stared into space incredulously.

"Yep. You're ready to leave, right?"

"I'm . . . I'm desperate to get out. You have no idea . . . ."

"Oh, I have an idea . . . ." she said coolly.

"Listen carefully. Put on something black, find a flashlight, and take anything that is valuable to you. You won't be going back. Take the path to the lake. There will be a helicopter waiting there for you, but you might have to get wet. Can you swim?"

"Sure can!"

"Good. Half an hour. We won't have a second chance. Be careful."

"Thank you . . . thank you!" Sheherezade was crying but it only took a minute for the tears to dry up and the survival instinct that had gotten her this far in life to shift into gear. She had a moment of uncertainty. Was the call authentic or a test? If it was authentic, could she trust this person with her life? The alternative was living with Lion in a virtual prison without Lila for the rest of her life. There was such strength in that voice. A chill made the hair stand up on her neck when she considered the danger she could face if she were to be caught—this would be her only chance to break away. *I have nothing to lose*, she thought. *Nothing*. Fierce resolve struck her like lightning.

Running into the dressing room, she looked around for a plastic bag of some sort. The voice mentioned that she might have to swim. She grabbed a dress, shoes, makeup, and her Marilyn Monroe wig. Lila flashed into her mind and she ran for her Bible that held the dried wild rose they had found by the lake. At the table she saw the brown envelope that had been delivered to her at dinner and she added those items to the bag as well. She walked over to her jewellery drawer in the dressing room but someone had seen fit to remove anything of value. She shoved the bag into a waist carrier and headed downstairs.

Everything appeared dark on the main floor as she made her way to the drawer where the flashlights were kept. Time was passing and she began to panic as she methodically went through the contents of three drawers. When she finally found a flashlight in the fourth drawer she stood still trying to catch her breath as she flicked it on to see if it worked.

Suddenly, her heart jumped as she realized she had seen a figure on the other side of the room. She turned the flashlight on again and froze as she saw Coral standing quietly in the dark.

"Oh, I am sorry if I startled you Coral. I was just looking for a flashlight so I could go out for a walk. It seems like a beautiful evening. Lion said something about having a lot of work to do tonight and I thought it would be better if I didn't distract him. I'll see you in the morning. Have a nice night."

I wonder if she bought that, she asked herself. She was not about to take any chances. She walked briskly toward the quest houses where the path started and then, as soon as she knew she would be out of sight, she turned on the flashlight and began to run as fast as her legs would carry her.

Coral walked over to the window and her eyes followed Sheherezade as she made her way down past the quest house. She ran into the study and found Lion sitting at his computer.

"Lion! Sheherezade is leaving! She had a little bag strapped to her waist and I saw her go down past the guest house!" He dropped what he was doing and began running through the house and out the glass doors of the kitchen.

"Send security to the lake!" he screamed back to Coral.

When Sheherezade entered the forest, the path changed; it was strewn with branches and jagged protruding rocks which made it more difficult to move quickly. Her breathing steadied as she felt the cool breeze of freedom on her face. Moss hung from the old trees. Darkness enveloped her and she prayed that someone was waiting for her at the other end of the path. *Maybe tonight she would be free.* As she slowed down to catch her breath she heard something and her head swung back. Her heart sank. The sounds were coming from behind her—someone was moving at a frenetic pace. In the distance she heard the sound of an approaching engine. Some light was beginning to peak through the trees up ahead indicating that she was getting closer to the lake. Her heart was pounding with exhaustion and fear as she used every ounce of strength she had to stay ahead of the person chasing her.

As she looked up to see the bright light of a helicopter flash through the trees, she stepped on a jutting rock which twisted her ankle and threw her to the ground. She landed on her right wrist sending a searing pain up her arm. As she pushed herself into a standing position again, she glanced backward and saw the dark figure of Lion running toward her in the moonlight that danced off the lake about two hundred feet away. Once again she began running as hard as possible.

When she was about ten feet from the shore, Lion reached out and grabbed her by the black hoody that she was wearing over a

T-shirt. They struggled for a moment until she slipped her arms out so that she was free from his grasp once again. The helicopter was now hovering above the middle of the lake and Sheherezade ran toward the shore. She jumped into five feet of water. Lion was right behind her. He grabbed her by the arm and they began to struggle.

"Stop! You bitch! You're not going anywhere!" Lion's voice echoed through the trees. Sheherezade brought her leg up and kicked him in the stomach, prying herself loose from his grip. Breathlessly, she began to swim toward the centre of the lake and the rope ladder that was waiting to take her to freedom. In a moment she became aware that Lion was no longer behind her and she remembered what he had told Lila. Cats can't swim. She reached the ladder and climbed upward. Two pairs of powerful arms lifted her into the helicopter as it jerked into full throttle.

"Thank you . . . thank you," she muttered breathlessly before she collapsed onto the seat in heap of nervous exhaustion. Both men were Lion's age. One had a long full beard and wore a leather hat. The other one had long hair that was pulled back into a greyish ponytail. They both had the strong physical presence that she had come to associate with bikers.

As she sat there shaking in a state of utter shock, they covered her in a blanket. Although her head was spinning and she felt like she was losing her grip on consciousness and her physical surroundings, she heard their victory yelps as the helicopter left the estate behind. Before closing her eyes she caught sight of a Purple Flame logo artfully tattooed on one man's shoulder. Amidst the panting and shaking, a small wave of relief passed over her tired body. An enemy of Lion was a friend of hers.

Chapter 50

It was only a short ride to her destination. The helicopter landed in a field not too far from an old railway station. In a couple of minutes a cargo train pulled up and came to a full stop. The engineer was introduced as Max and another man who appeared to be on duty in the control car, was introduced as Tom. Sheherezade barely had time to say thank you and shake the hands of the men who gave her her freedom before the train started rolling. She was sitting in the comfortable compartment behind the control room when Tom came back to speak to her. He told her how happy everyone was that she had made a successful get away. She had questions about who exactly he was referring to but she did not feel that she should ask too many questions since people were probably risking their lives in the operation to free her from Lion.

He explained that they were taking her to Boston airport where she would board a private jet which would take her out of the country. They were assuming that the Philadelphia and New York airports would be swarming with Pride members hoping to prevent her escape. The last leg of the trip was the most dangerous because she would have to walk from the entrance of the airport to the V.I.P. lounge on her own. Bodyguards would only serve to draw attention to her, so instead, they decided to have her disguise herself as best she could and they would keep a safe distance behind her. He told her it was important that she create a disguise for herself that would make her unrecognizable before they reached their destination in about four and a half hours. He presented her with a suitcase containing clothes, makeup, and wigs that she could use for the disguise. The look of sheer terror in her eyes prompted him to grab her hand, smile, and reassure her that everything would be fine, before he returned to his duties in the engine room.

She sat frozen in place imagining the walk she would have to make through a busy airport where any person there could be a threat to her life and liberty. Suddenly, she smiled. They wouldn't be looking for Marilyn. Who would guess that the person attracting attention is someone who is trying not to be noticed? She pulled out her wig, makeup, and dress, and in fifteen minutes she was transformed into her alter ego. Terrible thoughts fought to occupy her mind but she pushed them away with thoughts of being with Lila in a peaceful place far away.

She was shoving her bag into her suitcase when she looked down and saw the brown envelope. Just an hour ago she had felt so lost and hopeless that she could not face any further disappointment the letter might bring. *Destiny can change in the blink of an eye,* she thought. *Hope. Kind people. She wanted to live in a world like that. Dare she dream?* This new turn of events restored a dim hope she had always cherished—that it would be possible to live life on her own terms. She felt a renewed strength and resolve to get away from the bitter memories created by her life with Lion and Lucifer's Pride. Her jaw tightened as she told herself she would face it all head on and deal with whatever was thrown her way in order to have the life she had always dreamed might be possible.

She took the envelope in her hands and ripped it open with all the anger she had for the universe. It read:

Dear Mrs. Terkel,

> *We have concluded our search for your birth father Terrance Ivey. Unfortunately, it was discovered that he was killed in a plane accident in South Carolina, on July 12th, of last year. His fiancée, Jan Mucci was also killed in the crash. You are his only child. Your grandmother, Violet Ivey, is your only living relative on your father's side. She now resides in Westchester, New York. Her address and phone number are as follows . . .*

Sheherezade clutched the letter to her heart as she was flooded with feelings of sadness and hope. She would never know the father that had been the subject of so many childhood fantasies and, sadly, she had come so close to finding him. On the other hand her heart felt like it was going to explode with joy at the thought of meeting a grandmother that was her own flesh and blood. *I can call her,* she thought. *She will pick up the phone and I can actually speak to her. God, what will she think of me,* she wondered. *How am I going to explain my situation?* She dialled the number.

"Hello?" a soft woman's voice shocked Sheherezade into silence.

"Hello?" the voice asked again. Sheherezade took a breath and could not think of what to say, "Hello. Please don't hang up on me. I have to tell you who I am . . ."

"Who you are?" Violet repeated slowly.

"Yes . . . I know it's a strange story. I never knew who my father was until a few months ago when I found out his name. I hired a private investigation agency to find him for me and they gave me your number. I'm your granddaughter, Sheherezade."

There was a long silence on the other end and then Violet answered with trepidation. "I'm not sure I understand. I met my granddaughter, Sheherezade, in the summer time." Sheherezade closed her eyes and tears fell. Obviously, the poor woman was senile and Sheherezade became concerned that she was living alone.

"No, we have never met but I would like to meet you some day," she said kindly.

"Miss, I don't know who you are but I only have one granddaughter. I met with her just three weeks ago, so I'm sure I do not know what your game is but you cannot be who you say you are." The woman sounded so coherent and adamant that Sheherezade questioned her first evaluation of senility.

"You say you met me?" Sheherezade asked.

"Yes, I met my granddaughter and her mother just three weeks ago," Violet responded.

"Her mother? What was her name?"

"Regina, of course. Now, I'm quite finished answering your questions. You cannot be who you claim to be." Violet felt the pain of her meeting with Sheherezade and Regina come rushing back.

"No wait! Regina is my mother. There's some confusion here. I am your granddaughter, Sheherezade, but I didn't meet you three weeks ago. Where was this meeting and what was it about?"

There was a note of desperation in the poor girl's voice that confused and intrigued Violet. Pity, alone, accounted for her willingness to continue with the conversation.

"I met with them at the Ivey Building in Manhattan to discuss the inheritance."

"The inheritance? Who was receiving an inheritance?"

"I met with my granddaughter and her mother to discuss her inheritance of her father's estate on her twenty-first birthday," Violet answered.

"My birthday was three weeks ago, on the 25th of July. And you say you met with my mother, Regina?"

"Yes, my dear, and I met my granddaughter, so if you think you can fool someone into believing you are . . . ." Sheherezade eyes opened wide as if she were witnessing an atrocity.

"Oh my God! What colour were your granddaughter's eyes? Did you happen to notice?" Sheherezade's voice rose to a high urgent pitch. Violet hesitated as she relived the disappointment of discovering that her granddaughter bore no familial resemblance to her son.

"They were green. She had beautiful green eyes," Violet said coldly.

"Grandmother, the girl you met must have been my sister, Brandi. She must have been posing as me!" Violet was trying to take in this new information but it seemed too bizarre to have credence.

"Why would Regina take your sister to the meeting?" Violet asked as she felt a little bit of hope creep into her heart.

"Well, my mother and I have always had our differences. Well, to tell you the truth, she just never liked me. I'm sure she would prefer to see Brandi get money. She would have more control over it that way." She felt exposed and ashamed at what seemed to be her mother's deliberate fraud. Violet closed her eyes and tears fell furiously.

"Sheherezade! Oh my goodness, my dear. I cannot believe this! You have no idea what this means to me. If what you say is true, I have not met my granddaughter! My son's only daughter! I want to meet you now. I must. Where are you?"

"Grandmother! Nothing would mean more to me in this entire world than to meet you! But I'm in a real predicament at the moment and I'm in danger. I'm leaving on a private jet tonight and I doubt that it will ever be safe for me to return to the United States again. Maybe you could meet me somewhere outside of the country sometime and of course, I can call you and we can get to know each other that way."

"No! My dear. I want to see you. Is there anyway that we can meet before you get on the plane tonight?" Sheherezade thought for a moment.

"Well . . . I'm going to be at the V.I.P. lounge of the Boston airport in about four hours. Where do you live?" she asked.

"I'm about four hours from Boston airport, in Westchester, New York. I'm going to try to make it. Even if I could just see you for a moment . . . it would mean so much to me."

"Let's try but if we miss each other, grandmother, please forgive me because I have to make this plane."

"O.K., I understand . . ."

"Grandmother, I'll be in disguise. Watch for Marilyn Monroe. I hope I have the chance to see you tonight."

"Yes, my dear—I have to leave right now if I want to catch you. Goodbye."

Sheherezade hung up the phone and sat back in the chair in stunned silence. Suddenly, her thoughts snapped back to the reality she was living and the impending danger she would face on the way to the plane. *Would she be lucky enough to meet her grandmother for a few moments?*

Hours passed while Sheherezade sat lost in a state of hope and fear watching the trees outside moving past the window. It was getting close to midnight and the moon had floated to the surface of the world again. Rain had begun to fall in sheets and lightning danced to the east. Strange thoughts were ruminating in her head. She had been through so much turmoil and change in the past few months and now she was leaving that part of herself behind. She had become someone's granddaughter, someone she did not even know. As much as she yearned for that identity she was not sure who Sheherezade Ivey was, could be, or should be. And here she was disguised as another person surrounded by strangers who were helping her because of her past identity as the wife of the most powerful biker in the world. She felt like she was riding on a ghost train—just a cloud of uncertain identity flowing through time to an unknown destination.

And deep down there was that seed of her true nature—the strong self-reliant woman who was determined to survive anything the world could throw her way. Another part of her personality was beginning to come alive, feeding on the hope that was inspired by the events of the last few hours. Sheherezade clung to that small core of identity that was always there despite all the craziness that had surrounded her life. She knew that was the part of herself she could rely on to make it through to a brighter day if fate would allow it; the part of herself that would be there for Lila.

Tom came back into the car where she was sitting and stood there stunned at her transformation.

"Wow! You are Marilyn," he said as his eyes widened. She threw her head back and bit her lip to fight the emotion. "I guess I'm betting my life on it," she said wistfully.

Finally the train came to a stop and two men who looked more like policeman than bikers took her to a car that was idling in the rain. As they sped down the highway, they gave her final instructions on the layout of the airport. They told her that she would be watched by many of their men but they felt that keeping their distance would offer the best chance at having her reach the gate. She knew that no amount of protection could guarantee her life if Lion had decided she was expendable but she could not dwell on that now. It would not serve her at this point. She closed her eyes and began to get into character—the happy, carefree girl who's world was her oyster.

Chapter 51

Lion jogged back up to the house screaming wildly at his security men who had been right behind him on the run to the lake but useless none the less. Rage and self-recrimination resounded in his head. *He should have had her watched. How could he have been so naïve or was the word stupid?* He instructed the head of his security to dispatch as many men as possible to watch the international airports for his wife and to bring her back to the estate using whatever force was necessary to accomplish their mission.

Coral dreaded the storm that she knew was about to follow when she saw Lion's eyes shining black and hollow as he passed her in the kitchen and ran up the stairs. Entering their bedroom that Sheherezade had claimed for a refuge, he exploded at her rejection of him and her defiance of his will. He picked up a chair in the dressing room and smashed the vanity mirror, he pulled out the drawers of possessions she left behind, and lashed out at the wardrobe of designer clothes, ripping and throwing pieces in a frenzy of blind rage. Following the destruction of the dressing room, he entered the bedroom where he smashed the television, and the beautiful Pissarro landscape hanging above the fireplace. Suddenly, an eerie calm fell over the room as he stared down at the bed. He stood mesmerized by memories of what once was and then dropped to his knees as he grasped the mauve silk bedspread like a drowning man clinging to a life raft.

Sometime later Coral came to the door, tapped gently, and hearing nothing, opened the door to find Lion staring out the window.

"Lion, Dex is on the phone. He says it's important." Lion reached over and picked up the phone with the slow, deliberate movements of a person whose mind is otherwise occupied.

"What?"

"Hi Gov . . . I heard what happened at the estate, but there's another pressing matter that requires your attention. They've traced the cell phone that Ace is using and we know she is in Cannes. As soon as she turns the phone on again, we'll have her. You might want to make arrangements."

"Good Dex. Tell Jeff to be ready to make a flight plan to Nice airport. I'll call you right back with the exact location of departure."

"Done. Good luck, boss." Lion ran down to his office and found the cell number for the Swami.

"Swami, we will have a lock on the location shortly . . . it's time to go. Where are you right now?"

"I am at Boston airport as part of the surveillance."

"OK. I'll have the jet sent there to meet you and you know the rest. And don't forget—bring me back the tattoo. I want proof that I can see with my own eyes. I'm leaving now for the clubhouse. Call me as soon as you have a solid fix."

"Will do."

Sheherezade jumped out of the car at the far end of the parking lot and made the walk alone, with her suitcase, in high heels. Taking a deep breath, she threw her head back slightly, a la Marilyn, put a smile on her face, and turned on the wiggle as she made her way down the middle of the airport toward the V.I.P. lounge. People were ogling her and she pretended she loved the attention, turning to them, looking them directly in the eye, and giving them a little giggle. A girl with a teddy bear smiled at her and reminded her so much of Lila that she felt a rush of determination to do whatever it was going to take to live with her beloved niece again.

Swami turned to look at the beautiful Marilyn Monroe look alike who was smiling at the little girl holding onto the teddy bear. Her eyes reminded him of someone, somewhere—beautiful soulful eyes that shone with the same innocence and joy. *Lion's wife at the picnic when he was entertaining every one with magic tricks. Na,* he thought, *it couldn't be.* As he got closer he began to think that this girl had the same body type—not exactly Marilyn—thinner but definitely curvy. As he closed in on her he became more convinced that perhaps he was on the trail of Lion's wayward wife. He followed her through the long passageway, past stores and ticket counters until he saw her approach a distinguished looking woman standing with her chauffeur outside the V.I.P. lounge. *No, the pieces didn't fit. Sheherezade would not be meeting anyone at the airport.* He had to be mistaken. He turned and walked to the V.I.P. counter to make arrangements for his flight on the Pride jet to Nice.

Sheherezade's heart started to race when she saw a well groomed woman in a lilac coloured pant suit standing beside a man in a chauffeur's uniform in front of the V.I.P. lounge. When she was close enough to see her porcelain face touched with sentiment and teary eyed, she knew. It was like looking into a mirror. Dropping her suitcase, she ran up to her grandmother and they embraced like family that were being united after a long period of absence, rather than complete strangers. In the V.I.P. lounge Violet's chauffeur went over to the refreshment counter while Sheherezade and her grandmother sat down side by side on a comfortable couch.

"I just cannot believe it," she said as she grabbed Sheherezade's hand.

"You have your father's eyes, you *are* your father's daughter, and you are so . . . beautiful." Sheherezade indulged in a nervous laugh before her tears fell on her lap.

"I know where he got his eyes, grandmother," she said looking at a mirror image of herself. "I'm so thankful that I had a chance to see you before I left. I wish I could stay but it's impossible. I'm in danger here . . . I'm running from my abusive husband. It's a long story and I can call you now that I have your phone number and explain everything. I'm so afraid you will think I'm a flake when really I'm just trying to live a life I can be proud of with my niece, Lila. As soon as I can get settled and get some money together I am going to find a way to get her out of the private school where she is boarding and have her live with me. My husband doesn't know her whereabouts but he will be using his considerable resources to find her and I have to get to her before he does." Despair was settling into the corners of Sheherezade's eyes as she reflected on the hopeless situation she was describing.

"My dear, don't be so discouraged! You have me now and all the resources of the Ivey family. Firstly, you are wealthy in your own right. It seems your mother and sister took the first instalment of your inheritance but that was only a small portion of the entire trust. When I had the lawyers make up the terms of your inheritance, I made up two separate documents which dispensed the money in two totally different ways. Upon meeting your sister I was struck by how similar she was to your mother in many ways and how controlled she seemed to be by her. At that moment I decided to use the document that dispensed the money in controlled sums. If I had met the gentle, intelligent, sophisticated, young woman that sits before me I would have used the second document that assigned you complete discretion over the trust which is a considerable fortune by anyone's standards. Now it is yours, and when you arrive at your destination we will arrange to give you complete access. As for your niece, why not let me pick her up? There is nothing I would love more than to care for a little girl that would remind me of you until we can all be together again." Sheherezade face was lit up with joy and excitement and she reached over and gave her grandmother a hug.

"Grandmother, that is unbelievable . . . I don't have to worry about money?" she looked dazed and incredulous.

"No, dear your grandfather and father took good care of us." Violet smiled beyond the pain she felt for the difficult life her granddaughter had lived because of Regina.

"You could take care of Lila, until I got back?" she repeated, to test the reality of her luck.

"I would love to! Just tell me where to find her and I will pick her up tomorrow."

"This is too wonderful! She's in Toronto at the Bishop Stratton private school for girls. What I have not told you is that my sister, Brandi, died a few days ago and I don't want Lila to know until I can tell her myself. She only has me now. I speak to her almost daily and I've been preparing her for the day someone would pick her up from the school unexpectedly. The school is also aware that someone may come on my behalf to take her out on short notice." Sheherezade opened the suitcase and pulled out a small New Testament Bible which held the dried wild rose.

"Take this. I told Lila that our secret password was the wild rose and that the person sent by me to pick her up would have it." She gave the Bible to Violet and tears left one more trail of black mascara down her cheeks.

Just then a man in a crisp blue uniform came up to Sheherezade, leaned over and discretely informed her that he was the steward on her plane and that it was time to leave. Violet grabbed both of Sheherezade's hands and squeezed.

"You are a strong girl and you'll be fine. Don't worry, we will have this all straightened out in no time and then we are going to get to know one another. I want you in my life dear. You and Lila. You have family that loves you now. Just let me know where I can have some money sent to you as soon as possible. Try to relax, have a nice trip and don't worry about anything. I imagine you have been shouldering too much responsibility for a long, long time."

"I think I might be able to relax now that I have you in my life," Sheherezade smiled through tears. She stood up and looked over at the steward who nodded in her direction as if to confirm her decision to get going. Her grandmother went into her purse, pulled out a wallet, and pressed it into Sheherezade's hands.

"Take this, darling," she said softly as she gave her a hug.

"You have no idea what meeting you has meant to me grandmother. I just wish we had met under better circumstances and I hope I am able to see you again soon."

"Do what you must do and take care of yourself . . . we will be together soon." Violet assured her granddaughter.

Chapter 52

Sheherezade's spirit was so light she felt as if she could have flown to France without the airplane. It had been hours since she had any food so she dug into the sirloin tip steak dinner with relish as soon as they were airborne. The Merlot wine produced a warm glow throughout her body that seemed to calm down the tremor that had plagued her since she received the phone call from Ace. After seven hours of perfect sleep, the steward woke her and told her that they would be landing at Nice airport in about twenty minutes. The weather outside looked glorious. She went into the bathroom and examined the sorry remnants of Marilyn Monroe. In a few minutes she was showered and ready to meet her future.

A driver in uniform stood beside a long black limousine keeping a careful vigil for his passenger. There was a nod of recognition to her as soon as she exited the door from the airport. In fifteen minutes they were in downtown Cannes, the glamorous city which is the jewel of the French Riviera. She delighted in seeing the cute cafes and the white sandy beaches of the Mediterranean Sea, before they began navigating the steep road that led to the hills beyond the city. They pulled into a long driveway of a modern bungalow with a view of the sparkling Mediterranean far below. She had learned that the driver's name was Claude and that he had been employed by Ace for twenty-two years.

Sheherezade was greeted by a small dark haired woman with a kind face and a big smile.

"You're here! How marvellous! Where are my manners? Hello, my name is Denise," she said as she leaned over and gave Sheherezade four kisses back and forth from cheek to cheek.

"Hello, I'm Sheherezade. I can't convey how nice it is to meet you!" she giggled at her reference to her new found freedom.

"Ace was pacing most of the night. I must call her! She went down to the club to rehearse in order to get her mind off things—she was just beside herself until she heard you got out. Please, my dear, follow me and I will show you your room." Sheherezade followed Denise through the gorgeous bungalow to a bedroom with a window that overlooked the pool at the rear of the house.

"This is lovely, thank you so much!" Sheherezade smiled.

"Get settled and then we will see you by the pool for some real French cooking," Denise winked as she bustled out the door. Sheherezade walked over to the French doors that opened onto the back patio and gazed out over the pool area, taking in the clear blue sky and bright sun that was shining on her new life of freedom. Suddenly, a man emerged from the pool and stood by the edge drying his hair before walking toward the table under the umbrella that was set for lunch. Sheherezade could not help but stare at his perfectly proportioned body and handsome face. His cheeks had hollows that emphasized his square chiselled cheek bones and his hair fell in curls around his ears and neck. A small feeling of expectation in her stomach made her realize that the fear and shock were wearing off and that her reactions were becoming normal. After washing her face and brushing her teeth, she looked into the suitcase and realized that she had nothing else to wear. *Freedom is nothing left to lose,* she thought, *and smiled as she put on her white halter dress once again.*

She passed Denise, who was working in the kitchen, and found the large glass French doors that led to the pool area. The sun was shining brightly and there wasn't a cloud in the sky. *Bliss,* she thought. As she came toward the table set for lunch the man stood up. Sheherezade blushed as she looked into his beautiful face. There was an uneasy moment of silence before she stuck out her hand and said, "Hello, I'm Sheherezade."

"Hi, I'm Jim." Sheherezade looked a little puzzled and he quickly added, "I'm Ace's son. I guess I'm still a tightly guarded secret."

"You certainly are . . ." she said with a nervous giggle.

"We were all praying . . . it must have been harrowing," Jim said seriously.

"I'm still in shock. It was physically and emotionally exhausting but I couldn't be happier and I can't wait to thank your mother and you, of course, for helping me." She looked at him shyly and blushed again at the intensity of his gaze. Jim poured each of them a large glass of white wine and served the salad.

"You have a beautiful home, how long have you lived here?" Sheherezade asked.

"Well, we have a rather unusual lifestyle. Our general policy is to move every three months and when we move, it's usually to a different part of the world each time. This place is a rental and we have been here for a little more than three months. We were just saying this morning that we are due to find a new home, so in the next couple of days we are going to go to Paraguay for a few months. Lion still uses his considerable resources to track my mother so we don't have a choice. We both hope that someday we can settle down . . . ." Denise brought out Chateaubriand with frits and Jim served the food.

"That one man can create so much havoc in other people's lives is unbelievable," she said softly.

"Unfortunately, you are going to have to adopt the same precautions—he's indefatigable," Jim said clenching his jaw.

"I know it was the Purple Flames who rescued me and helped me get here so I take it you and your mother are still associated with the club?" she asked tentatively.

"No, my mother and father broke all ties with the club shortly after they got together but some of the guys who were with my father from the beginning still have loyalty to her and we needed their help to get you out of there, so we took it. But no, they do not support us financially. My father left my mother with plenty of money from his association with the club. She and I turned that money into enough money to support us for the rest of our lives—and in style," he said proudly.

"So what keeps you busy?" she looked into his warm brown eyes and did not want to look away.

"I couldn't have a career like the average person, so I earned a degree in business under an assumed name and travelled the world with my mother. Now, I look after our money and swim a lot," he grinned as he ran his fingers through his sun streaked hair.

"Well, I guess swimming as a vocation might work for me," she laughed. Jim fussed with the ice bucket as he stole a glance at her perfect face.

"Mum is going to like you. I can't wait until you meet her. The only positive thing I have to say about Lion is that he has remarkably good taste in women." Jim smiled and Sheherezade could not help but stare at his full curvy lips that did not quite cover his perfectly white teeth gleaming in the Mediterranean sun. Jim was simply the most handsome man she had ever laid eyes on and she was having a difficult time removing her gaze in a socially acceptable manner.

"Thanks . . . when will I have the pleasure of meeting your mother?"

"She was very worried about you last night and she had been a bundle of nerves ever since she made the plan. She thought if she lost herself in rehearsing, she could get her mind off of things. I know that Denise called her when you arrived so she shouldn't be long now."

"She actually sings in public?" Sheherezade was surprised.

"She loves to perform and it's her one small indulgence. Over the years she has only performed a few times and when she does she earns so much acclaim that we usually get out of town in a hurry. We knew we were leaving soon so she decided to do a show. There's a very good chance that this will be the last time. How would you like to go to the club to hear her sing tonight?"

"I would love to!" Sheherezade's hand came to her heart involuntarily as she smiled back at Jim.

Voices drew their attention in the direction of the house. Denise was following a slim woman who was pulling off a blond wig as she came through the French doors. Sheherezade ran to her and they embraced each other like long lost friends. Jim gave Denise a nod that indicated that they should leave them alone.

Ace put her hands on Sheherezade's head and looked at her square in the eye.

"You made it! Are you O.K.?" Sheherezade looked into her big brown eyes and was startled by her beauty. Her long black hair almost touched her waist and she had a serene intelligence about her that made Sheherezade's heart feel like it was bursting with trust and affection for this complete stranger.

"I'm O.K. This has been the happiest day of my life and I don't know how I can thank you. But I have one question that I have been asking myself since I received your phone call . . ."

"What's that?" Ace chuckled.

"Why? Why did you do it? Help me?" she asked as the tears fell down her face.

Ace's face was completely dead panned. "I just wanted to knock the smirk off Lion's face." The intimate knowledge of Lion they shared set them into a fit of nervous laughter that was sublimation for the pain they had both experienced at his hands. When they finally stopped laughing, Ace turned sombre. "I know about life with Lion. He was possessive, controlling, and abusive with me as well. He blamed Jimmy for our break up, but the truth was that I was looking for a way out and I just happened to find the man of my dreams at the same time. When I heard that Lion had a new victim in you, I just had to get you out of there. He likes to play God with other people's lives and we have to do whatever we can to stop him. And, besides . . . I owed him one." Sheherezade saw the pain in Ace's eyes and it was evident that no one had ever replaced Jimmy in her heart.

"Who told you that I was in a bad situation?" Sheherezade asked knowing that Lion only surrounded himself with loyal subjects.

"It's better if I don't tell you; that way I don't have to worry about that person's safety. You can imagine what Lion would do if he knew I had a friend in his lair." Sheherezade felt foolish for asking, but curiosity had gotten the better of her.

"He is everywhere, isn't he? I wonder what life will be like when I am looking over my shoulder all the time." Ace put her arm around Sheherezade. "You'll have a glorious and fulfilling life just to spite that asshole. We won't let him win. Never!" Sheherezade loved this woman's strength and admired her for living so long in fear of Lion.

"Never," Sheherezade reaffirmed. They walked back into the kitchen where Jim was standing with Denise.

"Well, we have tomorrow and forever to get to know one another but now I am going for a nap so I can put on a show tonight. Jim has convinced me that I shouldn't be taking these kinds of chances so it will probably be my last performance and I want to really enjoy it. See you later, guys!"

"Would you like to rest up for the performance or would you like to go sightseeing?" Jim asked, his eyes dancing with enthusiasm.

"I slept on the plane. I'd love to see Cannes!" Sheherezade said enthusiastically.

Jim and Sheherezade shopped at the outdoor kiosks swarming with patrons in the backstreets of Cannes. They collaborated on the choice of some vegetables but when they came upon a flower stand Jim knew exactly what he wanted.

"White roses for my mother when she finishes her performance, and pink roses for your room," Jim announced. Sheherezade blushed and put her head down to hide the tears of sadness and joy that were falling from her eyes. She had never gone shopping with Lion, and it was this tiny fragment of normal life that she had missed so much because of her strange childhood.

"Let's go down to the water and find a café. I know it is going to take a few glasses of wine to make those tears go away but we can make a start." Sheherezade looked up into his face and caught her breath, "Sounds nice."

Yachts, sailboats, and speedboats danced in the sparkling sea and bathers, topless in every shape and size, lounged on the beach below them. Sheherezade breathed in the sea air as they strolled down the Croisette, the glamorous street lined with designer stores and cafes with tables spilling onto the sidewalk. Many of the people walking by, looking for that perfect place to eat, were dressed in beautiful evening gowns and tuxedoes.

Sheherezade saw a long clingy white dress in a window and remembered that she had nothing to wear to the club. In the dressing room she peered at her reflection in the stunning dress and wondered if she could afford to buy it. Opening the wallet her grandmother had given her, she sat down on the small bench in disbelief. The purse had at least fifty one thousand dollar bills and an international cashier's check for one hundred thousand dollars. In the midst of the excitement the reality of what her grandmother had told her had not sunk in and, for the first time, she was being forced to acknowledge that she was an heiress. An heiress! She had an attack of the giggles and hoped that Jim and the salesperson had not heard her cackling like a mad woman alone in the change room.

They shared a glass of wine and ordered a plate of cheese in a quaint little café. "This town is so beautiful. I think I'll stay here for a while—until I can sort out my life. I just wish you and Ace were staying a while longer," she said wistfully.

Jim's face clouded.

"That's too bad. We assumed you would travel with us—for a while at least. We could help you out financially and maybe get you established somewhere. . . ."

"Well, you have no idea how much I appreciate your offer and your help. I left Lion without one pittance to my name and I would have been lost without your generosity at that point but I discovered that I have a grandmother that I did not even know existed until yesterday, and she gave me money so I have no reason to impose on your generosity." Jim took a sip of wine and was quiet for a moment.

"My mother has to leave for her safety's sake. But I could stay here for a while and help you get settled," he said watching her reaction closely. Sheherezade smiled and her violet-blue eyes crinkled at the corners. "I would love that," she answered sincerely hoping that he would not see her blushing in the shade of the awning.

Chapter 53

Regina sat in the holding cell waiting to be processed on charges of fraud. Her mouth twitched nervously as she tried to push the image of Violet Ivey out of her mind. She was attempting to concoct a positive spin for her present situation, however, the hubris she relied on to provide some modicum of comfort in tight situations such as these was failing her. What was worse was the niggling thought that Sherry was behind this and that she was now the beneficiary of all that money.

"Well, you're back and this time without your mink . . ." the Correctional Officer with the red pony tail commented sarcastically as she opened the cell door. When she heard that Regina was back, she switched positions with the Admissions & Discharge officer in order to experience this moment of karmic satisfaction.

"Remember me? I am the fuckin' loser who has nothing better to do than sit around a jail all day and get fat. What a coincidence! It seems you have nothing better to do either!" she said roaring with laughter. She invited Regina to join her in the strip room for processing.

"We'll see if we can find you some designer clothes. I hope you like orange . . ." she laughed again. "It's going to be your colour for a long time."

Regina was not the cheerful, animated, charmer that the staff usually saw in the admission area. Her nostrils flared as she was compelled to strip down and expose all of her orifices for inspection. When she finally got to the assessment unit she gave the girl on the phone such a look of indignation that she quickly hung up in order to free it up for Regina.

"Luke, ya, it's over now, so I just have to sit and wait." She threw her head back proudly but her gnashing jaw belied her words. "No,

I'm fine. You know me—I'm a chameleon. These little bitches are nothing. I can deal with anything they throw at me. I've been there and done that. Did you talk to the lawyer? It might take a while to sell Brandi's condo but her car and jewellery would be a start. There was a small fortune there. As soon as we get it you can post bail." A smug look passed over her face and then her eyes began to dart back and forth as she remained silent listening to Luke.

"Next of kin! No fuckin' way! I'm her mother. Lila is just a kid! What is she going to do with Brandi's stuff? That's ridiculous!" she fumed.

Regina was finished with this conversation. She did not like to hear news that contradicted her view of the world—the way she wanted it to be. Inheriting Brandi's things was her last hope and she knew it.

A woman she was acquainted with from the neighbourhood waved to her and she quickly used her as an excuse to end the call with Luke. She walked over to the common room with a big smile on her face as if she did not have a care in the world.

"Great to see you Debbie. Who would have thought we would be meeting here?" she chuckled.

"Reggie! Dennis saw Luke down at the bar and he was saying that you guys came into a lot of money. What are you doing here?" Debbie was an alcoholic who often did small bits for boosting. Regina made a dismissive gesture with her hand.

"It is just a big misunderstanding. I'll get it all sorted out when I go to court. You know the police here just get carried away with their power. Our congressman is looking into allegations against the police force in New Jersey for their corruption and for overstepping their authority. We have to do something about it; if we don't they are going to get out of hand." Debbie nodded in agreement and then said she was sorry about the death of Brandi. Regina face took on a sombre aura.

"Yes, it was a big shock. Real big. She was so young and successful. That girl was going places. She was living in a big penthouse in Manhattan. Very wealthy. She had the world at her feet. She reminded me a lot of myself. A real go-getter."

"Did you get to see her in the hospital before she passed?" Debbie asked sympathetically.

"No. No, the nurse called me when they brought her in and told me that she was unconscious and only had a few moments to live. It was a real tragedy . . ."

"Well, you still have Sherry. What a lovely person . . . such class! You did something right with that one. She's a real gem!" Debbie beamed. Regina's mouth pursed.

"I just remembered. I've got to call Luke," Regina announced dramatically as she left Debbie standing in the middle of the common room.

Fired by unmitigated hate, Lion sat in the tower of the clubhouse looking out over his kingdom and waiting for the call from the Swami. He told himself that Sheherezade's escape was a temporary situation and he would find her before long, just as he had found Ace. White heat flooded his brain whenever he was reminded that he did not know Sheherezade's present whereabouts. *One thing at a time*, he told himself. *He would prevail but he must focus.* The ringing of the phone ended his mental acrobatics. "Hello," he said impatiently.

"Ya, Lion. Everything is on target. The satellite located her when she turned on her phone at about three o'clock French time and we traced it to a club in Cannes. We found out that she is scheduled to perform there tonight with her band called The Exiles."

"Terrific. Call me beforehand. I want you to leave the phone on when you do it. I've waited a long time for this. I'm going to make you a rich man Swami."

Sheherezade spent some time fussing over her makeup and getting dressed for the club. Her mind drifted to a vision of Jim and her stomach did a small summersault. *Here I am, twenty-one years old and going on my first normal date.* She had to laugh. O.K., so falling for your ex-husband's, ex-girlfriend's son while in exile and on the lam was not exactly normal but it was certainly as close to normal as she was likely to get. Only one thing in her world was amiss. Fear gripped her but she forced herself to dial her grandmother's number.

"Hello," the voice came back cheerfully.

"Grandmother, it's Sheherezade."

"Hello, dear. Is everything alright?" her grandmother asked anxiously.

"Yes, just fine." She couldn't bring herself to ask about Lila as much as she wanted to hear something, anything, about the situation.

"Guess who I have with me?"

"Grandmother! Is Lila there? Sheherezade screamed.

"She sure is and she reminds me so much of you. Here I'll let you speak to her . . ."

"Hi, Meme! I'm with Grandma Ivey! She showed me the rose so I came home with her and she lives in a big house and I am going to stay here until you come back!" Tears ran down Sheherezade's face and she tried not to let Lila hear the emotion in her voice when she spoke, "I'm so glad you're back with Grandma Ivey. You're going to be so happy there and I can call you everyday. That's so wonderful Lila! You be a good girl for Grandma Ivey."

"When are you coming home, Meme?"

"Lila, I want us to be together more than anything in the world. You know that don't you?"

"Yes, I know that Meme. I know you would never forget about me . . ."

"No, my angel. I could never forget about you, and as soon as I can come and see you I will."

"I can't wait!"

"I know. I can't wait either . . . but I can't talk for long tonight. Let me speak to Grandma Ivey, now and I will call you tomorrow morning. Bye honey."

"I think she's going to like it here," Violet said as she looked at Lila and smiled.

"Thank you for helping me. I know she's not your relative and it is so very kind of you to help us out like this."

"Don't give it another thought. She's your family and that makes her my family. Finding my only granddaughter yesterday and now having a little girl to look after has surpassed my wildest dreams—I couldn't be happier. Are you sure you are O.K. there?"

"I think I might be having one of the best days of my life," Sheherezade said as she suddenly noticed she could breath deeper. "Knowing Lila is safe was my last worry. Oh, and thank you so much for the money grandmother. You are so generous. I just thank God I found you. You made my life possible and I will be forever grateful."

"My dear, it is *your* money. Just let me know when you want the accountant to send more."

"I think I should sit down and write you a letter explaining my weird situation before you decide to disown me," she said laughing.

"You are so much like Terry," Violet whispered as her voice choked. "And he was as solid as a rock. As long as I live I will be here for you, dear. I just hope that is a long, long time."

"Thank you, grandmother. I love you." Sheherezade was surprised as the words tumbled out of her mouth but she knew that they were sincere.

"I love you, Sheherezade. Your father loved you very much too."

"I'll speak to you tomorrow," she said soulfully. *Tomorrow. How wonderful it was to look forward to another day,* she thought. That was something that had not happened in quite some time but suddenly her world was changing.

She checked herself in the mirror and fixed the mascara that recently never seemed to stay where she put it, when she heard a knock on the door.

"Hey, Sheherzade, it's Jim. How's it going?" he yelled threw the door. "We should get going . . ."

She opened the door with a look of concern on her face.

"I'm sorry I ran late. I had a conversation with my niece and it took a little longer than I expected . . . ." Jim was standing in front of her staring at her. After a moment she became self-conscious and thought maybe she had missed some mascara that had fallen with her tears.

"Oh, do I have something on my face?" she asked.

"No. No. It isn't that . . ." he muttered.

"What?" she asked, suddenly becoming concerned.

"Has anyone ever told you that you are the most beautiful person they have ever seen?" She gave him a small poke on the arm and asked him how many times he had asked that question today. He laughed and looked into her eyes, "No, really." She returned his gaze and answered, "Well you aren't going to win any ugly contests either, Jim." They laughed and walked out into the fragrant night air.

The club was situated in the downtown core of Cannes, not too far from the beach. At the front door, a slat with thin bars across it opened to allow an inspection before it closed again and allowed them entry. Smoke hung in the air and the large room was filled with a mature, well-heeled clientele waiting expectantly and sipping drinks on the café style tables. The hostess seated them at a reserved table at the front and took their drink order. Jim looked over at Sheherezade with a look of admiration that said everything. She blushed and smiled back at him holding his gaze. He reached out and took her hand and she squeezed his fingers as if to return his sentiment.

The spell was broken when the band started to play and the crowd broke into applause as Ace walked onto the stage in a dramatic blue sequined dress with a split up to her hip on one side. Her long black hair brushed her waist and when she turned to face Jim and Sheherezade her beautiful face took on a youthful exuberance that told Sheherezade that, at this moment, she was doing what she truly loved. Sheherezade was in awe when Ace opened her mouth and began to sing. Many people had mentioned that she was blessed with talent but nothing prepared her for the sheer force of nature that stood before her. The crowd cheered and applauded after every song with such gratitude and appreciation that Sheherezade understood what Jim meant when he said that her performances created too much attention for someone who was trying to keep a low profile. After approximately forty-five minutes, the set ended with thunderous applause and Ace left the stage. Jim and Sheherezade joined her backstage as she had a cold ice tea between sets.

"You are in great form tonight, mum," Jim said proudly.

"You're such a musical genius, Ace. I'll never forget your performance tonight. I'm so glad I had a chance to see you sing before you quit. It's just a shame that . . ." Ace cut in before the evening took on a melancholy aura of what could have been, "Let's just enjoy tonight. I don't know about you two but I am having the time of my life."

"It's a very special night for us too," he said as he looked over at Sheherezade.

"I better get ready for the next set. I hope you like the last song Sheher. It is a song about Lion written by Soul's Gate. They gave it to me years ago because they said I did it better than they ever could. It was Lion's favourite song. Pity he'll never get to hear me sing it again," she said with a wry smile.

While Jim and Sheherezade waited for the next set to start they talked about going to the beach the next day and then having dinner at the Palm Beach Club where they would play roulette, and dance the night away in the adjoining disco. Before they could make more plans, the band returned to the stage and played a five minute instrumental before Ace walked out wearing a red satin dress that clung to her perfect figure. Her hair was pulled away from her face with a headband that sported exotic feathers also in red and her long hair cascaded down the front of the high neck dress to expose a very low cut back.

The songs in this set were somewhat slower and heartfelt. Sheherezade thought that they took on new meaning knowing that these were the last words she would probably sing to an audience. Jim took her hand in his and together they shared the sadness of what their life would never be because of Lion.

A man sitting close to the exit got up and walked outside. He took a position under a tree where he lit a cigarette, took a cell phone out of his pocket, and dialed a number.

"Yep. Got her."

"What does she look like?" Lion asked impatiently.

"The same boss. Decked out. Beautiful." Swami realized too late that his comment might have rubbed salt into an open wound. "But listen, you are not going to fuckin' believe this. Your little lady is here too."

"Sheherezade?! Sheherezade is there?" Lion yelled incredulously.

"Yep, and she's not alone."

"What do you mean she's not alone?" Lion roared.

"She came in with a guy about thirty years old and they have been holding hands. I asked the guy at the door who he was and he said he was Ace's son."

The phone was silent for a moment and then Lion asked quietly, "Swami, who does he look like? Could he be my son?" Swami searched his mind to recall the face of the guy who came in with Sheherezade.

"Christ! It never occurred to me! He's the image of Jimmy! He must be Jimmy's son!" Lion put his head back and closed his eyes. *It was happening again. First Jimmy. Now his son.* Standing in the middle of the control room, he clenched his fists and began to shake with such anger that his face looked like it would explode.

"Swami, I want you to go back in and kill them! All of them! Wait for me to give the final go ahead and leave this fucking phone on so that I can hear!" he commanded.

Swami walked into the club and looked up on stage to see Ace take the microphone in her hand to ready herself for the last song. She walked to the edge of the stage and Swami was shocked to see how little she had changed in all those years. He was mesmerized by her exotic beauty, and emotion, that had long since been lost with his youth, stirred in his heart. He had loved her; they all had. What man could resist a woman like that?

The room became quiet and then the guitar started to play a soft Spanish rhythm. Ace stepped into the spotlight, her black hair gleaming under the lights, as she began to sing.

> Entrance to the building,
> Holding a lantern . . .

Swami spoke into the phone, "Now boss? The time is right."

"No, Lion screamed. I want to hear her sing this song. When it's over I'll give you the final go ahead. Then, do it!"

> You make a gesture
> With your free hand
> Doorway with a shady figure
>> Oh Black Cat
>> Standing there beneath the moonlight
>> Oh Black Cat
>> Turn around now and he'll be gone

In the abandoned building adjacent to the clubhouse a Ruger tactical rifle was pointed at Lion's head. As the man adeptly adjusted the scope, his silver hair gleamed in the moonlight that was pouring in through the dusty window.

> Through a narrow street
> In the dead of night
> While faces bathe
> In the TV light

> A black cat gives you a start
> Through you go
> The streets you love
>> Oh Black Cat
>> Standing there beneath the moonlight . . . .

Lion knew the song well. It had been written as a tribute to him, the black cat, and Ace used to sing it to him. The song was about to end and he knew they only had a few seconds more of life. He had won. He threw his head back and laughed.

The sharpshooter lined up the scope with Lion's open mouth and pulled the trigger.

> Oh Black Cat
> Turn around, now, and he'll be gone . . . .

Epilogue

Hunger overcame Sheherezade. She bit into a slice of Marshall's thin-crust caviar pizza and felt her chest tighten involuntarily. Suddenly her mind was awash with the memories of the slice of pizza she had stashed away in her purse that day at Mick's knowing that there was not enough food in the house for everyone's dinner. The sting of poverty was still there; maybe it would never go away. The feelings of desperation and helplessness would sit dormant until some olfactory recall brought them to the surface and taunted her new reality. She could not believe the dramatic turn of events that had changed her life completely in just a few months!

Her mind wondered back to that day, when as the heiress to the Ivey fortune, she had walked into to the law offices of the Ivey building with her grandmother and they had listened to Lion's lawyer read the list of assets that were now hers as the only living relative of Lion Terkel:

> 1000 acres estate Ottsville, Pennsylvania
> 100 acres at Indian Lake, New York
> Villa Tunis, Tunisia
> Coop Condominium Manhattan, New York
> Commercial Properties, Index A
> Corporations Index B
> Yacht (Sheherezade), Helicopter, Jet,
> Vehicles, Sports RV's Index C
> Four billion, thirty-eight million ($ U.S.)

This news, along with the death of Brandi, were morsels of reality so incredible that she had to pause often to ponder them in the hope that her subconscious would eventually accept them as truth.

It was already Christmas Eve and Sheherezade stood on the deck wrapped in a velour throw, mesmerized by the moonbeams dancing on the lake. At the highest elevation on the horizon, a large white cross lit by spotlights glowed in the evening sky. Sheherezade turned and entered the glass doors that led into the grand room of the cottage. She and Lila had decided that they wanted to spend most of their time living by the lake. The construction of the cottage had been finished about one month ago, just in time for the interior decorators to take over and ready their new home for Christmas. Despite the fact that it had become a twelve thousand square foot marvel of architecture, her instructions to the interior decorator to make it cosy were translated with pure artistic genius.

On the first level, the grand room's bank of windows featured a full view of the lake. The ceiling was twenty feet high and tonight the eight foot Christmas tree, sheltering an enormous stack of presents, stood sparkling in the reflection of the huge wood burning fireplace at the far end of the room. Smells of cinnamon and vanilla wafted in from the oversized kitchen where Marshall was preparing a magnificent feast for the night's festivities. He often worked his magic preparing gourmet meals from the main house which gave her a chance to experiment with recipes in her new kitchen, including her favourite recipe for Couscous which she brought from Tunisia. The main floor also had a library, an office, a dining room, a family room, a home theatre, an exercise room and a large studio where Shcherezade painted. She had taken pictures of the lake when the leaves were turning in the fall and a four by five canvass waited patiently for her to put the finishing touches of red and yellow on the leaves of the trees. The first work completed in her new studio had been a portrait of her father which now hung on the main wall in the grand room. Her collection of French Impressionist Art was scattered throughout the house but she had not found a place for her collection of original work; she could no longer identify with the mood that had inspired her, and they felt eerily foreign to her now.

Upstairs, there were five bedrooms each with its own bathroom. The two main suites, occupied by herself and Lila, also had lovely sitting rooms that overlooked the lake. Outside, the magnificent pool with Jacuzzi awaited the completion of the stone patio and outdoor fireplace. The indoor pool with solarium was enjoyed almost daily by Sheherezade, Lila, and Violet.

Sheherezade heard footsteps and turned to see Natasha coming down the stairs.

"Everything looks wonderful Sher. Thanks for inviting me up for the holidays. I just love it here!" Natasha gushed.

"What's the matter? You look like you've seen a ghost." Sheherezade's eyes flooded with tears as she began to speak slowly.

"I did some blood tests last week and the office called to say the doctor wanted to go over the results with me. I was on my way to the tattoo parlour to get a wild rose tattoo where the Pride logo used to be so I thought I might as well stop into the office on my way." Natasha's stomach gripped her hard.

"What is it Sher?"

"They told me it was impossible . . . after what Lion did to me . . . ."

"Tell me . . . are you alright?"

"Oh, Natasha . . . I'm pregnant." Natasha's mouth fell open and stayed open as she hugged her friend.

"Sher, that's a miracle!"

"I know . . . I can't believe it. I'm going to tell Jim later when we're alone but I just had to tell you because you know . . . "

Sheherezade dropped her head so no one else would notice the tears falling from her eyes.

"Natasha, dear friend, you know what it took to get here . . . for girls like us to find this kind of happiness. Only you can appreciate how much it means to me."

Natasha hugged Sheherezade and whispered, "I know".

Lila came running into the room with Bugsy following behind her wearing a small pair of cloth reindeer antlers flopping around the top of his head.

"That is one funny looking reindeer, Lila!" Sheherezade laughed.

"Ya, but he doesn't know . . . he thinks he looks good!"

"I think you're right. We better take a picture of him in case he decides to run off and help Santa pull the sled. Don't you think?" She snapped a picture of Lila and Bugsy by the tree. Just then Violet walked downstairs dressed elegantly in a purple pantsuit. Amethysts surrounded by diamonds glittered from her ears. Sheherezade walked the length of the room to greet her.

"Grandmother! You look beautiful! But we are going to have to have a little talk. You are always wearing my favourite colour . . . and you are cramping my style somewhat," Sheherezade teased as she hugged her grandmother.

"You are an original, my dear. Trust me, all eyes are on you all of the time, so it doesn't really matter what anyone else is wearing," she smiled as she looked into her son's violet-blue eyes.

Lila and Sheherezade had lived at Violet's estate in Westchester when she returned from France and she supervised the construction of the cottage from there. The house where Dr.Lindsay had lived was being torn down and replaced with a new home for Violet. Once that was complete, Violet would bring the couple that worked as her housekeeper and chauffeur, down from New York.

Lila and Violet were inseparable. From the first moment they were together they seemed to love each other as if they were family members who had been together all of their lives. There had been no question that they wanted to live close enough that they could see each other every day and Sheherezade had the added bonus of getting to know her father through the stories that Violet never tired of recounting. They looked over at Natasha and Lila sitting quietly and talking by the fireplace.

"Funny, she hasn't mentioned Regina at all. Do you think she has forgotten about her?" Violet wondered.

"Honestly, grandmother, I don't think she cares. Regina was never a grandmother to her. She never paid any attention to her and when she did, it was never a positive interaction."

"And what about you, my dear?"

"When you are taught from the time you are a child that you are not important and that your parent is important you are bound to feel guilty when you are not dedicating your life to their happiness. It's a reflex that I will have to fight because it never goes away. But I do not believe I have to be tethered to her forever because we share some DNA. So grandmother, don't expect to bump into her at any of my family Christmas parties. Love is the only affiliation that should be cherished. Love defines who is in my family and I think everyone in my family will be here and accounted for tonight." Violet looked at her granddaughter with affection and reached over and gave her a hug.

"I agree with everything you said and the strange part is that I heard your father espouse a similar philosophy many times. He would have been so proud of you." Sheherezade giggled at the contradiction and looked up at the large portrait of her father hanging beside them on the wall.

"Meme, aunt Ace and Jim are here!" Lila yelled. Jim placed an enormous bag of gifts on the floor so he could take Sheherezade in his arms and kiss her.

"You look gorgeous tonight. Have I told you how much I love you today?" he whispered.

"No! You haven't. And I've been waiting all day," Sheherezade quipped.

"Let's see the Wild Rose! Did it hurt?"

Sheherezade looked deep into his eyes.

"I'm going to tell you all about my new Wild Rose later, when we're all alone." Jim saw the promise in her eyes and took a deep breath.

"Where were you two?" Sheherezade asked.

"You won't believe it! Mum's agent called and asked if she would be available to perform at Caesar's Palace on New Year's Eve. It was short notice so we spent the day making arrangements and I wanted to tell you the news in person." Jim beamed with pride.

"Did you hear that grandmother? Ace is going to be performing at Caesar's Palace on New Year's Eve!" Sheherezade exclaimed as she rushed over to Ace to give her a hug.

"Can we get seats?" Violet asked Jim. "We all want to go!"

"Yes," Lila jumped up and down. "Can we see aunt Ace sing, Meme?"

"Well, do you think we would miss that?" Sheherezade asked incredulously. Jim carried the presents over to the tree and Lila helped him find a place for each. Ace and Jim had been living at the main house while her turreted stone mansion was under construction at the other end of the property.

Ace looked stunning in a champagne coloured silk pantsuit with large diamond drop earrings that peeked out from beneath her long straight black hair. As they walked toward the tree, Violet turned to her, "I am so excited for you Ace! Sheherezade has never stopped raving about your talent and I can't wait to see you perform."

"I'm excited too. I never thought that I would have my life back and Jim . . . ." They looked over and saw Jim sitting on the couch with his arm around Sheherezade. "Well," Ace said as she choked up and her eyes filled with tears, "I'm glad he can finally have a normal life too."

"Yes, they were made for each other," Violet pronounced.

Ace's eyes danced with mischief. "I'm going to let you in on a secret. After dinner Jim is going to give Sheherezade a gorgeous diamond engagement ring and propose." Violets hands went involuntarily to her mouth and her eyes filled up. She put her head down quickly in case anyone was looking and was wondering why she was so surprised.

"How wonderful!" she said quietly to Ace.

"Yes. If I could have chosen my own daughter-in-law I would have picked that girl. This will be the happiest day of my life," Ace's voice cracked with emotion. Violet thanked her with her eyes and gave her a hug before they joined everyone in front of the fire where Tina was serving champagne and Jim was proposing a toast.

"Has everyone got champagne?" Jim asked. "Of course, I don't mean the Princess Lila. We had some concoction personally made by Shirley Temple herself flown in for her."

"No, you didn't," Lila corrected him playfully. "Marshall made it because I watched him." Everyone laughed.

"A toast," he said lifting his glass. "To our new life as one big happy family." Violet looked lovingly at Sheherezade and Lila. "Here, here, to togetherness!" she reiterated. Everyone took a sip to seal the sentiment.

Tina came in and announced that the buffet was ready and everyone made their way to the dining room to sample the delicacies Marshall had worked all day to prepare. The distant sound of the phone ringing broke the magical spell of the evening as Sheherezade wondered who could be calling on Christmas Eve. Tina came into the dining room looking shocked and quietly announced to Sheherezade that Boots was on the phone and asking to speak with her. She turned to Jim and Ace with a concerned look on her face as if to ask for advice. Ace raised her eyebrows and offered some information she had so far kept to herself. "I hear Shane is the suit that runs the whole operation now. Boots gets high and rides around on his motorcycle. He hasn't been the same since your sister's death."

"Murder," Sheherezade corrected as she walked off in the direction of the library.

"Hello?"

"Hi, Sheherezade, how are you doin'?" Boots distinctive voice asked innocently.

"Well, not too well. I'm having a family gathering and the only person who isn't here is my sister because you murdered her." The phone went silent; Boots was not prepared for this. Months of anesthetising his mind could not wipe the image of Brandi from his memory and he was being tortured by the emotion that the image triggered again and again. Love. Finally, he knew. Love was happiness and he had thrown it away. His one last hope—fantasy—was that he might have a chance with her sister and that she could help him forget Brandi, thus allowing him to forgive himself for his fatal error in judgement.

"Sheherezade, believe me, I had nothing to do with your sister's death. I wish she were alive—more than you know."

"Well I believe that you wish she were still alive. She was unforgettable. But I still believe you killed her."

"Sheherezade, just give me a chance . . . Please. I was hoping that we could get together and I'm sure I could convince you that I had nothing to do with your sister's death. She had a drug problem and I tried to keep an eye on her but she did her own thing sometimes," his voice trembled with desperation.

"Boots, I am not my sister! We're not interchangeable! Women are not interchangeable! You should have learned that lesson well by now."

"Oh! I know that. But the first time I saw you out at the picnic I . . . ."

"You just don't get it do you? Boots, I believe you murdered my sister! Just like you murdered Jimmy Bourke."

"Jimmy Bourke? That's just an old rumour! Complete bullshit," Boots stated emphatically.

"I'm familiar with the biker motto about three people being able to keep a secret if two of them are dead, but it didn't work in this case. One of them reached out from the grave and put the finger on you. Brandi told me the whole story before she died as told to her by Fancy before my sister murdered her. Dying words, Boots. They tend to be the truth. I have all of the details and I have the body. Do you want to bet the rest of your life that it's bullshit?"

Boots grimaced and looked off into space before he broke his silence, "Sheherezade, it was never my idea. Lion hated Jimmy but I got nothing out of it. Fancy blackmailed me for more than twenty years and made my life hell because of it. I was young and stupid. Really stupid. But I'm no killer. Please just give me a chance to explain what happened that day. We could . . . ."

"Murder is not something you can dismiss as a boyhood mistake! You robbed a woman of her husband and a boy of his father! You are going to have to atone for your actions! So if you don't want me to go to the police, I think you should listen to me. I've seen enough macho nonsense to last me a lifetime and it's time it stopped. I abhor everything an outlaw bike club stands for and I want you to announce the dissolution of Lucifer's Pride. Blame it on Lion's death. Whatever. I will give you three days to make the announcement or I will give the authorities the body." She looked out the window at the white cross glowing on the hill.

"O.K . . . O.K . . . ." Boots swallowed hard.

"If there is anything I can ever do for you . . . ." Sheherezade cut him off.

"I told you what you can do for me." She hung up. Sheherezade closed her eyes and listened to her heart pounding in her chest and then a broad smile crossed her face. She had found the best solution possible to the problem she, Ace, and Jim had discussed many times. Fancy had given up the location of the body to Brandi so when they had returned from France Ace asked Jimmy's friends to dig up his body and bury him on the hill by the lake marked by a big white cross, being careful to preserve any forensic evidence that might still remain. They realized there was very little chance that going to the police about the murder of Jimmy would be enough to convict Boots of the crime. They only had the hearsay evidence of Fancy on her deathbed as told to Sheherezade by Brandi—not real evidence in a court of law. That course of action would also inevitably lead to life on the run, once again. They would be hunted as enemies of Lucifer's Pride for the rest of their lives and they knew Jimmy would not want that life for them. *This was a good solution*, she thought. She would tell Ace and Jim about it when they had a private moment sometime tomorrow. Ace looked for her reaction when she came into the dining room and Sheherezade gave her a reassuring wink.

Boots had created his own hell and she could not help but think he deeply deserved exactly what he got. She often wondered what transgression Lion had paid for on that fateful day at his clubhouse. *That is something we will probably never know,* she surmised.

Silver hair glistened under a full moon as a man with a flashlight tramped through the wet and frozen patches of ground searching for the smooth black tombstone with her name. They had always had their own ritual on Christmas Eve, sitting by the fire, having a rum and eggnog, and enjoying a quiet evening. Now she was gone. Bending down on one knee, he placed a red rose on top of the black stone as he always did. He began to sob as he draped his arms over the stone as if to hug his wife. His heart. His love. Elise.

Lila ran over to Sheherezade and gave her a hug. Seeing that Lila was upset, she kneeled down to the child's level.

"What is it honey?"

"I wish mummy was here . . . ." Her little face started to pucker and tears fell down her cheeks. Sheherezade thought her heart would break for her niece.

"I wish she could be here too but she is in heaven with my dad, and his dad, and Jim's dad, and they are probably having a party tonight too. Someday we will all be together in heaven and then we will all be happy together won't we?" she asked smiling.

"Yes, we will all be together again," Lila said confidently.

"You know, when your mum was in the hospital, she told me how much she loved you and how much she wished she could be with you again. She wished she could play with you and spend a lot of time with you but she had to go to heaven." Sheherezade tried not to break down in tears.

"I had a necklace made for you that would remind you of your mother and I was going to give it to you tomorrow but I think I will give it to you now." Sheherezade picked up a box that was sitting on the tree and gave it to Lila. Lila lifted the necklace out of the box and beamed as she put the custom made gold figure around her neck.

"What does it mean, Meme?"

"This is an Ankh which is the Egyptian symbol for eternity, and inside I had them add a heart which stands for your love for your mummy. It means your love will last forever."

Her eyes told Sheherezade that she understood the deep meaning behind the symbol. I also bought a beautiful gold angel to remind us of your mum and I thought you should do the honour of putting it on the tree—right at the very top." Lila's eyes opened wide.

"Where is it Meme?" Lila asked eagerly. Together they walked over to the tree and Sheherezade brought out a box wrapped in gold paper and ribbons which she presented to Lila to open. Everyone watched Lila's face light up as she took the beautiful angel out of the box and examined the diaphanous wings that glistened from the reflection of the Christmas lights. Reverently, she carried the angel over to Jim. He lifted her up and she placed the angel at the top of the Christmas tree. Everyone paused and gazed at it in silence.

"We won't forget her Meme."

"No, my darling. LOVE NEVER FORGETS."

The End

Sheherezade's Tunisian Couscous

Ingredients:

3 tbsps olive oil
1 large onion
28 oz. canned whole or diced tomatoes (pureed)
Leg of lamb or three lamb shanks/ can be substituted for chicken
Three carrots traditionally cut into 4 pieces each
Can of chickpeas drained
1 cup of frozen peas
4-5 medium peeled potatoes
Stock to cover
Salt and pepper
1tsp Harrissa (Cap du Bon Harrissa from Tunisia made by Thyna gives a traditional flavour)
(Harrissa is a very potent spice that gives the dish its distinctive flavour. It can be found at most Middle Eastern Grocers in North America. If you do not like heat cut back)
1 package medium couscous (340 grams)

To prepare:

Cook onions in oil until they wilt

Add all of the other ingredients and enough stock to cover plus one cup

Cook for about two hours partially covered.

Couscous

Put contents of package of couscous into a heat resistant container.

Add an equal amount of boiling water and 1 tbsp butter and some olive oil for taste

Stir a bit to mix and cover for five minutes. Remove lid and fluff with a fork.

To Serve:

In a pasta bowl put a serving of couscous in the dish and then add stew over top. Very brave people add a bit of Harrissa on the side to enjoy with each mouthful.

Feeds a crowd

Edwards Brothers Malloy
Oxnard, CA USA
August 19, 2014